A RESOUNDING CHORUS OF PRAISE FOR LORI HANDELAND'S

FULL MOON DREAMS:

"This is my kind of story—a tortured hero redeemed by love. The circus setting adds sparkle; the hero and heroine provide the sparks!"

—Madeline Baker, author of
Embrace the Night

"...a fast-paced, exciting and delicious tale...Fans of both the supernatural and historical romance genres will rhapsodize over *Full Moon Dreams!*"

—*Affaire de Coeur*

AND *D.J.'S ANGEL:*

"*D.J.'s Angel* is a dazzling romance...resplendent with heart-stopping emotion and vibrant in its passion!"

—*Rendezvous*

MOONSTRUCK...

"Relax," John whispered, then brushed Emma's hair from her forehead. A slight wind through the open tent flap blew the strands back against her cheek. When his fingertips touched her flesh, she shivered and gasped. He smiled and lowered his head.

"Please, don't" she pleaded and put her palms against his chest, holding him away.

He frowned, hesitating. "Why not?"

"My grandfather. He—we—you—" she sighed. "I can't. You're a laborer. I'm a performer."

"True."

"We're not the same."

"No, we're not. I'm a man; you're a woman. That's the idea, Emma."

"I don't know you. You're not one of us."

"Doesn't that make me all the more exciting?"

"Yes." The word escaped her on a whisper. Her eyes widened at the admission.

John nodded, slowly. "You want to kiss me, Emma. You've wanted to kiss me from the first moment you saw me. Just like I've wanted to kiss you. It's time you grew up, Emmaline. Make your own decisions about the people you choose for friends. Think for yourself." He pulled her closer, and her eyes drifted closed as she lifted her mouth upward, unable to keep herself from wanting what she could not have. "Trust me," he whispered, just before his lips touched hers.

She stiffened. Her eyes opened, and fury snapped in their green depths. She shoved against his chest, catching him off guard so he stumbled back a few steps. She slid out of his reach, but she did not run. "Trust you?" she hissed. "I trust no one any longer. I don't plan to be the next victim, Johnny...."

Book Margins, Inc.

A BMI Edition

Published by special arrangement with Dorchester
Publishing Co., Inc.

Printed in the United States of America.

Digest format printed and distributed exclusively for Book
Margins, Inc., Ivyland, PA.

For Sue and Mike Spector
You've been my friends for over twenty years and
you still like me.
Thanks.

Chapter One

Southern Wisconsin, 1870

"Evil stalks us." Franz Gerhardt stepped into the middle of the platform. The crowd, composed of Gerhardt Circus performers, turned their attention to their leader.

Emmaline Monroe, accustomed to the melodrama inherent in her grandfather, did not react as the rest of the crowd did to his words, with gasps of fear and mumbles of apprehension. Instead, she watched and listened and kept her disbelief to herself.

At a gesture from the old man, the crowd fell silent. He continued, "The evil one murders the innocent beneath the full moon."

The people shifted and shuffled with unease, glancing up at the sky, then away. As one, they nodded. They had seen the two bodies, torn apart as if by a wild animal. Most of the assembled were immigrants from Germany, well versed in the terror of the full moon. They knew the signs. They believed.

Emma, a daughter of the New World, not the Old, did not. She, more than any of them, knew that wild animals were unpredictable at best. The two men had been victims of a renegade wolf or a rabid coyote, nothing more.

"The secret of these deaths must remain within the bounds of these wagons," Franz went on. "If outsiders learn of the danger, no one will come to our performances, and the law will not allow us to travel. This will mean the end of our world. We do not need anyone to tell us what we must do. We know the legends; we know what walks in our midst. Once we discover the *teufel,* the werewolf, the demon, we can end this."

Emma had heard enough. She perched upon the brink of great stardom—the first female tiger tamer in the United States, perhaps in the world. This summer's tour would prove her worth to everyone. Unless the old folks and their superstitions ruined everything.

She stepped forward, away from the crowd. "Grandfather." The old man frowned upon her. For the first time she could remember in her twenty years, she ignored his warning glare. She had to say *something.* If the entire circus believed that a werewolf stalked them, they would not look for the true culprit, and the murderer must be found. Now, before everyone's livelihood was destroyed, before her chance to become the performer she'd spent her life striving to become was ruined, before someone else died. "I can't believe what you are saying. Just because these deaths have occurred on two successive full moons, you think we harbor a werewolf? The culprit is most likely a mad dog or a starving wolf. Take a hunting party into the woods and destroy it."

The crowd gave a collective hiss of displeasure, and Emma turned to look at them in confusion. Why did they believe the unbelievable? She had given them a more sane explanation for the deaths, yet they clung to their belief of an evil one.

"Emmaline," Franz snapped, his authoritative voice commanding the attention of all who stood in the clearing. "You do not understand. You are a child of the New World. We are adults of the Old. We *will* go into the woods and hunt. But we will hunt the *teufel*. We will hunt the evil in our own way. Follow my orders and stay inside the bounds of these wagons. Especially tonight."

All around Emma faces turned upward once more, and eyes contemplated the round, silver moon rising into the night sky. Emma could smell the fear in the air, and despite her brave words, she feared as well.

John Bradfordini dried his hands on a towel next to the water pump in his office. He rolled his neck in a circle, wincing at the ache that had settled there after a sixteen-hour day. The work of a physician did not stop when the doctor tired.

He walked through the doorway leading from the examination room at the back of his house to the living area at the front. His housekeeper had left dinner on the table. Bless her. He was too exhausted to contemplate cooking for himself tonight.

Spring had returned to Andrewsville, and with the change of season came the chronic illnesses and injuries of rural America—broken legs and arms, sliced hands from any number of sharp farm implements, and the usual diseases that ran rampant through small farm communities. Today had been one of the worst days he could remember since he'd returned home from the war and opened his medical practice.

This morning, he'd lost a child to God only knew what disease. John walked to the front window and stared out at the night. Instead of his front yard, he saw the face of the little boy who'd died in his arms mere moments after arriving at the office. A wasting sickness. Just like the one that had killed John's mother. John had been unable to do a thing to stop death from coming, all his training nothing in the face of God's will. His vow to help the people of Andrewsville had been no more than useless words today.

In the window, John saw the reflection of his face, drawn, haggard, unhappy. On days such as today he missed his brother, Peter, with a longing almost physical. They had always been close, especially after their mother's death when John was nine and Peter eight. John had taken responsibility for Peter from that point on, their father having all he could do to keep the farm going without worrying about his sons.

The guilt over Peter's loss haunted John still. Moments before they'd marched off to war with the 26th Wisconsin, John had sworn to his father he would watch out for Peter. And he had, throughout countless small battles and skirmishes with no names. They'd even survived the bloodbath at Gettysburg. John dreamed about the battle yet: the screams of the injured and dying in the surgeon's tent where he worked; the cannon fire and gunshots on the hills and forests outside the tent; the horrible silence when the fighting ceased and so many thousands lay slaughtered. He and Peter had survived every battle, but John had returned home without his little brother. He hadn't seen Peter since Lee surrendered to Grant and everyone went home.

Everyone except Peter.

Peter had vanished with the tall officer he had spoken with the day before he and John were to return to Andrewsville. John's brother had always been the adventurous one, full of life, drawn to danger, the complete opposite of John, who craved the soothing peace of home and the staid existence he'd carved out for himself. Peter would have withered and died in Andrewsville. John had thrived, despite the niggling need for adventure that sprang up every now and again. John blamed his need on the lack of such spirit in himself, the spirit he had always found whenever he and his brother were together. He had depended upon Peter to put a spark of life into life. Without him, every day was the same as the rest.

John shook his head, sending the memories and the recriminations away. He had been over this ground countless times in the five years since Peter left camp with the officer and never returned. John should never have let his brother out of his sight. But he had, and he could do nothing about his mistake now.

John looked out the window once more, this time really seeing the out-of-doors instead of the window to his past. A full moon lit the darkness of the night, casting a silver glow across the front yard, a glow that illuminated the figure of a man trudging up the walk toward his house.

John sighed. Someone needed him. He would go. He opened the front door and waited for the man to reach him.

John narrowed his eyes. The figure looked so familiar, almost like . . .

But no, it couldn't be him. John only thought the man was Peter because he'd been thinking of his brother, missing him again. When he was tired, melancholy always set in.

The man stopped on the front porch. In one hand he held a Spencer rifle; with the other hand he pushed back the broad-brimmed hat that shaded his features.

John took in a sharp breath. "Peter?" he whispered, half afraid that any sound would make his brother turn to silver moonlight and disappear.

Peter nodded, once, and stepped inside. John wanted to grasp his brother's hands to prove the man in front of him real, but Peter held his rifle in a grip so tight his fingers had gone white. John frowned and looked into his brother's face. His chest ached at what he saw there.

The smiling, joking young man who had disappeared five years earlier was gone, and in his place stood a man whose face revealed the test of time—and something else. Lines creased his face, gray streaked his hair, and his eyes held a haunted, hunted look that made John cold deep inside. If he hadn't known better, he'd think Peter was nigh on to forty years old, not the single year shy of John's twenty-seven he happened to be.

Peter sat down at the kitchen table, placing his rifle on the surface within easy reach. "So, how have you been, Johnny?"

John blinked, stunned at the casual question. Did his brother expect to take up life in Andrewsville without some type of explanation? John refused to allow Peter to make light of all the pain he'd caused those who loved him. ''Where have you been?'' he snapped. ''We all thought you were dead.''

''I wanted you to think that.''

John's gaze narrowed. The coldness in Peter's voice disturbed him. He did not know how to approach the dangerous looking man who inhabited the body of the boy he'd once loved with all his heart. ''Why would you want us to think you were dead?''

''I didn't want anyone looking for me. I'm involved in something dangerous, Johnny. I shouldn't be here now.''

''Whatever has happened, Peter, whatever you've done, I'll help you. You know I will.''

Peter laughed. ''Of course. Johnny the helpful. I'd hoped you'd outgrown your tendency to take on responsibility for every lost soul you encountered.'' He stared at John's face as if trying to see into his very being. ''You still haven't realized you can't save everyone in this world. Some things can't be changed, no matter how hard you try.'' He laughed again, though this time the sound seemed wrenched from his gut. ''You're the doctor here now, just like you swore you would be after Mama died. How many souls have you saved today, Johnny? Do you have time for one more?''

The sarcasm in his brother's voice was another new aspect to Peter, one John found he didn't like any more than the cold, hard bedrock of a soul he sensed beneath that veneer of sarcasm. But his brother sat there before him, the brother he had feared dead, and the sight of Peter alive allayed any irritation John felt with the man Peter had become. ''What kind of danger are you in?''

The howl of a wolf pierced the night and Peter started. John ignored the sound, used to the call of the night animals from the forest surrounding his home.

Peter pulled his rifle toward him. A quick flick of his wrists, and the bullets poured into his hand, bright silver under the light from the lantern. Before John could ask where Peter had gotten the odd silver bullets and why, his brother reloaded the rifle, his face intent, his movements precise, almost as if he performed a ritual.

John took a step forward, putting his hand on the barrel of the weapon. Peter looked up at him, his eyes dark and haunted with the unknown. "I'm sorry," he whispered. "I shouldn't have come here. I should have known you would want to help me. You can't seem to stop yourself from helping others, even when they don't deserve it. I just needed to see you. To prove to myself there are people in this world worth dying for."

The voice and the words sounded more like the Peter John remembered. He removed his hand from the rifle and reached for his brother. Peter flinched away from his touch, stood, then crossed the room to open the door.

John followed. When he stepped onto the porch, Peter was already loping toward the dark shadows of the forest.

"Peter! Wait!"

His brother did not pause at his shout. John swore and ran after him. When Peter realized John followed, he stopped and turned, his face awash with fury.

"Go back, Johnny."

"No. You're talking crazy. I'm not going to let you out of my sight until you tell me what's going on.

What's been going on since you disappeared."

"I can't do that."

"You show up at my house at midnight, though I haven't seen or heard from you in five years. Then you leave with no explanation and expect me to let you go?"

"Yes." Peter took a step closer to John and laid a hand on his arm. "I don't want you hurt. You're all that's good in this world to me. If something happened to you, I wouldn't be able to live with myself."

"I haven't been able to live with myself since you disappeared. I promised Father I'd take care of you. Then I came home alone. Aren't you even going to see him? He's not going to live forever, Peter."

Peter's head jerked up, and he dropped his hand from John's arm. John could tell by the way Peter's gaze swept the grove of trees lining the field that his brother no longer listened to him. Peter's eyes—intent, watchful, wary—and the way he held himself, as if he expected an attack at any moment, made John feel the razor edge of readiness, too. He had never seen Peter like this, not even during the war when he'd fought with his usual abandon against the Rebels.

John took a step closer and raised his hand to touch Peter's shoulder. Peter stiffened, his fingers tightening on the Spencer. John frowned. This tense, pale reflection of his brother was a stranger to him—a man he did not understand or know how to talk to. John let his hand fall back to his side with a sigh. "You can't believe I'd let you run off and disappear again after you told me you were in danger. You're my little brother, Peter. I love you."

Peter's shoulders slumped, and his breath hitched in

his chest. "I love you, too. I was desperate tonight so I came to you. I'm sorry, Johnny." He tilted his head up, and John winced at the darkness that spread across Peter's face like the clouds drifting across the face of the full moon.

"What?" John whispered. "What is it? You can tell me. You know I'd do anything for you. What have you gotten yourself involved in?"

Peter hesitated, then opened his mouth just as a low, long howl erupted from the edge of the woods. His head snapped to the side, his gaze fixing upon the trees once more. The tension returned, killing any revelations Peter might have been about to make.

"*Teufel,*" Peter muttered.

John frowned. Their father had immigrated from Italy, their mother from Sweden, but in Wisconsin there were enough German immigrants for John to understand his share of the language.

Teufel meant demon.

"Stay here," Peter snapped, tightening his clasp on the rifle and stalking toward the woods.

John shook his head. Why did Peter behave as if the howl had been uttered by the devil incarnate? His brother knew there were coyotes in these woods. Wolves, too. Scores of them. Had Peter's mind become unhinged during his years of wandering God only knew where?

Ignoring the order to stay put, John followed in Peter's wake. He grabbed his brother's shoulder, and Peter spun around. The rifle hit John in the chest. He grabbed the barrel and pushed it to the side.

Peter wrenched the weapon away from John's fingers. "Dammit, Johnny, just stay out of my way. Go back to the house."

"I won't leave you out here alone. Come back with me."

"I can't."

"You're being ridiculous. I've never seen you act this way."

"You haven't seen what I have seen."

"Then tell me. I want to understand. I want to help you." Without conscious thought, John had begun to speak in his most calm and soothing tone. He hadn't trained as a physician throughout the years of war for naught.

Peter narrowed his eyes, obviously recognizing the words and the tone for what they were, a physician soothing an out-of-control patient. "You think I'm insane, don't you?" He laughed, the sound loud in the chill night air. "God, I wish I were. Then none of this would be real." His eyes took on a faraway look for a moment, as if he were remembering other times and places; then he focused once more on John's face. "But it is real, and I have to put a stop to it."

"Put a stop to what?"

Peter ignored the question. "Stay here, Johnny," he repeated. "For once in your life, let someone take care of you." Then he turned and disappeared into the darkness of the forest.

John hesitated for only a second. He couldn't let Peter walk the woods alone. He would do whatever he must to make his brother come back to the house and reveal the truth of his past five years.

John took a step after Peter. The snarl stopped him cold. The gunshot made him flinch. The wet, gurgling cry compelled him to run into the forest.

Where the full moon had lit the field almost as bright as dawn, its lack within the dense forest made the darkness loom all the darker. John blinked, cursing, until his eyes adjusted to the change in light. Once he could see, he wished he could not.

His brother lay on the ground in a puddle of blood; his rifle rested a few feet away, useless. John flung himself onto his knees next to Peter. His heart thundered in his ears. He could hear little beyond its cadence but the rasp of Peter's breath through a jagged gash in his throat.

"Get away, Johnny." Peter's voice sounded liquid, as if he spoke from under water. He opened his eyes. The haunted look remained. "You'll die next if you don't get away."

"I'm not leaving without you."

"You must. Leave me. I'm already dead."

"No!" John shouted, panic fluttering within him at Peter's words. He glanced around the thicket, searching for the animal that had done this to his brother, prepared to kill it with his bare hands. But within the darkened woods they were alone. He turned back to Peter.

The blood shone black in the shivering moonlight. John, who had never been bothered by the sight of blood, was bothered now. He swallowed against the bile at the back of his throat. "I'm a doctor. I've healed others; I'll heal you, as well."

Peter took another breath, and the rattle in his chest made John's heart catch in fear. "Dear God, no," John muttered, a prayer, a litany. "Please don't take him from me. I only had him back for a moment. Take me, not him. Please, please take me.''

"You can't bargain with God, Johnny. Believe me. I've tried. It's too late to change this.''

"Not if I get you back to the house. I can help you,'' he repeated.

"No one can help me.''

John looked into his brother's eyes and saw the truth of his words. No one could help Peter Bradfordini. Not even John. Not anymore.

He took Peter's hand. A howl began, low and sure, wavering higher and higher, longer and longer, until John wanted to scream for the sound to end. Peter's fingers tightened on his own, and John looked down into the face of his little brother.

"It's still out there and coming for you.''

"The wolf? Is it rabid?'' The thought calmed him somewhat. Hydrophobia was something he knew how to deal with.

"No!'' Peter's voice was surprisingly strong and sure in the denial. "You've seen rabid animals, and so have I. Don't make the mistake of believing it's that easy.''

John spied Peter's rifle on the ground and leaned over to pull the weapon closer. "I'll kill it, Peter.''

Peter's wan smile tore at John's heart. "Killing it won't help me now, Johnny.'' He coughed. A thin line of blood traced a path from his lips down his chin. "Gerhardt Circus.'' Peter's voice broke, and he pulled on John's hand, his grasp weaker than a moment before. John leaned forward, his face just inches from Peter's. "The answer is at Gerhardt Circus. If you get bitten . . .'' His eyes fluttered closed.

"Peter?'' John sat back and stared into his brother's

face. He shook him. "Dammit, Peter, don't die on me."

"*Jager-sucher,*" Peter whispered. "There are others."

And then he was gone.

John sat back on his heels. He raised his face to the moon and emitted a howl of agony to rival the howl of the wolf lurking somewhere in the forest. Not Peter. Once so full of life, now dead on the cold, hard ground. And for what? Why?

What would he tell their father? To lose Peter once had been hard, to lose him again would be agony. John knew, because the agony sifting through his gut made him double over in pain. Rage filled him, pushing back the grief. Though he wanted to gather Peter close and wail over the loss of his brother, he had other tasks to accomplish right now.

John picked up the rifle from the ground at his side and began to get to his feet. He balanced halfway between kneeling and standing when a dark shape leapt from the bushes. John had time to clench his fingers around the barrel more tightly before the body hit him and propelled him backward to the ground. The animal snarled, reaching for his throat. John pushed the mouth away, wincing when the teeth closed on his hand. He brought the barrel of the gun up with his other hand and smashed the weapon against the animal's head. He was free. Free of the animal's weight, yet still he could not move.

A black, creeping lethargy consumed him, blocking out reality. Just before the world faded into the dark void, the face of the animal that had attacked him rose up in his consciousness. He moaned a denial.

Peter had been right. This animal was not rabid. John had seen that madness before in the eyes of the dying—both animal and human alike. In these eyes John had seen something much worse.

Though the face was that of a wolf, the eyes—the eyes were human.

Unable to sleep after the gathering of her people, Emmaline lay upon her pallet and stared at the ceiling of her wagon.

The men had gone out to hunt in the woods. They should return soon. With any luck, they had killed the rabid wolf or coyote that preyed upon their people. Then the last two months of terror would end, and they could go on with their tour—safe and happy once more.

The night, unusually warm for May, made the air in her sleeping wagon stifling. The wagon was her home on wheels. It contained everything she owned in the world: her bed, her clothes, her costumes. Though she loved the place, her very possession of a private sleeping wagon showing her status in the circus as a star performer, the crowded state of the abode made any movement of air impossible. Emma stood and moved to the open end of the wagon. Though the moon was still visible, dawn approached. She should be safe enough if she stayed out of the woods, and to be sure, she would take along the best form of protection she possessed.

Emma jumped to the ground and glanced around the circus. Those who hadn't gone on the hunt slept, or pretended to sleep. Emma traversed the distance between her wagon and the animal wagons, whispering to Destruction as she released the tiger from his cage. "We'll just take a walk beyond the camp," she muttered to herself. "Then maybe I can sleep."

The elephants in the open field beyond the circus wagons shuffled with unease as she and Destruction approached. Emma frowned. The elephants should be used to the tiger by now. What could ail them?

She made her way to the large outcropping of rocks near the forest's edge. Most open fields in Wisconsin were surrounded by such rock piles, since the earth needed to be cleared of the obstructions before the farmers could plant anything. In such cleared areas, with the permission of the owner, the circus tethered their animals to graze. Both Emma and Destruction sat and stared at the fading stars while the hoofed animals of the menagerie milled nervously. After a few moments, Emma frowned in their direction. In the past, all that had been needed to calm the animals was her presence. Since childhood she had possessed a way with wild things, calming them with a simple word or touch. Emma felt more at ease with the animals than she ever felt with people. Destruction was her best friend. At times she thought she could read his mind.

Odd, but this time her presence seemed to upset the animals. "Shh," she called. "I'm here. It's all right."

Instead of calming them, her voice seemed to make the animals even more fidgety. One of the elephants lifted its trunk and trumpeted at the fading moon. The sound of fear from an animal that feared little made Emma get to her feet and start toward the menagerie. Either the storm of the century approached, or the animals sensed something she did not.

A low snarl from the darkness of the trees sent a

tingle up Emma's back. Slowly she turned her head and met the glowing eyes of a creature that glared at her in the semidarkness. She knew she should run, but she could not.

Emma's heart lurched with fear so deep as to be painful. The animal emerged from the trees, and a small cry of terror escaped her lips.

Destruction roared, and the animal at the edge of the forest froze. It glanced at Emma, for a moment uncertain—not afraid as an animal should be when confronted with a tiger, just confused. The confusion did not last for more than an instant before the cunning intelligence returned to those eyes. That intelligence frightened Emma more than anything else.

Not now, those eyes said, *but soon.*

The animal turned and retreated into the forest.

Emma, who had never before believed in werewolves, believed now. For though the body of the animal had been that of a black wolf, the eyes had been human.

Chapter Two

Destruction hovered, watching, waiting, licking his lips in anticipation before crouching to spring.

The massive Bengal tiger arched through the air, legs outstretched in a leap of perfection. He shot into the circle of flame and emerged victorious on the other side. A sigh of awe whispered in the silence. Thunderous applause followed. Destruction, accustomed to the sound, never flinched. In fact, he appeared to relish the adulation as his due in life.

Emmaline flicked her wrist sharply, cracking the thin whip she held more for show than necessity. Destruction rarely needed to be prompted in his routine. He knew his part as well as Emma knew hers. They had both been trained from childhood to excel in the ring.

The tiger stalked regally back to his perch next to the smaller female tiger, throwing a disdainful glance over his shoulder at his mistress. From past problems with him at rehearsals, Emma knew he hated the whip, taking its use as a personal affront to his professionalism.

She sighed. Sometimes Destruction could be downright irritating in his near humanity. Ignoring the tiger's implied rebuke, she turned toward the crowd. Raising her arms above her head, she bent at the waist to take her final bow, accompanied by a crescendo of music from the band.

Straightening, she glanced through the thin wire of the cage that enclosed her and the tigers, separating them from the crowd. The cage was too small to do all the tricks she wished to do with her animals, but it was a safety requirement. No one would bring their children to a circus that did not cage its wild animal acts.

Tonight Gerhardt Circus enjoyed a straw house: The seats, both the unreserved blues and the higher-priced grandstands, were packed to overflowing, and towners sat upon the straw spread up to the ring. Smiling faces of all ages peered at her, and she couldn't help but grin in return.

The circus was a place of magic, and every time she stepped into the ring that magic flowed through her. Each night the roar of the crowd, the smell of the oil lamps and greasepaint, the closeness of the people all straining toward her in wondrous anticipation energized her to a fever pitch. She would never grow tired of the thrill that accompanied a well-executed performance. From her first appearance in front of an audience at the age of four, she had been fascinated with the power she found there.

"Ladies and gentlemen, boys and girls," the ringmaster's voice cut across the excited whispers stirring the air. "Let's hear your applause again for Emmaline Monroe, the premier female tiger tamer in these United States. A genuine tribute to the Gerhardt family tradition of fine circus performers."

Stifling a grimace at the ringmaster's words, Emma waved one final time. The Gerhardt family tradition consisted of her grandfather and herself, and she had become who and what she was as a result of Franz Gerhardt's determination. At twenty years of age, she remembered no other life beyond the circus. She could not imagine existing anywhere else. Because of those feelings their present state of near collapse, financial and emotional, frightened Emma deeply. The circus and Emma were one and the same. If one died, how could the other expect to survive?

Emma led her tigers through a door in the back of the cage. The laborer who kept the back door of the tent clear of bystanders so she could return her cats to their wagons without mishap, gave a brief nod acknowledging her performance. She returned the nod just as the wire-walking act, Otto, Helga and Heloise, passed by, walking single file as always—an odd quirk that Emma rarely noticed anymore. She registered with half an ear the commands issued by Otto with the precision of an army sergeant. The commands were always the same, every night.

"Mach schnell! Bewegen!"

"Hurry up! Move!" The translation from German to English flowed through Emma's mind without a second thought.

The three siblings moved toward their places in a smooth transition while the brass band played a lively tune to distract the crowd between the change in acts. Once the wire-walkers were in place, the bandleader would slide the musicians into the waltz he'd written for use with the aerial acts of Gerhardt Circus and none other. He knew, as did all circus performers, that the musical arrangement was as much a part of the show as the acts themselves.

Emma paused outside the open tent flap and listened. As she had expected, the band switched from the first tune to the waltz in an effortless flow. Though the change might look easy, it was not. Hours of practice were required to make every detail of the music just right. Very little was left to chance at this circus. She wouldn't be surprised if her grandfather had spent part of the time he should have been asleep making sure the band lived up to his standards. Thanks to her grandfather's superb management, the Gerhardt Circus was a well-run reflection of his devotion.

Emma turned up her face and greeted the mid-June breeze with a smile. The sun slid toward the horizon, the days lengthening as summer advanced. Despite her enjoyment of performing, she always felt great relief when she escaped the warm, close air trapped beneath the canvas. Emma glanced at the open field with longing, then back at the tent. Did she dare take a few moments away from the circus? Her grandfather had warned her, had indeed warned them all, not to stray too far from the safety of their numbers. In the nearly four weeks since she had told him about her narrow escape from the black wolf, he had barely let her out of his sight. She needed some time alone, but after what had happened the last time she ignored his warning, she feared to do so again.

The full moon is still a night away. A little voice whispered the words in her ear. She pushed the temptation away, but the voice tried once more.

The sun shines yet. You will be safe enough.

Emma sighed. She must need solitude more than

31

usual if she planned to listen to the enticing little voice. And she did plan to. Now would be the best time to take a walk away from the simmering excitement of the circus. For all they knew, the *teufel* had moved on. For the first time in three months, Gerhardt Circus had escaped unscathed on the night of the full moon. Though Emma had to admit, if she had not thought to bring Destruction with her, she might have been the latest victim.

Not giving herself time to mull over the atrocities committed within her world for another second longer, Emma put the tigress into her cage wagon, then led Destruction toward the freedom of the open field.

Instead of following, the tiger stopped short, bringing Emma to an equally short stop at the end of the leash.

"Come on." She gave an impatient tug on the rawhide strap in her hand. "I don't have time for your nonsense now."

In answer, the tiger growled low in his throat, his gaze fixed on something beyond Emma's right ear. At that moment, a tingle between her shoulder blades told her someone stood there. Years in the public eye had trained Emma to know when she was being watched. From Destruction's reaction, he did not approve of this particular watcher.

Slowly she turned. At the last wagon parked on the edge of camp, a man lounged, watching her. She had never seen him before, but that in itself was not odd considering the nature of the traveling circus. What made her uneasy was the *way* he watched her. Not casually, as though he just happened to be outside for a smoke and she had crossed his path, but with intent, as though he waited just for her. A slither of fear snaked up Emma's back, replacing the tingle of a moment before. The images of death and murder and the full moon she had so recently banished from her mind returned full force. She bit her lip to keep a whimper from escaping her mouth. Emma glanced around, dismayed to find no one else about. Just like the last time she'd gone off on her own.

A glance revealed that the stranger continued to watch her, though he made no move in her direction. Destruction's presence soothed her unease. No one would be crazy enough to accost her with a tiger in tow.

"Ignore him," she muttered, as much to herself as to the tiger. Another imperious tug on the leash and her companion followed, though Destruction gave her a look that told Emma he did as she asked because *he* had decided to move on.

They continued toward the field. Another sideways glance showed her that the stranger still watched, though he did not follow. Emma breathed a short sigh of relief. Unfortunately, Destruction chose that moment to get playful and pushed her from behind. With her attention focused on the strange man, she hadn't been expecting the move and sprawled forward, landing on her face in the trampled grass and dirt. Luckily for her, the tiger was more agile and leapt sideways as they fell. If not for that, she would have become Emma-mush beneath five hundred pounds of Bengal tiger.

The big cat licked her cheek by way of apology.

"Thanks a lot, Dusty," she muttered.

"Do you need help?"

At the deep, unfamiliar voice above her, Emma drew

in a sharp, shocked breath. Whoever he was, he moved as quickly as the jungle cats she spent most of her time with—a frightening thought. The two murdered performers had been strong, able-bodied men, one a contortionist, the other the Gerhardt muscleman. Whoever had ended their lives had been quick and strong. This man was quick.

Emma raised her gaze from the dirt to encounter a very large and worn pair of boots. Looking further upward, she could see no more than his denim-covered legs. Though she would have preferred to crawl into the ground beneath her, she could not. Instead, Emma grimaced and struggled to her knees, dusting her hands together in an attempt to remove the damp earth from her palms.

Before she could get to her feet, Emma's hands were clasped in a firm grip, and she was unceremoniously yanked to her feet. She stumbled against his chest, and he grasped her upper arms to steady her. Emma rested her fingers against his blue cotton shirt. The muscles beneath her palms bunched, awakening her second fear. Not only quick, this man was also strong.

She took another breath for courage and looked into the stranger's face. His hair, the color of winter wheat, so light a brown as to be blond, hung nearly to his shoulders. Clean but slightly unkempt, the strands looked as if he ran his fingers through them often, whether in agitation or to keep them from his face Emma could not tell. His skin was much paler than the skin of most men she knew, as though he had been inside for a long time and just emerged into the sun. Still, he was attractive in a way that made her palms, which still rested against his chest, hum with awareness despite her fear of him.

He stared at her within the circle of his arms, his eyes seeming to draw her forward. They were very light, a strange cross between silver and blue. But what struck her most was the darkness she glimpsed within his eyes. There were shadows behind the light, shadows that haunted him. As she gazed into those eyes, she couldn't control a shiver of apprehension. She had never been one for premonitions, but this man meant trouble—serious and never-ending trouble.

They stared at each other for a long moment; then his gaze moved to her mouth. Emma's stomach tightened, just before Destruction growled low and pushed between them.

The man looked down, calm, cool and unperturbed at being warned by a tiger. Still, he let go of Emma's arms and moved back, his odd silver gaze returning to her face.

"Who are you?" Her voice quavered, and he frowned.

"Who do you think I am?"

"I don't know. I've never seen you before."

"I've never been here before. I arrived yesterday from Illinois."

A sigh of relief escaped Emma. If this man had just arrived from Illinois, he couldn't be the evil one they sought. Unless, of course, he lied.

What if he had been following the circus, preying upon them, knowing they would not go to the law as long as they believed that one of their own was cursed? If the people of the Gerhardt Circus looked to each other for the evil, they would not look to a stranger, and the stranger could escape unscathed. An unsettling thought with just such a stranger in front of her.

"You're Emmaline Monroe."

At the sound of the man's voice, Emma jumped and blinked. Since her encounter with the black wolf, her disposition had become quite skittish. "Yes, I am."

"The famous lady tiger tamer."

Emma cast a glance at Destruction, who had stopped growling but refused to budge from his position atop her foot. "I don't know how much fame I've achieved. But I do have the tigers."

"Yes." He turned his silver-blue gaze on Destruction, and the tiger glared right back. "I don't think he likes me."

"He's temperamental. Grandfather says I didn't begin to discipline him soon enough, and now he has a poor attitude. I raised him from a cub, you see, feeding him milk from a cloth and letting him sleep in my bed. Until the bed collapsed, that is. Now he sleeps in the cage with Hope." Emma heard herself chattering, but she couldn't seem to stop. The way he stared at her, first her face, then her neck and then the rest of her, made Emma want to hide. She must look a sight, her body-hugging tights stained at the knees and her hair clinging to her face. The outfit, which provided mobility in the ring, was downright scandalous in public. Never before had she wished for yards of petticoats and a breath-killing corset upon her person. She did now.

"How very enlightening," he said with a small smile. "Well, if you're all right, it's been nice meeting you, Miss Monroe." With a nod, the man started off toward the cook tent.

Before she could stop herself, Emma called after him. "I had the impression you were looking for me, Mr. ah . . ."

"Johnny," he said shortly. "And no, I wasn't looking for you. I was just . . ." His gaze drifted over her body, male appreciation in his eyes. Emma fought the urge to cover her breasts with her arms. He returned his gaze to her face, and she tilted her chin up to meet his eyes. She would not be embarrassed about her attire. Working with tigers required this costume, and working with tigers consumed her life. "I was just looking," he continued. "Your grandfather hired me last night as a canvasman."

Emma started with surprise. He didn't look like a laborer. But then he didn't look like a performer either, and his voice—deep, educated, almost cultured—was a far cry from the smoke-roughened tones common to most of the drifters who signed on for the summer season. Somewhere amidst his words she sensed a hesitation, as if English were not his first or his only language. She'd heard so many different accents among the immigrant-based populace of Wisconsin she couldn't distinguish the country of Johnny's origin.

A new canvasman, he'd said, a term circus folk used to describe those hired to take care of the tents—tearing them down at one site, loading them onto the wagons, then setting the canvas up again in a new town. Though with a circus of Gerhardt's size, the distinctions based upon work were few. Everyone helped where they were needed, whenever they were needed.

Emma continued to look him over with as much interest as he'd looked her over moments before. Her skepticism must have shown on her face, for when her perusal reached his eyes he looked away, refusing to allow her access to those windows on his soul.

"Excuse me." His voice was as cold as the silver-blue shade of his eyes. "I have to get to work." He turned away, leaving her to ponder.

Had she offended him? She couldn't see how. He possessed the air of a man with something to hide, or someone to hide from. She had seen his type often in her life with the circus. Workers came and went, drifters often on the run from their pasts or the law. The transient life-style of the traveling circus made them hard to locate, which was just what they wanted. If they did the work and didn't steal from the circus, her grandfather allowed them to stay on without prying into their pasts. But was that a good policy to continue with a werewolf on the loose?

"I wonder what's he's hiding," she murmured to Destruction, watching as Johnny crossed the yard, then disappeared behind one of the wagons. Perhaps her grandfather would enlighten her.

The music for the finale began, and Emma hurried toward the tent, yanking Destruction along with her as she dusted herself off. There would be no solitude for her this night. After a quick promenade around the ring, a few smiles and several waves, Emma returned the tiger to his cage, then went in search of her grandfather.

She found him nursing a cup of coffee at his desk in the ticket booth and main office of the circus, the wagon the circus folk always referred to as the "red wagon" no matter what its color.

"Good evening, Emmaline." His Old World accent

testified to his German heritage. "The show went well tonight, *ja?*"

"Yes, Grandfather. At least my act did. How were sales?"

"*Sehr gut, sehr gut.* If the weather holds, this should be one of our best tours."

Emma heard the hope in his voice. Though her grandfather had not said so outright, small things told her the circus wallowed in deep financial trouble: the paint on the wagons left to curl and peel until the mess could be ignored no longer, an elephant sold here, a llama there.

After the torrential rains that had plagued them during the summer of 1869, she wasn't surprised. They had barely been able to drag the circus wagons to ten towns last summer, and when they had reached a town, they'd been unable to do the usual parade through the streets because most of those streets resembled rivers. As a result, their ticket sales had been dismal. They'd retreated to their winter quarters a month early and spent the off season repairing the damage done by Mother Nature.

This season might be their last if the tour did not go well. The knowledge settled as an ache in her chest. Every year the costs to run a circus went higher, but the profits increased in minuscule amounts. They needed to add more animals to their menagerie, as well as publicize Emma's act, their biggest draw, farther and wider. Without publicity she would never become the star she'd dreamed of becoming all her life. But all those things took money—money they no longer had. The war had taken a toll on their savings. They had lost acts to recruitment and subsequent death. Then last season's disaster had exhausted their remaining funds. Many of the other circuses had begun to travel on trains, which allowed them to reach more towns faster.

But as her grandfather always said whenever she brought up the subject: "Gerhardt Circus is a mudshow. It has always been a mudshow, will always be a mudshow, young lady, until the day I die."

Emma knew better than to argue with that tone. She would do whatever necessary to make sure Gerhardt Circus did not die. The circus was all she and her grandfather had beyond each other.

So they buried their dead in the dark of night and kept their secrets from the local law. Circus people protected their own—and they punished their own. If the *teufel* lurked amongst them, the circus folk would learn the truth and take their own action. They couldn't afford to allow the law to stop them from traveling to all the shows they'd booked for the summer. Another short season such as the last would mean the death of their dreams.

Emma's mind turned to another problem. How could she ask her grandfather about their new worker without sounding too curious? Grandfather frowned on any interest in men on her part, and he did not condone fraternizing between the laborers and the performers. If he thought she had any special interest in Johnny, there would be hell to pay.

"Grandfather, I just met the new canvasman you hired." Emma paused, taking a deep breath in an attempt to make her voice casual and unconcerned. "What's his story?"

Her grandfather's gaze flicked up to hers, and she raised her eyebrows in what she hoped was a curious, yet innocent, expression. He stared at her for a moment before he shrugged. "He wanted a job. We needed the help, so I hire him."

"That's it? You didn't ask anything else about him?"

"I got his name. He is able-bodied. What else is there?"

"What if he's the one? And you've invited him to travel with us?"

"I doubt if the *teufel* would ask for a job, Emmaline."

Emma let out an exasperated sigh. "Why not? If asking for a job brings him closer to us."

"The werewolf has had no problem finding prey in the past. He would not need to resort to manual labor to get close to us. You are being ridiculous." He waved his hand at her in dismissal.

Emma didn't move. "If he's not the one, then he's in as much danger as the rest of us. Did you tell him?"

Her grandfather's gaze slid away from hers. He did not answer.

"Grandfather, did you tell him?" He refused to look at her. "You didn't, did you? How could you hire him and not tell him what we're facing?"

"We don't know what we are facing."

"I thought we did."

"You wish to tell a stranger about the *teufel?* You wish to tell an outsider, an Italian?" He said the last word as if being Italian were a curse. "They do not understand the ways of our world. He would probably go into the next town and tell the law we are a pack of lunatics. Is that what you want, Emmaline?"

Emma chewed her lip. She had to admit, when

Grandfather said things in that way, she didn't want to tell Johnny anything. She had a mission to accomplish—destroy the werewolf so she could get on with her career. Still, she didn't like deceiving anyone, especially when the deception would put his life at risk.

"I don't have to say there's a *teufel*. Just that we've had some trouble. If he's traveling with us all summer, he'll hear something eventually. And tomorrow night is the full moon. What then?"

"We will kill the evil one tomorrow. Then the problem will be solved."

"You didn't kill it last time."

"True, but the werewolf did not kill here last month. We were safe. We will take every precaution for safety again."

"And if you don't kill the *teufel*. What then?" she insisted.

Her grandfather sighed and looked away. "Then we will tell him. I swear. Right now, I want no further mention of the subject."

Emma ignored his order, something she seemed to be doing with increasing frequency of late. "This new man doesn't look like a laborer to me. I wonder—"

"Do not wonder," her grandfather interrupted, his stern gaze focused upon her once more. "He is here to work, like the rest of us. We need his help to make this season a success. Tell him nothing that would make him leave. Stay away from him, Emmaline. You have a great life ahead of you. Do not throw that away upon a drifter."

Emma frowned. "Who said anything about throwing away my life? I was just curious."

"I worry. After what happened to my poor Francesca, I trust no man."

Emma sighed. After so many years, Grandfather still mourned the loss of her mother, his only child. She had died alone in a broken-down cabin a few days past Emma's second birthday. At seventeen, Francesca had run off with one of the laborers, Karl Monroe, a handsome, no-good drifter, and given birth to Emma a year later. By then Karl was a memory, and Francesca died from a raging fever and a broken heart. Emma's grandfather had arrived to collect her and raised Emma from then on, just as he had raised Francesca after the death of Grandma.

Emma remembered nothing of her mother; she only knew what she had been told. Whenever Francesca's name was mentioned, she experienced two emotions, shame and loss, the litany she had learned from her grandfather. Love was never mentioned, nor forgiveness.

Emma pushed away the sense of emptiness that invaded her at the mention of her mother, and she comforted Franz as she always did in such a situation. "I understand, Grandfather. I don't plan to get married until I find another man just like you. Since you're one of a kind, I guess you'll have me around forever."

He smiled at her cajoling tone and returned his attention to the papers on his desk. Soon he was absorbed in his work, and Emma slipped out of the wagon.

The conversation with her grandfather had served to bring to the forefront of her mind the terror they faced. Instead of learning more about the mysterious Johnny, she had been given orders to stay away from him. Should she follow those orders? A little voice at the back of her mind kept whispering to her: *There is something odd about Johnny. Discover his secret before it is too late.*

Emma glanced at the expanse of canvas comprising the big top. The crowd had disappeared; the sun fell fast, leaving true darkness in its wake. It was the last night before the full moon struck. A shiver took her, and she hugged herself, hoping the minute warmth would chase the terrible chill away.

She needed to help with tearing down the canvas and loading the wagons so everyone could get some sleep. They'd be back up in a few hours and on their way toward the Door County Peninsula. At the circus, work always awaited beyond the sparkle and shine. Johnny what's-his-name would have to wait until later.

Chapter Three

John watched Emma stride through the midst of the organized confusion and make her way toward the big top. Her hair flowed in an unfettered red mass down her back, contrasting with the white tights hugging her body like another skin. Even after he'd seen her in costume earlier, the scandal of her attire still startled him. But she dressed no different than any of the other female performers walking the back lot.

He continued to study her, remembering in detail how it had felt to touch her, to hold her in his arms for a brief moment before the tiger had come between them. Her fingers were long and graceful, deceptively fragile since he knew their strength after holding them in his own hands. Though the skin had been smooth and supple, her palms were as callused as his own. No stranger to hard work was Emmaline Monroe. John found he liked that in a woman—among other things.

The first time she'd looked into his face her eyes had reminded him of the jungle cat at her side—wary, suspicious, watchful—their color a bright, pure green instead of the amber of her tiger's. Her skin, dusted to a pale gold from the sun, begged to be stroked.

He had given his name as Johnny, without thought supplying the name his brother had called him, a name which fit in better with his image of a common laborer. But when she'd said "Johnny," he'd felt things far and above what a childhood nickname upon a woman's lips should make him feel.

John gave a low growl of self-depreciation. During his stint with the circus, he needed to be wary, alert, suspicious, not distracted by alluring green eyes. She fascinated him, to be sure, but she was a part of the world he had come to investigate and perhaps destroy.

The full moon approached. The first since Peter's death. He could not endure many more nights of full moon dreams—memories of a wolf with the eyes of a human.

He put his fingers to his forehead where a pulsing pain had begun. He should know better than to agonize over his dreams. Such thoughts brought on pain, both physical and mental.

"*Jager-sucher,*" Peter had said. *Hunter searcher.* "There are others."

His brother's words were a mystery—a mystery John hoped to uncover at Gerhardt Circus. The place Peter had pointed him toward for answers. So far, all John had uncovered were more questions.

Following the attack, John and Peter had not been found until morning, after John's housekeeper had come to work and discovered him missing. After his night in the open, a fever raged through John's body. His father used remedies from his native Italy, but the herbs and poultices and bitter-tasting concoctions did not stop John's night sweats or horrible dreams. Since he was the sole physician for miles, there were no other options available in his treatment. But he was able to insist, amidst the delirium, that his father completely cauterize his wound. In that way, John believed, any poison or infection would be destroyed. Between the painful treatments and the debilitating fever, John's strength waned. By the time he recovered, Peter had been buried for three weeks. Though John had not thought the animal that attacked them had been rabid, when the usual two-week period for such symptoms to arise had come and gone, he was still relieved.

His father drifted around the house, his eyes as haunted as Peter's had been. The first day John got out of bed and went to sit on the porch, his father joined him. In one hand he held Peter's Spencer, in the other the silver bullets Peter had loaded into the gun, minus one. He sat next to John and stared into his face intently.

"Do you know what these mean?" He held out the hand with the bullets.

John shook his head.

"Peter told you nothing of what he'd done, where he'd been for the past five years?"

"No. He said he was in danger."

John's father nodded slowly. He turned his head to stare at the grave on the hillside above the house, a new stone next to the old one that marked his wife's resting place. "I will miss my son, but Peter is better off dead."

John frowned and opened his mouth to argue. His father gave a sharp shake of his head, and John subsided into silence.

The old man continued, "Kill the werewolf who

killed my son. Only then can Peter rest in peace.''

"Werewolf." John blinked. "Father, you aren't thinking clearly. It's the grief." John stood, planning to help his father inside and give him a dose of laudanum. When he awoke, he would be more lucid.

His father reached out a large, strong farmer's hand and shoved John back in his seat. John hit the chair so hard he rocked backward and had to scramble to keep from falling. When he righted himself, he returned his attention to the man staring at him with anger in his eyes. John feared that his father was losing his mind from grief. Paulo Bradfordini had never laid an angry hand on either of his sons in his life.

"Papa," John began, using the tone he'd tried on Peter that night. The tone didn't work any better on the elder Bradfordini.

He fixed John with a sharp glare. "You will not talk to me as if I am insane, young man. I know of what I speak. You know, too. You spoke when you were burning with fever. You told me of the wolf with the eyes of a man. You may choose not to believe with your mind, but in your heart you know the truth.''

A shiver passed through John. His father was right. He had seen a horrible thing—something his mind refused to acknowledge as the truth ever since his delirium had passed.

A shadow image of what he had seen that night drifted through John's mind. The wolf with the eyes of a man—human intelligence trapped within the body of a beast.

But a werewolf?

John was a man of science, of medicine. Accepting such superstition went against everything he believed.

But the endless nights of full moon dreams since Peter's death had shaken his grip on reality. Most of all he feared that if he believed, his belief would make the horror real. That he could not accept.

John looked at his father. The old man nodded. "The legend says—"

"No!" John held up his hand. "Tell me nothing about this legend, about Old World superstitions."

"But you must know what you face."

"I face a werewolf. All right, I have a hard time believing that, but I know I saw something. Something evil. That thing killed my brother. I will kill it before it kills again."

His father stared into his face for a long time. He seemed reluctant to let the topic go. But in the end he did. He handed John the rifle and the silver bullets. "Destroy it, Johnny. For Peter. For me." He leaned closer, putting his hand on his son's shoulder and looking into his eyes. This time the earlier anger was replaced by love and concern and something else. Might it be fear? "Most of all you must kill the *teufel* for yourself, my son. *You* must kill the evil wolf."

"Why?"

But John had said he wanted no more talk of legends, and so the old man refused to answer any more questions. He continued to wander around the house, not working, barely eating or sleeping, until John could stand to look at him no longer. He had to do something—and he knew what that something was.

So, despite his vow to heal the people of Andrewsville, to remain in his hometown so no more would die without aid as his mother had, John had closed his medical office and begun a search for Gerhardt Circus.

They were not hard to locate. The circus had given a show in town on the very night Peter was killed. The morning John lay in a delirium and Peter lay dead, the circus had moved on. But they left behind a well-marked trail, moving from one town to the next almost every night, at times remaining two nights if the town was large, and they always left plenty of flyers behind to say where they were going next.

Had Peter been at Gerhardt Circus before he'd come to John's home? Was that why he had sent John there for answers?

John removed his hand from his face, banishing the memories. He looked around the yard, only to discover that Emma had disappeared into the crowd awaiting the dismantling of the big top. As he watched, the canvas collapsed inward upon itself. A small cheer went up from the crowd before the circus people moved in to pack the tent onto the long wagon that served as a makeshift stage during the performances.

One of the men turned to John and shouted, "Hey, first of May."

John stared, unsure of what or whom the man addressed.

"That's you, Bradfordini, you're a first of May. The lowest of the low. The newest of the new. Get on over here and lend a hand."

John hurried forward, crossing the short distance to the now-collapsed canvas and pitching in next to the others. The circus people knew the routine so well they joked and laughed, making the hard work a pleasant task. Though the teasing and the nicknames were uttered with good-natured smiles, John still got the message. He was the outsider. He had hoped they would consider him a part of their circus family, that they would learn to trust him with their secrets. But though they were friendly, they remained reserved. They did not trust him. Not yet. Even the other laborers, drifters who came for the summer season and moved on when the circus retired to winter quarters, treated John like someone apart from the rest.

Because they hid something or someone? Most likely. If he could get one of them to trust him, to confide in him, he could discover the secrets he sought. John was sure of it.

But who? And how?

Everyone retired to their beds, lumpy pallets within the brightly painted circus wagons, around ten o'clock. Top performers, such as Emma, had their own wagons; everyone else shared. John found himself sharing a wagon with four other men. He was so tired, he didn't care. And not just from the physical labor. He had never liked duplicity, and the practice of it did not sit well upon his conscience. The thought of sleeping so close to others when he dreamed such horrible dreams did not appeal to him either. Though he'd become used to the nightmares to the point that he was able to keep from screaming out his brother's name, he would still awaken sweating, shaking and sick almost every night.

Tonight, despite his concerns, John fell instantly into a deep and dreamless rest, only to be awakened in what seemed like an hour by one of the men.

"Hey, Bradfordini, time to get on the road."

John opened his eyes and blinked, amazed that the dreams had not haunted him. He glanced out the open rear end of the wagon. Stars shone, brilliant white against the indigo night. He'd slept for perhaps four hours, and it was time to get up and work again.

Groaning, he rolled out of bed. Muscles he hadn't known he possessed screamed for mercy. He had believed himself in good physical condition. But the years of working as a physician and helping out on his father's farm had not prepared him for life as a laborer in a traveling show.

The sounds of the awakening circus drifted through the doorway. John moved to the end of the wagon and glanced around the area. Oil lanterns hung upon some of the wagons, casting an eerie glow around the camp. The scurrying figures of the circus people wavered in the artificial light. A dwarf ran by, his short legs pumping like the wheels of a locomotive. He raised a hand to John in greeting. John nodded back, unable to keep from staring after the man. Though the dwarf's three-foot stature gave him the illusion of youth, his gray hair had thinned into a crown upon his head, and a hundred wrinkles lined his face.

The sideshow freaks were another aspect of this life that John needed to explore to learn the secrets of Gerhardt Circus. They were part of the group, yet their physical deformities kept them on the periphery. Perhaps they would be more willing to tell John any secrets they might be party to. Or they might be fiercely loyal to the people who gave them a livelihood and a place to belong when the rest of the world treated them like blights upon humanity. Still, somewhere within this seemingly innocent company lurked the evil that had killed his brother. He could never forget that fact, and he would watch and learn about every aspect and being of this place, be they common laborer, star performer, or sideshow freak.

The wagons were loaded in an amazingly short time. John climbed onto the seat of the one he'd been assigned to drive. Just as he opened his mouth to call to the team of Percherons, the dwarf clambered onto the seat next to him. John stared at the little man, nonplussed.

"Hello, I'm Wade Thumb." Wade stuck out his hand for a shake.

John enveloped the tiny fingers in his own. "Johnny," he returned. "Johnny Bradfordini."

"I know. You're new. Franz told me to keep an eye on you. Help you out. Teach you the tricks."

Interesting, John thought. Franz is keeping an eye on me. Why?

John glanced at Wade. He had just reminded himself not to leave any part of the circus family free of his questions. Perhaps befriending the dwarf would be a first step toward enlightenment.

A long whistle shrieked from the front of the caravan.

"Yahoo! Here we go," Wade cried, his voice high-pitched and youthful. John couldn't help but smile at the dwarf's enthusiasm. He couldn't remember smiling in real pleasure since Peter had died.

With a jangle of their harnesses, the team of mighty draft horses surged forward and they pulled out of camp. Within two minutes, John understood why all the wagons were hitched to Percherons. The roads, if you could call them roads, were full of ruts—mud-bogged in some places and hard as stone in others. Just getting to the next town would be a miracle, let alone getting there in the dark.

"You do this every night?" he asked Wade.

"Yes. The advance man goes out and marks the road. See?" He pointed to a trail of white dust, which looked like flour to John, on the road ahead of them. "We follow the trail and by morning we're at a new town. Then we parade down Main Street, to get the people excited about the show, you see?"

"Do you sleep?"

Wade grinned. John half expected him to bounce up and down on the wooden seat in his jubilance. "Not much. My wife, Devora, she's a Gypsy, the fortune-teller here, she is always tired. And you know how women are when they are tired." He shook his head, rolled his eyes and shrugged in the way of a man commiserating on the foibles of females with another man. "But I've gotten used to the lack of sleep. I hardly ever feel tired anymore, though I can fall asleep at the drop of a hat." He snapped his fingers in front of John's nose to illustrate his point. "Anyway, once we're done with the parade, we'll set up in whatever farmer's field Heinz has commandeered. Then we can sleep until the matinee."

"Heinz?"

The happiness on Wade's face faded. "The advance man. He's also a clown, though he only performs in the matinee, then leaves to mark the trail to the next town. You haven't met him yet?"

"No."

Wade smiled again, though the expression did not reach his eyes. "You won't see much of him. He keeps to himself. He is from the Old Country. Odd bird. Never takes off his clown makeup in public."

John frowned. He would have to search out this Heinz. If the circus folk considered the clown odd,

John wanted to meet him. Perhaps another outsider would be able to enlighten him on what everyone else hid. Or perhaps the outsider was the one doing the hiding, just like John.

"So, Johnny, tell me about yourself," Wade said.

John stared at a point between the horses' heads and considered. Had Franz asked Wade to question him? Or was Wade just a curious man? Either way, John could not tell the truth.

He gave a shrug. "Not much to tell. I needed some work. I heard the circus needed help. Here I am."

Wade nodded. "Many like you come and go. Have you ever considered settling in one place?"

John frowned. "Is there a point to this inquisition, Wade?"

The dwarf laughed. "Devora says I'm too curious for my own good. She is probably right. I can't seem to help myself. You've got sad eyes, Johnny Bradfordini. I don't like sad eyes. Whenever I see them I have the need to make the sad eyes happy."

John's lips twitched. "Thanks for the concern, Wade. You've made me smile for the first time in a long while."

Wade's face split into a delighted grin. He clapped John on the shoulder. "I think we're gonna be good friends, Bradfordini." He leaned back and closed his eyes. As he had predicted, within seconds the little man slept, despite the rutted roads.

John turned his attention back to his driving. He found that the prospect of making a friend at Gerhardt Circus lightened his heart. He pushed aside the guilt at the lies he'd told Wade and everyone else. At this point, the lies were a necessity.

The circus reached the outskirts of Cherry Bay, a small town at the base of the Door County Peninsula, just after sunrise. The performers bustled around, dressing in their luminous costumes and unloading the animals they would parade through the town. John was impressed with the workmanship of the costumes. Heavily beaded and form fitting, representing all the colors of a rainbow and more, he had never seen such craftsmanship in his life. When he mentioned the fact to Wade the little man nodded.

"Everyone does their own costumes. In larger outfits they might have a seamstress, but not at Gerhardt. Part of a performer's training is learning to sew a costume that will complement their act. If you can't make your own costumes, you can't perform in Gerhardt Circus." Wade jumped down from the wagon seat. "Got to get dressed for the show," he said. "Today I get to ride one of the elephants." With a grin of happiness at the thought, Wade trotted off.

A glimpse of Emma flitting through the crowd drew John's attention. Today she wore bright blue tights studded with silvery beads, a long half-skirt trailing from the back to end just above her ankles. Now that he knew she'd made the outfit herself, he was even more impressed with the craftsmanship. What couldn't she do?

Taking up a position at the head of the parade with Destruction on a leash, she led the way down Main Street as the band, perched atop a bandwagon, played "The Flying Trapeze" to draw the attention of the townsfolk.

John drove his wagon at the tail end of the parade. He kept his gaze focused upon Emma at the head. She didn't trust him, that was clear. In fact, in her eyes the day before, he'd seen a spark of fear.

Why fear?

She had no reason to fear him unless she was hiding something, something she feared he had come to discover. Did she think he would use silver bullets on one of her circus family? He would. If she feared such an action, then she was as much at fault as any other. Harboring a monster made the protector a monster, too. John needed to learn what fired the fear at the back of Emmaline Monroe's eyes. He *would* get her to trust in him, to confide in him. But how?

The crowd on the sides of the street cheered at their first sight of Emma and Destruction. She smiled and waved, her bright red hair glinting in the morning sunshine, the blue of her tights outlining the curves of a woman's body, curves that should be properly hidden beneath yards of material. Or at least he'd believed such a thing until he'd seen Emma in her costume. She was a beauty, in body and in manner. Her love of the circus and of life in general shone through her eyes whenever she performed. The idea of denying such beauty to the world because of a convention showed the stupidity of those conventions.

Yet despite her manner of dress, Emmaline's face, her manner, had been that of an innocent. The contrast intrigued him. How would she respond to overtures from a man she feared? Could he seduce the information from her?

The thought, which in his past life would have made him cringe, took on a glow. He was a changed man. He had sworn over Peter's grave that he would do whatever he must to learn the truth. If Emmaline Monroe stood in his way, she would pay the price, despite any lingering tendrils of decency he might possess deep within him. Something indecent had killed his brother, and John would have to adopt different standards of behavior if he were to have any hope of discovering, then destroying, the evil one.

"Ladies and gentleman, boys and girls." The ringmaster's voice drifted over the assembled crowd. John glanced up and saw the man, dressed in his black suit and stovepipe hat, perched atop one of the wagons. "Come one, come all to Gerhardt Circus, which boasts the only female tiger tamer in the world. Come see the menagerie. We have animals from the most exotic corners of the earth. Barbary apes, kangaroos of New Holland, horned owls of Lapland, a Chinese cockatoo and many more. Our first show begins at three. Tickets are twenty cents, ten cents for kiddies under ten."

How could the ringmaster make the usual sound so unusual and exciting? John shrugged. Promoting the circus was the man's job. He'd better do a good job or the ticket sales would reveal his ineptitude. John had an idea that Franz Gerhardt would not be a forgiving taskmaster. One mistake, one bad night, and an employee would soon become an ex-employee. John would do well to keep that in mind. He didn't need to lose this job before he accomplished what he'd come to accomplish.

Behind Emmaline and her tiger followed the elephants, six of them in a line, each hanging onto the tail of the preceding elephant with its trunk. Upon the back of each elephant sat a performer in full costume—wire-walkers, aerialists, acrobats—all looking as excited about the parade as the people lining the streets waiting for them. John caught a glimpse of Wade perched upon the lead elephant, smiling and waving with childlike exuberance, and he couldn't help but like the man. He would have to curtail such softer emotions, with Emma, with Wade, and with anyone else he might develop a fondness for. He could not allow his natural affinity for people to cloud his judgment in the days to come.

The clowns followed after the elephants, rolling on the ground and shouting riddles to the crowd. John tried to see which one might be the mysterious Heinz. But to him, a clown was a clown. Bringing up the rear rolled the painted circus wagons, each a work of art in itself. The band sat upon the top of the bandwagon, first in the line of wagons. Next rolled the animal wagons, which housed some of the menagerie, separated from the crowd by iron bars. Bringing up the rear were the sleeping wagons, disguised as such by their brilliantly painted tableaus, ranging from fairy tale depictions to biblical scenes. John drove a wagon that sported a painting of a wolf in an old woman's clothing, slavering over a small, red-haired girl—a tableau representing the children's tale of Little Red-Cap and the Wolf. John hated the painting already.

As John passed through the center of town, he found himself looking at the children lining the street, their faces filled with wonder, their eyes glazed from the glory. For one shining moment, John experienced a sharp sting of pride at being part of that glory. Then the cold realization of why he traveled with the circus returned, and he forced his attention away from the wonder of the parade and focused on guiding the Percherons to their new camp.

Two hours later John walked toward the cook tent. Though lack of sleep made him bone weary, lack of food would keep him awake despite his exhaustion. He promised himself immediate bed rest as soon as he filled his rumbling belly.

When a new camp was struck, the cook tent rose first. The men and women of the circus worked hard night and day, and to keep up their strength the circus cook kept his fires burning whenever the circus remained still for longer than a few hours. As the Wisconsin River meandered through Wisconsin, hot coffee flowed through the circus lot. The featured fare of the day was whatever game had been shot most recently and whatever fresh food had been bought from the farmers along their route.

Sitting on the ground with his back against a tree, John dug into the plate of venison and mashed potatoes with an appetite reminiscent of a hound dog on a rampage. He frowned when he took his first bite of meat, the taste of overdone wild flesh unpleasant on his tongue. He'd never before preferred his meat rare, but right now he craved the seasoning of blood.

"Here you are, Johnny." The soft female voice made him pause in mid-chew. "I've been looking for you all morning."

Emmaline.

John winced and swallowed the meat, which then lay like a cooling lump of coal in his stomach. His plan to seduce her would not be furthered if she continued to think of him as a common laborer. Yet here he was, stuffing food into his mouth like an animal while the sweat of those labors still dried upon his back. Though he'd been on the lot a mere day, he'd seen the line of social demarcation between laborer and performer. The line was slight but there nevertheless.

He glanced up and she smiled. He narrowed his eyes. Yesterday she had been afraid of him. At the least, she should still be wary. What was she up to? He replaced his spoon on the plate and put his dish aside, gritting his teeth against the rumble of his belly. Then he raised a brow in question. "You've found me, Miss Monroe. What can I do for you before I get some sleep?"

She lowered herself onto the ground at his feet, tucking her legs beneath her with unconscious grace and spreading the half-skirt out on the grass so the material would not become stained. "Please, call me Emma. We're all family here."

She smiled again, this time with greater hesitancy. Her confidence seemed to wane the longer she spent with him.

John glanced at her costume. Why did she still wear the revealing outfit she'd worn during the parade? She acted as if *she* meant to seduce *him*.

Interesting. What did she want to know? And how far would she go to learn what she wanted?

John leaned back against the tree, crossed his arms over his chest and stared at her. Emma flushed. John smiled. She might pretend to be a woman of the world, for a moment, but her reactions to his scrutiny revealed she knew nothing about seduction.

"You've got a few more minutes, haven't you?" Without waiting for an answer, she continued. "We never finished getting acquainted yesterday. I thought we should talk some more."

Their brief encounter the day before had already told him she chattered when nervous. She was nervous now.

Good. He needed information. He would keep her off balance, slightly frightened of him, yet interested despite her fear. He didn't want her to think of him as one of the family. He needed her to think of him as so much more.

"What would you like to know, Emma?" The slight lowering of his voice, almost to a whisper, when he spoke her name, caused Emma to look up. The uncertainty he saw in her eyes before her gaze danced away told him she felt the attraction between them, too; she just had no idea what to do about it. He did.

"Emma?" he said again.

"What?" She looked at him once more. This time her eyes revealed the unease his nearness brought her. Despite her uncertainty and fear of him, his attraction for her deepened. When she licked her lips, John had to force himself not to imitate the movement.

"You said you wanted to talk."

"Oh, yes. I do." She took a deep breath, swallowed and wet her lips once more. So unconsciously alluring, so fascinating in her innocence, John had to stifle a groan at the response of his body. Who was seducing whom?

"Though I don't take much interest in the management, I do own half the circus. At the very least I like to know the full names of the people who work for us."

John went still. Why so curious about his name? Might she have heard of him when she passed through Andrewsville last month? If so, any chance of keeping his identity a secret would be destroyed. He couldn't lie about his name, since he'd already told the truth to Franz. "I told your grandfather my full name," he said slowly, watching her face for any telltale sign of knowledge. "Didn't you question him about me?"

"I—ah—I forgot to ask your last name." Her flush deepened at the admission. Emma might pretend to be interested in a purely business manner, but she was interested in a personal manner, as well. All the better for him.

The twinge of conscience he felt at the direction of his thoughts flew away with the memory of Peter. That memory and his own disgust with his lack of spine to accomplish what must be done caused John to answer more sharply than he'd intended. "Bradfordini," he snapped. "Johnny Bradfordini."

She showed no recognition of the name, only concern at his manner of stating it. Emma bit her lip. "I'm sorry if you think I'm prying. I know laborers are here for their own reasons. I won't ask you anything else."

His eyes narrowed. "What do you mean by that?"

She shrugged. "The nature of our life makes the circus appealing to those with something to hide. Or someone to hide from."

"Who says I have anything to hide?"

"No one. You asked me what I meant. You're only proving my point by getting so defensive."

She'd hit too close to the truth for John's comfort. He had to make her abandon that line of thinking immediately.

"In my experience, it's those who are hiding something themselves who see secrets in the eyes of others."

From behind Emma, a male voice interrupted, "How interesting. Tell me more."

At the sound of the voice, Emma frowned, and her

shoulders stiffened. She did not turn but continued to stare at John as though she hadn't heard the interruption. As John looked past her and met the eyes of the man who had spoken, a quiver of disquiet stole up his spine, and he went on the alert.

Though the man wore work clothes, denim trousers and a long-sleeved cotton shirt, the face that stared back at John was painted brightly, garishly, in the likeness of a smiling clown. The single, black tear that dripped down one cheek created a distinct contrast with the initial image of joy. His head completely bald, the top shone in the mid-morning sun. Despite the theatrics inherent in the makeup, the man's eyes held John's attention. They were bright blue and piercing, burning with an inner flame.

Heinz, the advance man and sometime clown, if John didn't miss his guess.

John stood and stepped past Emma, who continued to sit on the ground, her gaze fixed forward. He offered his hand to the newcomer. "Johnny Bradfordini."

The man nodded a greeting but did not extend his hand. After a second's hesitation, John dropped his own hand back to his side. The clown smirked. John didn't like him already. "I am Heinz Kirshner, performer and advance man for Gerhardt Circus." The man's voice, though not as heavily accented as Franz Gerhardt's, still betrayed his German heritage. "I heard Franz hired a new worker." He glanced at Emma, who continued to ignore him. "But what are you doing here, Emmaline? Shouldn't you be exercising your cats instead of relaxing with the help?"

Emma stood. Her shoulder brushed against John's, and she took a quick side step away from him. The tingle that passed between their bodies at the accidental contact had affected her, too. He resisted the urge to draw her back.

The breeze slid a hint of her scent past his face. John took a deep breath, and his body responded to the perfume he already identified with her—warm woman and lilac soap.

John glanced at the clown and found the man watching him. The expression on Kirshner's face was difficult to read because of the makeup, but John could have sworn he saw anger.

"We'll talk again later." Emma's voice broke through his thoughts, and he turned toward her. The warmth in her tone had vanished, lending a trace of a threat to her words.

She left as abruptly as she'd stood, never once looking at the clown. John watched her go. Bad feelings existed between the advance man and the tiger tamer of Gerhardt Circus. John would have to find out why.

He returned his attention to Heinz. More questions flooded his mind. Why did the man hide behind makeup? Did the quirk add to his image as a clown? Was he just eccentric? Or perhaps something worse?

John had to admit that most of the performers he had observed so far leaned toward the odd—the juggler juggled his dinner, one of the acrobats walked around the circus on his hands all day, waving at people with his feet, and the wire-walking act insisted on walking in single file, one behind the other wherever they went—but then odd had always been one of the earmarks of the circus.

The clown watched as Emma walked toward the tiger cages. When he noticed John observing him, he shrugged fatalistically. "She does not like me. I will change her mind one day."

"How?"

"Anything is possible at the circus. Didn't you know that, young man?

"No. Why don't you explain?"

Heinz chuckled. "The origin of magic. Of mystery. Of legend." He swept an arm out in a theatrical gesture, encompassing the circle of wagons. "Do you doubt that your most secret dreams and fears will be realized here?"

"That depends on what my secret dreams and fears are, doesn't it?"

"Are they not all the same, young man? For everyone? We dream of life, and we fear death."

"Both those things can be realized here?"

"Of course. The circus is life at its best. Color, magic, the world at your feet."

"And death?"

"Everyone dies, young man. Some worse than others."

"Heinz!" Franz's voice reached them through the open rear doors of the red wagon. "*Mach schnell!*"

"Hurry up," the clown mumbled. "Franz is always in a hurry." With a nod, he left John to his thoughts.

An odd man, and one prone to theorize, as well. An interesting man. An educated man. Out of place in this setting.

As out of place as John himself.

Emma paused at the site where the big top would stand. The workers were about to raise the huge tent. She waited, knowing such a spectacle never failed to lift her spirits, and since her encounter with Heinz at the cook tent, her spirits needed uplifting.

Lord, how she detested that man. If he wasn't such an asset to the circus, she would have insisted that her grandfather get rid of him long ago. But even if she had found a good reason to demand Heinz's dismissal, her insisting would have done little good. The clown had come over from the Old Country, the same as Grandfather, and Grandfather had a soft spot for any-one from Germany. But where her grandfather charmed with his Old World accent and impeccable manners, Heinz revolted with his slick and calculating ways, al-ways on the lookout for the shortcut. She had tried on several occasions to point this out to her grandfather, but he insisted she did not understand the life he and Heinz had led in Germany during their childhood, amidst the wars for unification. Though they no longer lived in the Old World, people of the same origin and faith helped each other.

Emma's gaze sharpened as the trainer whistled to the elephants and the three animals moved forward to-gether, pulling on the ropes to lift the huge canvas into the air. The expanse of white fluffed toward the sky, then peaked upward and settled into place. Canvasmen secured the tent and led the elephants away to be teth-ered in an open field downwind from the rest of the circus.

Emma looked out over the tents and wagons with pride. She loved what she did—the travel, the adven-ture, the excitement of the ring. Sometimes she imag-ined herself with a normal life—a husband, a home, a family. But there the fantasy always ended. She had no idea what life away from the circus was like. What would she do? How many positions were there for lady tiger tamers out there? How many men would want to marry a woman the world considered to be half a step above a whore?

She could not exist outside the bounds of her circus. Of that she had no doubt. Though she might be dissatisfied with the emotional emptiness of her life, if something happened to the Gerhardt Circus she did not know how she would cope. She never tired of watching the kaleidoscope of colors, hearing the symphony of sounds and smelling the myriad scents inherent to her world. The thought of those pleasures ending terrified her. All her life she had pursued the dream of becoming the first female tiger tamer in America. Now that she had achieved her dream, she needed a bit of luck to become the toast of the circus world. But the luck she'd had lately had been nothing but bad.

If, in the dark of night when she couldn't sleep, she lamented the childhood she had missed, the cheers of the crowd at her next performance always dispelled any lingering melancholy.

Her grandfather had strict rules about performers and workers mixing socially, especially workers of different national origins and religions. Despite the bustling nature of the circus, such rules had contributed to Emma's constant sense of loneliness. The United States might be the one country where all nationalities could blend into one, in theory anyway, but Emma knew her grandfather would condone no blending between herself and any man unless that man was German and Lutheran and a performer without peer.

Emma often wondered if he believed his own lectures, which always began "Those boys, they are no good," or if he simply couldn't bear the thought of losing her the way he had lost her mother to Karl Monroe. Still, she had been raised in the ways of the Old Country, taught to respect her grandfather, professionally and privately, and though she often gritted her teeth at the frustrating restrictions in her life, defying him had rarely occurred to her.

But in the past day since Johnny arrived on the scene, rebellion had crossed her mind often. Despite his cool response to her overtures, she was drawn to him. The sadness that hovered just behind his eerie silver eyes called to her. She had always harbored a soft spot for hurt creatures, and Johnny Bradfordini seemed to hurt more than most. Still, she'd seen a wounded animal turn snarling and snapping upon its rescuer. She would have to remember that image whenever she dealt with Johnny.

Emma sighed. She was so tired, and the tension within the circus became harder to bear with each passing day. The full moon approached, and the older women among the circus crew muttered of werewolves and demons, twisting their fingers into the forked sign against evil whenever the murders came up in conversation. If they continued to whisper about curses, Johnny would learn the truth on his own, and then her grandfather's orders would be for naught. Johnny would leave, and perhaps that would be the best for them all.

Emma moved toward the wagons that housed her tigers. She needed to work them a bit before she slept. The night of travel followed by the parade always excited them to the point they would not rest unless she allowed them into the performance cage to practice.

An hour later Emma threw up her hands in disgust. "I've had it with you two," she snapped.

Edgy and inattentive, Hope growled back at Emma's every command and deliberately disobeyed. Destruction obeyed, but grumbled under his breath more than usual. Both seemed to sense something in the air. They sniffed the breeze often and shifted with unease. Several times Emma went to the open tent flap and scanned the horizon for signs of a coming storm. Animals did not react well to changes in weather, and there was always a chance of a big top blow-down if the wind picked up too quickly. If such a thing happened in the midst of a performance, the consequences could be deadly.

Despite the tiger's odd reactions, the sky remained clear and the wind calm. The only explanation Emma could come up with for their behavior was the full moon that would rise in a few hours. Did the animals already smell the evil one that stalked them? She suspected they did. After several more futile attempts at practice, Emma gave up and took the tigers back to their cages, hoping their attitudes would improve before the coming performance.

As she walked past Hope's cage, the animal reached her paw through the bars and took a swipe at her. Emma drew back with a gasp of surprise, then stared at the cat glowering through the bars.

"What on earth is wrong with you, Hope?" Emma exclaimed.

At the sound of her mistress's voice, Hope lay down and put her head between her massive paws. Emma frowned. She hoped the tigress hadn't eaten bad meat. She knew that a tiger could become very ill, perhaps even die, from eating rotten meat. They could not afford the death of such an expensive animal, and just the thought of losing one or both of her tigers made Emma's heart thump with fear. They were her children, her responsibility. What would life be like for a tiger tamer without tigers? She would keep a close watch on both of her animals for the next few days, and she would leave Hope out of the show today just to be safe. If the tigress's bad temper had nothing to do with the meat, any number of things could be wrong with her. Emma didn't relish turning her back on a three-hundred-pound kitty with a surly disposition.

Her decision made, Emma turned away from the cages and started back to her wagon, deep in thought over how she would change her show to make up for the absence of one tiger. She was halfway across the open area in the midst of the circus when she sensed someone watching her. Probably Johnny, as before. She continued on her way. She needed sleep now, not a confrontation with a man she did not understand. When the feeling persisted, Emma glanced around the lot. Her steps slowed when she spotted a strange man leaning against the red wagon. Tall and thin, with longish blond hair and weather-roughened skin, he had the look of a laborer, though he seemed older than most of the men they hired. His eyes were shaded by a broad-brimmed hat, the type worn by outlaws of the West, depicted on the covers of the dime novels she read on rainy days. The man was out of place here, and frightening because of that fact. Even more unsettling to Emma was the knowledge that beneath the shadows cast by the hat's brim, he watched her. He had most likely been watching her for a long while if the behavior of her cats gave any indication. They liked strangers no more than she. The thought of this man scrutinizing her when she was unaware made Emma shiver. He was a stranger, and strangers meant trouble.

Unable to shrug off her unease, Emma tilted her head down and hurried toward her wagon. Seconds later, she slammed into someone and, with a startled gasp, lifted her gaze.

"Emmaline, where are you going in such a hurry?"

Emma let out a sigh of relief at the sight of a familiar face. "I'm sorry, Grandfather. I wanted to get inside my wagon."

"And what is so interesting inside your wagon?" Franz raised an eyebrow.

"Ah, nothing. It's just . . ." Emma paused and glanced over at the man who had been watching her. He stood straight now, his head cocked as though he attempted to hear their conversation. Franz's gaze followed the direction of Emma's. He stiffened, swore in German, then bore down upon the stranger.

"Grandfather," Emma called. "What's the matter?"

Franz shouted without breaking stride, "*Gehen!* Go! Inside, Emmaline."

"Grandfather?"

Franz whirled to face her. "*Gehen!*" Pointing a bony finger at her wagon, he glared. "Do as you are told."

Before she could think clearly, years of obedience made Emma move in the indicated direction. Looking back over her shoulder, she saw her grandfather waiting. He would not move any farther until she complied with his order. Emma risked a glance at the stranger. His gaze was focused so intently upon her that she ducked inside her wagon to retreat from the almost physical touch of his eyes. Once inside, she peaked back around the edge.

Franz reached the stranger quickly, and across the distance that separated them, Emma heard the anger in his voice. "Why are you following us?" he demanded.

The stranger glanced at her, then back at Franz. He answered too low for Emma to hear. Though her grandfather remained angry, he, too, lowered his voice so she could not hear his next words.

The stranger listened to her grandfather's tirade with no show of emotion on his face. When Franz took a deep breath several moments later, the man glanced over at her wagon once more. Emma yanked her head back inside.

After a short time, she peered outside once again, only to find the stranger and her grandfather gone. The thought of her grandfather alone with the unknown made Emma jump to the ground and run to the red wagon.

There was no sign of either man outside, so Emma climbed the steps to the office and knocked tentatively on the door. When no one answered, she looked inside. The room was as empty as a big top on a Tuesday morning.

What was going on? Obviously, Grandfather knew the man and didn't like him. The stranger seemed to know her, though she could swear she had never met him.

Pondering where to look next for the two men, Emma stood in the doorway of the wagon and let her gaze drift over the camp. A slight movement caught her attention, and she turned to the large farmer's field surrounded by piles of rocks.

Emma relaxed a bit at the sight of her grandfather walking alone through the crowd of elephants, llamas, camels and horses comprising his circus menagerie. Something about the way he walked clenched at her heart. Head down, shoulders slumped, he looked every bit his fifty-five years and more.

Whatever had passed between the two men could not have been good. The suppressed fury in her grandfather's voice had revealed that. But as Emma watched him huddle alone between the animals, she recalled the words he'd shouted at the man before they lowered their voices—"Why are you following us?"—and a sudden fear shafted through her.

The man was following them? And her grandfather knew? Could this stranger be the evil one they sought? And if so, why had her grandfather allowed the man to leave?

Did Grandfather know more about the murders than he was saying?

Chapter Four

As the new man on the lot, John drew the easiest job for the matinee performance. Assigned to protect the rear opening of the big top and ensure that the doorway remained clear of gawkers who might impede the performers' entrances, he watched in fascination the parade of players who passed him on their journey toward the ring: clowns with their painted faces and crumpled hats, bareback riders with their waving headdresses and glittering costumes, elephants with their slow gait and sad eyes. He had attended such shows countless times during his youth, yet he remained dazzled by the energy, the light, the colors of the circus.

Heinz Kirshner passed by, this time in a garish costume reminiscent of a harlequin's suit, his face painted as it had been on their first meeting. He nodded at John but did not speak until he entered the ring. Once there he shouted to the crowd, "Here we are again!" in a comical manner and then posed a silly question for the ringmaster. The ringmaster, as he did at every performance, admitted he did not know the answer to the puzzle. From there, the clown continued with his act. Amazingly, Kirshner was a very funny man. The crowd roared at his jokes. The clown possessed a charisma John could not fathom. He had asked some of the other men about Heinz, and they had shrugged, saying Kirshner always wore his face paint, no one knew why. An eccentric from the Old Country, he kept to himself and rarely talked to anyone but Franz.

John spotted Emma walking across the lot toward the tent. She paused to release Destruction from his cage wagon, snapped a short leash onto his collar and led him toward the entrance to the big top. She wore a costume the color of evergreen. The tights hugged her figure, outlining her ample upper curves. The long half-skirt flowed over her lower curves but left little to the imagination since the cloth swayed from side to side as she walked, revealing the length of her legs encased in material of the same color. As she walked past him, she gave John a slight nod, her attention focused on her coming performance.

She was the queen, no doubt about that. Despite his intention to remain aloof and keep his attention focused on learning the secrets of this circus, he could not help but be intrigued by her. Try as he might, he could not keep his gaze or his thoughts off of Emmaline Monroe. Her confidence in her art, offset by shy, little-girl eyes, created an irresistible combination. He had yet to see her perform, and the desire to do so was nearly overwhelming.

John glanced around the area behind the canvas. Deserted. With a shrug, he moved forward to stand inside the entrance to the big top where he could watch Emma work.

Only when he saw Emma and Destruction in the performance cage did he realize that the tigress was missing from the act. He stepped outside to look toward the tiger wagons. There the second tiger paced restlessly. What could ail the tigress enough to warrant her exclusion from the main act?

A roar from Destruction in the performance cage drew him back into the tent. There was an answering roar from the tigress outside. She must be angry at being left out of the show. The tigress continued to roar periodically, the sound becoming angrier as the moments passed and no one came to release her. John glanced around the tent. The music and the crowd's excitement covered the sound of the roars. But he could hear her quite well from his position just inside the door—as could half the countryside, he had no doubt. Emma would have to do something about the tigress later, or they'd be taken to task for terrorizing all the livestock in the county.

John watched as Emma put Destruction through his routine. She amazed him. Whatever she did, she did with a grace both beautiful and unconsciously alluring. No wonder Destruction never took his eyes from her. The cat was in love.

Something hit the back of John's knees, and he fell forward to the ground. He raised his head just as the screams began.

"Dear God!"

"Help!"

"No, please no!"

Seeing immediately the cause of the panic, John leapt to his feet. Emma's second tiger had escaped from her cage and now stalked the horrified crowd.

People who only seconds before had leaned eagerly toward the performance now screamed and climbed over each other in an effort to get away from the snarling animal. But there was nowhere to run since the tigress paced between them and the exit.

People scrambled to the top of the bleachers and leapt down behind them, while others dove underneath the seats, huddling together. Parents slid their children behind them, stiffening in preparation for an attack from the snarling wild animal. The screams continued. The tigress flinched and skittered backward every time a shriek erupted.

John saw the exact second Emma's attention focused on a prey. She stopped moving backward and went very still. Her head tilted sideways, and she crouched low, focusing upon a girl of about two who crawled out from under the bleachers.

"Kitty, kitty," the child chanted as she crawled just beyond the reach of her mother's grasping fingers. The woman, with three other children clinging to her, could not fit through the small opening between the seats. She began to wail as her daughter crawled closer to the waiting animal. The sound of the mother's agony did nothing to halt the design of the tigress. Hope's tail switched back and forth, her haunches wiggling as she prepared to launch herself at the child.

"Hope! Come!" Emma punctuated her command from inside the cage with a crack of the whip, which sounded unnaturally loud and sharp above the cries of the crowd, the frenzied mother and the tigress.

Hope hesitated, cocking her head toward the sound as if hearing a voice she recognized but could not quite place in her memory.

John glanced at the cage where Emma stood, face pressed against the thin wire. The cage, designed to protect the crowd from the wild animals within, had prevented Emma from getting out in time to stop the cat.

Emma attempted the command in German. "*Nein,* Hope. *Kommen.*"

Instead of obeying, the tigress roared, a furious sound that made the hair on John's arms tingle; then she turned back toward the child.

John sprang into action. He ran toward the child, hoping he could shove her close enough to the bleachers so her mother could yank her to safety. His movement drew Hope's attention, and instead of springing at the child, she switched her tail once, twice, three times. Her shoulders bunched, her haunches inched upward. She charged John.

With no time to retreat and nowhere to go if he tried, John froze. He stood dumbfounded as death stampeded in his direction.

Hope leapt. She seemed to hang suspended in the air, as though springing through a ring of fire. A loud pop echoed over the shriek of the crowd. Her body jerked once, then her outstretched paws hit John in the middle of his chest. He fell backward to the hard-packed ground. His eyes closed. He had a fleeting memory of the last time an animal had pushed him to the earth. This time he had no weapon, and this animal outweighed him by at least a hundred pounds. He was as defenseless as the child he'd sought to protect. John braced himself for the bite of fangs at his throat or the slash of a claw across his face.

Nothing happened.

Hope, the tigress, lay as dead weight upon him.

Three hundred pounds of tiger pushed all the air from his lungs. John tried to take a breath. A sharp pain in his side warned him that if he didn't move her soon, his ribs would break.

He shoved at the expanse of fur and muscle pinning him to the dirt, but nothing happened. He sensed movements nearby, and seconds later, the inert body of the tigress rolled off him.

Emma and two of the laborers peered at him from what seemed a long way off. "Are you all right?" Emma's brow was creased with concern. Her voice shook with fear.

He nodded, uncertain if his voice worked. Emma helped him sit up, then supported him when he would have fallen back to the ground on a groan of pain. A blurry glance around the tent revealed that the big top had cleared of people in record time. The now motionless tigress lay a few feet away.

"What happened?" he managed to say, gingerly touching his ribs, then his chest. He took a deep breath. No sharp pain. Excellent. At least she hadn't broken any of his bones.

Emma picked up a rifle from the ground at her feet. "I've always got one close at hand. I never trust a wild animal. Even my own."

"Thank God," John mumbled and got to his feet. He stumbled, and Emma grabbed his arm until he steadied himself. His chest hurt where the tigress had lain on him, but other than that, he was unharmed— and very lucky.

The laborers left to assist the performers in calming the crowd outside. Emma approached the inert body of

Hope. She went down on her knees and reached out a shaking hand toward the animal's still face. As she smoothed the fur over and over, her shoulders shook with sobs. A roar from the performance cage made both John and Emma jump. Destruction paced on the other side of the wire, heartbroken at the sight of the still form.

"I didn't have any choice," Emma whispered, using the back of her hand to wipe away the tears.

"No, you didn't." John wanted to take her in his arms, and he would have if her grandfather hadn't chosen that moment to shout, *"Mein Gott!* What is going on here?"

John turned to see Franz running through the rear entrance of the tent. Gerhardt searched out Emma. After finding her unharmed, he assessed the scene, then pointed a gnarled finger at the prone tigress.

"Explain this, Emmaline."

Emma stood. She swallowed her tears and straightened her back before meeting her grandfather's anger. "Hope ran inside from the back entrance. She was going to attack a child when Johnny distracted her. Then she charged him, and I had to shoot her." She let her breath out on a long, watery sigh. "She's dead."

"How did she get out of her cage?" Franz's face creased in bewilderment, then he pierced John with a glare. "Was anyone near the wagons while you were watching the back?"

"I didn't see anyone. But . . ." John hesitated as he remembered what he'd been doing just before the tiger knocked him down the first time. "I went inside the tent to watch Emma. Hope kept roaring. She sounded very angry. I thought it was because she'd been left

81

out of the act. Then suddenly, out of nowhere, she knocked me down.''

''Someone released her.'' Franz scowled at him, almost as if he believed that John had done the deed himself. ''Perhaps we should look at the cage.''

John preceded Emma and Franz outside, arriving at the cage first. The chain, which was usually wrapped around the door, lay upon the ground. The door yawned open.

All three of them stared at the evidence. ''I don't understand,'' Emma said. ''Whoever did this had to have been waiting for Johnny to turn away. Hope doesn't roar unless she's furious. So I doubt she liked whoever set her free. They had to have been insane to release a furious tiger. Why do such a thing?''

''For no other reason than to cause trouble,'' Franz muttered. He glanced around the back lot as though looking for the culprit. John followed his gaze. The place was deserted.

''Why did you leave Hope out of the act in the first place?'' John asked.

''She took a swipe at me this morning. I thought she might be ill. Or maybe a storm was on the way or even the wo—'' She broke off and cast a glance at her grandfather. Franz shook his head. John watched the interplay with interest. Another secret to uncover. Emma continued, ''I decided to leave her out of the show until her disposition improved.'' She tilted her head in thought. ''I'm shocked she went on the attack. She's accustomed to the noise and movement of a crowd.''

''You said if she was roaring she must have been angry,'' John reminded Emma. ''What if the person who released Hope worked her into a fury before opening the cage?''

"Why? They had to realize she might hurt someone. I can't understand why anyone would do such a horrible thing.''

"I doubt we will ever know the truth,'' Franz said. "And the truth will not bring Hope back to life. That tigress cost hundreds of dollars, Emmaline. We cannot afford another.''

Emma winced. "I know, Grandfather. I'm sorry.''

John frowned. Someone could have been killed, and Franz worried about money? "Emma had no choice but to shoot her,'' he said. "The tigress might have killed me.''

Franz rounded on him, his face red with fury. "You are replaceable. The tigress is not.'' He paused, then narrowed his eyes. "Who gave you leave to address my granddaughter by her first name?''

"She did.'' Out of the corner of his eye, John saw Emma wince again.

Franz blinked, surprise lighting his eyes before he turned away from John without further comment. With a final glare for Emma, the old man stalked toward the red wagon, disappearing inside.

There was more going on here than either Franz or Emma was saying. John glanced at Emma, but she had already started to walk toward the big top.

She was upset now, even a bit frightened. His medical training had taught him that people in such a state were at their most vulnerable. Especially when someone stronger offered them help. Once, he would never have considered taking such an advantage. Once, but no longer.

He followed in Emma's wake.

When John entered the tent, Emma stood over the prone body of the tigress. Destruction continued to pace and growl and roar within the confines of the performance cage. Emma ignored him, her grief focused upon Hope.

Though she made no sound, her shoulders shook with the force of her sobs. John stepped forward and placed his hand on her shoulder. She started, then turned toward him, coming into his arms and burying her face against his chest. He stroked her back and held her close while she cried, damning his body for wanting her despite his plot. He was not as detached from her as he needed to be.

She looked up into his face, and the lost-little-girl look he found so touching had returned. Suddenly his mind was freed of all the questions and the need for their answers. No one existed but John and Emma. Not Peter. Not Franz. Not the nameless, faceless being he had come to discover.

She must have seen the change in his face, the exact moment when the stroke of his palms against her back became so much more than comfort. She tried to step away from the circle of his arms, but he held her tight. He would not let her go.

He could feel the heat from her body call out to his. "Relax," he whispered, then brushed her hair from her forehead. A slight wind through the open tent flap blew the strands back against her cheek. When his fingertips touched her flesh, she shivered and gasped. He smiled and lowered his head.

"Please, don't," she pleaded and put her palms against his chest, holding him away from her.

He frowned, hesitating. "Why not?"

"My grandfather. He—we—you—" she sighed. "I can't. You're a laborer. I'm a performer."

"True."

"You're Italian. Catholic."

"Half Italian, though I don't see what difference that makes. Or my religion either."

"We're not the same."

"No, we're not. I'm a man; you're a woman. That's the idea, Emma."

"I don't know you. You're not one of us."

"Doesn't that make me all the more exciting?"

"Yes." The word escaped her on a whisper. Her eyes widened at the admission.

John nodded slowly. "You want to kiss me, Emma. You've wanted to kiss me from the first moment you saw me. Just like I've wanted to kiss you. It's time you grew up, Emmaline. Make your own decisions about the people you choose for friends. Think for yourself." He pulled her closer, and her eyes drifted closed as she lifted her mouth upward, unable to keep herself from wanting what she should not have. "Trust me," he whispered just before his lips touched hers.

She stiffened. Her eyes opened, and fury snapped in their green depths. She shoved against his chest, catching him off guard so he stumbled back a few steps. She slid out of his reach, but she did not run. "Trust you?" she hissed. "I trust no one any longer. I don't plan to be the next victim, Johnny."

He went very still. "Victim?"

Emma's lips tightened. She had let something slip. He had begun to wonder if Peter had made a mistake in sending him to Gerhardt Circus. If these people harbored a werewolf, they were doing an excellent job of hiding their secrets. He had uncovered nothing out of the ordinary with his questions and quests. They mistrusted him; mistrust was to be expected. But the fear in Emma's eyes, the way she put her fingers over her trembling lips . . . She hid something. A secret John planned on knowing very soon. The word *victim* made him think she was not as innocent as she pretended in her knowledge of the *teufel*.

John took a step toward her. This time she ran.

He let her go. She had nowhere to run. Nowhere to hide. He'd let her worry awhile. Worry when he would come to her next. Worry what he would do, how she would keep her secret from him. He watched her until she disappeared from his view.

She did not understand yet; he was as determined to wrest her secret from her as she was to keep it hidden.

Emma ran. She didn't know where she was going, she only knew she had to get away. From Johnny. From his ice blue eyes, his mocking words and his beautiful, tempting mouth.

When he'd stood so close to her that she could feel his body whisper against hers, the yearning need had frightened her.

Was that how it had been with her mother and father? Had Francesca known that Karl would spell her doom, yet been unable to keep herself from wanting him?

Even if there had not been the danger of a murderer in their midst, the differences between herself and Johnny would prohibit anything lasting between them. Laborer—performer, Italian—German, Catholic—Lutheran. Though she'd never entered a church in her life, religion was one of the things her grandfather had carefully taught her throughout childhood. She had never understood his insistence that they stick to their own kind. But he did insist. If she went against him now, she would be relegated to the limbo where her mother existed, no longer a child of Franz Gerhardt, but a disappointment he refused to acknowledge. She had no doubt he'd disinherit her as he'd done her mother. She could work for another circus, but another circus would not be the same as *her* circus.

Make your own decisions about the people you choose for friends. Think for yourself.

Johnny's voice came to her as if he stood near enough to touch. But she was alone. She was always alone. Despite the milling throngs of people forever present in her world, Emma stood apart. *Separate. Different. Lonely.* She had been so preoccupied with pleasing her grandfather and becoming a performer without peer, she had neglected to see how often she allowed Franz to make her decisions for her. Before now, she hadn't cared who she spent time with or what she did. She had no other life beyond the circus, no friends but her tigers. In the past few days, her life had shifted. Johnny had brought change to her mind and her world. He had made her think, and now she could not seem to stop. She was twenty years old. She should take control of her life. If she could only figure out how.

Emma paused at the edge of the camp and leaned against a tableau wagon. No one could see her here, and she needed time alone to deal with the other problems Johnny brought to mind.

Why had kissing Johnny made her so nervous? Men

had wanted to kiss her before. Every year there had been at least one summer laborer or townie who found himself fascinated with her exotic life-style. She had learned to destroy their hopes quickly and efficiently. Once they saw she was not the woman in the ring when she left the big top, they left her alone. That had always been fine with her. She had not cared about them; she had not wanted to kiss them. She wanted to kiss Johnny Bradfordini back—and so much more.

Then she had compounded her stupidity by blurting out her fear of becoming a victim. She had not even realized she equated her fear of Johnny with her fear of the unknown, unseen murderer in their midst. Logic declared he could not be the one. He had not been in the state when the murders were committed. Or at least he said he had not been here.

She wondered. The way he walked, like a jungle cat, almost as if he were stalking them all, made strands of fear shoot through her whenever he glanced her way. But tangled within those strands was a deep-rooted attraction for the danger she sensed within him. She understood danger and its allure better than most, as she courted death every time she turned her back on a tiger, but she had never played so close to oblivion as she did when she played with Johnny Bradfordini. She suspected the only way to keep him away from her would be to cage him like a wild beast. Showing him the truth of herself would do no good. His silver eyes had seen her for what she was immediately, and he came to her still.

He watched them all when he thought no one was looking. What did he want from them? What did he want from her? Besides the obvious.

She'd promised her grandfather she would not reveal the secret of the murders to Johnny. But did she need to hold to her promise when her grandfather lied to her? He knew more than he was saying. His conversation with the blond stranger had proved that. She had had no time to confront him yet over what she had seen and heard. When she did, she would tell him she had rethought her promise.

If she told Johnny of the murders, perhaps he would leave them and take her desires along with him. She doubted that her grandfather would object to losing the help if she told him Bradfordini had tried to kiss her. He would throw the man off the lot himself.

Emma touched her lips with her fingertips. She couldn't do it. She couldn't tell her grandfather of the moments she'd spent in Johnny's arms. They were too exciting, too special, and hers alone to cherish forever. She took a moment to lament the lost kiss. She could take out that memory in the dark of night whenever the longing kept her awake.

"Attention!" the ringmaster's voice echoed over the lot. Emma stayed behind the wagon. She could hear and still remain unseen. "Herr Gerhardt has canceled this evening's performance. We will move on in the morning."

Emma had forgotten the scheduled evening show. No one would come once word of the tiger attack spread. And tonight they would not move on. Tonight the moon would be at its fullest. Tonight the men would hunt the *teufel*. If all went well, by morning their problems would be solved.

Emma stayed hidden behind the wagon, needing time alone to come to terms with the loss of Hope. She heard the noises of the circus lot being cleaned and swept—familiar sounds that soothed her further. This was her world. Tonight they would do whatever was necessary to save that world.

As the sun set, Emma walked away from the wagon toward the edge of the woods. The hoofed menagerie animals were tethered there. As she walked among them, they welcomed her with pushing noses and soft snorts. She understood animals and they her. Whenever she felt alone, she came to the animals, and the loneliness faded for a brief time.

A large, flat rock sprouted from the field. She sat upon it, then lay down so she could watch the setting sun paint the sky above her. The bright pink and orange fingers of light warred with the blue and white sky. She had always been fascinated by color and light, perhaps because those things were part and parcel of her circus world.

The sky darkened but the colors remained, and Emma continued to watch them ebb and flow. The tears she'd shed over Hope's death had exhausted her. Her last thought before she fell asleep was a vague unease she couldn't quite understand, but it had something to do with the slow fading of the bright colors toward night.

John watched Emma reclining upon a rock in the midst of the field where the menagerie animals milled about. He left her alone as he'd promised himself he would. Tonight he would remain awake while the others slept. When the werewolf made an appearance, he would be ready.

John used his lingering aches from the tiger attack

as an excuse to sleep while the others worked. He awoke just as darkness fell.

Stepping to the open doorway of the wagon, he glanced around the circus. A chill wind ruffled his hair, emphasizing the deserted aura of the place. The full moon rose, casting silver shadows across the empty lot. He had to be mistaken. Everyone could not have disappeared.

John jumped to the ground and headed for the red wagon. "Franz?" he called as he opened the door. No one answered. The office stood dark and deserted.

His next stop was the wagon where Wade Thumb lived with his Gypsy wife. John hadn't seen the dwarf except in passing since the day before, but he liked the little man better than any other he'd met so far, and Wade seemed to know everything about anyone. That characteristic made him John's first choice for a special friend.

The doors of Wade's wagon were closed. John climbed up on the small platform at the rear and yanked on the door. The portal swung outward with a harsh whine. A startled gasp from inside revealed the circus was not as deserted as it appeared.

The sound of a pistol being cocked made John freeze in the doorway. The interior of the wagon held no light, but the brightness of the moon behind him illuminated John like the center of a target. He held his hands up in the age-old gesture of surrender.

"I'm looking for Wade." John squinted into the blackness of the interior. "Wade? Is that you."

"He is not here." The voice, as heavily accented as that of Franz Gerhardt, was neither German nor male. A woman moved forward from the darkness. A trace

91

of silver drifted across her face. She looked as old as Methuselah, and her eyes held the wisdom of the ages. Tall, rawboned, she dressed as a Gypsy. When she moved, the bracelets on her wrists clanked together with a cheery sound at odds with the Navy Colt clasped in her hand. John had seen enough of them during the war to know the weapon on sight. He could also tell on sight when a person knew how to use one. She did.

"I mean you no harm," he said. "I just wondered where everyone's gone."

She took a step closer, squinting as she studied his face. "You are the new worker, no?"

"Yes. I'm new."

She nodded. "They have all gone to hunt the evil one. The *teufel* as they say, though demon is not the exact word for what they seek."

"No," he agreed. "It's not." His mind worked frantically. If the men had gone to hunt the werewolf, they were not party to keeping it safe. They wanted the *teufel* dead as much as he.

The Gypsy's dark, knowing eyes studied him once more. "You wish to hunt the evil one, as well?"

John blinked. His father had insisted he must be the one to kill the werewolf. John had promised to do so. If he planned to keep his promise, he'd better get into the woods before someone else accomplished his revenge for him. "Yes," John answered. "I want to hunt, too."

She nodded as if she understood the underlying need in him. "The men left at dusk. The women are huddled within the wagons. Tonight the men will attempt to destroy once again the evil that has stalked our world."

"Again?" John frowned. *How long have they been*

hunting the werewolf? And failing to kill it?

She ignored his voiced question. "The evil one is strong. He is cunning. He is elusive. If you wish to hunt, you must go now. When the moon is at its highest, the hunted becomes the hunter." She uncocked the pistol and held the weapon out to him. "Use this. It is loaded with the silver."

He shook his head and pushed the gun back toward her. "I have my own."

John returned to his wagon and retrieved Peter's Spencer. He loaded the weapon and stalked toward the woods. He would make sure the evil one did not escape. He would not sit idly by with the women while the others did the work. Work they had failed at before, since the werewolf still roamed free. He must keep his vow to his father so Peter could rest in peace.

John approached the rock where Emma had been earlier. He came to a stop, a curse upon his lips, when he saw her sleeping on it. What on earth was she thinking to sleep unprotected? Reaching out, he shook her ankle.

"What?" she gasped, sitting up so fast her hair flew forward over her shoulders. She blinked at the night sky, her eyes widening when they found the full moon high above. She came to her feet with a lurch, a startled cry of dismay escaping her lips. Then she saw John in front of her, a rifle in his hands. The fright in her eyes made him swear once more.

Emma knew the full moon meant danger. If she knew that, she knew more, maybe even the identity of the one he sought. Though the circus folk might be hunting the wolf now, perhaps they had kept the odd creature in their sideshow—until it escaped. Or perhaps

93

they were as much victims of the evil one as he and Peter had been.

John glanced at the moon as it moved ever closer to the apex of the heavens. He and Peter had been attacked when the moon reached its highest point. He needed to be in the woods when the moon arrived there tonight. Whatever truth Emma knew, he had no time to question her now, and if he found what he sought in the woods, there would be no need for questions later.

"Get back to camp, Emma." He started past her.

"Wh-where are you g-going?" Her teeth chattered with cold, her eyes full of fear.

The fear stopped him. He knew about fear. He could not leave her out here alone and so afraid. "Go back inside where you'll be safe. Go to Devora if you don't wish to be alone. She won't let anything happen to you. I'm going hunting with the rest of the men."

She frowned. "You know?"

The distant howl of a wolf saved him from answering. Emma flinched.

"Go," he ordered. She complied without further argument, running past the shuffling, twitching menagerie animals without glancing back. He watched until she entered her own wagon and drew the doors closed. He should have known she would not go to the Gypsy. Though Emma might allow her grandfather to make too many decisions in her life, she was still quite capable of taking care of herself. If not, she never would have survived in this world for so long.

He turned away from his contemplation of Emma's wagon home, ignoring the pull to go to her. She would be safe enough if she stayed where she belonged. His gaze fell once more upon the elephants and llamas and zebras tethered throughout the field. Without exception, each animal strained at the rope binding it to the earth. They grunted and whined, sniffing the air and tossing their heads in fear. Their eyes rolled in his direction, whites glaring in the midnight light, then rolled away toward the murky shadows of the forest where danger must lurk. Living on a farm all his life, John had learned to trust the instincts of animals. These sensed danger somewhere close.

John entered the darkened woods, intent on destroying an inhuman foe. He walked for many miles and saw no one, nothing beyond the occasional squirrel or raccoon. Not only had the evil one escaped him, but the hunting party, as well.

A low howl in the distance made John spin toward the sound. He had come a long way, but he could still discern that the howl came from the direction of the circus. Instead of traipsing out after the others, he would have been better off remaining on the outskirts of the circus, awaiting the werewolf. But he had wanted to do something, to take some type of action after so many days of waiting. He hadn't thought, and that lapse could very well mean the death of another.

John started to run in the direction of the circus, but after a half hour, he knew he must stop and rest. The fever had weakened him, and he had yet to recover his full strength. Sitting upon the cold ground, John leaned his head back against a tree and closed his eyes for a moment. He could feel the light of the moon shining through the trees and touching his eyelids. He had noticed the moon before only as it related to the task at hand. Now the silver sheen pained him.

He drew up his legs and rested his cheek against his knees. The light shone upon the back of his neck. He could feel it there, a burning sensation on the exposed flesh of his nape. John rubbed at the sting. His hand ached.

Was he having a relapse of the fever that had overtaken him on the morning after Peter's death? If so, he would have to get back to camp before he lost consciousness and lay unprotected in the night. He sat up straight and began to get to his feet but found himself fascinated with the swirling play of silver shadows across his face. Instead of standing, John lay back on the grass and stared at the perfect, round moon visible through the trees above.

Chapter Five

The dream came again, bearing down on him fast and hard from the blessed peace of sleep. He struggled against the too-familiar images, hoping, praying they would leave him this time. Not strong enough, his mind succumbed to the inevitable.

Darkness all around. Shifting, stifling, clinging night. Then, in the midst of the darkness, a sudden shaft of light. Silver, round, ice.

He looked up, his face bathed in a sheen from the heavens. But not a heavenly light. *No.* If there could be light from hell, this would be it.

The sight of the full moon, heavy in the sky, transfixed him so completely he didn't see the leaping form until it came upon him.

The struggle was always the same. A fight with a demon he could not see and did not understand. The searing pain through his hand, the bright shaft of agony in his head. Then the tumble into a darkness more black than any he had ever known.

When the darkness lightened, the dream grew worse.

He became the dark, leaping figure. The hunter not the hunted.

His senses deepened. He could hear for miles, smell the slightest hint of a scent, taste the warmth of the meat upon his tongue before the flesh even entered his mouth. The hair on his body whispered in the breeze as he ran through the darkest night, never stumbling on the unknown path.

He did not see his victims, but he heard their screams. Painful, shrill cries that grated on his sensitive hearing. They never screamed for very long—the wet, gurgling sound of their deaths replaced by the sound that always awoke him from his slumber.

He started up from the dream, heart pounding, chest slick with sweat. A cool breeze drifted across his heated flesh, and he shivered as he saw where he lay. Instead of awakening in his bed with the knowledge he'd only dreamed the horror, this time he rested in a clearing, deep in the woods.

Naked. Bloody. Alone.

The light of the moon on his bare flesh pained him. But he could do nothing to stop its glow. Just as he could do nothing to stop the sound echoing within his brain. He covered his ears with his hands.

There was no escape. As always when he awoke from the dream, he could not purge from his ears the horror that had yanked him from slumber—the moist, spine-chilling sounds of an animal feeding.

But this time John knew the truth with a certainty that chilled his inner being. The dream had not been just a dream as on all the other nights since the last full moon. This time the dream had been a reality. This time John had become the beast he sought to destroy.

He sat up with a howl of anguish. How could such a thing be? He had done nothing to deserve this horror. He was a man who had devoted his life to saving others. How could he become an animal that destroyed them?

He understood now why his father had told him to save himself. He, too, was cursed. As cursed as the evil one who had made him so.

Why hadn't his father told him the truth? Why had he allowed John to wander around where he would hurt someone else when the full moon arose?

Because you told him not to tell you the legends, you fool!

John winced at the voice in his head. And if his father had told him, what then? Would he have believed a superstition? Probably not. He would still be right where he was. Hoping to find a way to deny the truth, despite the evidence of the blood on his body and the memories in his mind.

He had planned to search out and destroy the werewolf that had killed his brother. But now he needed to discover the identity of the *teufel* for another reason. His father had insisted that John end the life of the werewolf. Could his cure come about only if *he*—John and no other—killed the evil one?

Throwing back his head, John stared at the night sky. The tops of the trees swayed and dipped as they danced with the descending silver moon. Every time the moon's light flashed across his eyes, John winced. How he hated that bright, shiny moon.

John looked down at his flesh, covered with dried blood. He flexed his fingers. They ached in reaction to the movement, almost as though the skin had been stretched to its breaking point, then returned to this form. He cast a covert glance around the clearing, half expecting to see a dead body, throat torn asunder just as Peter's had been. But he was alone.

Perhaps the blood had come from an injury to his own body? Perhaps he could not remember the past few hours as a result of the fever he'd endured after the attack? His last coherent thought before the full moon dream had been the fear that he was experiencing a return of his fever and delirium.

John's fingertips traced over his flesh, searching for a cut that would explain all the blood. But even as he did so, he knew he lied to himself. Some things he could not remember. Others he remembered very well. And the screams of the dying still echoed in his mind, though he had no sight images to match those sounds. Still, he would know who those screams had belonged to soon enough. As soon as he returned to Gerhardt Circus.

The moon slid out of sight, the disappearance of the eerie silver light helping to clear John's mind of the panic that had threatened to overtake him while it continued to shine above. The sky remained dark, though his inner clock told him the sun would cast a hazy gray light over the trees to announce its appearance very soon. Maybe then he could discern where he was. Right now, he had no idea, and he did not relish the thought of thrashing through the forest naked.

John stood, eyes straining against the darkness, trying to catch a glimpse of anything in the distance that might give him an idea of which direction to walk to get back to the circus. But the trees surrounding him reached higher than the big top, and he could not see even a swatch of the pale canvas through the thick summer foliage. A light breeze blew against his raised face, and he sniffed the air, then relaxed in relief.

The animals. They were tethered downwind from the circus wagons. If he headed into the breeze, he would eventually run across the camp.

John ran in that direction, his steps swift and sure despite the dark and unfamiliar forest. He splashed into a small, cold creek and paused long enough to wash the blood from his face, hands and torso. The cool water against his heated flesh made him shiver. He winced at the sensation of the hair on the back of his neck rising in response. Never before had he felt the reactions of his body so acutely.

He started to stand, then fell to his knees once more as the horror of the night washed over him full force. He threw back his head and blinked at the sky through burning, tearing eyes. "Dear God, dear God, what have I done?" he whispered. "Why did you let me live? You gave me a gift to save lives. I can't bear to be the one who has taken them."

Just because he had washed away the blood from his skin did not make the stain disappear. He would see the blood on his body for the rest of his life, however short that life might be. John covered his face with his hands and breathed deeply until the pain in his chest, which he knew to be a sob, receded.

He dropped his hands to his sides and shouted, "What am I going to do?"

His answer was the whisper of a breeze, nothing more. But somehow that warm breeze calmed him enough to stand. A purpose filled his mind, pushing the horrors away for a moment. He had to return to the circus and learn the truth. No more time for self-recriminations right now. There would be an eternity for those.

Going onward, he reached the thinner trees at the edge of the clearing in a much shorter time than he should have for the distance he'd calculated. His night vision was much better than he could remember it being before, and he'd smelled and heard the animals from what must have been over a mile away. He recalled the dream that had not really been a dream and how his senses had sharpened with the change. Though his body had returned to the shape he recognized as his own, all the changes had not disappeared with the return of sanity.

John slowed to a stop behind the trees nearest the rock upon which he'd found Emma asleep.

Emma.

His heart pounded with fear. She was the last person he remembered seeing. He blinked, focusing upon a foggy image of Emma walking away from him and disappearing into her wagon. Was that image the truth or merely a wish?

He took a step forward and his bare foot fell upon soft cloth instead of rough grass and twigs. John closed his eyes and took a deep breath, terrified to look at what he'd stepped upon.

Dear God, he hadn't hurt Emma. Had he?

Knowing he had to look sometime, John braced himself before tilting his head downward. A sigh of relief rushed through his lips at the sight of his clothes in a tangled heap beneath his foot. He bent and grabbed his shirt, stuffing his arms into the sleeves. When he reached for the buttons, his fingers froze. The buttons were gone. The places where they'd been sewn to the cloth sported small holes, as if the buttons had been torn from the shirt by force. John picked up his pants. The buttons that closed the front were also missing, and the seams strained almost to the breaking point in several places. He glanced at the ground once more. The buttons lay across the grass as if sprinkled like dew from the sky. John scooped them up and, after donning his trousers, hid the evidence in a pocket.

If he had not before believed the changes that had taken place within him under the full moon, he did now. His clothes looked as though his body had burst from beneath the cloth. He marveled that his shirt and pants were not in shreds after the beating they'd taken.

The trumpet of an elephant drew his attention away from the perusal of his tattered clothing. John moved from the shadows of the trees to the edge of the clearing. The sky was no longer black but tinged with a gray and pink dawn. The animals, which had been tugging on their tethers in fear the last time he saw them, had calmed quite a bit, though they still milled restlessly amid the cropped grass.

He needed to return to the circus. He must find out what had happened last night. Perhaps the others had killed the werewolf that had marked him. Perhaps he was wrong and *he* did not need to kill the evil one, the evil one just had to be dead to remove the curse upon him. Then he could return home with no one the wiser.

In his heart, John knew such hopes were unfounded. Despite the disappearance of the full moon, he could still see farther and better than ever before, the smell of blood nearby made his stomach clench, and the sound of someone crying grated on his sensitive eardrums. If his curse had been broken, he would not still have these abilities. The question was, had the *teufel* been killed by someone else, leaving John a werewolf forever?

John walked toward the camp. The animals edged out of his way, though they did not react so much in fear as in distaste. They could sense the difference in him, too.

His foot slid in what he thought was a patch of mud. John looked down.

His gorge rose when he recognized blood beneath his feet. Nothing else remained to tell him what had died here. No fur, no clothes, no body. Only blood. The sickly sweet smell rose to invade his nostrils, and he swayed, light-headed with hunger as his stomach clenched in response. Then he wiped the back of his hand across his lips in a ferocious gesture. He sickened himself.

"Hell and damnation," he muttered, then clamped his lips shut when he realized what he'd said. The sound of the words brought home to him the state of his soul—cursed through no fault of his own—just as the puddle of blood beneath his feet showed him what he and his kind had done.

John closed his eyes and reaffirmed his vow. He would discover the identity of the werewolf before the next full moon. He would destroy the evil one.

Before John Bradfordini became a werewolf and killed again.

Helga and Heloise had been wailing since the men brought the body of their brother, Otto, back from the woods. Emma tried to calm them, but to no avail. They cried in jumbled German as they rocked their brother's body back and forth between them. At least Wade Thumb's wife, the Gypsy fortune-teller Devora, had taken her husband back to their wagon and locked herself away with him in blessed silence. Emma could understand the sisters' grief, but all the wailing and shrieking made her want to scream herself.

How had this come to pass? The men had gone out to hunt the werewolf and returned with two more dead men, and this time some of the menagerie animals had been slaughtered as well. The appetite of the evil one seemed to have doubled with this full moon. If Johnny had not come and sent her back to her wagon, she might well have been the dead body in the field this morning.

"Emmaline!" Her grandfather's voice brought Emma to her feet. He beckoned to her from the door of the wagon. A glance at the sisters assured Emma they would not even notice her absence. She moved to the opening and jumped to the ground.

"Everyone has been told to keep the tragedies amongst ourselves. We will move onward today, away from this place, then bury our dead as we have done before."

"Who are we to keep this secret from, Grandfather? We all know what happened."

"Not all. But then Bradfordini seems to have disappeared. So we need not worry about him."

Emma's heart gave a leap of fear. "But I saw him last night. He went off to find the rest of you. Do you mean to tell me he never reached you?"

"No." Franz frowned, then grabbed Emma's upper arm in a tight grasp. "What do you mean he came to find us? Did you tell him our secrets, Emmaline?'' He shook her, once, hard. ''Did you?''

''No. I think he already knew. He had a rifle and told me to get inside. Then he went into the woods.'' Emma took a deep breath as the meaning of her words sunk in. Johnny had gone into the woods, but he had not returned. Perhaps there were more victims out there than they had yet discovered.

Emma turned, the long skirt of her blue day dress tangling with her petticoats. Whenever she wore the clothes of a young lady, she often tripped over her feet. She was used to the freedom of her costumes. She bit off a curse word she'd learned from working next to the laborers and pulled her foot free from the hem. Before she could take a step, her grandfather yanked her back by her skirt.

''Where do you think you are going, Emmaline?''

''To find him. He could be hurt. He could be . . .'' her voice broke on the word she didn't want to imagine. She didn't pause to wonder why the thought of Johnny Bradfordini dead upset her so deeply.

''If he is gone, so much the better for us.''

''You told me not to tell him anything so he'd stay. Now you want him gone?''

''I said that before we had another—incident. Last night changed everything. Now we must use all our resources to find the *teufel*. We cannot allow another full moon to come upon us without discovering who is killing our people. We cannot afford to lose any more performers. Or any more animals.''

Emma sighed. ''I know.''

''If Bradfordini returns, tell him nothing. I do not trust him. For all we know, he is the one.''

Emma, who had been looking at the ground and trying not to remember the sight of the dead zebra that had greeted her when she'd gone to feed the menagerie animals this morning, jerked her head up to meet her grandfather's intent gaze. "But he didn't come to us until after we'd lost two people. How can he be the one?"

"Anything is possible, Emmaline. We can no longer trust each other, let alone a stranger."

"I suppose not." Emma glanced at the woods, wondering if she should go looking for Johnny anyway. Another wail from within the wagon made her flinch and return her attention to the problems at hand.

"Calm them as best you can," her grandfather advised. "We must leave within the hour."

She nodded, and after an awkward pat on her shoulder, the usual extent of his comfort or affection for her, he left. Emma climbed back into the wagon, but just before she went inside, something made her turn and glance out over the circus lot.

Johnny approached from the woods. His shirt hung open, revealing a muscled chest covered with hair a shade darker than the brownish-blond hair on his head. That hair hung in disarray about his face, giving him a wild look that matched the rest of his appearance. His denim trousers gaped open at the front in a careless fashion. Emma could feel her cheeks heat at the image of what lay just out of sight beneath the open pants. She wanted to run to him. To ask where he'd been. If he was all right. What he had seen. She would have, if Devora had not chosen that moment to open the doors of her wagon and step onto the small platform at the rear.

The Gypsy's gaze lit on Johnny, and as she raised her arms, Emma heard her bracelets clank together, loud and harsh in the stillness of the new morning.

Johnny heard them, too, for he raised his head from an intense contemplation of his boots and sought out the source of the noise. His gaze stopped at the sight of Devora, standing at the back of the wagon, her arms raised like an avenging angel.

The Gypsy said nothing. She did not need to. With no other sound but the music of her bracelets crashing together like the drums during a circus parade, Devora twisted the fingers of both hands into the symbol against evil.

John stared at the Gypsy. He had seen that symbol before in his dealings with the superstitious immigrants in his care. She made the sign against evil in his direction. How did this woman know what he was when he'd just learned for himself? More importantly, what did she plan to do with her knowledge?

Before he could ask, the Gypsy turned and disappeared into the wagon. She slammed the door behind her. John frowned.

That was all? No screaming, no finger pointing, no shooting him with the Navy Colt she'd possessed the night before? The pistol loaded with silver bullets to destroy the evil she now recognized within him?

The sound of crying, which he had been following ever since he'd retracted his boot from the puddle of blood in the field, came to him once more. Turning his head, John saw Emma standing at the rear of another wagon. She stared at him, green eyes wide and frightened in her tired, pale face. Just the sight of her alive and well sent a rush of relief through him so strong he stumbled in reaction. As he righted himself, the thought crossed his mind that Emma meant so much more to him than a means to discover the identity of the werewolf. He wanted to keep her safe from whatever threatened them all—himself included. His joy at seeing her safe caused him to smile. She took a step backward at his expression. The smile died upon his lips. She was afraid, more afraid than he had ever seen her.

"What happened?" he called.

When she didn't answer, he strode forward. Her gaze flickered to the side as if she wanted to slam the doors to the wagon in his face just as the Gypsy woman had done. John stopped short. Emma must have seen Devora make the sign against evil in his direction.

Since the people of Gerhardt Circus had been out hunting the werewolf last night, they did not know any more than he the identity of the evil one or they would have killed the man before he changed. They knew they were being stalked, but that was the extent of their knowledge. For all Emma knew, the *teufel* could be Johnny Bradfordini. The sad truth was, she would be right.

Still, he had to put her mind at rest. If she believed and told the others, he doubted that he'd last another hour before a silver bullet rested within his body. He did not want to die before he avenged Peter's death, and if he'd read his father's cryptic comments correctly, he must avenge his brother's death for his own curse to be lifted. He needed the twenty-eight days until the next full moon to search out and destroy the killer.

Somehow he would make Emma trust him. Emma

and the old Gypsy woman both. But how?

"Emma," he tried again. "Who is crying?"

She jumped at the sound of his voice. He had shouted at her, letting his own fear of the situation cloud his judgment. He needed to act lucidly or he would be dead. "Emma," he said more softly. "Please, tell me what is wrong."

His gentle tone worked, for she relaxed and opened her lips to speak. Then her eyes widened as she stared at something behind him, and her mouth snapped shut with a click of her teeth that John heard quite well across the distance because of his improved hearing. He also heard the rustling of grass as someone approached behind him. He spun around to meet Franz Gerhardt's scowling countenance.

"Bradfordini, we thought you had deserted us."

"No. I got lost in the woods."

Franz stared at his clothes, and John had to fight not to flinch under the old man's scrutiny. If he acted like a man, no one could prove him a beast—until the next full moon anyway. When Franz raised his questioning gaze to John's face, John smiled and shrugged. "I tried to find you and the men, but I ended up sleeping in the woods. When the sun rose, I found my way back."

"Why did you try to find us?"

John wrinkled his brow in what he hoped was a convincing imitation of confusion. "The Gypsy told me you were hunting. I thought I'd help. I've always been a very good shot."

Franz turned and stared at the wagon where the Gypsy woman had disappeared. Then he slowly turned back to John.

He doesn't believe me. He'll ask her for the truth.

John stood his ground under Franz's continued perusal. He had to admire the old man. Gerhardt's interrogation tactics would have made him useful during the war. With his stern face and stiff German voice, he reminded John of a school headmaster. John stifled the urge to tell him everything before Franz beat him with a hickory switch.

"If your sense of direction is so poor, next time stay with the women," Franz snapped. He glanced up at Emma, who had said nothing during the questioning. A silent communication passed between the two of them—an order from Franz, an acknowledgment from Emma. Then he turned back to John. "We are ready to load up. Get to work, if you please." He stalked in the direction of the red wagon.

John couldn't believe he'd been allowed off so easily. Franz had not even questioned him about the sorry state of his clothes. The old man knew John lied, but he had said nothing. A thought occurred to John. If Franz believed him to be the werewolf, he would not want John to know that for fear John would kill him. Franz would also want to keep John near the circus until they could destroy him. He would not allow John to wander about the woods, trailing the circus from the depths of the trees. In order to keep John where they wanted him, Franz would have to pretend everything was fine, even if everything was not. An unpleasant thought, but John had to be prepared for everything. Somehow he would have to find a way to make the circus people trust him.

The slam of a door interrupted his thoughts. A glance revealed that Emma had shut the doors of the wagon. The sounds of crying from inside became muffled. John winced as guilt stabbed him. The sobs were a result of his actions, or the actions of one other. He needed to discover who had died last night. Since Franz chose to pretend that nothing had happened, and Emma couldn't seem to find her tongue this morning, he would have to question the others while they worked. Perhaps Wade Thumb would be a good place to start. He had always been a talkative fellow.

John hurried to his wagon and changed, stuffing his ripped clothing to the bottom of his carpetbag. The circus folk spent the next few hours loading up, and John spent the time asking questions. But no matter how many people he asked, the answer remained the same. No one knew where Wade had gone. No one knew who cried within the wagon, or why. They had gone hunting for meat and returned empty-handed. They lied, but John could not prove it.

They traveled all afternoon through the bright sunlight and heat of a late June afternoon, bound for the lumber towns of the north. The thick, towering forests of upper Wisconsin would be the home of Gerhardt Circus for a month as they made a circuit of the large area. Though not as populated as the southern region of the state, the north woods boasted little in the way of entertainment, and families would travel for a day or more just to see a performance.

A twinge of unease assailed John at the realization that they would be deep within the north woods when the next full moon rose. *Better for a wolf to hide in, my dear,* his mind taunted. John scowled at the tableau upon his wagon—Little Red-Cap and the Wolf. The painting had invaded his thoughts.

The caravan stopped right after dark to rest. Though

the moon did not look any smaller than the night before, still the silver orb waned. Tonight, heavy clouds
drifted over and back across the face of the moon, making travel difficult. Several kerosene lamps were hung
on the lead wagons to help light their way. The lamps
swayed to and fro, throwing wavering fingers of flame
into the shadows. They used a minimum of light to
save on kerosene and lessen the chance of mishaps.
Many a wagon had been lost when a spark from a lamp
ignited the paint of a tableau. But the circus still had
an hour's ride before they reached their destination, a
small town called Haywardsville, and they needed the
extra illumination not provided by nature.

Many of the larger towns in the state had Indian
names, taken from the natural wonders around which
the city had grown. Milwaukee, for instance, meant city
by the water. But in the north woods, the small villages
were often named for the town's leading citizen, and
they were often moved from place to place as the lumber camp moved. As a result, a village in one place
last year would be up the road a piece the next year.
That's why Heinz always went ahead and marked the
way.

Heinz.

The thought of the man brought a frown to John's
face. He hadn't seen the clown since the last performance. Kirshner must have been out marking their way
last night, as he did nearly every night, instead of hunting with the rest of the men. John sighed and jumped
down from the wagon seat. He walked away from the
caravan, stretching his aching muscles in an attempt to
loosen them before he had to climb back into the driv-
er's seat. He had hoped the odd clown was the were-

wolf. But how could such a thing be when Kirshner had been miles ahead of the circus marking the trail? And if all the men had gone out hunting, then why had no one discovered the identity of the *teufel?* Someone must have disappeared long enough to kill.

''Onward!'' The ringmaster's booming voice came from the lead wagon and echoed down the long line of conveyances. Those who had been walking, like John, turned back toward the caravan and remounted their wagons. John followed more slowly than the others. He hated getting back on that damn seat. Driving alone after spending the last trip with Wade Thumb made the long trip seem all the longer. Since John had seen no sign of the dwarf, he feared the worst. The fear that he might have been the one to end the man's life burned like a lump of coal in his throat. John swallowed, trying to make the pain go away. Instead it intensified. He had many things to hate himself for, but Wade's death would be the worst thus far. The man had befriended him when no one else would, and it looked as if Wade's friendliness had been his downfall. No wonder the Gypsy had made the sign against evil at John. He should count himself lucky she hadn't aimed her pistol at his head if Wade had been the latest victim.

The other wagons began to move, and John, bringing up the rear, put his team of Percherons into motion. They weren't on the trail more than five minutes when one of the horses began to favor its hind leg. John swore and ordered the animals to stop. The caravan continued on without him. John didn't bother to hail them. They wouldn't hear him anyway above the noise of the wagons and animals. He would catch up once he tended to the Percheron.

It took John longer than he expected to check the horse. Every time he came near the animal, it snorted and pawed and tried to back away from him. Then its huge haunches would bump against the wagon and the horse would roll its eyes in fear. John released the Percheron from the harness, and only then would the animal allow him to remove the stone from its shoe. By the time he'd put the horse back into harness and started down the road, the rest of the circus had disappeared from view up the winding trail.

The Percherons plodded along the path, their heavy feet making a muffled clip-clop on the packed dirt road. Every so often John would hear the sound of a man's voice or the snort of an animal in the distance. With his improved hearing, those sounds could be miles up the road for all he knew.

The night pressed upon him, reminding him of the night Peter had died. He had been afraid that night. Afraid of the unknown. Afraid of what Peter knew and would not tell. But now, despite the fact that he was alone in a strange place, John knew no fear. The worst had already happened to him. He had nothing more to fear until the next time the moon reached its fullest point—twenty-seven nights away.

The horses slowed as a fork appeared in the road. A fence rail had been borrowed from a farmer's fence to rail the route. This one indicated the road to the right. John tilted his head to the side and listened. He could swear the circus sounds came from the left. He turned his head back toward the fence rail and studied it.

Right.

The wind must be playing tricks with his hearing. He wasn't yet accustomed to the heightening of his senses. John turned the Percherons onto the marked path.

He drove for over half an hour and probably would have kept going for another hour if the trail hadn't become so overgrown that the huge Percherons could not get through. Then John admitted the truth. The circus had not come this way. Someone had changed the trail marker. They intended to send him in the wrong direction.

John drew his Spencer from beneath the seat of the wagon and lay the rifle across his lap. If they planned to get him alone so they could kill him, he would not die without a fight. He had revenge left to take. John's gaze raked the darkened forest. He saw nothing, heard no one, smelled not a thing amiss.

Jumping down from the seat, he held the Spencer in one hand and used the other hand to guide the Percherons backward, the trail too narrow at that juncture to turn them.

"A-ma-zi-ing grace, how sweet the sound—"

The horses froze, their ears twitching in response to the song.

"That saved a-a wretch li-ike me."

John's ears strained to determine the direction the sound came from. His heightened hearing sharpened with his will, and when the words drifted to him upon the night air, he flinched at the volume.

"I-I once wa-as lost but now am found, was blind b-ut now I see."

John left the horses and crept toward the sound of male and female voices raised in song. While they finished the hymn, he traversed the short distance toward them.

The forest, dense and thick, provided perfect cover for John to hide. He peered from behind a clump of shoulder-high brambles and observed the secret ceremony.

Chapter Six

Thunk.

Emma winced as a shovel hit the dirt.

Scrunch.

Her grandfather's boot pushed the tool into the earth.

Scrunch. Scrunch. Scrunch.

Three of the laborers followed his lead and pushed their own shovels into the earth around the grave.

"Ach, mein Gott," Franz swore as he lifted a shovel full of dirt. The rest of the men accomplished their job with stoic silence.

Wunk. The clump of dirt landed on top of the hastily constructed wooden coffin.

Ssss. The dirt broke into pieces, cascading down the sides of the coffin and rejoining its brothers within the grave.

Helga and Heloise leaned against Emma, emitting nothing louder than a sniffle every few seconds. They had exhausted themselves crying, thank God. Emma didn't know how much longer she could have stood being confined with the two of them and the dead, mangled body of Otto within the wagon. She had done her best to calm the girls, but in the end, she had given up and let them vent their grief without interference. She could not imagine what it felt like to lose a brother in such a way, and Helga, Otto and Heloise had been triplets. What they'd shared had been closer than the usual sibling relationship.

Emma glanced up. Devora stood alone, silent, thoughtful, next to Wade's newly turned grave. Emma had not had a chance to speak with the woman yet. But she would.

They made quite a picture, all the circus folk standing in the woods dressed in their Sunday best or, if they had none of those, their most elaborate performance costumes. All dressed up and no place to go— except a funeral.

The burials were secret, as the others had been before them. If the townsfolk learned the truth, Gerhardt Circus would die. If the law discovered what they'd done, someone would go to jail, or worse. Everyone within the small, darkened clearing knew these things and would keep their own counsel.

The only one not considered one of them was Johnny. Grandfather had hoped their new worker would not return this morning. When he had, Grandfather made sure he would not know of the secret burials. A small stone in the Percheron's shoe had ensured that Johnny remained behind. A mismarked turn and he was lost. Grandfather's schemes had worked for tonight, but soon they would have to tell Johnny the truth, or make sure he went away for good. The thought of losing him before she'd had a chance to explore the strange but exciting way he made her feel upset Emma more than she cared to admit or examine. But the circus was what mattered, and she would do whatever was necessary to protect it.

Her grandfather straightened and handed his shovel to one of the other men. Though the clearing had been devoid of sound beyond the sniffles of the sisters and the natural noises of the forest since the group had finished the hymn, when Franz Gerhardt stepped to the head of the grave, the area became completely still. No wind, no sniffles, not even a bird dared twitter.

"We have lost two more of our men. The appetite of the *teufel* grows stronger. This time the wolf took two human victims and two lives from our menagerie, as well. I am sorry we cannot have a proper funeral or the correct words from a man of our faith. But we all know why we do what we do." Several heads nodded in assent. "Otto and Wade were good men. Good performers. Hardworking until the end. I feel responsible for this tragedy. I should not have divided our people into pairs to search for the werewolf. I had hoped to end this last night. Instead, I made our situation worse."

"No, Grandfather," Emma whispered.

He made a sharp motion with his hand for her silence, then stepped toward Helga and Heloise. "I am sorry, girls. I will make sure the *teufel* pays for this."

"You have said that before." Devora's heavily accented voice broke the silence. All in the clearing turned toward her. "Please forgive me if I no longer believe you."

"He has done the best he can," Emma said.

"Please, Emmaline, I have no need of your defense."

"But, Grandfather—"

"Be silent, I say. She is right. I have done nothing but talk." He sighed, a sad, hopeless sound that tore at Emma's heart. "Talk and get more of our people killed."

The gathered circus folk shifted and muttered at the admission of their leader. Emma wanted to shout for her grandfather to stop, for Devora to leave him alone. They could not afford to let their people become afraid and demoralized. If Franz and Devora wanted to argue fault, they could do it without an audience.

The burden of Helga and Heloise, who made no response to the argument but continued to lean upon Emma so heavily her shoulders ached, became too much for her. Before she could ask one of the others for help, the acrobats, for once walking on their feet and not their hands, saw her dilemma and stepped forward to lead the girls away. At a nod from Emma, the rest of the people followed the procession back toward camp.

She turned toward Devora and her grandfather, who now stood on opposing sides of Wade's fresh grave. Devora stared at Franz's bowed head impassively. Emma's lips thinned in frustration as she crossed the short distance to stand next to the Gypsy woman. She put away her anger at the woman's words. Devora had just lost her husband and had every right to be upset.

"I know you must be angry," Emma ventured.

Devora's black eyes snapped. "You know? What do you know, Emmaline? Do you know what it is like to hold a man you love in your arms—both when he is alive and when he is dead?" Devora glanced at the grave and winced. Taking a deep breath, she returned her gaze to Emma's face. The fire in her eyes had died,

121

leaving the ashes of despair. "No, you do not. Though someday soon you might. I pray what I see for you is not so." She shrugged. "But who am I to say what is truth and what is dreams?"

Emma frowned. Devora had the sight and made no secret of the fact. "What are you talking about?"

"Never mind that now. I speak ahead of myself." Devora stepped around the grave and put her hand on Franz's forearm. The old man did not respond.

"Boss man, I know you have tried your best. It is not your fault the evil one is so clever. You search out a demon from hell with the methods of a good man. There is no other way for you. But for me there is."

She squeezed Franz's arm once before turning to walk away. Emma glanced at her grandfather. He stared at the grave without moving. When Emma looked again for Devora, the woman had disappeared.

The moment John saw what they were doing, he knew his trip up the wrong path had been planned—most likely by Franz. He counted himself lucky the old man had not ordered his burial along with the two other men. Since there had been two other deaths before these, they had been fighting the evil for several months now. Gerhardt Circus meant to keep their werewolf a secret from everyone they considered an outsider. To them, John was the enemy, as much or even more so than the evil one who stalked them. The evil one they knew they must kill. They did not yet know they should do the same with Johnny Bradfordini.

Pain racked him when he heard the identities of the dead. He had not known Otto, but Wade—Wade he had considered a friend. The image of the smiling, life-loving dwarf dead in the grave made John close his eyes and utter a prayer for forgiveness. Had he been the one who ended Wade's life?

John turned away from the scene and silently made his way back to the wagon. He frowned as he drew near the stalled conveyance. Devora sat upon the seat awaiting him.

He glanced back over his shoulder. How had she gotten from the clearing where they'd buried her husband to the wagon without his seeing her? And how had she known where to find him?

John moved forward and stood at the side of the wagon. She did not look at him, staring instead at a point between the massive rumps of the Percherons. John remained silent, as well. What could he say to her?

"Come here."

John's gaze flicked toward her. She still did not look at him.

"Ma'am?"

"Up on the seat, boy. Sit next to me. I wish to talk with you."

John climbed up on the seat as he'd been ordered. Devora reminded him of his father's mother, who had lived with them on the farm until she died when he was five years old. Though *Nona* had spoken to him in Italian, her tone had brooked no argument from her young grandson. Devora used the same tone, and John, who remembered well what happened when you argued with a woman like her, obeyed.

She turned toward him, her bracelets clanking as she reached for his hand. John flinched away from her touch.

"Give it to me."

He looked into her eyes. The grief within her soul pierced him as a physical pain. He could deny her nothing. Silently, John put his marked hand into hers.

"I thought you were the one last night, but I could not be sure." She stared for a moment at the smooth perfection of the back of his hand. Amazingly, the teeth of the wolf had left no marks where they could be seen at a glance. The truth lay hidden. She turned his hand over to reveal the bite marks that marred his palm and traced them with the tip of her gnarled finger. "You were bitten, but you survived. You are one of them."

"I didn't know."

"You did not know that being bitten by the werewolf and surviving would make you a werewolf, as well?"

John shook his head. The thought had occurred to him often since the night Peter had died, but he had never believed it until this morning. With childlike stubbornness he had clung to the hope that not believing in the curse would make it not so. "I didn't know the legends. I didn't want to know." He sighed. "My father knew, I think. He wanted to tell me. But I refused to listen. And I don't think he wanted to believe it either."

She gave an exclamation of disgust. "You young people think we old folk know nothing. But we know so much more than you about things like this." She smoothed her thumb over the scar once more.

"I know." John hung his head.

"Why did you come here?"

John looked up. Devora stared at him, her black eyes intent with an inner purpose. "I came to kill the werewolf. To destroy this place if you were protecting it. I see now you are all as much victims of this evil as I. But when I came here I did not know I would become a wolf, too.'' He looked up at the night sky, remembering the perfect silver moon of the night before. Then he returned his gaze to her face. ''I didn't know until I awoke this morning covered in blood.''

Devora flinched at his words, but she did not draw away. She continued to hold his hand, stroking the scar with her thumb. Her touch soothed, and for the first time since he'd awoken that morning, John relaxed.

One of the Percherons snorted, stamping its foot in impatience, and John straightened, drawing his hand away from Devora's hypnotic touch. ''What do you plan to do with me?'' he asked.

''Do? What should I do?''

''Kill me now? Or will you tell the others and let them do it? Franz seems defeated. Perhaps it will help him to be the one to destroy me.''

''Destroy you? I don't think so, boy. You are our key to the evil one.''

''But you just said—I mean, I'm evil now, too.''

She interrupted him with a quick shake of her head. ''Not evil. Or at least not truly evil. Not yet. You have been made a werewolf through no fault of your own. Eventually the inner you will disappear, and the evil beast will take its place. But for now, the good man is still stronger than the evil wolf.''

''I might have been the one who murdered Wade. Though I don't remember doing it, your husband is still dead. I'm sorry.''

''I know you are, boy. The man is sorry, the wolf was hungry. That is the way of the beast.''

"You don't seem very upset."

Her eyes flashed. "I loved him with all my heart. I am dead in my heart now that he is dead. But crying and fainting will not accomplish what I need to accomplish. I have one thing left to live for now."

"I don't understand."

"I will explain. You heard Franz. We have been stalked by the werewolf for months now. Either he is one of us, or he follows us from town to town—listening, learning, waiting for the next moon. Whatever the truth, we have been unable to uncover his identity and destroy him. He knows what we do before we do it. But you, boy, will help us."

"How?"

She ignored his question, instead asking one of her own. "Why did you come here if you did not know you were cursed?"

"He killed my brother. I want him dead."

She smiled. "Excellent. Revenge is a good motivation. It is my motivation. But you have an even better one than that now. If you don't kill him, you will continue to turn into a werewolf yourself. With each successive moon you will become more the wolf and less the man. Right now you are a victim. As time passes you will become as evil as the one who made you. You must destroy him before this happens."

"Then what I've heard is true? If I kill the one who bit me, the curse will be lifted?"

"That is what the legends say."

"What if someone else kills it?"

"The curse upon you will remain."

"And then?"

She stared at him for a moment, then raised her hand

and brushed a lock of hair away from his forehead with a sad, regretful expression on her seamed face. ''Then you will have to die, as well.''

No surprise came to him at her words. He had known what she would say before she said it. Still, knowing didn't make hearing the pronouncement of his death any easier. He had considered taking his own life after he'd awoken covered in someone else's blood. Only the fact that the other could continue to kill unchecked without his interference had stopped John from using the silver bullets in Peter's rifle on himself.

He had a month to save himself and the rest of the circus folk. He saw the irony in the fact he had come to destroy Gerhardt Circus, and now he wanted to protect it and its people. One person in particular. Though his mind and body were in a turmoil, he spared a moment to acknowledge his relief that he would not have to destroy Emma's circus in his quest for revenge. Then he turned to Devora with his questions. ''What made you suspect I was also cursed?''

She smiled, a small, sad smile. ''I have the sight, though my powers do not extend to those I love too much. I could not save Wade. I had no warning of what would happen last night. But I have seen you before. In my dreams. You and Emmaline.''

''Emma?'' A cold wind slashed across his face. ''What about me and Emma?''

''I am not sure. I dreamed she would find love and then lose it. Then I saw your face. I do not know if you are her love or the instrument by which she will lose her love. Maybe you are both.''

''I'll stay away from her. I don't want her hurt.''

Devora laughed, a dry, breathless sound that reminded John of dead leaves kicked up by a winter wind. "What is fated cannot be stopped, boy. This much I know."

"You won't tell the others what I am?"

"No. They would shoot you where you stand, and there would be nothing I could say to stop them. Your secret is safe with me. Make sure the truth of your nature remains between the two of us."

He had one more question he needed to ask the old woman. "Are there any signs that indicate a werewolf in human form? Behavior I should look for in the *teufel* and be on the alert to disguise in myself?"

She tilted her head, thinking. "A good idea. One I should have thought of. I will look. Perhaps we can solve our problems before anyone else dies."

"I hope so."

"Remember, tell no one what you are." She grasped his forearm in her talonlike grip. "Show no one your mark. You might not have known its meaning, but everyone here does, and they will not hesitate to destroy you should they see that scar. I mean what I say. If you die, the true evil one will go on killing. I feel this in my heart. You are our last hope of survival."

Dawn dusted the horizon when Emma and her grandfather returned to camp, and silence hung over the lot. Her grandfather had not spoken on the walk home, his silence telling her all she needed to know about his state of mind. Otto and Wade had been his friends. He felt responsible for their deaths.

Would this horror end only when they all lay dead? What had Gerhardt Circus done to deserve this?

Emma walked with her grandfather to the red wagon

where his bed awaited him. "Get some sleep," she told him.

"There is a performance today. I have much to do."

"You have time to sleep for a while. You must."

He sighed, a sound dredged from deep within, then smiled at her and patted her cheek. "All right, Francie. I will sleep awhile."

The smile forming upon Emma's lips froze at his words. "I'm Emmaline, Grandfather."

He frowned and squinted into her face. Confusion flickered in his eyes for a moment before he said gruffly, "Of course you are. Who else would you be?" He turned and left her alone.

His manner frightened her. He was old, Emma knew, but he had never been frail or forgetful. This sudden change, coming so quickly, made Emma's heart thump with fear for him, for them all. What would she do without him? He had been the rock upon which she built her life. His circus, his dream, had become hers, as well. Right now both were slipping away before her eyes, and she could not do one thing to stop it from happening.

A sound from the road drew Emma's attention. Seconds later, the Red-Cap tableau wagon came into view with Johnny and Devora upon the wagon seat. Emma frowned. After Devora's behavior this morning, Johnny would be the last person Emma would expect her to ride in with.

She cast a glance at the closed doors to the red wagon. Her grandfather was in no condition to bother now. She would talk to Johnny Bradfordini herself, and Devora, as well. She had been meaning to do so since this morning when she'd witnessed their exchange outside the wagon of Helga and Heloise. Devora had made the sign against evil when she'd seen Johnny. Had she made the sign to keep the evil in Johnny away from her, or to keep the evil surrounding them all away from Johnny? Emma needed to learn the answer to that question. She wanted to trust Johnny, to share with him the secrets burdening her heart. But she could not. Not yet. Not when he had as many secrets in his eyes as she had in hers.

Before she could hail them, Devora jumped down from the slow-moving wagon and disappeared inside her own abode. Emma sighed, then shrugged. She would have to make allowances for Devora's grief. She would talk with Johnny now; then later, after Devora had some rest, Emma would speak with her.

As Emma crossed the distance separating her from the wagon, she passed Destruction's cage. He roared in protest and Emma paused. Did she want to talk to this man alone? Perhaps she would do better to bring the tiger along.

As she removed the chain from the door of the cage wagon, Emma worried her bottom lip with her teeth. What should she ask him?

Have you lied to me, Johnny? Did you kill my friends? Will you kill me, too?

She pulled Destruction's leash from the pocket of her best dress, which she had donned in deference to the burial services, even though the depth of the neckline would not be considered appropriate for such a solemn occasion. The dress, an emerald green silk, had been bought by her grandfather for Emma to wear to a dance at the governor's mansion last fall. Though circus people were often considered little above tramps by some, those who understood their talents treated them like American royalty. Emma had been as uncomfortable at that dance as she'd been every time she entered any town on their tour. Whether people treated her like a tramp or a queen, they still treated her differently from everyone else.

Destruction jumped to the ground, but before Emma could attach the leash, he snarled and pushed himself in front of her. Emma gasped and spun around, her startled gaze meeting the silver-blue eyes of Johnny Bradfordini. She frowned at the tiger, which had placed himself in front of her and now crowded her backward with his body as Johnny advanced upon them.

The man walked toward her slowly, his long legs eating up the space between them too quickly for Emma's liking. He stopped, too close to the tiger, and she tensed, her breath coming harsh and fast in the still air that hung between them. Destruction snarled again—a warning, a promise.

"Call him off," Johnny whispered, the trickle of sound all the more demanding for its lack of volume.

Emma looked into his eyes and hesitated. She had been afraid of him before. She was afraid now. But mixed with her fear was an attraction so deep she could not resist its allure. Still staring into Johnny's eyes, Emma snapped her fingers, and the tiger's snarl faded to a low rumble. A word of reproach and he lay at her feet.

Johnny looked as if he might touch her, and she was astounded to find she wanted him to. Where on earth did all these strange yet wonderful desires hail from?

"Good choice, Emmaline." To her relief and dismay, he did not touch her, but continued to stand as close as he could with a Bengal tiger lying between them. The silence chanted unspoken questions, and after a few moments, Emma could no longer stand the noise. She had to know where the truth began and where the lies ended, despite her fear of this man.

"I saw you return from the forest this morning."

Something flickered in his eyes, then died. He raised his eyebrows. "You knew I'd gone hunting with the men. What of it?"

"You never found the men. They never saw you, Johnny. Where were you all night?"

"Where do you think I was, Emma?"

She didn't know. She didn't want to know. Or did she? What should she believe? She found it hard to fathom that Johnny Bradfordini, this man with the haunted eyes and beautiful lips, could turn into a monster under the light of the full moon. Just the idea seemed ludicrous, would be ludicrous if she hadn't seen for herself that such things were possible.

"I don't know where you were. That's why I'm asking you."

"And you'll believe whatever I tell you?"

"Do you plan to lie?"

He laughed, then looked surprised to have done so. "One thing you need to learn, Emma, men often lie. But they never tell you when they're going to do it."

She didn't appreciate him treating her like a child. She knew men lied. She knew that very well. The memory of her father's desertion was never far from her mind.

"Where were you?" she asked again.

"In the woods." He stared into her eyes, daring her to ask the next question.

She swallowed and did. "What were you doing?"

"Hunting."

"Whom, I wonder?"

His hand snaked out, and his fingers circled her upper arm. She gasped at the pressure against her flesh and tried to pull away. He held her tighter. Emma glanced down at Destruction, but the tiger stared placidly back. She had told him to lie down and be quiet, and unless she told him to do otherwise, he would not disobey. She looked back into Johnny's face, and what she saw there made her breath catch in her throat.

"Don't," he said firmly. "Don't wonder, Emma." He pulled her toward him, and she stumbled against Destruction. Johnny grasped her other arm and lifted Emma off her feet, stepping backward and bringing her with him until her toes touched the ground on the opposite side of the tiger. The ruffled train of her dress slid over the tiger's fur with a rustle only silk could emit. The big cat grumbled in displeasure but did not move.

Johnny released the pressure upon her arms but did not remove his hands. She stared wide-eyed into his face and something changed between them. As her body moved downward, her heels headed toward the ground, she slid against him, breasts against his chest, hips brushing his upper thighs. His jaw tightened. Emma wanted to touch the muscle that leapt in his throat, with her fingertips—or her tongue.

She blinked at the shocking desire. Where had it come from? A little voice, the voice of reason she supposed, told her to step away, call her cat, do anything but continue to stand so close to this man. A man such as he meant trouble. But she couldn't make her body move or her mouth call out at the command of the little voice. Instead she continued to stare into his face, fascinated with the play of shadows in his eyes.

Without her realizing it, her hand moved upward and touched the pounding pulse at the base of his throat. He gave a harsh sigh and grabbed her wrist, pulling her fingertips away from his heated flesh.

"Don't, Emma," he said again.

"Don't what, Johnny? Don't wonder, or don't touch?"

"Both. You don't know what you're doing."

"Yes," she whispered. "I do. I just shouldn't be doing it."

Unable to stop herself, Emma used her other hand, the one Johnny didn't possess in his iron grip, to reach around his neck and pull him downward. He hesitated, his strange light eyes darkening; then he came to her with a curse on his lips.

She stilled the curse with a kiss. His lips were cold, so cold she gasped. When she opened her mouth, he took control of the kiss, slanting his lips across hers and brushing the inside of her mouth with his tongue. Her body seemed to have a will of its own, slipping ever closer to his. Her hand, freed from his grasp, crept up to join its mate at the back of his neck. His hair drifted over her wrists and tickled her skin.

When he circled her hips with his arms and pulled her against him, the proof of how much he wanted her pressed against her stomach. She moaned into his mouth and tried to move ever closer. He kissed her harder, deeper, and she gave herself up to the new sensations, allowing him to teach her without words all she wanted to know.

When he lifted his mouth from hers, his lips were no longer cold. His eyes were no longer dark. They glittered silver in the gleaming sunshine. He stared at her for a long moment, his eyes focused upon her lips. His arms tightened a bit, almost as though he wanted to hug her, but decided against doing so. Emma smiled, hoping to reassure him. She ran her tongue across her lower lip, tasting Johnny there and wanting more. Tightening her grasp on his neck, she raised her mouth toward his—an offering to the unknown.

His breath hissed out—half sigh, half curse—and he reached up to pull her arms away, refusing the sacrifice. She resisted, but he was stronger.

"What's the matter?" she asked.

He pushed his hair out of his face, fingers tangling in the strands. Then he looked toward the woods, but the sight of the tableau wagon seemed to bring him up short. He focused upon the story pictured there, Little Red-Cap and the Wolf. Ever since she had seen the werewolf, Emma had hated that wagon. The similarities to real life were too close for her peace of mind. Johnny continued to stare at the picture for a long moment, then gave a self-derisive snort before shaking his head.

Emma wanted to step in front of him and make him look into her eyes. What had happened between them had been wonderful, despite all the horror and mistrust around them, nearly magical. She needed to understand why.

"Johnny?" she tried again.

He continued to stare at the painting. "Listen to your grandfather, Emma, and stay away from the help. I'm nothing but trouble. Men like me eat little girls like you, just like the big, bad wolf did to Little Red-Cap.''

His words struck so closely to her earlier thoughts that Emma winced. Did he know the truth? Or did he guess? What had Devora told him?

She had no chance to ask, for with those parting words, Johnny left her, never once looking her way again. Though she wanted to go after him very badly, Emma made herself stand next to her tiger as she watched him lead the horses away. She would not run after him. She would not beg him to touch her.

Johnny was right. He was trouble, and trouble she had enough of already.

Chapter Seven

He should never have kissed her, John berated himself that afternoon as he aimlessly raked the already raked dirt inside the big top. In the distant past, he had been a calm and rational man. Before events beyond his control had sapped whatever patience he possessed, he had been able to restrain his desires. Now another man, or was it a beast, lived inside him. He desired Emma, even though he could never have her. Any plans he might have entertained for seduction had disappeared with the knowledge of what he was. He had no business starting something he could never finish; he didn't dare to want her. He could hurt her, badly, irreparably—or worse. He might be lost, but he knew what was right.

What was it about Emma that called out to him? She was different from any woman he had ever known, not that there had been so very many. He had lived all his life in the town where he was born, leaving only to serve in the war. When he returned, he'd opened his medical office and spent the last five years helping others. He had called on a few girls, but he had never felt anything for them beyond a mild interest. He felt so much more than a mild interest for Emmaline Monroe.

Why now, when his life could end at any moment, did he meet someone who moved him as she did? Even if he destroyed the evil one who had cursed him, he must then return to his old life. People needed him. Emma would never be able to exist in small-town Wisconsin. The circus was her life. She would wither and die without it. His future was murky. Theirs was impossible.

John muttered a curse as he propped the rake back in the corner where he'd found it. He had no business thinking about Emma when he should be thinking of a way to draw the werewolf out of hiding before the next full moon. He needed to speak with Devora. Perhaps she had learned something new.

Leaving the big top behind, John strode across the lot. With a mere hour until show time, everyone bustled about in preparation for the performance. Though murder had occurred within their ranks two nights before, show people went on with the show, especially when the rest of the world knew nothing about the grief that Gerhardt Circus hid behind the music and the laughter.

Just as John came around the back of Devora's wagon, Emma jumped down in front of him.

"Oh," she gasped, startled, and stumbled forward into his arms.

John caught her, pulling her close for a short, sweet moment. He could smell her hair, a warm, earthy scent distinctly Emmaline. He brushed his cheek against the top of her head, clinging to her for one second longer before he put her away from him. In that direction lay danger for them both.

She looked up into his face in confusion. She must

have felt him hold her too long and too tightly for the mere act of steadying her. She reached for him, but he took a step backward. Her face fell at his withdrawal, and he wanted to step toward her and take her back into his arms. Instead, he put his traitorous hands behind him and stared at her with a face devoid of the emotion roiling within him. Before either of them could speak, Devora appeared in the doorway of the wagon.

"Boy," she snapped to John. "Get inside. I wish to speak with you."

He glanced at her, then back at Emma, but she'd already walked away without a word.

John jumped into the wagon. Devora closed the doors behind him. The kerosene lamp hanging from the ceiling threw golden shadows against the darkened interior.

"Sit," she ordered, waving her hand at a pile of cushions. Her bracelets clanked with the movement. John did as he'd been told. She spared not a moment for small talk but went right to the heart of her need to speak with him.

"Both Emmaline and Franz have been here before you."

"What did they want?"

She snorted, her version of laughter. "What do you think? They wanted to know what I had told you. What you had told me."

"What did you say?"

She kept silent as she lowered herself to sit next to him on another pile of cushions. "I told them you were looking for the men last night. When you asked me where everyone was, I told you they had gone hunting. You went out to help. They wanted me to tell them if you knew anything about the deaths.''

"In what way?'' John frowned. Did they already suspect him of killing Otto or Wade?

"They wanted to know if you'd heard the funeral service or seen the graves while you were lost in the woods yesterday.'' She gave a slow smile. "They think you have a terrible sense of direction, boy.''

"If their belief in my terrible sense of direction makes them see me as I wish them to see me, I'll live with the embarrassment.''

She nodded, not hearing the sarcasm in his tone. "As far as you know, a hunting accident occurred. A renegade wolf is on the loose. The creature attacked Wade, and Otto was shot by mistake. That is the story to be told if anyone from the outside asks.''

John raised his eyebrows. "A renegade wolf?''

"It is always best, when one lies, to remain as true to the truth as possible. Remember that.''

"Both Franz and Emma believe I know nothing about the werewolf?''

"They don't want you to know. They don't trust you. I told them you know nothing. They believe me.'' She pointed to herself with a flick of her wrist and a clank of her bracelets. "I follow my own rules, boy, and those words that were not truth sounded like truth when I spoke them. I am a very good liar.''

"So am I, now.''

"Excellent. You will need to live the lie if you want to remain alive.''

John nodded. "How will we discover the evil one? I take it you've tried to discover his identity before?''

"Of course. I've tried every trick I know, but he is old in the ways of evil. He knows all the tricks I might use before I use them. But now"—she nodded with satisfaction—"now I have something he wants."

"What?"

She smiled, her crooked eye teeth lending the expression a canine cast. "Why you, of course. You, dear boy."

"Me? Why would he want me?"

"He knows who you are since he marked you. He'll wonder if you are here to join him or destroy him. Either way, he will have to come to you sooner or later."

Though the thought of the wolf in human form searching him out to destroy him before he could destroy it sent waves of disquiet through John's mind, another thought disturbed him even more deeply. Before he could stop them, the images appeared before his eyes—the blood, the screams, the mind-numbing horror of what lurked beneath the surface of John Bradfordini. "What if he comes for me later?" he blurted out. "What if he waits for several months?" John heard the note of panic in his voice and forced himself to stop, take a deep breath and push the horrific images back to the place he'd relegated them to from the moment he'd understood what he was. Only then was he able to continue in a quieter, steadier voice. "I don't want to kill anyone else."

Devora flinched at the mention of killing, and John berated himself for his insensitivity. Devora appeared so calm, in control of herself and everyone else, that he kept forgetting she'd lost her husband two nights before, quite possibly as a result of John's transformation.

She recovered her composure quickly, waving away

his apology. "I am fine. If we are to solve our problem, you must be able to speak to me without worrying about my feelings." She pointed at a stack of ancient, dusty volumes next to her bed. "I have been looking through my books, searching for a hint of other ways to uncover one such as he."

"Have you found anything? Have you discovered a way to break the curse?"

"Thus far the single cure I've found is to kill the one who bit you—a common remedy and one you planned to execute all along. You must kill the werewolf with the silver. Only you and no one else, or your curse will not be lifted. I have also learned what signs we must search for in order to discover a werewolf. We must study everyone in the circus for these signs. But let no one else know what they are," she warned.

"Why?"

"Because you will exhibit these signs, as well. If others are searching and know the signs, their search will lead them to you."

John took a deep breath. Not only would the *teufel* be stalking him, but every other being at Gerhardt Circus, as well. Suddenly he knew what it felt like to be hunted, and he did not like the feeling at all. "What are the signs?"

"Dreams of bloodshed, murder and transformation."

John blinked. He had those. Nearly every night.

She watched him as she named the next symptoms. "A craving for bloody meat."

John recalled the burnt taste of the last meat he'd been able to stomach at the cook tent. Since then, he'd avoided eating meat at all.

Devora continued. "Extreme thirst."

John shrugged. Not being accustomed to physical labor in the sun, he'd attributed his thirst to hard work. Now he wasn't so sure.

"Clumsiness."

When he drove a stake into the ground to secure the big-top canvas, he often hit his thumb. The other workers joked at his ineptitude. John had merely thought he needed more practice.

"Excessive lust."

John winced. Now he understood his sudden and inexplicable fascination with Emma.

John stared into Devora's black, knowing eyes. "Stay away from her," the old woman whispered.

John didn't even pretend to misunderstand her meaning. "I thought what is fated could not be stopped," he said, bringing her earlier words back between them.

"Perhaps. Still, why tempt fate? Maybe our destinies can be changed if we try hard enough. I do not know." Devora put her hand on his in an imploring gesture. "I've known her since she was two years old. She's lived enough heartache."

Though he knew he should not, John could not stop himself from asking, "What heartache?"

Devora hesitated, clearly uncertain if she should divulge circus secrets. Then she heaved a sigh, her large shoulders moving up and down with emotion. She gave him a brief pat on the back of his hand before moving her hand to rest in her lap. "Her mother ran away with a drifter. I arrived here soon after she left, so I never knew Francesca, or Karl, Emma's father. But I heard the story. We circus folk keep to ourselves, but within the circus there are few secrets." She paused and fixed him with a glare.

Be careful, her eyes said. *Trust no one.*

He acknowledged her warning with a sharp nod, and Devora continued with her story. "Francesca was a talented aerialist. Franz had her trained by the finest from the Old Country. His heart broke when she left, but she loved that drifter, and nothing could stop her from going with him. Three years later a message arrives. Francesca has died. Karl has disappeared. Emmaline is alone. Franz brought her back here, and she became his replacement for her mother. Emma knows nothing beyond this place and this life."

"She loves it."

"Yes. And she loves Franz, and he her. He has taught her well. He keeps a close watch on her. He won't let her leave as her mother left."

"If Franz is so protective of her, why does he allow her to work with tigers? She could be killed at any time."

Devora shrugged. "One thing you must understand, with circus folk the circus comes first. He loves his granddaughter, but if making Emmaline into the first female tiger tamer in the country makes his circus the best, he will sacrifice her to that end." She made a sharp gesture, stilling John's opinion of Franz before the words left his mouth. "Emmaline understands the rules. She wanted to work with tigers. Ever since she could walk, she's been with the animals. They understand her. They love her and she loves them. She wants to be the best, I think, because she wants to prove to her father that he left someone important when he left Emmaline Monroe." Devora sighed, a sad, wistful sound. "Until she triumphs for her own reasons and not for others', she will not be a happy woman in her success."

"Why are you telling me this?"

"I see how you look at her, and she at you. There is much between you two. And as I told you before, I have dreamed of you both. You will hurt her before this is through."

"I don't want to."

"No, you don't want to. But you will. My dreams always come true. I can pray that things will be different this time and try to make them so . . . I can tell you to stay away from her and soothe my conscience, but I doubt that whatever I do or say will change what is meant to be." She shrugged. "All I can hope is that you will not kill her."

Devora's words so closely echoed John's hopes that he wondered if she could read minds as well as foresee the future.

She said her dreams always came true. He prayed that this time she would be wrong.

Nearly two weeks passed, and Emma's heart lay heavy within her. She had not seen Johnny except from afar since leaving him outside Devora's wagon. Her life had been filled with traveling, parades, unloading, performing, loading and traveling again. She had little time for sleep, too much time to brood on her own stupidity.

She had made a fool of herself. For just a moment Johnny had clung to her, and she'd hoped he needed her comfort as much as she craved his. She'd been wrong. When she had reached for him, he moved away.

His retreat had been as painful as if he'd slapped her face.

Emma slammed Destruction's dinner down in front of him, ignored the big cat's grumble, and then banged the cage door shut with more force than necessary. The physical outlet for her anger with herself felt good, so she stomped across the back lot toward her sleeping wagon as she fumed some more.

She had spent hours telling herself he was not for her. Her grandfather would disown her. Her life would be over. And for what? For a passing infatuation with a man she could never have.

For all she knew, he could be a monster beneath the face he presented to them all. She had tried to speak with Devora, but the Gypsy only confirmed Johnny's statements, and though Emma had an odd feeling that the Gypsy lied almost as much as Johnny, she couldn't quite believe that Devora lied on purpose. If Johnny were a monster, then he had killed Wade, and Devora would be the first one to put a silver bullet through his brain.

Wouldn't she?

Franz had consulted the old woman about setting a trap for the werewolf so they might kill the beast before the next full moon. Whatever Devora had said made her grandfather abandon his idea. Devora possessed countless books in several languages that dealt with the beings who walked the night. She also saw things no one else could see. Thus far, her sight and her knowledge had not helped them enough. But she still knew more than anyone else, and the circus folk trusted her to point them in the right direction for an end to this horror. If she said they must wait another month to kill the thing that stalked them, then another month they would wait.

Emma had just reached her wagon when an uneasy feeling of being watched overtook her. Since this was becoming a common occurrence, Emma took the warning and paused before climbing inside. She glanced around the area, and the low sun revealed what her eyes could not see: On the ground next to her wagon stretched the elongated shadow of a man. Emma stopped in mid-stride, uncertain of what to do. Though she could not determine the man's identity from the shadow, she did not believe him to be any of the workers or performers of Gerhardt Circus.

The shadow moved toward her. Emma's breath caught in her throat, and her gaze darted around, searching for a place to hide. With half an hour until the matinee, all of the circus folk, performers and laborers alike, had disappeared into their wagons or the big top to make final preparations for the show. If she screamed, would anyone reach her in time? Or would she look the fool for shrieking in fear over a townie who had come early to the show?

Emma did not wait to find out. Instead, she lifted her long skirt and petticoats above the ankles of her high top boots and ran back across the open area to take refuge behind Destruction's cage wagon. Destruction roared a greeting.

"Shh, Dusty. He'll see me," she hissed. The big cat subsided at the warning note in her voice.

Emma could see straight through the open bars of the cage wagon. She kept her gaze upon her own wagon until the hidden man appeared. At her first sight of him, Emma gasped.

147

There stood the blond stranger who had watched her once before. The man Franz had argued with; the man whose existence she had forgotten with all the other mysteries and horrors crowded into her life.

The man looked around the open area, acting as if he belonged at the heart of her circus. His gaze touched upon the cage wagon and halted. Emma ducked lower, hoping Destruction's huge body blocked the stranger's view of her. What should she do? The last time this man had been on the grounds, her grandfather had ordered her from his sight. The two had argued and her grandfather had asked the man why he followed them.

He still followed them. Were they looking in the wrong direction for the *teufel?* Was the werewolf not one of them as they'd suspected, but this man who followed them from town to town? Her grandfather knew him. If the stranger was the one preying upon their people, wouldn't her grandfather have destroyed the man while he had the chance?

Then again, the stranger could be from another circus, come to lure her away from Gerhardt's. She had dealt with such people before, though none of them had made her as uncomfortable as this man did. But her discomfort was more likely a result of the situation they faced than the man himself.

Emma straightened from her crouched position. Destruction mumbled and grumbled. She ignored him. She was tired of being afraid. She was tired of hiding. She was tired of being treated as a child when she was a woman grown. Johnny had told her to grow up, to think for herself. He was right. This man had invaded her circus. She planned to find out why.

Emma came around the edge of the cage wagon and

began walking toward the man. He saw her and froze. She was still a good distance away when a wagonload of hay rolled between them, cutting the man off from her view. She stopped, waiting for the conveyance wagon to pass, tapping the toe of her boot on the hard-packed earth. When the wagon passed by, she took a step forward to continue on her way. She stopped as her skin went cold and clammy.

The man had disappeared.

Biting down on her lip, Emma surveyed the area. He had to be here somewhere. Pushing away her unease, she walked through the rows of wagons until she reached the outskirts of the circus. Townspeople streamed up the dirt road, some walking, some riding horses, others in carriages. Squinting against the late afternoon sun, she attempted to see whether one man walked in the opposite direction within the crowd. But she could not distinguish the man she searched for among the rush of humanity.

Emma turned and began to march toward the red wagon. Her grandfather knew the stranger. She had meant to talk with him about the argument she'd witnessed between the two men, but the latest murders had made the situation flee her mind.

Emma squeezed between two closely positioned wagons, intent on taking the shortest route to her grandfather. Just as she reached the end, a man turned into the small opening, blocking her exit. A gasp of shock escaped her lips before she could stifle the sound, and Emma looked up to meet the gaze of Johnny Bradfordini.

"Excuse me," he said, though he made no move to retreat and allow her to pass. Instead, he leaned against the side of a wagon, crossed his arms over his chest and studied her with a half smile.

In the time he'd worked for the circus the sun had bronzed his skin several shades deeper, and his hair now possessed blond streaks slashing through the light brown strands. The change in coloring made his silver eyes shine brighter.

"Where are you going in such a hurry, Emma?"

"I need to speak with Grandfather."

"About what?"

Emma frowned. "None of your business."

"Isn't it? What if you're going to speak with him about me? Is it my business then?"

"This has nothing to do with you." She paused and studied him. He stared at her with equal intent. "Why would you think it did?"

"I just wondered if, perhaps, you and Franz were thinking of firing me."

She blinked at his statement, so far from her true intent at the moment. "Why would we fire you? You're a good worker. Or maybe you'd rather leave us?" she suggested, though she held her breath, half afraid he would agree with her and be gone from her life forever.

"Where would I go, Emma? On to another circus? Another job? I like working here."

She remained silent a moment, contemplating the freedom of his life. What would it be like to just move on whenever she chose? See the world on her own terms and not on the terms of others? Emma shook her head and the tempting image dissolved. She returned her attention to the man who waited for an answer to his questions. "We've lost two men. Perhaps you're afraid. We seem to be having a run of bad luck, and bad luck doesn't pick and choose its victims.''

"Victims. An interesting choice of word. One you seem to use quite a bit, yet you don't strike me as much of a victim.''

Emma recalled the last time she'd used the word *victim* when he'd kissed her and told her to trust him. She hadn't trusted him then, and she trusted him less now, even though she had no real reason to mistrust him.

He smiled, a slow, sensuous smile that set Emma's lips tingling. "Don't worry about me, Emma. I have little to be afraid of anymore. If I were you, I'd worry about myself.''

For some reason Emma felt there was more to his words than what they said. Almost a warning, but why? Devora had assured her that Johnny knew nothing about the werewolf they sought. If he did, he would have been long gone by now. No man wanted to face a supernatural enemy. Especially a man such as Johnny, who had no ties to Gerhardt beyond his weekly wages. Why would he risk his life for them?

Emma experienced a moment's guilt at the keeping of their secrets. They were putting Johnny's life in danger. Maybe she should suggest that her grandfather fire him, but she had a feeling that if they did so, Johnny would become more curious about the secrets they hid. They did not need someone else sneaking around the circus looking for the truth.

Emma took in a startled breath of air. *The stranger.* She needed to talk with Franz. Right now. Before the man got too far away.

"Please move." She took a step closer to Johnny. He continued to stare at her. "I have to speak with Grandfather."

"About what?"

She let out a sigh of irritation. "We've had this conversation already. If you must know, I saw a man. A stranger. Blond, very tall and thin."

Johnny frowned and straightened away from the wagon. "Was he bothering you?"

"No. He was just watching. But he made me uneasy."

"Where is he?"

The glitter in Johnny's eyes and the tension in his arms made Emma hesitate. He looked ready to kill. The thought frightened her.

When she continued to hesitate, he glanced at her. In the shadows between the wagon, his eyes shone oddly silver, and Emma found herself mesmerized by their too-bright sheen. He grasped her arm in a tight grip and shook her. "Where did he go, Emma? Tell me."

She blinked, and when she looked at him again, his eyes no longer shone with what she'd imagined for a moment was a nearly unholy light. "He left. He was here one minute, and then he was gone. I looked everywhere, but with all the people coming for the show, I couldn't see him anymore."

"Have you seen him before?"

She hesitated again. He shook her. "Yes." She yanked her arm from his grip, confused at his insistence for information. "Once before. Over a week ago. He and Grandfather argued."

Johnny glanced over his shoulder toward the red

wagon with a thoughtful look on his face. "Franz knows him, then?" He looked back at her, his eyes intent upon hers, searching for the truth.

Emma shrugged. "He seemed to."

"What did he say when you asked him about the man?"

"I didn't. Yet. That's where I was going right now."

Johnny turned, his shoulders bumping the closely confined wagons. He stepped out into the afternoon sunshine, then waited for Emma to join him. "I'll go with you." He strode toward the red wagon.

Emma stared after him a moment, then snatched up her irritating skirts and hurried in his wake. "Why?" she asked as she trotted next to him. "What business is this of yours?"

He stopped, and the fury in his face gave her pause.

"Despite the fact that each and every one of you insists upon treating me like an outcast, I am a part of this circus now. I want to make sure everyone is safe. Strangers mean trouble. Especially men who watch young women and then disappear. You're too naive, Emma. You need a keeper."

He stalked past her. She grabbed his arm. He halted, staring at her fingers on his shirt before he looked into her face. Emma caught her breath.

So beautiful he was. His long hair looked leonine as the strands rushed about his tanned face. A short stubble of beard, darker than his hair, roughened his chin, giving him an air of danger. The muscles of his forearm bunched under her fingers, and she stroked them once beneath the fabric of his shirt, unable to stop herself. The anger in his eyes faded, to be replaced by something just as hot but much more compelling.

153

Emma tilted her head. *How much can I trust you?*

Not much, she decided. He had the air of someone hiding something. She suspected that two beings existed inside Johnny Bradfordini—the calm, cool, collected man with the cultured voice and intelligent eyes who made her world seem not quite as bright or wonderful as she'd believed it to be and the rough, wild stranger who made her feel dangerous longings whenever he came near and who fit into her world all too well.

"Let me go," she said softly.

"I'm not touching you, Emma. You're touching me." He leaned closer, and his breath brushed her temple. "But I like it when you touch me."

She looked up, meeting his gaze head on. A moment ago he had been angry with her, and she with him. Now their anger had changed into something more for both of them. His eyes, those strange, haunted, silver eyes, searched her face for an answer to his unspoken question. He must have found one, for his eyes narrowed and he slowly lowered his head.

He's going to kiss me, her mind stated matter-of-factly, as though she were kissed often by strange men in the light of day, in the midst of her circus. Her body tightened with excitement at the image of his lips on hers. Without a second thought, she tilted her face up to accept the kiss.

"Emmaline Monroe!" A voice thundered, and she leapt away from Johnny with a cry of dismay. "What are you doing?"

Something very stupid, Emma thought as she turned to confront her irate grandfather. Johnny took her hand in his and squeezed her fingers. She squeezed back, touched by his support.

"Johnny and I were just talking, Grandfather."

Franz jumped down from the red wagon and stalked toward them, a dark frown spread across his face. "*Ja,* it looked as though you were just talking." He turned to Johnny and pointed his finger at the younger man's chest. "Get back to work. We have a show in fifteen minutes." Franz glanced at Emma with a scowl. "What are you doing out here dressed in such a manner?" He waved his hand at her day dress. "Get into your costume, young lady."

"I wanted to ask you a question, Grandfather."

He glanced at Johnny, then back at her. "There is no time for questions now. The show is everything, and it will start soon. With or without you. Get dressed." He glared at Johnny. "*Gehen!*" he shouted. When Johnny hesitated, he shouted in English, "Go!"

Johnny squeezed Emma's hand once more, then leaned down to whisper in her ear. "We'll come back and talk to him after the show."

She nodded and released his hand with reluctance. Facing her grandfather's wrath with Johnny's hand clasped in her own had made the ordeal much easier than usual. For the first time she could remember, she had not felt alone. Emma turned away to follow her grandfather's orders.

"Just one moment," he said. She turned back. "Have you lost your senses, Emmaline? That man is no good. A drifter, a loser. You know how I feel about his kind."

"I know, Grandfather. But nothing happened."

He snorted. "*Ja,* it looked as though nothing was

happening. Little you know, *mein Liebchen.* Men!'' He waved his hand in the air dramatically. ''Bah! They are after one thing. I know about men. I am one myself.'' He took her hand and squeezed her fingers urgently. ''You know I speak the truth. Remember your mother. She should have listened to me, but she did not. She was sorry in the end, I think. You listen to me now, Emmaline. You are the light of my life—the only part I have left of my''—his voice dropped to a whisper— ''my darling Francesca. Don't ruin your life as she did.''

The mention of their shared loss never failed to melt Emma's anger. ''Grandfather, I won't let you down. You know that. I understand what you're telling me and I won't forget.''

''You cannot trust men. Especially one such as Bradfordini. Especially now, when we are being stalked by the evil one. I would not be able to survive if I lost you, *mein Liebchen.*''

''I'll be all right. Johnny won't hurt me. Of all of us, I know he is not the one.''

''How do you know this?''

''The werewolf killed before he came. Johnny came to us from Illinois. He wasn't even near Gerhardt Circus at the time of the first two deaths.'' She recited the reasons she'd repeated to herself countless times over the past few weeks. At times she believed them, at others she did not. Franz did not seem convinced. She tried again. ''I'm safer with Johnny than anyone, Grandfather.''

''Safe from one evil, perhaps, but not another. Stay away from him, Emmaline, he is not for you.''

Emma sighed. No one would ever be for her if Grandfather had his way.

She turned and watched Johnny walk toward the big top. She could hear her grandfather swearing in German under his breath as he left her. Just as Johnny reached the tent, he turned and looked back. Their eyes met over the milling crowd of townsfolk, animals and performers between them, but for Emma it was as if no one else in the world existed but the two of them.

If only that could be true.

Chapter Eight

John went about his work for the rest of the afternoon, watching the back door for the matinee as well as for the evening performance, but his mind remained on Emma. On what she had told him about a stranger in their midst, and on what had passed between them before her grandfather interrupted. Devora had told him to stay away from Emma, that one of the signs of the werewolf was uncontrollable lust. His reactions to Emma proved the Gypsy correct. No matter what he told himself about right and wrong, good and evil, innocence and degradation, he couldn't keep his mind from wanting her or his hands from touching her.

But what could he do about it? If he remained with the circus, Emma would be forever near, but he needed to stay with the circus to search out the werewolf.

Shaking his head, John watched Heinz Kirshner perform his act in the evening show. Why had the clown broken his pattern of going ahead to mark the trail after doing the matinee? John wondered. He gave a mental shrug; no one else seemed to be bothered by the clown's being there tonight.

In the past few weeks of traveling with the circus, John had come to understand the vast distances between towns and the time it took to get a wagon drawn by Percherons from one town to the next. Those weeks of traveling had convinced John that Kirshner could not be the one he sought. To have marked the trail to the next town on the night of the murders, which Kirshner had done, and commit the murders, he would have had to be in two places at nearly the same time. It seemed impossible.

Still, John didn't like the clown. But he pushed aside his mistrust and turned to the problem at hand, confronting Franz about the stranger who was no stranger to the circus owner. He would have to use Emma to get the answers he sought from her grandfather. At the thought, John swore under his breath. Part of his problem in discovering what he needed to know lay right there. He needed Emma's knowledge of her people, and the access she provided to them. No one trusted him here, except perhaps Emma. Devora knew what he was and would use him for her own purpose, but she did not trust him. Emma did, and that trust could be her downfall. But what choice did he have? He needed her right now. He had to use her or others might die—himself and Emma among them.

The band began to play a march, and the townsfolk filed out of the tent. A good thing the lines of communication in northern Wisconsin were so primitive. By the time word reached this town of the tiger attack, Gerhardt Circus would be gone.

John waited until everyone had left the big top and the other workers were occupied with the tear-down, then slipped off and made his way to Emma's wagon.

Her door was shut, so he tapped upon it. Seconds later, her face appeared in the opening.

"Let's go see your grandfather before he becomes too busy."

Emma nodded and slid through the door. She was dressed in her young-lady clothes, though to his mind the long skirts and petticoats were more hazardous than becoming. He'd seen her stumble over them enough to know her difficulties when wearing all that material. She moved with such grace when dressed in her costumes, the lack of mobility afforded by the long skirts and rib-constricting corset must seem twice as bad after she'd worn the other.

He reached up to help her down from the wagon, catching her around the waist and swinging her to the ground. Her feet landed next to his, and when he released her, she took a step back, feet tangling in her skirts. He caught her before she could fall and pulled her up next to him.

He had told himself countless times in the few hours since he'd last touched her that Emmaline Monroe was off limits. They could help each other, but no matter how he craved her soft, full lips and tempting body, he could look but he must never touch her again. He had no right to make promises he could not keep, and Emma was the kind of woman to believe that a kiss constituted a promise. He'd like to promise her the world, but what good was a promise from a man whose deepest secret was murder?

John started to step away, but to his surprise Emma followed. Startled, he frowned. She entwined her arms around his neck and leaned upward to press her lips to his. John froze.

His changed body at war with his logical mind, John at first did not respond—could not respond. Then her lips parted under his tight mouth, and with a groan John gave in to his physical demands.

She was as sultry as he had imagined in the seconds before he slept. She was as sweet as he had dreamed in the seconds before he awoke.

John clenched his hands at his sides, determined not to continue the madness, but when Emma pressed against his hardening body, he couldn't help but cup her hips in his palms and pull her nearer to his aching center. He slid his hands along her sides, encountering the bone structure of her corset. A low growl of disapproval for the strictures of society rumbled in his throat. He continued to move his palms upward until he encountered warm flesh and brushed his fingertips beneath the neckline of her dress, tracing the tops of her breasts. Her entire body shook in response, and he delved lower, palming one full breast as his tongue swirled around her mouth. He tasted her, a scalding mixture of sweet woman and tart desire. He rubbed a thumb over her nipple, and the scent of her flesh aroused him further. Any thought of where they were and what they were doing fled his mind as other images took hold of his senses.

As suddenly as the embrace had begun, it ended, and John was left breathing heavily, his lips still hot from hers. He watched Emma warily through half-closed eyes as she backed away from him, her trembling fingers pressed to her swollen mouth, the top of her dress rumpled where he'd touched her. The shadow of a nipple peaked above the material. His eyes fastened on the rosy skin, unable to look away.

161

When she saw where his gaze rested, she gave a half sob of shock and yanked her dress back into place. She kept her hand over her chest. As if her hand could stop his mind from seeing what his palm had touched.

He had frightened her, and he cursed his desire, honed to a razor-sharp edge from God only knew what changes had ravaged his body. Still, he had been warned to be careful, by Devora and by himself. No matter that Emma had initiated the embrace, he should have stopped it before things went so far.

"I'm sorry, Emma," he ventured. "That shouldn't have happened."

"No." She turned her head away, embarrassed. "It was my fault. You kissed me once and I—" She stopped and swallowed, then pushed her hair from her face with an impatient gesture. "I just wanted to know more."

"More?" John echoed. "Haven't you ever been kissed before? I find that hard to believe, Emma."

"I didn't say that," she snapped, then stalked away without looking back.

John hurried after her, intrigued. "You didn't answer the question."

She kept walking.

John reached out and took her elbow, bringing her to a halt. He gritted his teeth against the flush of awareness that touching her brought him. "Emma, talk to me."

For a long while she remained silent, staring at the ground. Her hair, the color of flames in the light of the last quarter moon, shielded her face from his gaze. Finally she sighed and her shoulders sagged. "If you must know, I've never been kissed by a man other than my grandfather." She glanced up at him through her hair. "I'm twenty years old. Most women are married with several children by the time they're my age. But me, I've never been kissed." She jerked her arm away from his grasp. "I'm sure someone like you must find me amusing."

John found her many things, none of them amusing. Her embarrassment over her naiveté he found endearing. He pushed those feelings away, well aware of their danger. He liked Emma too much, admired her, desired her. Any further softening in his feelings would hurt them both.

"Come on," he said, allowing his frustration to make his voice short and gruff. "We have a meeting with Franz."

She nodded, turning in a swirl of skirts to follow. He hesitated a moment, prepared to catch her if she fell again. But this time, she navigated the yards of material without mishap. He breathed a sigh of relief. He should not touch her again. To do so would court disaster.

He took several quick steps to reach her side. She did not acknowledge his presence, and the silence between them hung heavy. John attempted to dispel her unease with a change of subject. "I've noticed Heinz is away quite a bit. Marking the trail."

She gave him a quick sideways glance from beneath her lashes. "That's his job. He's the advance man."

A sudden flash of insight caused John to start with surprise. Such a simple explanation. Why hadn't he thought of it before? "Does he have someone to help him? Someone who could lay the trail if he had something else to do?"

His voice sounded too anxious, too interested in

what should have been a casual question, for Emma stopped and turned to him with a frown. "You work here, Johnny. Do you see any extra help around? Heinz is our clown, our advance man and the trail marker. He has no one to help him. He never has. The day he needs help is the day he'll need to retire."

John sighed. So much for his brilliant flash of insight. In doing his job alone, Kirshner had an alibi for the murders. Demon or no, a man couldn't be in two places at once.

John and Emma reached the red wagon. The doors were shut, all seemed dark and quiet. John glanced at Emma. She shrugged and looked around the lot. No one paid them any mind, all going about the business of tearing down. There was no sign of Franz among the milling circus folk.

Emma climbed onto the wagon and opened the door. "Grandfather?"

A mumble came from inside, and she stepped into the darkened interior with John following. A few steps and she fumbled in the dark, then as the low glow from the lantern she'd lit illuminated the area, Emma straightened away from the desk. She turned toward the pallet in the corner where a shape shifted.

"Grandfather, are you ill?" Emma knelt upon the ground next to the old man.

He squinted into the light, then blinked at Emma. "*Ach, nein, mein Liebchen.* Just tired." He sat up.

"We wanted to talk with you about something."

"We?" Franz looked up. John stepped out of the shadows near the door, and the old man frowned, then glanced at Emma.

"Yes. Remember several days ago a man came

here? He was watching me, and when I pointed him out, the two of you argued.''

Franz continued to frown. Then he rubbed his forehead as though trying to bring the memory forth.

''A man?'' His voice sounded frail, old, no longer capable of the bellowing fury John had heard on so many occasions. He peered at John. ''He is right there.''

Emma looked at John, concern etched on her face. ''No, Grandfather, not him. The blond man. Remember? You argued with him. You wanted to know why he followed us.''

John took a step forward. He had not heard the situation described that way before. He'd thought the man and Franz had argued and the man's return had made Emma nervous. But a stranger who *followed* the circus? He could be the one John sought.

''He is nothing but trouble,'' Franz said. ''Make him go, Francie.''

Emma froze at the mention of her mother's name. ''I'm Emma, Grandfather. Mother is gone.''

''Everyone I love is gone. Or soon will be. You and that Karl Monroe.'' He waved his hand at John, obviously mistaking him for Emma's father. ''If you go with him, Francie, don't come back.''

Emma sighed and put her hands on her grandfather's shoulders, pushing him back on the pallet. ''Go to sleep, Grandfather,'' she whispered. ''I'll take care of everything.''

He closed his eyes, and in a few moments his chest rose and fell in an even rhythm. Emma stood and walked past John without a word. He joined her outside.

"He's never been like this before," she said.

"Perhaps things are becoming too much for him to handle."

Emma glanced at him sharply. "What do you mean by that?"

"He's not getting any younger. There are a lot of responsibilities with this circus. I can see you are in financial trouble. You have lost two of your performers and a tiger, which makes that situation worse, and the loss of your mother still preys upon his mind."

"I suppose you're right. I will try and take on more responsibility."

John frowned. He didn't want Emma putting herself in any more danger than she was in already. "If you see this man again, you come and find me. Do you understand?"

She nodded, but he could tell that her mind had drifted away from him. She stared at the closed doors of the red wagon, her lovely face creased with concern. John put his hand on her shoulder and she started, turning toward him with a question in her eyes.

"Don't go anywhere near this stranger when you're alone, Emma. Promise me. You don't know why he's here or what he'll do."

"I promise. I'll come and find you if ever I see him again. Though you know, Johnny, he is probably from another circus, sent to lure our best acts away. That would explain why Grandfather was angry with him."

John considered her explanation. She could be right, but somehow he doubted it. With the rampant secrets of Gerhardt Circus, John doubted that the blond stranger's presence could be explained away so easily.

He left Emma to tend to her grandfather and returned

to his wagon to change into a work shirt. The wagon loomed dark and deserted, all the other men hard at work. John pulled his carpetbag to the edge of the wagon, using the moon's glow to see inside.

He found the shirt he desired, but right next to it lay the shirt he'd worn the night of his transformation. His hand brushed that shirt, and the rough texture made him yank the material from the bag and turn it toward the light. The silver moon darkened the patch of blood in its center to a dull, rusty brown.

When Emma went inside the red wagon once more, her grandfather still slept. She would have to supervise the loading. She didn't have the heart to awaken him.

If she was honest, she didn't have the courage. Emma was terrified that when she awakened Franz he would be worse instead of better. What if he slipped into the past permanently? She would be left alone to manage the circus, or what would be left of it once the werewolf finished with them.

Emma looked at him one more time before dousing the lamp. He looked so frail and old lying on his pallet. She'd never seen him like this before. In her mind and heart, Grandfather had always been the strongest of men, full of boundless energy and love for the life they led. Now it seemed as if his life force waned along with the circus fortunes. Emma had no doubt that if Gerhardt Circus died, so would Franz Gerhardt. She would do anything to keep that from happening.

When she left the wagon, a glance around the lot showed her that the tearing down and loading up proceeded without any problems. Their people had done the task so many times they did not need overseeing,

167

though Franz usually oversaw them anyway.

She saw Johnny standing behind his sleeping wagon, staring at something in his hand. Emma flushed at the memory of their earlier kiss. What had possessed her to behave in such a way? Maybe the haunting sadness clouding his face when he wasn't aware that anyone watched. She couldn't help but be drawn to a man with such pain swimming in his eyes. She wanted to soothe away his pain by whatever means available, and she'd found that whenever she touched him, the pain in Johnny's eyes faded and another emotion took its place— an emotion that called out to her and made her behave in ways she never would have considered before she met him, ways she should not be considering now. Despite her arguments with her grandfather to the contrary, she should not even trust the man.

Emma glanced up, noticing the object of her concern walking toward the forest. Knowing they had only a few more minutes before they must be on their way, Emma hurried after him.

"Johnny," she called.

He continued to walk onward, not even pausing to indicate he'd heard her call.

"Johnny!" she called again, running to catch up to him. She put her hand on his shoulder. At her touch, he stopped and tensed, then turned to look at her. For a moment, his eyes didn't focus and his vacant gaze drifted over her face. Emma frowned. Then he started and looked at her, really looked at her. The depth of agony in his eyes made her cry out.

"What's wrong, Johnny?"

"Nothing," he said, his voice clipped and hoarse. "I'm fine. I just have to do something right now."

He tried to move away, but she caught his arm again and he stopped. He carried his carpetbag. Where could he be going? Did he plan to leave the circus altogether? How could he go now, when she needed him so much?

"Emma, I have to go *now*," Johnny said through clenched teeth, yanking his arm from her grasp.

"But we're about to leave. We have to go or we won't get to the next town on time. We can't wait for you."

"I'll catch up." He turned away once more.

"How will you know where we are?" She stopped, biting her lip, hating the fear within her that made her blurt out her next question, though she knew she should not. "Are you leaving forever?"

He did not even look at her, did not respond to the quavering plea that colored her voice. He just walked away.

But his words drifted back to her on the night breeze. "I'll be back, Emma. Trust me."

Trust him? He kept saying that.

If only she dared.

John walked into the woods, continuing onward until he reached a clearing so far into the forest he could no longer hear the calls of the laborers as they finished packing up the circus. There he paused, then fell to his knees. He opened his carpetbag and pulled out the stained shirt. Next came the stained pants he'd discovered when he went through all of his clothes. The same pants he'd worn on the night of his transformation. The shirt and pants that had been ripped but not bloodied.

They had blood on them now.

Someone had put the blood there to place blame for

the deaths upon him. John knew who that someone was: the evil one. Just as Devora had said, the evil one knew him. The evil one wanted to throw the blame in John's direction. If the circus folk believed John to be the werewolf, they would kill him and think themselves safe. The werewolf could either move on to another place unhindered, or kill for at least one more full moon without being hunted.

John needed to destroy the evidence so cleverly planted in his possession. He made a small fire, then fed his shirt and pants into the flames. The orange tendrils licked his clothing until they lay a pile of ashes.

A movement at the corner of his eye brought John to his feet, poised for flight or a fight, his gaze darting around the small clearing as he tried to pick up the movement again.

The tree branches swayed and a bat started up, flying low over his head. John flinched and ducked away from the ugly, black rodent, its screeching cry grating on his sensitive hearing. The breeze brushed his heated flesh, and John looked up. He could smell the animals from the circus—and something else. Something wild and dangerous. Something evil.

He was being watched. He knew it as well as he knew his mother's name. The one who had done this to him hovered near.

John stood in the clearing, feeling the evil on the breeze swirl around him. The old, dead leaves from the autumn before danced at his feet, creating a hollow, lonely sound that emphasized his isolation.

He should run forth and discover who, or what, watched him, but John found himself unable to do anything but listen and wait. He heard a slight shuffle to his left, and he glanced in that direction, but nothing moved except the wind. A skittering sound from behind made him whirl around. Again, nothing. His skin crawled with the feeling of a hundred eyes watching him from all directions, and he wanted to rage at his helplessness. Then, as abruptly as the feeling of being watched had come, it faded, and he felt alone once more.

Freed from the inertia that had gripped him, John sprang into action. He kicked apart the remains of the fire, then grabbed his carpetbag and loped in the direction of the circus. No longer could he smell evil. No longer did he feel the presence of the other.

Where had the *teufel* gone? Why had it left him alive?

John approached the lot where the circus had camped. He smelled no animals on the breeze. He heard no shouts from the workers or creaks from the wagons. He had traveled a great distance to destroy the evidence he'd found, then traveled back as great a distance. Not yet used to his newly acquired speed of movement, John didn't realize how great the distance or how long he'd been gone until he burst through the brush into the open.

The moon shone upon a deserted field.

Gerhardt Circus had moved on without him. He should have known. Emma had warned him.

John took a deep breath, grasped his carpetbag tighter, and loped off down the dirt road in pursuit.

Where had Johnny gone?

Emma held the reins of the Percherons that drew the red wagon and contemplated the question over and over. Her grandfather slept on, which caused Emma no small distress. If he could sleep while the wagon jounced over the countless holes in the dirt path they used for a road, he was very ill, in body and in spirit.

Emma had put off leaving for as long as she could, but in the end she had been forced to allow the ringmaster his call of "Onward" or they would never reach their destination in time for the next show. She did not dare leave a wagon or horses behind for Johnny, either, since she did not know for certain if he would return. The thought tore at her heart, even though Johnny's disappearance would be the best for all of them, including Johnny.

The night had darkened as time passed, thick, dark clouds covering the moon. Every so often a shaft of silver would penetrate the clouds and send a ray of light across the backs of her Percherons, only to disappear again, leaving the night even darker. Emma brought up the rear of the caravan, hoping against hope that Johnny would follow and she would be the first to see his return.

"Emmaline." Devora's voice jerked Emma from her contemplations. The Gypsy walked next to Emma's wagon, long legs eating up enough ground to keep pace with the plodding Percherons. "Franz. Where is he?"

Emma sighed. The absence of Franz concerned the older performers. He had never missed a night of traveling, and the fact he did so now, when the circus needed him most, proved how different life had become. Still, Emma hoped he would be back to his usual strong, bullheaded self after a bit of rest. "He is exhausted, Devora. I made him rest."

Devora gave a sharp nod of approval. "Good. We

need him at his best when the full moon returns. Our people are ready to fight, but they must have a leader.''

Emma agreed. She prayed that Franz would be fit to lead when the time arrived.

''Where is Bradfordini?''

Devora's question made Emma jerk on the reins she held in her hands. The Percherons threw their heads back in protest, and she released her grip. The horses required no guidance; they would follow the wagon in front of them even if that wagon went over a cliff.

''Johnny?'' Emma said, her mind reaching for an answer.

Devora scowled at her. ''Is there another Bradfordini, Emmaline? Of course Johnny. Where is he?''

Emma made a great show of looking at the occupants of the other wagon seats within her line of sight. Finally she returned her gaze to the Gypsy. The woman stared at her with narrowed eyes. Emma shrugged. ''I haven't seen him.'' That much was true.

Devora turned her sharp gaze on the forest. As if in answer to an unspoken question, a long, low howl began deep within the woods. The tone rose, higher and higher, the sound drifting toward the cloud-covered moon, then echoing away into the darkness.

Emma's flesh tingled at the sound. Destruction roared an answer from his cage several wagons ahead. Another howl began, this one from the woods on the other side of the road. The forest came alive, cries of the wolves, children of the night, swirling at them from all directions. Emma's fingers clenched the leather straps in her hands so tightly they cut into her flesh. She dropped them, staring with horror at the slash of blood across her palm.

Her people had been silent tonight, the absence of Franz upsetting them. All who knew him understood that nothing but a dire problem would keep him from them. Now, with the howls of wolves filling the air all around them, they began to call out to each other in fear. The animals' voices joined the chorus as pandemonium threatened. Emma rubbed her palm on her skirt and glanced at Devora.

"Calm them," Devora ordered. "You are our leader when Franz is not here. Tell them."

"What?" Emma whispered.

"The truth."

"The truth?" Emma had a sudden vision of herself throwing Johnny to a mob of circus performers with the bodies of people and the countenances of wolves. She shook her head to dispel the startling image.

"Pay attention," the Gypsy hissed. "Look." Devora flung her arm up at the sky. Her bracelets clanked an emphasis to her words. The moon, as though under her spell, came out from behind a cloud and shone upon them. Emma saw and understood.

"Go," Devora urged. "Do what you must to calm them."

Pulling back on the reins, Emma brought her animals to a stop. A nod from her and the ringmaster shouted, "Halt!" All the wagons followed his order.

Emma climbed up on the top of the red wagon. All eyes turned toward her. Emma shivered, then stared, wide-eyed, at her circus family. Their fears, whispers in the night, washed over her. Devora was right, they depended upon her now, and she would not fail them. Gathering her courage with a deep breath, Emma raised both hands toward the sky. The moon shone down, a slim ray of silver lighting her from the heavens.

"Look!" she shouted above the howls. "Look at the moon and know the truth. The evil one cannot transform tonight. What you hear are wolves. True wolves. Animals of the forest, not beasts of death and destruction. They smell the menagerie. They hunger, but they will not harm us. They fear us more than we could ever fear them. We are safe."

The whispers died. The howls ceased. Emma lowered her hands. The moon went back under a cloud.

Without another word from her, the people dispersed, and moments later the caravan rolled forward once more. Emma climbed down onto the wagon seat. She looked for Devora, but the Gypsy had gone.

Emma, drained of energy, put her face into her hands, promising herself she would rest for just a moment. When she looked up again, she sat alone in the shadowed night.

Chapter Nine

John followed the trail marked by Heinz Kirshner. He doubted that anyone had changed the fence rails or flour trails to lead him away from the circus tonight. Even so, he would locate them eventually. Though his increased abilities in sight and smell had faded a bit with the moon, they were still strong enough to enable him to find Gerhardt Circus, but he had no doubt that in another few days the abilities would fade back to near normality.

The time he'd spent alone as he trailed after the circus had been agony, giving him the opportunity to contemplate the horror of what he was, what he might become again. Though being cursed was not his fault, neither were his victims at fault for being in the wrong woods near the wrong man.

He might say he would use the silver bullets upon himself if he was unable to break the curse, but as the Gypsy had said: Each full moon he would become more the wolf and less the man. In that case, the wolf within him would fight for its life. What match was a man like he—a gentle man who valued healing above all else—for the evil beast that would fight for control of the body they both shared? Had the one who made John a werewolf once fought this dilemma also, finally giving in to the evil that ate his soul alive?

John's musings were interrupted when, from a mile or so away, he heard the others: the jangling of the harnesses, the snorts of the Percherons, the creak of the wagons. He could smell them, too. *Animals, people.* John paused in his loping run and sniffed the breeze. *Warm woman and lilac soap.*

Emma. Much closer than the rest.

He had caught up with them quicker than he'd thought possible. His ability to run must be even stronger than he'd believed. Could that be how Kirshner was able to complete his job marking the trail and commit the murders, seeming to be in two places at once? John considered the possibility. The distance between the towns the circus traveled to was much greater, miles and miles of twisting roads and hazardous trails, than he had traversed tonight. And he had come through the forest, ignoring the trails, cutting the time necessary to reach the circus in half. No, even considering the increased abilities of a werewolf, Kirshner could not have committed the murders.

Damn. He was getting tired of having every theory thwarted.

John started to run once more, then stopped as another scent drifted by him, the scent of evil he'd caught a few hours before when he'd burned his clothes in the forest. John turned his head and searched the black shadows of the trees. Nothing moved but the leaves in the wind. But something was out there. It followed the circus, followed him. John walked off the path and into the thick woods. Now was the time to discover who lurked in the shadows. Now, when John was alone with the *teufel,* when no one else would be hurt if he made a mistake. He would be prepared for the creeping lethargy that had overcome him earlier and halted his discovery of the evil stalking them all.

He slid through the trees, flinching every time a branch snapped or a leaf crackled. The other would have the same heightened senses John possessed. If John could smell the evil, then the evil could smell him. He paused, sniffing the air once more. The scent faded away. The *teufel* was on the run.

John increased his pace, no longer caring if the werewolf heard him. Up ahead, though a break in the thick trees, he saw a swatch of white. A shirt? A face? He could not tell, but something that did not belong in this forest.

Slowing as he neared the place where he'd seen the white flash, John heard the stamp and snort of a horse. He glanced toward the road, which he'd run parallel to during the chase. The horse shifted again, and the low murmur of a woman's voice reached him. He knew that voice.

Emma.

John crept forward until he could see the road through the trees. He swore softly under his breath. She sat, alone, on the seat of the red wagon, head in her hands. A rustle to his left drew John's attention away from Emma. He glanced that way and saw a man watching her just as John watched her. Or maybe not just as John watched. This man wanted to touch her, and he would if John did not stop him.

Backing away from the road, John circled around

behind the other man. He had not recognized the face from Gerhardt Circus, but the face was familiar. The features tugged at John's memory, but he could not place where he had seen the man before.

John crept toward the place where the stranger watched from the trees. Rage flooded him, and he had to fight to keep from launching himself at the man in a mad fury. He had to keep the beast within him in check or he would not win this fight.

A deep breath, a silent admonishment, and John made his way forward once more. When he stepped from the dense shadow of the forest into the sparser ground near the road, John's heart leapt into his throat. Where the man had been, there stood no one.

Had the man reached Emma before John could prevent him? He had heard no cry of distress. In fact, he had heard nothing. No sound, no movement. He sniffed. Nothing. No longer could he smell the evil on the breeze.

John hurried forward and peered through the brush lining the road. Emma still sat upon the wagon seat. Silent, sad, alone.

A shuffle from behind made John spin around. Nothing there, but a shadow, deeper within the forest, shifted and the scent of a horse reached him. Using his newfound speed of movement, John left Emma on the road and went after the stranger.

He reached the man just as he mounted his horse.

The sound of John crashing through the brush made the man turn toward him. Though he wore a broad-brimmed hat and the long leather coat of the West, this time John recognized him. The shock of his recognition stopped John in his tracks.

The stranger who had watched Emma was none other than the Union officer who had spoken with Peter on their last day in the army—the officer who had lured Peter into the secret dangers that had killed him. The man looked much older, a bit ragged and worn, but still the same man.

John's eyes met those of the man on the horse. The stranger's gaze narrowed, almost as if he recognized John, but the officer had not seen him at the battle site. John had only caught a glimpse of the man as he left with Peter. The man pulled a Colt from the holster on his hip and aimed the weapon at John.

John stared at the barrel of death and wondered if the officer knew he needed silver bullets to do the job right. John's gaze flicked from the Colt to the man. They stared at each other, and understanding lit the older man's eyes. He cursed and lowered the pistol, reaching for the rifle holstered on his saddle.

As his fingers touched the hilt, the sound of someone crashing through the trees in their direction made both John and the stranger freeze. John kept his gaze on the man on the horse; the man glanced out over the forest. What he saw made him look back at John in disgust. He removed his hand from the rifle and kicked the horse into motion. Man and beast disappeared into the darkness of the night. But in the look the stranger had given John there had also been a promise. He would be back.

Emma tripped into the clearing, her feet tangled in skirts that had caught upon a thorn bush. John caught her before she hit the ground.

"Johnny." She clutched at his forearms as she

180

straightened, pulling her boot free from the hem of her petticoats.

Her voice, breathless, a bit frightened, spurred his anger. Yanking his arm from her grasp, he reached behind her to free her skirt from the thorn bush. The material tore, the sound echoing in the silence of the clearing. She gasped, pulling the skirt around so she could assess the damage. He caught sight of a stain, a rusty slash of what looked to be blood.

"What the hell is that?" He grabbed the skirt again, yanking her toward him so he could see the stain closer. The metallic tang of blood filled his nostrils, and his mouth flooded with saliva. John cursed in disgust and dropped her skirt as if the torn, bloodied material had caught fire and burned him.

She frowned at him in confusion. "I cut my hand. I guess I wiped the blood on my skirt without thinking. Stupid of me, now I'll have to take this dress and wash it in the river tonight or the stain will be there forever." She plucked at the tear he'd made. "Maybe I shouldn't even bother. Whenever I wear a dress like this, all I do is trip over my own feet."

John's disgust with himself heightened his irritation at Emma's preoccupation with her clothes. The man who had just left had been watching her as if she would be his next meal, and she hadn't even known he was there. "Emma, you need a keeper more than your tiger does," John snapped. She dropped her skirt and turned toward him with a frown of confusion. "What are you doing out here alone?"

Her chin tilted up at his tone and her lips thinned. She crossed her arms, hugging herself as if for comfort, even as anger filled her eyes. "I heard something."

"And you came into the woods to see what it was? Are you insane?"

Her lips thinned. "Maybe I should ask you what you're doing out here."

"Ask if you wish, but you won't get an answer."

"Why not?"

"What I do is none of your damned business, Emma." He was overreacting, but coming upon the officer from Peter's past watching Emma in the forest was too much of a coincidence. John needed time alone to sort out all he'd seen and learned.

"I think it is. I'm your employer, Johnny."

John contemplated Emma. In her high fury, the red tingeing her cheekbones warred with the shade of her hair as the strands curled wildly about her face, loosened from their pins during her run through the forest. If she knew what he'd seen, she'd be frightened, not angry. Maybe he needed to frighten her a bit. Maybe then she'd realize the danger she invited by sitting alone in the forest. The evil one lurked here; in fact, a part of that evil stood with her right now in this very clearing, and she should know better than to tease a wild beast.

His scrutiny of her made the red on Emma's cheeks fade to pink and then to white. Her eyes, which had been narrowed in anger, became round as she saw the change in him. She took a step backward.

"Poor Emma," he whispered. "Do I frighten you?"

"N-no." Her stammer told him the truth to that lie.

"Do you want me to?" He smiled slowly and reached out to touch her cheek.

She went very still, like a doe who'd sighted a hunter. John could smell the heat from her body, heavy

182

on the damp night air. He was distracted from the danger of her questions by the danger of her fragrance. Just the smell of her made him hard and ready in seconds. Devora had warned him of the uncontrollable lust that could take control of his body, and he had seen for himself the beast he became despite his efforts at control. The deeper feelings beneath the lust, the feelings he fought to deny, only made him want her more.

His desire had been to frighten Emma into leaving him alone; instead she had stayed, and he could not think clearly with her so close and the two of them all alone.

"Tell me," she whispered. "Trust me. What were you doing out here, all alone in the forest?"

Instead of an answer, John wrapped his fingers around the back of her neck and crushed his lips to hers.

Her mind full of fears and suspicions, Emma stiffened when Johnny pulled her closer. But when his lips touched hers she forgot to think, forgot to be afraid, forgot to distrust. She knew only Johnny and the way he made her feel with his slightest touch.

His mouth was hard and demanding, as was another part of him that pressed against her stomach. Emma reveled in the proof that he wanted her. She had been frightened of him before, was frightened of him still, but for some reason she couldn't fathom, the fear did not make the wanting go away; the fear made the desire burn stronger.

Johnny brushed her lips with his tongue, and she opened her mouth on a sigh, luxuriating in the liquid warmth dipping inside her mouth. Such new and wondrous sensations contained in a mere kiss. Hesitantly she met his tongue with her own, and the groan her response evoked from him gratified her. He had called her naive once, and he'd been right. But she would not be naive forever with this man to teach her.

His hands moved from her neck into her hair, and he tangled his fingers in the long strands. She wanted to touch him as well and framed his face with her palms, pulling him closer, half afraid he would break off the kiss before she had enough. As if she could ever have enough of such intoxicating sensations.

Then his mouth left hers, and she uttered a whimper of protest. His lips touched her jaw and traced a warm path to her neck. His teeth grazed against the vein pulsing there, and she moaned at the contrast of the slight pain and the intense pleasure. Impatient fingers tugged at the buttons of her dress, opening just enough of them to bare her neck and the swell of her breasts. The night air had been warm until it swept across her heated flesh. She shivered in response, and his arms circled around to pull her tighter. He nibbled and sucked on the tender flesh above her collarbone, his tongue tracing the outline of that bone outward to her shoulder.

He paused and raised his head, silver eyes searching hers in the waning moonlight. What had begun as a kiss became a question, or perhaps a promise. She said nothing, only stared back, her breath heavy and aching in her chest.

Don't stop, her mind begged, though she couldn't bring herself to say the words. She had been waiting for him to touch her for a lifetime, and now that he had, she couldn't bear for him to stop before she experienced the pleasure he could bring her, the release of the eternal aloneness that possessed her every waking moment and haunted her every dream.

Johnny must have found an answer to his unspoken question in her eyes for he gave a small sigh, as though he couldn't stave off the inevitable, and tugged his shirt over his head, spreading it on the grass beside them. After sitting on the ground next to it, he pulled Emma down to sit on the fabric. Looking into her eyes all the while, he unbuttoned her dress to her waist. She had not put on her corset tonight, a fact that pleased her now. Her breasts spilled over the edge of her lace chemise. He reached out a finger and traced their swell. She caught her breath at the contrast of his callused skin against the softness of her untouched flesh. His finger caught the edge of the material and pulled downward until her breasts sprang free of the confinement; then his gaze dropped from hers to feast on the flesh revealed to his eyes.

His gaze caressed, and her nipples hardened from the nearly physical touch of his eyes. He stared at her so long she felt as though she would scream if he did not touch her soon. As if he could read her unspoken thoughts, he pushed her back gently to lie on the improvised bedding of his shirt.

"God, Emma, you're too beautiful," he said on a whisper.

He lowered his head toward her, and she bit her lip when his warm, wet tongue touched her breast. Around and around his tongue circled her nipple before he turned his head, using his hands to bring her other breast in closer proximity to his mouth. Then he proceeded to tease both breasts until Emma grew mindless with the need for more. She had never imagined such pleasure, never known her body could respond with such fervor to another human being's touch.

He kissed her again and again until her mind numbed with swirling sensation. If Emma had a coherent thought left in her mind at that moment, it would have been burned to nothing with the heat shooting through her as his mouth and tongue warred with hers.

He pulled back, leaving her alone once more. She opened her eyes. He stared down at her, the silver of his gaze now gray-blue with desire. A question haunted his eyes. Another question she did not understand. All she wanted was for him to continue what he had begun. She reached out and touched the blond hair on his chest, then kneaded the tight muscles of his shoulders. Curious, she traced her fingers down until they reached his flat male nipples. As if in answer to her curiosity, they hardened under her touch. Emma's hands brushed the flat plane of his belly, and Johnny jerked as though burned, then rolled over on top of her, bracing himself with his elbows on either side of her shoulders. A hardness pressed at the juncture of her thighs, and unable to help herself, she arched against that hardness. Johnny gasped, a hissing breath which made her breasts tingle and her heart pound.

"We should stop this, Emma. Now, before it's too late."

"Too late?" she questioned, her mind full of the smell and feel of him.

"If you keep pushing against me like that, I won't be able to stop. Do you understand what I'm saying, Emma? I'll finish what we've started. Right here on the ground. Is that what you want? Because I sure as hell do."

His voice sounded rough and dangerous, no longer the voice of the man she'd wanted to trust, despite the knowledge she should not. Emma gazed up into his face, shadowed by the fading moonlight behind him. She could no longer see his eyes, and for some reason that bothered her. Her grandfather had always said the eyes mirrored a man's soul. But what about his heart? She needed to know the essence of this man's heart before she gave herself to him. He had secrets, secrets he refused to share with her. If she wasn't careful she could end up just like her mother—alone, abandoned, dead. Used and then deserted by a drifter.

Drifter? her mind sneered. *What about murderer, Emmaline? What about werewolf?*

Emma clamped down on those thoughts, the fear and uncertainty they brought too much to contemplate right now with the man in question so close she could feel the heat of his breath upon her cheek. She'd professed his innocence to her grandfather, and thought she'd believed it, too, but with so many lives at stake she found she did not trust him as much as she'd hoped. The ease with which lies had begun to slip from her own tongue made her all the more aware of how easily Johnny could lie to her and to them all.

Emma looked up at him, trying to keep her confusion from showing in her eyes. But he could obviously see her better than she could see him, for he rolled to the side and sat up, presenting her with his back.

"That's what I thought," he muttered.

Emma hesitated, sensing his anger and wanting to do something to erase the distance her confusion had put between them. She didn't know what to say, her inexperience with men hitting her full force and making her even more uncertain of her actions than before. After a moment she sighed and then sat up, straightening and then buttoning her dress.

Presentable once more, Emma stood and glanced at John's stiff back. She wanted to touch him again, to soothe him as she would a hurt animal, but she dared not. "We should return to camp."

Johnny stood, grabbed his shirt from the ground and, after shaking the cloth free of dirt and grass, pulled the garment over his head. He turned toward her, and Emma took a step backward at the blazing awareness in his eyes.

Johnny followed her retreat, crowding too close as he looked down into her eyes. "I understand you don't trust me, Emma. I can't blame you. But I don't want you any less. Every day I want you more. I shouldn't. God knows I shouldn't. But what we should do and what we actually do are often two very different things." He reached up and smoothed her hair back from her face, then kissed her on the forehead. "That's my problem. Among others."

He stepped away, and the loss of his warmth created an ache deep inside her. She wanted to ask him what other problems he spoke of, but she knew he would not tell her. After the closeness they'd shared, then lost, she didn't think she could bear to have him push her away any more this night.

"I'll take you back," he said.

Emma remained silent, looking up into his still face, hoping, irrationally, that he'd kiss her again. She remembered the feel of his warm lips on her body. She wasn't sorry he had taught her what it felt like to be wanted. In the loneliness of her wagon in the nights to come she would crave those feelings again, but she could not give in to the wanting as long as the secrets remained unanswered. No matter how much her body cried out for release and her mind cried out for companionship.

With a nod of acquiescence, Emma allowed him to lead her back to the red wagon. His hand at her elbow warmed her skin through the material of her dress. What was it about this man that caused her to burn with desire whenever he came near? Was it her fear of him? The haunted sadness in his eyes? Or the danger around them that made life look so much sweeter against the possibility of its loss?

Whatever the reason, she doubted she'd be able to stop the wanting, no matter what his secrets turned out to be. Even if he had lied, if he was the evil one they sought. Even if the men killed him, she would remember until the day of her own death the passion that Johnny Bradfordini had awakened within her.

John cursed himself all the way back to the red wagon. He had wanted to frighten her, to show her the dangers that awaited a naive young woman alone. Yet the moment he touched her, all thoughts of teaching Emma a lesson had fled his mind, leaving only a nearly all-consuming urge to throw her upon the hard ground and rut like a beast. He disgusted himself. Why hadn't the lust that signaled the beast at rest within him begun to fade as his hearing and sight enhancements had? Instead, his desire for Emma seemed to increase with each passing day. If this continued, he would hurt her before he was through. Just as Devora had predicted. He would be unable to stop himself from taking her innocence. No matter that the beast within him would do the taking, Emma would suffer.

They came from two different worlds, as different as the sun and the moon, one rising as the other falls. She the sunshine and laughter and color and life. He the night and tears and darkness and death.

Even if he killed the evil one and ended the curse upon him, there could never be a future for himself and Emma. The circus was her life, her ambition to become the premier female tiger tamer in the world. He had vowed to spend his life healing others. Andrewsville still needed him, and when his mission here was complete he must return to his duties.

"Francie?"

The sound of Franz Gerhardt's voice, weaker and softer than usual, drifted to them from the red wagon.

Emma drew in a sharp breath and started to run toward the sound of her grandfather's voice. After tripping once, she righted herself without John's help. She burst through the bushes and onto the road, just as Franz jumped down from the red wagon.

"Grandfather, what are you doing up?" Emma reached him and put her hand upon his arm.

"Francie, where is everyone?" He grabbed her hand and squeezed, causing Emma to wince. "Why are we out here alone?"

John stood at the edge of the road and observed Franz. The change in the man was incredible. Where a few days before he had been strong, able-bodied and in charge of a large operation, today he appeared weak, addled and totally dependent upon Emma, who he continued to refer to by her mother's name.

"I'm Emmaline, Grandfather. Mother is dead. Do you remember?"

He wrinkled his brow, then shook his head. "I know your mother is dead, Francie. I just don't like to remember. She didn't want to leave her family in the Old Country, but I made her. I told her of the riches we would have here. How famous our circus would be. She always believed in me, and I brought her here to die."

"Grandfather, that's not true. You couldn't have stopped the fever that took Grandma. No one could have."

John found himself nodding in agreement, recalling his mother and all the others he'd lost to mysterious illnesses. The reminder of what he neglected while traveling with Gerhardt Circus brought a wave of sadness through his mind. If there had been an epidemic in Andrewsville while he was away, he would have to live with the responsibility of those deaths for the rest of his life. As Peter would have said, Johnny the responsible one would never forgive himself.

Franz shook off Emma's comforting embrace and headed toward the wagon. "Come on, girl. We have to catch up with the others."

Emma glanced at John, panic on her face. John shook off his melancholy and crossed the short distance to join Emma behind the wagon. He resisted the urge to hold her close and tell her he would take care of everything. He knew where such an action would lead them. Besides, Franz would most likely take a shotgun to him if he touched Emma in the old man's presence. Not that John needed to fear a lead bullet. But when Gerhardt shot him and he did not die, the circus owner would dig out his silver bullets and finish the job right.

"He's never acted like this before." Emma's voice wavered on the last word, and she stopped and swallowed before continuing. "I don't know what to do."

John glanced at Franz. The old man talked to the Percherons as he patted them on their noses. John had seen this type of behavior often in his elderly patients. Sometimes they came back to reality and sometimes not. The mind was a secret even physicians could not unlock.

"We'll have to keep a close watch on him. Make sure he doesn't wander off. I've seen old folks return to normal with rest. Don't let him become upset."

Emma glanced at him sharply. "You sound like a doctor."

John blinked and attempted to keep his face from betraying his chagrin. So accustomed to prattling off a diagnosis when questioned, he hadn't remembered to act the unskilled, uneducated laborer.

John shrugged. "My grandfather was like this. I'm just repeating what the doctor told us."

Emma stared at him for a long moment, then looked away toward Franz. "Did your grandfather improve?"

"Yes." John's grandfather had died in Italy, long before John had been born. But Emma needed to hear something positive right now, and what was another lie upon all the others he'd already told?

"Emmaline, *mach schnell!*"

Emma's face lit with a joyful smile at her grandfather's use of her name. She glanced at Johnny. "He's better," she said and ran to join the old man on the wagon seat.

John followed. Franz looked at him and glowered.

"What are you doing here?"

John frowned back. Franz acted as though he hadn't seen John until just that moment, but he'd been standing in the clearing all the while. Perhaps the old man's eyesight was failing, too. "I work for you, sir."

"I know who you are. I just want to know why you're here." He turned his glower upon Emma. "And why you two are out here alone."

"We're not alone," John said. "You're here."

"I was asleep. I do not trust you, Bradfordini. Especially with my girl."

John nodded. Franz was right not to trust him. John could not argue with the old man. But since the circus owner seemed more lucid, he did have a point to argue with Franz.

"A man followed the red wagon through the forest." He paused at Emma's gasp of shock and glanced at her. Two circles of pink stood out in stark contrast to the pale skin of her cheeks. He'd frightened her again, this time the way he'd meant to in the first place. "He was watching you when I caught up to you," he said to Emma, "but he rode off before I could catch him."

"What did he look like?" Emma asked, her voice tight, her lips stiff.

"Tall. He wore a hat so I couldn't see his hair. Looked like an outlaw almost, with a long leather coat."

Emma nodded. "That's him. The man who's been following us. The one you argued with, Grandfather."

John looked away from Emma and back at Franz. The old man stared into the air above the Percherons' heads.

"Who is he?" John asked.

"Francie went away and she never came back. He took her away from me. She was all I had left of my Magda."

Emma's shoulders slumped, and she gave a long sigh before looking at John, dejection in her eyes.

Franz had not stayed better for long. In fact . . . John narrowed his eyes focusing on Franz's face. The old man seemed to conveniently lose his grasp on the present whenever they questioned him about the blond man.

"We need a *jager-sucher,*" Franz mumbled.

John's breath caught in his chest. His gaze flicked to Emma. She looked as confused as John was excited. He took a step closer to the wagon and put his hand on Franz's arm. The old man turned to look at him. His glower had disappeared, in its place a serene, thoughtful expression. Gerhardt gazed into John's eyes, but John didn't think the old man saw him.

"Why?" John asked. "Why do we need a *jager-sucher?*"

"The time has come. I can no longer do this alone."

"What is he talking about?" Emma demanded.

John didn't spare her a glance this time. All his attention remained focused upon Franz. *Jager-sucher.* Peter had said the same words. Words John had remembered but not understood. Words he had not questioned anyone about.

Until now.

"What do they do?" John asked, his urgency causing his voice to come out a near growl. "The *jager-sucher?*"

"Hunt. Search. Destroy."

"Where are they?"

"Everywhere. Nowhere."

John resisted the urge to shake Franz until the answers tumbled from him like the leaves from an oak tree in the autumn wind.

"How do we get one?"

"Johnny," Emma hissed, "leave him alone. What is the matter with you?"

He ignored her. "Franz, how do we get a *jager-sucher* to come?"

But Gerhardt had heard enough questions. He shook off John's hand and clucked to the horses. The Percherons started up and the wagon rolled past John.

"Get on the back," Emma shouted above the jingle of the harness and the creak of the wagon wheels.

John caught the edge of the red wagon and swung himself onto the tail. He had all he could do to hold on as the conveyance jolted and jerked along the rutted dirt road. Though his hands were occupied with clasping the rough wood, his mind flew forward to what he would do once they reached camp. He had more questions for Devora and her books and notes—questions he should have asked long ago about the nature of the *jager-sucher*, and whether one could be employed to save his soul.

Chapter Ten

To reach the others John, Emma and Franz had to cross the Wisconsin River in the darkness. Luckily for them, the dry summer heat had lowered the river. They crossed at a narrow curve, but still Franz and John had to shove the heavy red wagon from behind while Emma encouraged the Percherons from the front. When they reached the opposite bank, all three of them were soaked and shivering in the gray light before dawn.

By the time they reached camp, everyone slept. The ability of circus folk to sleep whenever an opportunity arose never ceased to amaze John. Sometimes at night, sometimes during the day, when the order came to rest, circus folk obeyed.

"Halt," Franz ordered the Percherons and they did with a jerk. John bumped his head on the wagon door. Rubbing the spot with his palm, he walked around the edge of the wagon to find Emma assisting Franz to the ground.

"*Ach,* leave me be." Franz pushed away her helping hands. "I am not an invalid yet. I just wish to get rid of these wet clothes and be left alone to sleep.'' He stomped past John without a glance, and seconds later the sound of the wagon's doors creaking open, then closed, echoed in the dark of the night.

John turned to find Emma removing the Percherons from the harness. He moved forward to help her. The way she kept her face averted revealed her embarrassment over what had taken place between them in the woods. He hated to think of her discomfort over what to him was a joyful memory. One of the few he had.

''Emma, promise me you won't go in the woods alone again.''

She continued to unharness the horses without replying.

''Emma.''

''I wasn't alone. Grandfather was with me.''

John let out an exasperated sigh and placed his hand over hers. The warmth of the horse beneath their joined fingers reminded him of the warmth of her flesh against his lips. He tightened his hand, and she glanced upward into his face. ''Franz wasn't the only one out there with you. There was me and there was the stranger.''

''I didn't know that.''

''My point exactly. You're too trusting.''

''You make it sound like that's a bad thing. Trust.''

John looked away from her searching gaze. ''Can be. When you trust the wrong person.''

''Like you?''

Her voice was a whisper falling between them with the volume of thunder. John removed his hand from hers and stepped away.

''There's a renegade wolf on the loose, remember? You've lost two men. With all the animals in this circus

I wouldn't be surprised if the damn thing followed us, as well. Until it's destroyed and we learn who this outlaw is who's following you, I think you'd better stay close to the wagons, Emma.''

"You aren't my father. You can't tell me what to do.''

He looked at her then and saw the fear and the longing in her eyes. He steeled himself against the answering need within him. "No, I'm not your father, and I'm sure by now you understand I don't want you to think of me as one. Don't argue with me about this, Emma. I know what I'm talking about.''

Despite the warning note in his voice, she looked about to argue. Instead, she gave a sharp nod and returned to her task.

John left her to it. He needed to speak with Devora—now, when the memory of Franz's words was fresh in his mind. Not to mention the mystery of the blood-stained clothes he'd burned in the forest. Devora was the only one he could speak with about these mysteries.

He stalked across the quiet camp. She'd parked her wagon beneath a large oak tree, shaded from the intermittent light of the moon that peeked from behind the clouds at will.

At his approach, a long-fingered, sun-browned hand appeared through the open doorway and beckoned him inside. He should have known that nothing would get past her notice, especially his late arrival with Franz and Emma.

She reclined on her cushions, the candle on a low table throwing a flickering light around the dark interior. He sat next to her and waited.

"What happened, boy? You're wet and you smell of fear and the forest."

He ignored her question, putting forth one of his own. *"Jager-sucher,"* he said and waited for her response.

Her sharp black gaze narrowed upon his face. "What do you know of them?"

"Nothing. My brother said the words just before he died. He told me there were others."

She remained silent, thinking. He did not interrupt her silence. Long moments later she looked at him once more. "In Germany there is a secret society of men who hunt the werewolves. They devote their lives to the hunt. No one knows who they are, just that they exist. Perhaps your brother was one."

"Peter?" John shook his head. "I don't think so. He would have told me."

"He could not. They are sworn to secrecy on threat of death. He told you what he could before he died. If he said there were *others,* he could have meant other than himself. Why didn't you tell me of this before?"

"The words made no sense to me, so I had forgotten until Franz said them tonight."

"Franz? What did he say?"

"A lot of nothing. He's not himself. He keeps calling Emma by her mother's name. When I try to question him, his mind wanders."

Devora nodded. "The deaths have been too much for him. He's tried, but he is no match for the one who stalks us. His mind cannot cope." A shrewd look came over her face. "He's also a very smart man. He might be acting this way to keep the questions at bay and to keep Emmaline near. He'd do anything to keep her from leaving him.''

"I had the same thought. Still, he won't answer my questions.''

"I doubt if he knows much more than I. I'm sure he heard the legends during his childhood in Germany. I learned them from Wade.''

"Do the legends say how we employ one of these men?''

"They say that when the beast is at its strongest, the *jager-sucher* will come.''

"How will we know if he's here?''

"We won't. He looks like everyone else. He acts like everyone else. He kills, then disappears into the night without pausing for thanks or recognition. He is the mist, the fog, the dew upon the grass, a part of this world that hunts something no longer a part. If he comes, he will hunt you, boy. Watch yourself.''

John nodded an acknowledgment of the warning. "I found bloody clothes in my carpetbag today.''

Devora, who had been staring into the candle's flickering flame, turned her head slowly in his direction. She raised her eyebrows and waited.

"They weren't bloody when I put them in the bag. Torn and dirty, yes. But not bloody. They were the clothes I wore the night of the full moon.''

Devora winced at the reminder. "The evil one wishes to put the blame on you. If the circus folk or the *jager-sucher* turn their attention to you, the evil one can move on unmolested. By then it will be too late for us to do a thing to stop his evil from spreading to others. What did you do with the clothes?''

"I burned them in the forest.''

"Good. No one saw you?"

John hesitated. He remembered the swirl of evil all around him. The smell of death and hate. Someone had been watching him. He did not know who, but he knew what. He told Devora.

She sighed. "He knows you know. He will try again to put the blame on you."

"He wants to implicate me? That's why he didn't kill me in the woods today?"

"Yes. If he kills you before he has thrown suspicion upon you, his plans will be for naught. You must be careful. We do not have much time to discover his identity. If something happens to you before then, we might never learn the truth. He could drift away forever, or he could come back when we are not looking for him and kill again."

"How am I going to discover his identity if you haven't been able to? Shall I set some kind of trap?"

"Trap," she spat. "Franz wanted to do the same thing. Stupid idea. This *teufel* is ancient, I believe. He knows every trick. He knows what we do. We could never fool him with something as simple as a trap. We would only infuriate him."

"Well, what then? I can't just sit around and wait for the next full moon. I'll change, too, and then how will I kill him?"

"A wolf can kill a wolf, my boy."

"No!" John swallowed against the bile that rose in his throat at the thought of again becoming a monster who murdered. The images came fast and furious through his mind. Blood, death, screams. Were they real or were they a dream? He strove to breathe deeply and not plead out loud for the memories to stop. John swept away the sweat that had broken out on his brow, swallowed and looked the Gypsy in the eye. "I don't want to change again."

Devora waved her arm back and forth; clank-clank went her bracelets. "Never mind that now. We still have some time. He will come to you, and when he does, you watch for the signs. If he admits anything at all, kill him."

John started. As disgusted as he'd been at the thought of changing into a wolf and killing the evil one, the idea of killing another human being was worse. He had devoted himself to saving lives; he had taken a vow to that end. He had come here to kill a werewolf, believing he could shoot a demon with ease. But to shoot a man? He didn't know if he could. "What if I'm wrong and kill the wrong person?"

"Don't be wrong."

Easy for her to say. John rubbed his forehead, which now pounded viciously. "What if I can't do it?"

Her strong, bony fingers grasped his and pulled them away from his face. "You *can* do it. You must. Think of your brother. Think of yourself. You will save many more lives in the end with this action. And be more than careful, boy. Let nothing prevent you from your true purpose here—finding the evil one. Especially Emmaline."

"What do you mean by that?"

"You are enamored of her. And she of you. The lust of the beast clouds your sanity. You are not watching for danger when she is there. Remember, the evil one is amongst us. If he is not one of us, then very close. He can see how you want her. All he would have to do is take her, and you would follow. You would do whatever he wants to save her, wouldn't you?''

John didn't need to answer. He didn't think Devora needed him to either. Icy fear and burning fury washed through him. Nothing would touch Emma. He would do whatever he must to keep her safe. So innocent, so trusting, if she thought an animal hurt, she would help it. She might even walk right up to a wolf and bare her throat for its kiss.

Emma turned the Percherons out into the field to graze with the other horses. The darkness faded toward dawn. She should be exhausted after traveling throughout the night, then fording the river in her long skirt. She'd had to hold on to the Percherons with all her might as her heavy, wet dress became caught up in the river's current and tried to pull her downstream. She should change her clothes and get some sleep, just as her grandfather was doing. But if she went to her bed, she would not be able to sleep. There were too many conflicting feelings and memories and fears within her now to allow for rest.

Destruction roared a welcome as she wandered toward his cage wagon. She had not been spending much time with him since Johnny had come upon the scene. Emma walked up to the bars and put her arms through the openings, circling the tiger's neck for a hug. Pleasure rumbled in his throat as he rubbed his furry face against her cheek. Destruction gave her unconditional love—the type of love she'd longed for all her life.

Living without parents, she had never experienced such love until she raised Destruction. Oh, her grandfather loved her, but his love came with a price. Follow his edicts. Be the best. Don't fall in love. Stay with me. If you don't, you're not welcome.

Of course, he had never said the last, but his comments about her mother told Emma the story. Francesca had not followed the rules. Look what had happened to her.

Emma straightened away from the bars of the cage. Destruction mumbled his displeasure. She patted his head as consolation. "I'll be back later, Dusty," she said before turning away.

Her heart leapt into her throat at the sight of the man who watched her from the edge of the forest. She took a step backward. Destruction, sensing her fear, roared, a furious sound that should have struck terror into any man.

The blond stranger did not spare him a glance. He approached Emma, his long legs eating up the distance between them too fast. She glanced around the camp.

Deserted. Everyone asleep. Only herself, a tiger in a cage, and a stranger who could be a werewolf.

The man stopped a few feet in front of her. He no longer wore the long coat, but the wide-brimmed hat still sat on his head. The hat's shadow combined with the dawn-tinged sky obscured his face. He looked like the drawings she'd seen in western novels of outlaws—men with no names, no faces, just the pasts that made them legends. His clothes were ordinary—blue jeans, boots, spurs, cotton shirt. Nothing to make this man memorable, but memorable he was, would always be in Emma's mind, if only for the fear pounding through her body as he continued to stare at her from beneath the shadows.

He took a step toward her. Destruction snarled. The stranger paused and removed his hat.

For some unknown reason, Emma relaxed at the sight of the man's face. Just a man, nothing more. At least not right now.

Streaks of white shot through his blond hair; age and the elements lined his face, making it difficult to determine his age. Older than herself, younger than Grandfather. But his age did not interest her. His purpose at her circus did.

Emma found her voice. "Who are you and why are you following us?"

"You needn't be afraid, Emmaline." His voice held the same soothing tone she used to calm her cats during a thunderstorm. His accent was German, but not as pronounced as her grandfather's. Still, she did not find the accent in itself unusual. Over half the population of Wisconsin had immigrated from Germany. "I am following the circus because I enjoy the circus. Is there a law against watching something you enjoy?"

"No," Emma said, drawing the word out as she studied him. She sensed, with the innate knowledge of a woman used to sensing things in animals, that this man meant her no harm. At least not at the moment. With that reassurance in mind, she took the advantage and questioned him. "I saw you and my grandfather arguing. You know each other?"

The man looked up at the sky as though considering his words. "Your grandfather and I knew each other long ago. The memories are not pleasant for either of us."

"What happened?"

He shook his head and looked at her once more. "I didn't come here to talk about Franz. I shouldn't be here at all, but I wanted to warn you. There are those at Gerhardt Circus who are not what they seem, even those you think you can trust. Keep to yourself until the murderer is found.''

Emma gave a start of surprise. How did this man know of the deaths? They had done all they could to keep the secret. If news of the murders became public, the circus would be ruined.

''I don't know what you're talking about.'' Emma tried to sound indignant, and she did a good job until her voice broke on the last word.

The man cocked an eyebrow. ''You don't have to pretend with me, Emmaline. I won't tell anyone what you're hiding.''

Emma clamped her lips shut over the questions. If she said any more, she'd confirm his words.

''Listen to what I'm saying. Trust no one. Bradfordini, for instance. I've seen you with him. He is not who you think he is. Keep away.''

Emma frowned. This man had watched the circus for longer than they knew. He had seen more than he should have seen. ''What do you know of Johnny?''

''Not enough. Perhaps too much.'' His face hardened, taking on a ferocious cast, and Emma caught a glimpse of another man behind the cool, calm, almost gentlemanly facade. His gaze narrowed upon her, and she had the urge once more to run away and hide. She stifled the urge by twisting her fingers into her long skirts until they ached. He glanced at her hands, then back at her face. ''In any case, I will learn more about him, you can be sure of that.''

''Why do you care? Who are you? Why are you warning me?''

''I admire your talent. Call me a connoisseur of the

circus, and you, my dear Miss Monroe, are a wild-
flower I would hate to see trampled before you reach
your full bloom.''

''I don't believe you.''

He laughed, a short, dry sound without humor.
''Good. You're learning. Trust no one. Especially a
stranger.'' His voice choked on the last word, giving it
a bitter sound that made Emma's brow crease in confusion.

Destruction roared, and Emma turned toward him,
glad for an excuse to break the tension strung between
herself and the stranger. She murmured nonsense
words to the tiger until he lay down on the floor of the
cage wagon with a thump and a grumble. She turned
back to the stranger.

He was gone.

Emma hurried to the open area at the middle of the
camp. Step by step she turned in a full circle, searching
all around for a glimpse of the man.

Nothing. No one. Nowhere.

He had disappeared as quickly as he had appeared,
and she had not even learned his name.

John spent the rest of the predawn hours speaking
with Devora, looking through her books and notes, trying to discover a concrete answer to his most desperate
questions. He was no more successful in his search
than she had been before him. They would have to
continue on the way they had so far, floundering in the
dark, hoping to hit upon a discovery and learn the truth.
He had no other choice.

The thunderstorm began at dawn with a crash of
sound and a flash of lightning. Devora slept on her

cushions. Even the earth-shaking thunder did not awaken her. John covered the old Gypsy with a blanket, pressed a kiss she would never allow him when awake upon her brow, then blew out the candle before he left her to sleep.

As he walked across the empty yard toward his sleep wagon, the rain came in earnest, torrents of water against his back that soaked him to the skin in seconds. The rain was warm, the morning new and fresh and quite beautiful to his tired eyes.

Even more beautiful was the sight of Emma standing in the field with the menagerie animals. They milled around restlessly, starting and flinching whenever the lightning flashed or the thunder crashed above them.

John leaned against his wagon and watched her. She had a gift with the animals. He'd seen her talent before, but never so much as right now. Just her presence within their fold helped to calm them. They gathered around her like the multitude at the foot of a prophet, and like a prophet she reached out and touched each one—gently, reverently—leaving peace and joy in her wake.

With all his heart and soul, John wanted to be one of the multitude, but he knew in that same heart and soul he was not. He was different. Separate from all but one.

Cursed.

Forever? a voice asked, with the quaver of a child frightened by the truth.

God knows, answered the voice of the man. *Only God knows. Not I.*

The animals calmed down, despite the escalation of the storm. He should turn away before she saw him.

He should go inside and rest. But he wasn't tired.

Just one more moment, he told himself. I'll only stay for another moment. She'll never know I was here, and, God help me, I need the sight of her right now.

So he watched for another moment. A moment he should not have taken. For despite the fury of the storm, the wind, the rain, the distant but approaching thunder, she sensed him there and turned.

Their eyes met over the animals and she tensed. The zebra she'd been stroking felt the difference in her and threw back its head, braying at the flashing zigzag of lightning above. Her lips moved, a sound John could not hear, but the meaning was as clear as the silver slash of electricity lighting the sky.

Be calm. Everything's all right. I'm here.

If not those words, words that gave the same peace, for the zebra relaxed once more and dipped its head toward the ground. She came toward John through the rain, her long skirts heavy with the wet. They dragged upon the ground, and their hems darkened with mud. He remained where he stood, unable, despite the shout of reason within his head, to run away.

She represented everything safe and beautiful in the world. Everything he craved but could not have. Not now. Perhaps never. And still he wanted her with a need and a burn he could not kill no matter how he tried.

His past pressed upon him. In another life, another world, he was Dr. John Bradfordini, savior of Andrewsville, the man everyone wanted a piece of. He had a duty, a calling, a responsibility to the people he had promised to protect. But all his duties and vows had become mere words when Peter died. His logical mind told him he must return someday. But here, where all knew him as Johnny the canvasman, he'd experienced a freedom he had never known before. A freedom he had not known he craved. A freedom personified in Emma and her thirst for all that life had to offer. With her, he became a different man, a man he had never dreamed of being, but one that intrigued him nonetheless.

She didn't speak when she reached him; she stood before him as the water trickled down her face like tears. There, in the rain, just the two of them existed, along with the animals she had calmed with her presence. He wanted it to remain so, if only for the duration of the storm.

He didn't give her the chance to speak, the chance to ask more questions he could not answer. His mouth crushed down on hers and she gave a small whimper. At first he thought it was fear and started to pull away. But she circled his neck with her arms and drew him back, opening her mouth beneath his. He relaxed. The sound had been desire, not fright.

He leaned back against the wagon and she came with him, laying her length against his. Wherever they touched, heat emanated, making a startling contrast between their warm bodies and the chill of the rain upon them.

He had wanted to hold her, to feel her life and her goodness within his arms for a moment, to show himself there were still things on this earth worth living for. Or perhaps dying for. He remembered Peter saying those words, and he finally understood his brother's need.

She kissed him more deeply, using her tongue and

her teeth and her lips in ways he had so recently taught her. His fingers tangled in her wet hair, holding her head still as he took control of the kiss. She took a deep breath and relaxed against him, total trust in the circle of his arms.

John lifted his head and stared down at Emma's face. Her eyes were closed, the auburn lashes dark against her skin. She had freckles across the bridge of her nose, very light, but still there. They made her look like a little girl.

Like Little Red-Cap?

John winced at the question that echoed in his mind.

Little Red-Cap and the Wolf.

On the heels of his mind's answer, Emma opened her eyes and gazed into his. Her brow wrinkled, and she straightened away from him, though she continued to study his face. Reaching out, her hand trembled, from the damp or the desire he knew not which. She touched his cheek, her fingers cold against his skin. He shivered and grasped her wrist, pulling her touch away.

"What is it, Johnny?" Her voice, low, almost a whisper, held an intensity that frightened him. She'd seen something in his eyes. Perhaps the darkness in his soul, the evil that resided there for a time or maybe for always. He waited for the compassion in her eyes to turn to fear or horror, for the heat of her body to disappear when she ran from him forever.

Instead, she turned her wrist in his grasp and tangled her fingers with his. The captive become the captor as she brought his hand to her lips. Unable to stop her, he stood amazed as she kissed his fingers gently, like a mother kissing a child's scrape to take away the pain. But the response within his body was nothing like the response of a child. She started to turn his hand, to kiss the center of his palm.

The mark of the werewolf glistened red against his flesh. As he stared at the scar in horror, the mark began to burn like hellfire. With a curse, he yanked his fingers away from her mouth and wrenched himself from her grasp, putting the incriminating hand behind his back. As soon as he removed himself from her touch, the fire went out—in his hand but not in his body, not in his mind.

Her lips tightened at his callous withdrawal, and he thought she might turn and leave him alone in the rain. Instead, her mouth relaxed and she glanced away, her shoulders lifting, then lowering on a sigh. She had opened herself to him, then he had thrown her gentle, caring caress back in her face. And he could not explain why.

When she spoke again she did not look at him, but the pain in her voice told John all he needed to know. "Can't you tell me what hurts you so? Every time I look into your eyes I see the agony. I feel the pain, too."

The sky rumbled; the lightning blazed, illuminating her face for a moment. She turned back to him, the emotion in her eyes so intense he had to swallow against the answering feelings at the base of his throat.

She reminded him of Peter, he realized with a start. Her love of life, her adventuresome spirit. The hole in his gut that had opened when his brother disappeared and then had become a permanent bleeding sore when Peter died in his arms, stopped aching when he looked into Emma's eyes. In the short time he'd known her she'd become the missing part of his soul.

God help him, he wanted to tell her everything. He wanted to confess the truth and have her comfort him as she'd comforted the terrified animals in the field. He wanted to lay his head in her lap and have her stroke his hair and tell him everything would be fine. Even though nothing might ever be fine again.

She saw his indecision and pressed the advantage. "Let me help you. Please, I want to help you."

For a moment he let himself believe that Emma could help him. He allowed himself to imagine what it might be like not to exist alone with the horror of his truth. He began to reach for her.

The howl of a wolf began deep in the heart of the forest, far enough away to be no danger, close enough to remind John of all he had forgotten in the one brief moment he had reached toward salvation.

Emma gasped and jerked her head toward the sound. John's hand, which had been outstretched in supplication, fell back to his side untouched. He watched her face as the howl escalated to a peak, then faded away to an echo. The terror he saw there brought reality back to his mind. John turned and left her alone in the waning storm.

Chapter Eleven

Emma watched Johnny walk away from her. She could still feel the pressure of his lips on hers, the need in him calling out to the need in her. He might frighten her, but he was frightened of her, as well.

She could tell herself her desire for him was based on the lack of love in her life. She did not want this man so much as she wanted someone, anyone, to love her for herself and not for what she could do for them and the circus. But she would be lying. Something in Johnny, perhaps the darkness that hovered in his eyes, the fear upon his lips whenever he kissed her, called to her heart. She could not deny comfort to any animal she sensed in pain. How could she do any less for a man who affected her so deeply? She could deny the truth all she wanted, but the truth was still the truth. She wanted him to touch her, to kiss her and more.

Emma touched her fingertips to her mouth, the soft caress reminiscent of Johnny's lips. She closed her eyes and let the rain fall on her face as she held their embrace in her mind, then stored the memory away with the others she would hold close forever.

She should stop the relationship now, before it went too far. The passion between them could only end in pain. A drifter, he would leave her soon enough. Perhaps even now he had left. And if so, she would survive. But if she gave in to their mutual passion, if she let herself love him, and then he left, what then? Would she die like her mother had died when Karl deserted her?

"Emmaline, what are you doing out in the rain?"

Emma froze at the sound of the voice so close behind her. Her eyes snapped open, and she spun around. Heinz Kirshner, his clown makeup shining bright white beneath the brim of a large hat, stood too close to her. She stumbled when her feet caught in her skirts, and he grabbed her forearms to steady her. He did not let go when her feet found firm purchase on the ground. Instead, he held her still in his grasp. When she tried to pull away, his fingers tightened until she winced.

"What do you want?"

"Why, I wish to talk with you, of course. I came looking for you." His lips curved, emphasizing the smile painted around his mouth. "But you were occupied, so I waited."

Emma caught her breath at the implication. Heinz had watched the exchange between herself and Johnny. The beauty of the experience paled with the knowledge that they had been observed by someone such as he. She looked into the clown's eyes, then lifted her chin. She would not let him ruin the moment for her. What had happened between herself and Johnny was between them. They had nothing to be ashamed of. If anyone should be ashamed, that someone should be Heinz— the sneaking, treacherous, spying harlequin.

"Let me go." Emma allowed her disgust with the man to enter her voice. "If you wish to speak with me, speak. I'm tired and I need to get to bed."

Heinz released her arms, though he continued to stand too close to her. Emma took a step back, putting a more comfortable distance between them.

"I want to be your friend. That's all I've ever wanted. Yet if it weren't for your grandfather, I believe you'd spit upon me."

When Emma didn't answer, the hope in his face faded toward fury. "Does your grandfather know what you do in the rain, Emmaline?"

Her hands tightened into fists. She struggled to keep the fury from her voice. Anger would fuel his spite. "I am an adult. What I do is my business. Now state yours or go away."

"Your *friend,* Johnny, is it?" He looked to Emma for confirmation. She refused to acknowledge his question. He knew very well Johnny's name. Emma turned to leave, but his next words stopped her in mid step.

"He has secrets, Emmaline. Secrets I know."

She didn't want to turn. She didn't want to give Heinz the satisfaction of telling her Johnny's secrets. But she couldn't deny her need to know them either. Too many lives depended upon her.

She faced Heinz again. He smirked. She took a deep breath and waited. She would not ask him to tell her. That she could not do.

She did not have to. Heinz was more than willing to share his knowledge with her. "He left the circus yesterday. Took a walk into the woods."

"Yes. Is there a law against walking in the woods?" Her gaze swept the trees surrounding them. The storm had blown away. A new day dawned. The same problems remained. "We have little choice here about where we walk."

"No, there is no law against walking. No law that I know of against burning things either."

"Burning things?" Emma's brow creased into a frown. "Why?"

Heinz shrugged. "I'm not sure. When I was leaving the lot, I smelled something burning. When I went to investigate, I found a small fire. I heard a sound and followed. I saw Bradfordini walking away."

"That doesn't mean he burned something."

"No? I suppose not. Though the ashes were still hot and he very close. Don't you want to know what he burned, Emmaline?"

Emma raised her eyebrows and waited once more. Heinz did not disappoint her.

"A pair of pants and a work shirt. There was enough left unburned for me to see what they were."

"I don't understand. Why would he go into the woods to burn some clothes?"

"Perhaps they were stained. With blood, possibly?"

"Why would you say that?"

"Just a thought. Maybe you should ask him what he was doing. He is hiding something. We do not need strangers with secrets here, Emmaline. Make him go."

Emma glanced sharply at Heinz. "You're not the boss here."

"And you are? I can tell Franz, but we both know he won't dismiss Bradfordini because of a suspicion, even if he might want to. He needs the help too much. But if I tell him what I saw out here he will throw

Bradfordini off this lot without a second thought. Is that what you wish?''

Emma's breath caught. Though she was not ashamed of kissing Johnny, she didn't want her grandfather to hear of the incident from Heinz, who would make the situation sound so much more damning than it was. In Franz's current vague state, she did not know how he would react.

''Why do you care, Heinz? If Johnny leaves, there will be more work for us all.''

''I care because I'm tired of seeing my friends buried in the forest.'' His voice, which had until then been calm and rational, lowered to a vicious snarl. ''I don't trust Bradfordini, and you should not either.''

''He came to us *after* the first men were killed.''

''That means nothing and you know it. Men lie. He is an outsider. We don't need him.''

Emma sighed. Much as she hated to admit the truth, Heinz was right. But if she dismissed Johnny, and he was the one they sought, he would then have the opportunity to follow the circus and stalk all of them from the forest. Weren't they better off with an evil they could see than one they could not? She said as much to Heinz.

''We can always kill him.''

Emma started at the coldness of the clown's voice, so at odds with the smiling paint on his face.

''Are you insane? We can't kill a man because we *think* he has secrets. Half of the people at this circus have secrets. You included.''

''I suppose you are right. I tell you this because I see how you look at him. You want him and he wants you. You are young, impressionable. You do not understand the ways of men, or their beast. Beware this man, Emmaline. I do not want to bury you in the woods like the others. You don't like me, but I still care for you. Family is family.''

He nodded once and turned from her, striding away toward clown alley, which housed the wardrobes, props and sleeping wagons of all Gerhardt's clowns.

Emma watched him go. When he reached his wagon, Kirshner turned back toward her. Despite the shadow of his hat and the makeup on his face, she recognized his fear for her, and a chill seeped into her blood. If Heinz, always so unfeeling and sarcastic, feared for her, then she should fear, too. The wondrous memory of Johnny's kiss, which she had tucked away close to her heart, faded and died.

Instead of going to her sleeping wagon as she should, Emma made a sharp turn and headed for the red wagon and her grandfather. She would not be able to sleep, and she certainly didn't want to lie awake and think. Checking on her grandfather would keep her mind occupied for a little while.

Emma stepped into the wagon without knocking. A glance around the interior revealed him asleep on his pallet. She crossed the room and stared at him for a moment. He slept peacefully. She would not disturb his rest. Perhaps when he awoke he would be himself once more. She could always hope.

Emma's gaze fell upon some papers lying atop the desk. They looked like letters. Old letters. Some had been torn, some burned.

She glanced back at her grandfather. He slept on. Emma picked up one of the pages. Both ends had been burned, and when she touched the paper, parts fell away, drifting onto the desk in a slow waltz with the air. Only one line remained readable.

I have reasons for what I do. I loved Francesca with all my heart and

The rest of the letter crumpled away, ashes and soot. She picked up another, which had been torn until a mere quarter of the page remained. On that page she read:

I want to see her. She is my
You have no right to keep
She should know I
Every summer I will
Karl

The signature leapt out at Emma, making her breath start and freeze in her chest. Her father's name. This letter had been from her father to Franz.

When? How? Why?

Her grandfather had said Karl Monroe left Francesca and Emma without thought, never to return. Her father cared nothing for her, and she should forget him. But in her hand she held the proof he had not disappeared. He had written how much he loved Francesca. Emma glanced down at the torn paper—and if she had deciphered these words correctly he had wanted to see her.

She frowned. What was this line about every summer? Every summer he would write again? She glanced at her grandfather. Had he refused to let Karl see her? The first hint of anger blew through her heart, warming the cold that had lodged there since she'd seen her father's name written in his own hand. She had gone through a lifetime believing he did not care about her. She had agonized over the pain for many years. Had everything she'd believed about Karl Monroe been a lie? And if so, then all she'd believed about Franz Gerhardt was a lie, too.

Emma took the three steps between the desk and her grandfather's pallet and grasped his shoulder. He did not awaken. She shook him—once, twice, three times.

He sat up, questions in German on his tongue. *"Was? Wer?"* His gaze darted around the wagon, fear shining in his eyes.

"It's Emma, Grandfather."

He relaxed at the sound of her voice. "Ah, *mein Liebchen.* You startled me. Is it time for the matinee?"

He sounded like his old self. He had not called her Francie. She would question him now before he slipped back into his confused state. "I found this, Grandfather." She held out the paper. His gaze flicked to her hand, then up to her face. Carefully blank were his eyes. He said nothing.

"A letter from my father. Why didn't you tell me he'd written? This I needed to know."

He plucked the paper from her hand with surprising quickness and crumpled the note into a ball in his fist. "Karl Monroe is nothing but a drifter. His interest in you was no more than a way to take the circus away from me. He is no good, has never been any good. He would just hurt you. I cannot allow him to cause you any more pain."

"I spent my life believing he never cared about me when all the time he wanted to see me and you wouldn't let him?"

"He does not care about you. He only cares about what he can get from you. He only cares about the circus."

"Is he any different from you, then? Or me? We

221

care about nothing but this place. How we can keep it going. How we can continue to live in this world and none other. Why is my father any different?''

''Do not call Monroe your father,'' Franz shouted. ''He did nothing but create you. I raised you. I made you what you are. Without me you would be nothing.''

Emma went very still as tears pricked her eyes. She blinked them back. She would not cry. She would not show him how much his words and deeds had hurt her. ''I could never be nothing. Will you ever see that I am more than your star performer, Grandfather? I am your granddaughter. Karl's daughter. A woman with a mind and a heart and a soul separate from yours. You will have to learn this or I cannot stay here.''

Her grandfather's face whitened. He opened his mouth to speak. But before he could, a knock came on the door. They both turned toward the sound, then looked back at each other. Franz stood, then brushed past her and yanked open the door.

A tall, broad-shouldered man wearing what looked to be a Union captain's hat stood on the ground next to the wagon. Emma caught her breath for a moment, thinking it to be the stranger. Then her gaze caught the badge of authority fastened to his shirt, and she winced.

''Franz Gerhardt?'' the man asked.

Her grandfather gave a short nod.

''I'd like to have a talk with you. I've heard here 'bouts you've got people missin'.'' He glanced at Emma, nodded respectfully, then returned his attention to Franz. ''Could you step outside with me while I ask you some questions?''

Emma saw her grandfather's shoulders tense, but he held himself tall and proud as he walked to the edge of the wagon and jumped down. He looked back at Emma, in his eyes a warning. The truth must continue to be hidden at all costs.

Emma took a moment to thank God her grandfather was lucid now. They needed him at his best.

The law had caught up to them at last.

John meant to return to his pallet and sleep the morning away. He told himself that only in sleep would he forget the taste of Emma's lips upon his own. But he knew better. In sleep, the memory would become so much more vivid. He winced at the thought of how his mind would embellish the encounter.

Suddenly the need to get away from Gerhardt Circus consumed him. He reached the field where the menagerie animals and the horses were tethered. Emma was no longer there. He had to get away from the secrets and the strangers. He had to get away from Emma and the frightening need she made him feel, a need he could not trust since it hailed from the beast sleeping within him. She deserved so much more from a man than lust. He'd heard that lust could grow into love, and maybe it could if given a chance, but he doubted that lust that stemmed from a curse could grow into anything more than hate.

John grabbed the nearest horse, one of the bareback rider's mounts, released the tether and swung onto the animal's back. One kick and they were on their way, thundering down the dirt trail and away from the circus.

Although accustomed to riding, very often at top speed and in the dark of night, John was not used to a horse that responded to the pressure of a rider's legs like an Indian pony. John held onto the horse's mane and let the animal run. The feel of the wind, fresh from the storm, whipping against his face and through his long hair blew away some of the tension coiled within him. If he didn't look too closely, he could almost believe himself back at home, riding the dirt roads around Andrewsville. Just the thought sent a wave of homesickness through his belly. He loved his hometown, his life's work of helping the people he'd known since childhood and the ones he'd brought into the world since his return from the war. He hated the thought that people could be dying without his help. But if he'd stayed home, he would have been the one killing them.

The thought made him flinch. If he continued to think of all the things he might have done or could yet do, he would go insane before the next full moon. He had come out here to forget about the darkness in his soul. He would take this short time and enjoy his freedom without torturing himself over what might have happened and what could happen still.

The problem was that he had always been one to stay in the same place, never one to wander. The first time he'd left home had been to go and fight the war; the second time he'd come here, run away to join the circus.

John's lips twitched at the thought. He and Peter had often spoken of doing just that, every year after their father took them to a circus matinee. After they'd spent an afternoon amidst the color and magic, their life on the farm had looked so much more dreary. They would go home and stay up late, whispering in their room about what they would do once they escaped to the circus. Or rather Peter would speak and John would listen, marveling at the spirit of adventure that coursed through his little brother. John had no doubt Peter would have been a performer without peer in the circus world, and his personality would have thrived under the attention of the crowd.

"Peter should see me now," John said to himself. The horse snorted an agreement, and John patted his neck. "Yeah, he'd love everything about Gerhardt Circus." John paused, then sighed. "Or almost everything."

The horse slowed to a stop and tossed his head back. Without knowing what he did, John must have given the animal a signal with his legs. John glanced back the way he'd come. There was no help for it. Try as he might to forget his problems, they were too much a part of him to leave his mind for long. He must return to Gerhardt's now and attempt to catch some sleep before the matinee.

John pushed with his right knee and the horse turned around. A brisk kick and the animal trotted. Once the horse understood they were headed home, he began to gallop. When John made no move to stop him, he settled into a run.

They returned to the circus at the same speed they'd left it. The horse slowed when he reached the outlying wagons. In the time he'd been riding, the circus had come back to life. Performers and laborers alike milled about the back lot. One sight drew John's attention—the sight of Franz speaking earnestly with a tall man wearing a Union captain's hat. The stranger's back faced John, but the way the man held himself seemed familiar.

John frowned and urged the horse forward. Franz

saw him coming and stepped around the man. He frowned at the horse, then glared at John. "*Dummkopf!* Idiot! That horse is not yours to ruin."

The tall stranger turned to see who Franz shouted at. His eyes widened when they lit upon John. Shock shot through John's body. Before he could stop himself, his legs clenched. The well-trained horse bucked. John, unprepared for the move and with nothing to hold on to, flew head first over the horse's head.

"Umph!" A grunt of pain sprang from his lips as he hit the hard ground face down. The impact knocked the air from him, and he lay gasping for breath as pain blossomed in his gut.

When his lungs allowed him to take in air, he lifted his head from the ground. His hair hung in his eyes, and he shoved the strands from his face with impatience before turning to glare at the horse.

The animal stared placidly back as if to say, What are you doing down there?

"What do you think?" John growled. He pushed himself to his knees.

"John?"

John froze when the tall stranger spoke his name. He glanced up and focused upon the silver star attached to the man's shirt.

"Sheriff," John greeted, hoping the man would take the hint and not reveal their association.

He stood. The sheriff removed his hat, revealing short, graying hair and a wide, ruddy face, which split into a grin as he stepped forward to clap John on the shoulder. John glanced at Franz, who watched them closely. A movement behind Gerhardt drew John's attention. He looked up to see Emma standing in the open door of the red wagon; her long skirts blew in the slight breeze, and he glimpsed a pair of high-topped boots and several petticoats beneath yards of material.

John swore under his breath, then turned his attention back to the man in front of him. He tried to ward off the inevitable question with a sharp shake of his head, but Captain Marcus Birkelund had never been one to understand subtlety.

Instead of keeping quiet, he squeezed John's shoulder, grinned ear-to-ear and bellowed, "Lieutenant, what the hell are you doin' here?"

Chapter Twelve

"Lieutenant?" Emma's voice wavered on the word. John glanced up and swore again when he saw the distrust flash across her face.

"Lieutenant?" Franz echoed.

Think! Move! Do something before Marcus calls you doctor and ruins everything.

John stuck out his hand, and Birkelund replaced his hat, then put his hand in John's. John squeezed hard on his friend's fingers, and Marcus looked up into his eyes. "Follow my lead," John whispered.

The intensity in his voice reached the sheriff, and Marcus nodded once, then returned John's handshake.

John glanced over at Franz. "I met the captain in the war. We both served in the 26th Wisconsin."

"You were in the war?" Emma asked.

Stifling his irritation at the shock in her voice—for he had given her no reason to think of him as anything other than a drifter—John looked at Emma. The distrust had left her eyes, surprise taking its place. "Yes," he said shortly, "I was."

"I would have thought a drifter like you had no time

228

for such things,'' Franz said.

Marcus frowned when Franz said the word *drifter,* and his gaze flicked back toward John. John shrugged. ''I drifted into the war, then out when it was over. A lot of men with no place to go did the same.''

''But you were an officer?'' Franz insisted. ''How did you accomplish such a feat?''

John had accomplished nothing. He had been appointed an officer because he'd apprenticed as a doctor. But he couldn't very well say so. ''They needed me. I did my job. They rewarded me for it. Isn't that how the army works, Captain?''

''Uh, yes. True.'' Marcus sounded confused, but his words at least supported John's statement.

''What brings you here?'' John asked. He needed to turn attention away from his past before either he or Marcus said the wrong thing.

Marcus stared at him for a long moment, then turned back to Franz. ''I've come to ask Mr. Gerhardt some questions. There have been rumors passed about that this circus is missin' some performers. Since others have turned up missin' from the towns the circus has passed through, people are talking.''

''Other people?'' The shock of the sheriff's words caused John to speak, even though he did not want any more attention upon him.

''Uh-huh. One in Cherry Bay. Another in Haywardsville.''

John nearly choked at the sheriff's words. Marcus watched his face, catching every expression John was unable to control. John took a deep breath and kept any further comments to himself.

''We do not have them here,'' Franz snapped, and

thankfully Marcus turned away from his contemplation of John.

"I didn't say you did. But I do need to ask your people if they've seen anything along the way that could help me find out what happened to 'em. Or if they might have seen anyone resembling 'em."

Franz's face took on a sly look. "There is one man who has been following our circus. Tall, blond, with the looks of an outlaw. You would do well to seek him."

"Really?" Marcus glanced at John. "Have you seen this man?"

"Yes." John looked over the sheriff's shoulder at Franz. Whenever he and Emma had asked about the stranger, Franz's mind had wandered. Now he remembered the man quite clearly. Interesting. Too bad John could not question Franz further with Marcus listening. He turned back to the sheriff. "I saw the man in the woods one night. I haven't seen him since."

"I have." Emma's quiet voice from behind Franz made them all turn. Her face was pale, and she clasped her hands tightly in front of her, but when she spoke, her voice held steady and strong. "He was here one night and I spoke with him."

"You what?" Franz bellowed.

Her gaze flicked toward her grandfather once, then away. She stepped past him, ignoring his question. "I spoke with the man, then he left. He has not been here since that night."

"When did this happen?" Marcus asked.

"Two nights ago, perhaps. I cannot recall."

"What did you talk about, Miss . . . ?" Marcus let the question hang in the air.

"Monroe," Emma answered. "Emmaline Monroe. I asked him why he followed us. He said he admired talent. My talent."

Franz snorted. "He is a troublemaker."

The sheriff sent a sharp glance Gerhardt's way. "You know him?"

Uncertainty flickered in Franz's eyes. "Not really. I've seen him. I told him to go. We do not need his type following us."

"What type might that be, sir?"

Franz nodded at John. "His type. Drifters. No-goods."

Marcus raised his eyebrows. John held his breath, then let it out on the sheriff's next question. "You've hired John to work for you, is that right? Yet you think he's no good?"

"I hire help when I need help. They come, they go. His type are not responsible."

"So the missin' performers have disappeared?"

"Who says they have disappeared?" Franz demanded.

Marcus shrugged. "Rumors fly in small towns."

"Well, that is all they are. Rumors." He glanced at Emma, and a long look of understanding passed between them before he turned back to the sheriff. "We have had some trouble with a wolf following us. The animal must be mad since it stalks us and does not relent. When we have gone out hunting, we have lost four men."

"Four?" John asked, recalling that he was supposed to know nothing about the first two deaths. "I'd heard two."

Franz scowled at his interference. "You were here

231

when we lost two. We lost two others before you came.''

"And you didn't tell me this?''

"You did not ask.''

" 'Scuse me,'' Marcus interrupted. "Two or four, you've still lost men but you haven't asked for help from any local law along the way. Why not?''

"We need no one else. We will take care of the animal ourselves.''

"Isn't it a bit odd for a wolf to stalk a group so long and so far?''

Franz shook his head. "Not when the wolf is mad and not when we have so many animals with us.'' He pointed at the field of menagerie animals.

Marcus followed the direction of Gerhardt's hand and nodded slowly. "Odd, though, that a rabid animal would last this long. Most die off on their own. But this has been going on for what? Two months?'' He looked back at Franz. "Three?'' His polite and curious voice belied the expression on his face. Marcus did not believe a word Gerhardt was telling him.

"I know nothing about mad animals. I only know I have lost four men and I am tired of it. Since you are here now, perhaps you can do better?''

John had to give Gerhardt credit. He played a good part—the outraged circus owner who did not understand why he was being questioned. If John hadn't seen for himself the midnight burials, he would have believed Gerhardt's lies.

"Maybe I can. Tell me, what did you do with the bodies? Can I see 'em?''

Franz blinked, nonplussed at the question. "Of course not. It is summer. We did not drag them along with us, we buried them in the forest.''

''Without a priest or a minister or even an under-taker?''

''Is there a law against conducting a burial in the forest?''

''None I know of. Too bad, I would have liked to take a look at those bodies.''

''You are a very odd man, Sheriff,'' Franz mumbled.

''Maybe. Or maybe there's just somethin' odd going on around here.'' He narrowed his gaze upon the circus owner. Franz stared right back. Neither gave way until Marcus shrugged and glanced at John. John shrugged, too. The sheriff turned back to Franz. ''I'd like to question your people. That all right with you?''

Franz hesitated a moment, staring at Marcus as if measuring the amount of trouble a refusal of permission would bring their way. Then he waved his hand in acquiescence. ''Do what you wish.'' He turned and stomped away.

Emma, who had watched the sparring conversation with as much interest as John had, took a step after her grandfather. Marcus stopped her. ''Miss Monroe?''

She turned back; her gaze touched on John's then slid away. He clenched his teeth. Something had made her distrust him even more than before. Something that had occurred since they'd kissed in the rain, but before she'd learned of his military service. Had Franz told her more lies?

''Sheriff?'' she asked, and the husky quality of her voice called to John despite the tension in the air.

''I'll begin my questions with you, if you don't mind,'' Marcus said.

She glanced at the red wagon where Franz had disappeared. Then her shoulders lifted and lowered with a sigh. "I'm afraid I can't help you. We have a show soon and my grandfather is unwell. I have to make sure everything is ready." She rubbed her forehead with her fingers. "And I haven't slept since yesterday."

"Shouldn't take too long."

Emma looked at John, and the plea in her eyes made him step forward and clasp the sheriff's shoulder. "Why don't you start with me, Marcus? Emma does have to take care of a few things."

Marcus hesitated, then threw up a hand. "All right." He turned back toward Emma. "But if I don't get to talk with you before the show, I'll need you to come into town later, Miss Monroe."

John glanced at Emma just in time to see her flinch as if struck. He narrowed his eyes. For some reason, the thought of going to town upset her.

"Miss Monroe?" Marcus pressed. "You'll come to town after the matinee?"

She looked around as if searching for an escape. She found none.

"I'll bring her later," John said.

Her gaze flicked to his, relief in her eyes. He smiled, but she did not return the expression. Instead, Emma turned away and strode off toward the milling throng of elephants and canvasmen who were just about to raise the big top. John watched her go, wondering how he would get her to confess why she looked at him with so much pain and distrust in her eyes.

"What's the story, Doctor?"

The sheriff's voice made John turn back, glancing around the lot to see if anyone stood close enough to hear. Fortunately, everyone went about the business of setting up for the first show.

John shook his head at Marcus and motioned for him to follow as John led the bareback pony to the open field. Once there, John began to rub the horse down with dry grass. They were alone but for the menagerie surrounding them.

"Aren't you goin' to answer me?"

"Yes. I'm just trying to decide where to start." John was trying to decide how much he could tell Marcus. He couldn't tell him the truth. Either Marcus would drag him away to an insane asylum, or he would lock him up in jail until the next full moon, then shoot him like a rabid animal. Neither option was very appealing.

"Why don't you start with why you're here pretendin' to be a common laborer when we both know you're a skilled physician? And why you let Gerhardt talk to you like you're dirt under his feet?"

John sighed. "He talks to me like that because he believes I am little better than dirt. That's what I want him to believe."

"Why, John?"

John turned away from the pony. "It's a long story. I have my reasons. Good reasons."

"Is Peter with you?"

John frowned. "No. Peter's . . ." He took a deep breath. He had not had to say the words to anyone yet. He hadn't known they'd be so hard. John tightened his lips and forced himself to voice his pain. "Peter is dead."

"Huh?" Marcus blinked, shock passing across his face. "I just saw him a few months ago."

John went still. "Here?"

Marcus nodded. "Of course. I've been the sheriff in

Michel's Pond since the war ended. What happened to him, if you don't mind my askin'?"

"Rabid wolf," John said without a second thought for his lie. Lies tripped off his tongue these days.

"Really? How odd. There seem to be a lot of rabid wolves around these parts. When Peter came through he was after a rabid wolf. Did it get him?"

"Yes."

"I've never heard of a mad wolf killin' so many. You sure that's what killed 'em, Doc?"

John went still. He didn't like Marcus's questions any more than Franz had. "What else?"

"I don't know. In these woods we're so isolated, the old stories are passed around a lot. There are evils in this world we can't begin to understand."

"I could."

Marcus looked into his eyes. "Yeah, I suppose you could. Once you've been in a war like we were, nothin' surprises you. But there's somethin' goin' on in these woods, John. Somethin' real strange."

John didn't comment on his friend's observation. Marcus was right. "How did you hear about the missing performers?"

The sheriff looked out over the milling animals toward the woods. The slight slump of his shoulders revealed an inner pain. "I wouldn't have heard, except the missin' boy is my nephew."

John's face drained of blood at the man's words. *A child. A little boy. Gone.* John knew quite well what had happened to him. Luckily, Marcus kept staring at the trees as he spoke and did not see John's discomfiture. "He went to the circus, then he never came home. I went down to Haywardsville to talk to my sister, check around a bit for her, and some of the townsfolk told me about the missin' dwarf and wire-walker.''

John cleared his throat, hoping his voice would not reveal his agony. "How did they know the men were missing?"

"These outfits rarely change, John. Oh, the canvas-men might come and go, but the performers are part of the family. They don't disappear from one day to the next. After I did some more checkin' I found out the muscleman and the contortionist weren't around anymore either.''

John didn't know how to explain the disappearances without telling the truth, so he said nothing.

Marcus returned his gaze to John's face. Despite his large size and usual bluff, hearty manner, Birkelund was a smart man. John cursed the fates that had made Marcus Birkelund the sheriff in this town, that had made John, or one other, steal away Birkelund's nephew during the last full moon. Marcus would not rest until he learned the truth.

"What do you know, John?"

"Your nephew isn't here. He didn't run away to the circus, if that's what you're thinking.''

"I was hopin', to tell the truth. Any other option sticks in my gullet and burns.''

"I suppose so.''

"The wolf that killed Peter, is it the same one stalkin' the circus?''

"I'm not sure.''

"You seen it?''

"Yes.'' John recalled when he had seen the *teufel*—the black wolf with the eyes of a man that had killed

237

his little brother and cursed him.

"Then that's why you're here? To kill the wolf?"

"Yes. I'll kill it. You can make a bet on that, Captain."

"Why are you pretendin' to be what you're not? Why didn't you just come here, kill the damn thing, and go?"

John had known the question would come eventually. He took a step closer to Marcus and lowered his voice. "I need a favor." The sheriff narrowed his eyes, his suspicion renewed. "Don't tell anyone who I am. Please, Marcus. No one here knows, and I don't want them to know."

"Why?"

"Because you're right. I want to kill the thing. But the people here don't trust outsiders. They wouldn't allow me to travel with them if they knew who I really was. So I pretended to be a drifter. No one asks questions of drifters. It's against circus rules."

"This entire place smells, John. They're hidin' somethin'. I can always tell. If I don't find some answers, I'm goin' to have to make 'em stay here until I do. A mad wolf that kills four or more people and doesn't die as mad wolves should makes me think of another kind of wolf. One that isn't always a wolf. Do you understand what I'm sayin'?"

John understood very well. "I might. But I wouldn't pass your theory around town, Marcus. Some people might lock you in your own jail."

The sheriff nodded. "I know. But I've heard the old tales same's you. I've seen what a werewolf can do." He glanced up at the sky, remembering. "In the war, sometimes after a fight when the full moon would shine on the dead, I'd see wolves on the battlefield. One or two, not a pack like real wolves run in. These were lone wolves, and after a time I figured out why."

John held his breath, fascinated with the sheriff's tale. This was the first person who had seen what he had seen, except for Peter. John wanted to hear all Marcus could tell him about his experience. "Why?" he whispered. An encouragement, a prayer.

"These wolves follow the meat. They prefer live victims, but dead will do in a pinch. And in a war, they can gorge themselves on the dead. They can even gorge themselves on the livin', and with all the death around no one is any the wiser." Marcus glanced at John with a raised brow. "You must think I'm crazy."

John shook his head, captivated by the story, unwilling to break the string of Marcus's words with words of his own.

The sheriff continued. "I saw one, John. One night I couldn't sleep so I took the watch. A wolf came out of the river bottom. He started chewin' on a man. The man wasn't dead, and he started to scream. I drew my Colt and walked over there. Shot the damn thing right in the chest." Marcus closed his eyes as if he were seeing the event again and did not want to watch. "It howled, I could almost make out a word, the thing sounded so human. I waited for the animal to die, but it just stared back at me, a wolf with the eyes of a man. Then it ran off."

"And the man this creature bit?"

Marcus opened his eyes and stared at John for a moment, considering. "I took him to the surgeon. You."

John frowned. "I don't remember."

"You never saw him. By the time his turn came in the tent, he was gone."

"Dead?"

"No, just gone. He was shot up real bad, but he walked away from camp, and I never saw him again."

"Delirious," John pronounced. "Must have gone off to die in the woods."

"Maybe."

John didn't answer. He knew what had happened to the man bitten by the werewolf. He knew very well, and so did Marcus.

"So, if a mad wolf is followin' this circus, I'm gonna have to make you stay here until we kill it." The sheriff's voice was all business once more. John had no doubt that if he questioned Marcus about his story, the man would deny ever telling the tale. To the world, a mad wolf followed the circus, not the evil they both knew lurked in the forest somewhere.

John's lips tightened at the thought of what Emma would say when she heard what the sheriff planned to do. She would fight with everything she had to keep Gerhardt Circus from dying. "I wish you wouldn't make them stay here." John looked Marcus straight in the eye. He had to make the man understand the severity of such an action. "If the circus can't move on to their next show, they won't complete their tour. From what I've heard, the war and last year's floods hurt them. They've got to have a good season or die."

"Not my problem, Doctor. There are too many missin' people." He narrowed his gaze, as if he saw a trace of the shadows within John's eyes. "You know somethin', somethin' more than a legend about why those people are missin'. Why don't you tell me and save everyone else the trouble?''

Marcus was honest, hardworking and trustworthy. He was also the law. The law who believed in the curse of the werewolf and would not hesitate to destroy one if he could. John did not dare tell his friend the truth, so he told him nothing.

''Will you keep my secret, Captain?''

Marcus's mouth tightened at John's use of his former title and the memories it aroused. John hadn't wanted to use his influence over the sheriff, but he had little choice.

Marcus made a sound of disgust and kicked a stone with his boot. The rock skipped several feet upon the grass, startling a zebra enough to make it bray in response. ''You know I'll keep your damn secret, Doctor. I owe you. You saved my life at Gettysburg. My leg would've festered if you hadn't been so stubborn and kept cleanin' it every chance you got. I saw enough men die in those tents to know how lucky I am. But this makes us even. If I find out you or the folks at Gerhardt are protectin' a murderer or worse, I'll haul you off to jail or a hangin' as fast as any other man.''

John looked into the sheriff's eyes. Marcus would be true to his word. He'd keep John's secret, and when he learned the truth, he'd make sure John hung—or worse.

The matinee went well, considering the sheriff's conspicuous presence. Emma was aware of him wherever he went—asking questions of anyone he could corral long enough to speak to and poking his head into every wagon, tent and cage. The unease that had assaulted her when she'd first seen him at the door

241

of the red wagon turned into fear as the implications of his search and interrogation sunk into her mind. This man meant to uncover their secret, even if uncovering it meant the destruction of her world.

She'd watched him speak with Johnny, marveling at the revelation that they'd served together in the war. The knowledge added an entirely new facet to Johnny Bradfordini's character. If he'd served his country, been promoted to an officer in fact, then he wasn't the irresponsible drifter she'd believed him to be. Emma had a feeling that Johnny wasn't anything she believed him to be, and that fact scared her just as much as the threat to her circus.

Her grandfather had disappeared, to avoid more questions about Karl Monroe, she was sure. His defection left Emma responsible for making sure the show went on, as well as doing her part in the performance cage. When the matinee ended and the townsfolk streamed back toward town, she went looking for the sheriff. She didn't want to speak with him, but she had to, and she'd rather talk here than in town. She'd been to town before—it didn't matter which town, they were all the same to her, and she didn't want to go back again. Just the idea made her skin crawl.

"Emmaline!" Devora's voice snapped across the open lot. The Gypsy beckoned from her wagon. Emma rubbed her tingling arms and followed the woman's order. "That man from town has upset us all," Devora said.

"He's the sheriff. He has the right to question us."

"Perhaps. But you know if he continues to question people, sooner or later someone will tell him what he wishes to know. Then what will you do?"

Emma sighed. Without being told, the circus folk had come to the conclusion that Franz no longer possessed the capabilities to lead them. As if by some silent vote, they now turned to Emma for answers. Even Devora, who usually found her own answers. "I don't know what I'll do," Emma admitted. "What *can* I do?"

"Lie."

Emma blinked. "What?"

"You must lie. Give the sheriff an answer. Any answer will do, as long as he leaves us alone. Do you want to stay here until the next full moon? Do you want him to see what happens then? Do you want him to learn how we've traveled on, knowing the danger that follows us?"

"Of course not."

"Then lie, Emmaline. And do it right." With that advice, Devora turned in a swirl of colored skirts and disappeared into her den.

"Lie." Emma turned the word over on her tongue. Not a new concept really. She'd been lying to Johnny from the first moment she'd met him, and he'd been lying right back. She could lie to Sheriff Birkelund. She would do whatever she had to. Even go into town and face the people there.

Emma hurried to her wagon and yanked off her costume. She would go to town dressed as a lady. She would give the old hens there nothing to peck about. She had a purpose for visiting Michel's Pond. She must focus upon that purpose and not her own problems with facing the rest of the world.

Emma pulled out her green walking dress and all the ladylike trimmings—chemise, drawers, petticoats, crinoline, corset. She even had boots to match and gloves. Emma decided to wear the boots and forgo the gloves. Driving into town would ruin the lace anyway.

Though she owned the appropriate wardrobe, she detested wearing any of it and only did so under duress. There was also a trunk full of her grandmother's clothes brought over from Germany, but the heavily embroidered bodices, aprons and tight-fitting hats would only make her look more out of place in small-town Wisconsin. She had never worn any of the dresses, despite the beauty of her grandmother's craftsmanship. Emma held up the first layer of undergarments and began to don the ensemble; by the time she tied the ribbon of her green silk hat beneath her chignon, sweat dripped between her breasts and she could barely breathe. Emma braced herself and opened the wagon door.

She froze when she saw Johnny waiting for her. He turned at the sound of her indrawn breath; the smile on his lips became fixed at the sight of her, and his eyes widened. He looked her over from the tip of the feather in her bonnet to the toe of her high-topped boots. Then he let out a long, low whistle and met her gaze once more.

Emma frowned. He acted as if he'd never seen her in a skirt before. He'd seen her in a lot less. Yet he seemed more impressed by this costume than her others. And this was, in fact, a costume. She pretended at being a lady to suit a purpose. Her tiger tamer attire was less a costume and more Emmaline.

"Very nice, Miss Monroe. Where are you going so dressed up?" Johnny reached up to assist her to the ground.

Emma considered ignoring his offer of help, unaccountably miffed at his compliments. But from past experience she knew she'd more than likely fall flat on her face in the dirt if he didn't help her down. So she swallowed her pride and moved to the edge of the wagon.

The odd tingling that always accompanied Johnny's touch began the second his work-hardened hands touched her waist. Despite the layers of undergarments, she could feel the heat of his skin through the cloth. He swung her to the ground, her crinoline swirling round and round her feet with the movement. When her boots touched the earth, he let her go, but the warmth of his touch remained. He stared down at her, standing as close as the wire of her hoop would allow, his legs just touching the leaf green material of her dress. Emma couldn't seem to take a deep breath, whether from the tightness of her corset, which seemed to squeeze any air from her chest, or the desire reflected in Johnny's silver blue eyes.

He smiled at her, a crooked half smile that made him look like a little boy when combined with the sun-darkened skin of his face and the sun-lightened brown of his hair. He reached out a hand and brushed the feather, which had fallen forward on her forehead, back into place. His callused fingers scratched against her temple, and her eyes widened in shock that such a casual touch could cause such a flustered response within her.

"I-I-ah have to go into town." She stopped, blaming the breathless quality of her voice on the corset.

"I know. I'll take you."

"No. You don't have to. I can manage."

"I said I would and I will." He turned away and studied the circle of wagons. "Which one should we take?"

"What?"

"Which wagon. It's too far to walk, and you can't ride in that outfit. So which one should we take?"

"Oh." Emma hadn't thought past getting dressed. Johnny was right, she couldn't ride a horse, but the thought of driving a circus wagon into town and drawing attention to herself made her want to go back inside her wagon and hide. Emma stiffened her spine. She had to do this, and she would. If she had to ride a tableau wagon into Michel's Pond, then so be it.

"Pick whichever one you want," she snapped and stomped off toward the field.

Before she took three steps, Johnny grabbed her elbow and spun her around. She hissed at him, and his eyes widened in surprise at her uncommon show of anger. She yanked her arm from his grasp and glared. "What do you want?"

"Where are you going?"

"To get some Percherons. Or did you plan to pull the wagon?"

He laughed. "No, not today. But I don't think you'd better go near the animals wearing that dress. You'll spook 'em for sure. Pick a wagon. Sit on the seat, and I'll bring the horses."

Emma scowled at his orders. She hated being a lady if it meant she had to sit by and watch everyone else be a part of life. But for one hour she would make herself endure it. Giving Johnny a sharp nod, she stalked toward the least colorful tableau wagon Gerhardt Circus owned, a painting of heaven, all whites

246

and blues and pinks, with cherubs gracing the four corners.

By the time Johnny returned with the two large horses, she had hoisted herself into the seat, not without great difficulty and no small amount of awkwardness, and rearranged her skirts so she looked like a lady, even though she sweated like a canvasman. Emma smirked. She'd heard that ladies never sweat, they perspired. Well, whatever was making the back of her dress stick to her skin sure felt like sweat to her. She'd never fool a soul into believing Emmaline Monroe was any more than who she was—the tiger tamer in a traveling mudshow.

When had she ever wanted to be anything else? Emma watched as Johnny whispered to the Percherons, coaxing them into harness and hitching them to the wagon. The answer stood before her now. Since Johnny Bradfordini had come to the circus, Emma had begun to see her world in a different way.

Until this summer's tour, the circus had been everything, her one goal to become famous and bring glory to her name and therefore her world. But with the advent of the murders and the stench of evil that permeated her world now, she had come to value something else above fame. Her life and that of her loved ones were more important than anything else. She did not fight merely for the survival of the circus but for survival.

Right in the midst of everything stood Johnny Bradfordini, a man who had shown her she could be a woman and not just an asset. Despite his drifter's ways, he represented another world—the world outside the circus—a world she could never survive in. Still a small, secret part of her wanted to try.

Johnny climbed up on the seat next to her. When he saw her pensive face, he smiled—a gentle, encouraging smile—and squeezed her hand. What would life be like if she had this man at her side for the rest of her days?

The thought came, unbidden, making Emma blink and pull her hand away from his. He frowned at her withdrawal but did not comment. Instead, he picked up the reins and clucked to the horses. The heavy tableau wagon rumbled away from the circus and toward town. Emma pushed aside any dreams of a life with Johnny. Right now she had to face the real world—and the thought scared her to death.

Chapter Thirteen

To John, what should have been a short trip to town seemed to stretch for hours. Since Emma had inexplicably yanked her hand from his, she had not spoken beyond noncommittal murmurs to any question he voiced. He could smell her apprehension in the air, along with the tantalizing scent of her body, warm beneath the yards of material she'd encased herself in.

The first sight of her in the doorway to the wagon had shocked him. He'd seen her in a dress before, but never so starched and formal as now. She pretended to be like all the other women in the world, and she hated it. But not as much as John did.

The tableau wagon rumbled past the hand-painted sign at the outskirts of Michel's Pond. Despite the approach of the dinner hour, townsfolk still milled about on the street. Several people stopped and stared at them. John smiled and nodded, but no one returned the greeting, instead turning away to go about their business. John shrugged. He supposed they looked odd driving a tableau wagon through town, but that was no reason to be rude.

John glanced at Emma to see if she'd noticed. Though she gave no indication if she had, the stiffness of her spine as she stared forward between the horses' heads told him that whatever had upset her before upset her still. Had she gotten this same reaction from the townsfolk whenever she'd ventured into town? That would explain her earlier attempt to avoid coming to Michel's Pond and her sudden affinity for young-lady attire on this trip.

When they came to the sheriff's office at the end of the street, John called a halt to the Percherons. He jumped down from the wagon and walked around to Emma's side. Before he could get there, a young woman wearing a dress in the latest style—one with a bustle and not a crinoline—her hands encased in lace gloves and her bonnet set at a fashionable tilt upon her perfectly coiffed hair, stepped from the sheriff's office. When she saw John, she gasped, one hand fluttering up to the high-buttoned neck of her dress. Her face paled. John frowned.

Did he look so dangerous that his appearance would frighten a woman? He glanced down at himself. His hair fell forward, and he shoved it impatiently away from his face. He could use a haircut, or a length of leather to keep the strands out of his eyes. His pants were worn, his shirt wrinkled from being out in the rain that morning; his hands were browned by the sun; his skin, a legacy from his father's Italian forebears, had served him in good stead in his outdoor work. He had no doubt his face was as dark as his hands, which made his light blue eyes, from his mother's Swedish side, appear almost silver. He probably did look quite dangerous now, no longer the staid Dr. Bradfordini he had once been.

John glanced up at the woman, who sidled back toward the closed door of the sheriff's office. He smiled, but the expression only served to make her face turn whiter. With a hiss of irritation, John gave up trying to placate a stranger and moved to help Emma down from the wagon.

When she stood next to him on the ground, John whispered, "What's the matter with her?" He looked around and saw several other townsfolk watching them avidly. "With everyone?"

"They don't want us here." Her voice, though low and calm, held an undercurrent of tension that made John glance down at her. Emma did not look at him, instead keeping her gaze upon the young woman behind him. When John turned, the woman gave a startled little cry and ran back inside the sheriff's office.

Emma laughed. "Little does she know there are things more frightening in this world than you."

Little do you know, Emmaline, you should be frightened of me, too.

The truth of his thought angered John and made his question come out sharper than he'd intended. "Do they always act this way?"

Emma glanced up, her eyes wide at the anger in his voice. She shrugged, though the gesture did not match the hint of pain on her face. "Of course. They might come and see the show, but they don't want people they consider little better than tramps in their town."

"Tramps? Isn't that a bit strong?"

"Hardly. We wander from place to place. No one knows us. They certainly don't trust us." Emma sighed. "They're right not to. There are circuses about who hire thieves to rob a town while the people attend the show. Outfits like those give the rest a bad name."

As he listened to Emma's explanation, John allowed his gaze to wander over Main Street. The women retreated behind their men. The men watched him, hanging on his every move as if they expected him to charge up to them and rip open their throats with his teeth. John winced at the direction his thoughts had taken. If they waited around until the next full moon, their fears would be realized.

Never before had John experienced people's disdain. In his world, everyone treated him with a respect bordering on awe. At first, such behavior had been hard to get used to from people who had known him as a child. With time he had become accustomed to it and barely noticed the behavior any longer. Not until now, when he experienced its opposite.

How did Emma stand this? She was more isolated than he'd imagined. No wonder she seemed so innocent of the world, despite having traversed the countryside all her life. Her world was the circus, literally. If people treated him like this, he would not venture into town either.

The door to the sheriff's office opened once more and Marcus appeared. He nodded at John, then turned his gaze upon Emma. Admiration replaced surprise, and a flash of jealousy assaulted John. He put his hand under Emma's elbow and guided her forward. Marcus turned his attention from Emma, to John's hand on Emma's elbow, to John's face. He stared at John a moment, considering; then understanding dawned in his eyes and he smiled. John ignored his friend's expression. Marcus could believe whatever he wished, as long as he left Emma alone.

Marcus stepped out of their way, ushering them inside the combination office and jailhouse. John looked around the room, frowning when he did not see the young woman who had escaped inside. He glanced at Marcus.

"She ran out the back." Marcus nodded at the open door behind his desk. "Muttered something about a man who frightened her and took off." Marcus raised his eyebrow and smirked. "Was she talkin' about you, Bradfordini?"

John ignored the taunt. Marcus was one of the few people from his old life who had never treated him with awed respect. Maybe because Marcus had been his superior in the war, or maybe because he was just Marcus and not in awe of much—except werewolves.

John had to behave as close to his usual self as possible or risk Marcus seeing his other nature. Marcus was a believer, and all the sheriff needed was a reason to put a silver bullet through John's heart. Sure, Marcus was his friend, he owed John his life, but in Marcus's mind ending John's life would be the right thing to do. John would be better off dead than a werewolf. John had to agree with that assessment, but he wasn't ready to die just yet.

John held out a chair for Emma. He sat next to her and looked at the sheriff in expectation. The sheriff shrugged and took his seat behind the desk. He waved a hand at John, indicating his unkempt appearance.

"You have to admit," the sheriff said, "you've let yourself go a bit."

John glanced at Emma, who had been staring at Marcus. At Birkelund's words she frowned, and her gaze shifted sideways toward John. John stifled a sigh of exasperation. Marcus had agreed to keep his secret. Why did he have to throw out little barbs that served to raise Emma's curiosity? She already mistrusted John, with good cause, but he didn't need her asking more questions of him right now. The full moon approached, and he had a werewolf to destroy, maybe even two.

"You wanted to speak with Miss Monroe," John said, fixing Marcus with a narrow glare. "I've brought her here, so speak. We have a show to do tonight."

Marcus remained silent, assessing John, then he gave a slight nod and turned his attention to Emma.

"Miss Monroe, you are the owner of Gerhardt Circus?"

"Me and my grandfather."

"I spoke with him this afternoon. He seems . . ." The sheriff paused, as if searching for the appropriate word to describe Franz. He glanced at John, then back at Emma. Finally he let out a disgruntled sigh and plunged ahead. "Well, forgive me, miss, but he seems a bit addled. I couldn't get a thing out of him that made a lick of sense."

Emma's fingers tightened in her lap, grasping a wad of material and twisting as if she meant to wring the green right out of the cotton. But when she spoke, her voice and her gaze were steady on Marcus. "He has not been quite 'right' for a while now. He forgets people, places. He is old. We cannot fault him for what he cannot help. I am the one you need to talk to if you want to speak with the owner of Gerhardt Circus."

John didn't voice his and Devora's opinion about

Franz being deliberately vague to suit his own purpose. Franz had been quite lucid when the sheriff arrived, had been perfectly capable of yelling at John for taking a bareback pony off the lot, but when the sheriff asked questions about the missing performers, Franz remembered nothing. However, in John's association with old folks he had noticed that upsetting topics contributed to their memory loss. With that in mind, he would continue to give Franz the benefit of the doubt.

"All right," Marcus said, interrupting John's thoughts. "I've questioned most of your people. Looked the place over and I haven't found a thing."

"What are you looking for?"

"I'm not sure."

"We told you we've lost our men to a mad wolf. We can't help that. We know nothing about the townsfolk. They must have been dragged away by the same animal."

"Probably."

"Then we can leave tonight?" Emma's voice went up on the last word, revealing the hope within her.

"No."

Her harsh intake of breath shafted through John like an arrow.

"Why? You said you've found nothing. We know nothing. Why must we stay here?"

"Because it's been my experience that those who say they know nothin' the loudest are the ones with the most to hide. If someone in your circus doesn't know what happened to the missing townsfolk, I'll eat my horse."

"But—but . . . you can't do this!" Emma lurched to her feet, her boots catching in the hem of her dress.

John grabbed her elbow before she tumbled onto the sheriff's desk. She wrenched her arm from his grasp without sparing him a glance or a word of thanks and slammed her palms onto the desk. "We have to move on. We can't stay here. You'll kill us if you make us stay here."

Marcus stared at Emma for a long moment, then glanced at John. He sighed and pushed his fingers through his short, graying hair. "I'm sorry, Miss Monroe, really. Until I get some answers, I have no choice. I can't let you traipse across the countryside. People have a habit of disappearin' wherever you people go."

"It's not our fault," Emma cried.

"You still have to stay."

"You can't do that!"

"Yes, miss, I can. I have just cause to detain you. Even if I didn't, I can pretty much do what I want in this town. I'm the law here, which means I'm in charge. Don't have no mayor yet. We get a judge comes through maybe twice a year. So when he shows up again, 'long about October I'd say, you can take up the subject with him."

Emma spun away from the desk toward John. "Do something, Johnny." Her face had paled until her fiery hair looked even more red against the starkness of her skin. Her green eyes beneath the brim of her out-of-date bonnet were pools of anguish calling out to him. He tore his gaze away from hers to confront Marcus. His friend spread his hands wide and shrugged.

"Is this really necessary, Sheriff?"

"You know it is."

Since John did know that if he were in the sheriff's position he would do the same thing, he said nothing more. Emma saw the truth in his face before he said a word, and she turned away from him with a sound of disgust.

"How do you plan to make us stay, Sheriff?" she asked. "Are you going to put deputies in a circle around us?"

"I won't have to. If you leave, I'll make sure you never perform in this state again. News might move slowly around here, but not as slowly as Gerhardt Circus moves. If I find you gone, I'll send a man to every town on your tour to tell them you're fugitives and murderers."

Emma gasped. "That's not true!"

"It ain't? Prove me wrong, Miss Monroe."

The two stared at each other for another moment, two wills at war. Then Emma looked away. "I don't like your friend, Johnny," she whispered. "Take me home."

John guided her to the door, but when she stepped outside he nodded toward the wagon. "Go ahead. I'll be right there."

She looked up at him, her eyes bright green with unshed tears. A single, sad nod, and she did as he'd said. John went back inside and closed the door. He leaned his head against the wood so he wouldn't bang it against the door in frustration. When the urge passed, he turned to face his friend.

"Dammit, Marcus, I told you what it would do to the circus if you made them stay."

"I heard you. I have no choice and you know it."

"What do you expect to find?"

The sheriff shrugged. "When the next full moon arrives, I'm sure something will turn up. Or someone will tell me what I want to know.''

"If you believe that, you don't understand these people.''

"And you do?''

John gave a short nod. "Yes, I think I do. I'm still an outsider. They don't trust me. But I've been traveling with them for almost three weeks now, and I believe I understand them.''

Marcus leaned back in his chair and folded his hands over his stomach. "So explain things to me, Doc.''

John frowned at the nickname but understood the sheriff's need to throw barbs his way. Marcus was angry. John had coerced a promise from him that Marcus did not want to keep, even though he would. Of all things, Marcus Birkelund was an honorable man. A man John had once liked and would like again if given the chance. John glanced at the sheriff and saw he awaited John's explanation. "They're a family, united against everyone else. You saw how your people acted when Emma and I came into town. They only have each other. They aren't going to tell you anything, Marcus. No matter how long you keep them here.''

"You're saying there's something to tell? They know who's doing this and they're protecting him? It?''

"No,'' John snapped, then took a deep breath and pushed his hair out of his eyes as he fought for calm. "I'm just saying they wouldn't betray one of their own. They'd take care of the situation themselves. You're wasting your time.''

"We'll see.''

John could tell by the set of the sheriff's mouth that he would not be swayed from his decision. John turned to leave, but at the door, Marcus stopped him.

"Maybe you'd like to exchange another favor?"

John didn't turn, but he didn't leave either. "What kind of favor?"

"You keep an eye on things at Gerhardt for me, and when the truth comes out, I'll make sure your little friend goes free. Unless, of course, she's the one I'm lookin' for, but somehow I doubt that. I'd believe you were the one before her. Those sweet green eyes don't lie too well."

John considered the sheriff's offer. If he did what Marcus asked, he'd be betraying the trust of the circus folk, a major circus sin. But betraying the circus folk was not what bothered him about Marcus's request. Though he had come here to destroy Gerhardt Circus, he had long ago decided not to take such an action. The circus folk were as much a victim of the evil one's appetite as Peter had been. Still, he would have spied upon them were it not for a single pair of bright green eyes that haunted him day and night.

He could not agree to Marcus's request because he would be betraying Emma's trust, and betraying her was something he could not do. Emma had done nothing wrong, and despite the sheriff's veiled threat, he could not put her in jail—at least not for very long. Even if John weren't around to object, Emma wouldn't let the sheriff push her around. She might have, a few weeks past, but no longer. With each step of Franz's deterioration, Emma became stronger.

John looked straight into the sheriff's eyes. "No, Marcus, I won't be your spy."

The man frowned. "I don't understand why not. They're travelin' tramps. Sure, they put on a good show, but they're little better than riffraff.''

Anger flooded John at Birkelund's words. Emma had been right. He just hadn't wanted to believe that such prejudice existed. ''You don't know what you're talking about, Marcus. These people are strong, talented, loyal. More than I can say for any other group I've been associated with.''

''Even the Union Army?'' The sheriff's voice was belligerent. ''I'd say we were plenty strong and loyal.''

''Yes, we were.'' John's anger rushed out on a long sigh. ''You'd have to live with them to understand. They're fighting to stay alive. To keep their traditions intact. They bring color and laughter and music to places that have very little of those things. They're doing something noble, and you're destroying it.''

Marcus snorted. ''I'm destroyin' nothin'. They're the ones who are gettin' people killed.'' He looked at John for a long moment, then snapped his fingers. ''It's the girl, ain't it? I wondered, but I couldn't quite believe that you and her—'' He shook his head sadly. ''You're lettin' yourself be led around by somethin' other than your brains. The John Bradfordini I knew was a smarter man than that.''

John sighed. Marcus wasn't getting his point. He wouldn't bother to explain any further. ''I won't be your spy,'' he repeated. ''I can't.''

''Then you'll face the consequences, and so will she.''

John didn't answer, but just opened the door and stepped outside. Emma sat on the wagon seat, spine stiff, eyes straight ahead. The ridiculous feather on her bonnet twitched as though shivering. Several men stared at her from across the street, but one glare from

John and they dispersed. Looking dangerous had its advantages. He climbed up next to her and took her hand. *Ice cold.* He squeezed her fingers. She did not respond, so he let her hand drop back into her lap.

"What did he ask you, Johnny? Did he want you to be his spy?"

John clucked to the Percherons, guiding them around and back toward the circus before he answered. "Yes, he did."

"And are you?"

He glanced at her. She remained stiff as a washboard, her gaze fixed straight ahead.

"What do you think?"

"I think he's your friend."

"Yes, he is."

"And what am I?"

If possible, her body became even more stiff and straight as she awaited his answer. She still refused to look his way.

"You're my boss."

"So if I order you to remain loyal, you will?"

"No. You can't force loyalty, Emma. You have to earn it."

She turned her head until she looked him straight in the eye. "And have I earned your loyalty, Johnny? Are you one of us, or are you one of them?"

He looked into her eyes, down deep where the fear hovered, and his chest ached with the need to pull her into his arms and soothe the pain away. At that moment he knew he was not only loyal—he was in love with her.

She awaited his answer.

"Yes, Emma. You've earned my loyalty," he said,

then returned his attention to the road before she saw the answer to her second question in his eyes.

Are you one of us or one of them? she'd asked.

He was neither. He was something else entirely.

Emma rubbed at the ache between her eyes. The wagon jerked and slowed. She looked up. They had returned to the circus. Emma closed her eyes against the sight.

She had failed.

The circus. Her people. Her grandfather. Herself.

She was responsible for Gerhardt Circus, and she had been unable to prevent disaster from overtaking them. Devora had told her to lie. Anything to get them out of this mess. But she had been unable to think of a believable lie to make the sheriff release them. What would she tell Grandfather?

As soon as the horses came to a stop, she jumped to the ground.

"Emma?" Johnny's voice stopped her. "Where are you going?"

"I have to tell my grandfather what's happened. We have to decide what to do."

Johnny slid across the seat and jumped down next to her. He put his finger under her chin and turned her face toward him. Her mouth tingled when she looked up into his face, and she bit her lip to stop the response. His gaze flicked to her lips, hesitated, as if he had to stop the rush of feelings just as she did; then he tore his gaze from her lips and met her eyes.

"What is there to decide? I know Marcus. He'll follow through with his threat. We can't leave."

Fury and frustration assailed Emma, and she stepped

back, out of Johnny's reach. "He's your friend. Couldn't you do something?"

"I did everything I could. He wouldn't listen."

"We'll die. You know that, don't you?"

"Yes. Unless you can tell him something he wants to know."

Emma went very still. He sounded almost as if *he* knew something. She glanced at him but could discern nothing in his eyes to tell her the truth. No, she must be mistaken. "What can I tell him that others haven't already?"

"He doesn't believe the rabid-wolf story." Johnny took a step closer crowding her between his body and her crinoline. She fought the urge to pull at the starched collar of her gown. "You know what, Emma? Neither do I."

Her eyes widened. Panic flared. Had she been unable to hide their secrets from him? Was she able to lie to no one on this earth and make them believe her? Had Johnny discovered their truth long before today and told his friend the sheriff? He'd said he wouldn't be the sheriff's spy, but he had said nothing about telling Birkelund what he already knew. Had Johnny Bradfordini, the man she had begun to trust with her heart and soul and body, betrayed everything she held dear in this life?

"What have you done?" she whispered.

He frowned, then a flash of panic lit his eyes before he doused the flame. "I don't know," he said, and the stark despair in his voice made her anger disappear. Perhaps his aura of mystery stemmed from something other than the problem at hand.

"Did you come here to hide? You can tell me, Johnny. I'll help you."

He didn't answer her. Instead, he turned away and began to release the Percherons from their harness. Emma blinked at his withdrawal. He'd been on the verge of admitting something to her, then she'd ruined any confession with her ill-timed question.

"Johnny?" she ventured.

"Go to Franz, Emma. Tell him what's happened. But remember, you won't be able to fool Marcus. He won't let you leave. You're up against the wall here."

Emma took a step toward him, her hand reaching out toward his back. He stiffened, and she did not dare touch him. He was angry. Or frightened. Either way, he did not want her comfort now, and she did not know what else she could do to prove to him that he could trust her with his pain. She left him with the horses and went in search of her grandfather.

Franz was not in the red wagon. Emma looked around the lot but could not find him. She had begun to worry when she saw the open door of Devora's abode. Perhaps he resided with the Gypsy. Emma crossed the lot and climbed into the wagon.

The interior loomed, shadowed and empty. Emma turned in a slow circle, looking for some indication of where Devora might be. An open book on the low table next to Devora's sitting cushions caught her attention. Emma knelt to look at the vividly colored picture.

A wolf with the eyes of a man leapt at a woman. In her hands, a rifle, in her eyes fear—and something else. She needed to kill the werewolf or die, yet she could not bring herself to hurt it.

Emma frowned at the agony of confusion she recognized in the woman's face. Her gaze dropped to the words below the picture. She read them aloud. "Another legend advises that the sole way to save the man within the wolf is for the woman who loves the man to kill the wolf. The love must be true or the man will die with the beast."

"What do you think?" Devora said. Emma looked up to see the Gypsy standing inside the doorway. Emma let out a startled gasp and dropped the book on the table with a thump. She had heard no one approach. How had Devora gotten inside without her knowledge?

"Wh-what do you mean?" Emma said once she recovered her breath.

Devora walked closer and pointed a long finger at the book. "About the cure? Do you think you could do it?"

"What?"

"Kill the one you love in order to save him?"

Emma glanced back at the picture, then up at the Gypsy. The woman asked more than a casual question. "Where did you get this book? I thought you'd looked through everything you had and found nothing to help us."

"I'd forgotten about this book. A children's storybook. Very expensive. Very rare. I had put it away for my children, but when I never had any . . ." She shrugged. "Well, that's neither here nor there now. Answer my question. Could you kill the one you love in order to save him?"

"I don't know what you mean. What does it matter if I could do such a thing or not?"

"It matters, girl. It matters more than you know. Answer the question."

"I, ah . . ." Emma stared at the picture. She looked at the face of the woman who held the gun, experienced for a brief moment the woman's agony of indecision. "I would have to believe, truly believe, that the curse would be broken."

"You would have to love, truly love, for it to work."

"How does one know if they truly love?"

Devora looked away, but not before Emma saw the pain. *Wade.* The Gypsy had truly loved him. Emma ached for the old woman's loss.

"You will know. At the moment it most matters, you will know." She looked back at Emma. "I pray your moment comes before he is dead."

"Who?"

"Bradfordini, who else?"

Emma started in shock. "What are you talking about? I don't love him. I barely know him. He's not one of us. Can never be one of us."

Devora gave a short bark of laughter. "You aren't talking to your grandfather, girl, you're talking to me. I see. I know. I have dreamed you would hold your love in your arms and watch him die. I pray this dream is wrong. That this"—she pointed to the book—"is the answer to our problems. I do not wish for you to suffer so."

"I don't understand what you're saying."

"Yes, you do. Fool yourself for a while longer and then know the truth."

"Love?"

The word sounded foreign upon Emma's tongue.

"Yes, love. And pray your love is enough to save him."

"From what?"

"From the beast within himself."

Emma stared at the Gypsy as her heart froze with dread. Her question and Johnny's answer echoed in her mind.

What have you done?

I don't know.

He had not been referring to his talk with the sheriff, he had been referring to the night of the last full moon. He did not remember what he had done.

"He is the one?" she whispered, though in her heart she knew the answer.

Devora gave a sharp nod. "One. But there is another."

Emma swallowed, shook her head and tried to lie to herself and Devora one last time. "I don't believe you."

Devora smiled, a sad smile. "You don't wish to believe me. Ask him. The time has come for truth."

"He wasn't here when this all began."

"He wasn't, but the other was."

Emma recalled the times she'd kissed Johnny, the words he'd whispered to her in the heat of their passion. Her heart ached with dread. "Does he know of this cure?"

The Gypsy blinked in surprise. "I have not told him."

Devora had not, but had she needed to? Had Johnny not learned of this cure on his own? Were all his embraces merely a way to seduce Emma into loving him? Were the emotions in his eyes as much a lie as the man himself?

Emma stepped past the Gypsy. She stood in the

doorway of the wagon and allowed her gaze to wander over the back lot.

No sign of Johnny. No sign now, but that did not matter.

She would find him. As Devora had said, the time had come for the truth. For both of them.

Chapter Fourteen

There he is!

Emma jumped from Devora's wagon and headed for the big top. She'd seen Johnny's brown-blond head bobbing amidst a sea of laborers raking the dirt around the performance tent.

"Emmaline, *kommen.*" Her grandfather's command brought Emma to a halt. She glanced toward the red wagon and saw him waving her inside. He must have returned while she had spoken with the Gypsy. Emma looked longingly at the big top, then turned away. She had to tell Grandfather what had happened. For now, a confrontation with Johnny would have to wait.

Emma climbed inside the wagon. Her grandfather was seated at his desk. He waved her into a chair.

"Where have you been? I've been waiting for you to return and tell me what happened in town."

"I looked for you. You weren't here."

His eyes slid away from hers. "I had things to do."

"Where?"

He cleared his throat and looked back at her with a stern gaze. "What happened in town?"

Emma bit back a sharp retort. She should know by now the extent of her grandfather's stubbornness. He would not tell her anything he did not wish her to know.

"We must stay here until the sheriff's questions have been answered."

"No! That is impossible, and well you know it, young lady."

"Grandfather, I did not give the order. The sheriff did. I did what I could. So did Johnny. Birkelund suspects something."

"What could he suspect? We have told no one." His gaze narrowed upon her. "Unless you have told that drifter the truth? He and this sheriff are friends. Perhaps Bradfordini is the source of our troubles."

"I told him nothing, though I think he suspects. He can't very well travel with us all this time and not suspect something, Grandfather." She took a deep breath, preparing herself for his explosion. "I plan to tell him the truth tonight."

He stared at her as if she'd lost whatever sense she had. Amazingly, he did not scream and shout as she'd expected. "You will do no such thing."

In the past, there had been little room for argument with Franz Gerhardt. In the present, Emma saw the vast space between them and waded in to her hips. "The full moon is only a week away. He has a right to know what he is facing."

"He has no rights here. He is an outsider."

"Believe what you wish. I will tell him the truth."

"I forbid it, Emmaline." Though her grandfather's voice was deceptively soft, his face had reddened with anger. Emma found that the threat of his fury no longer frightened her. There were so many other things in the world worth being frightened over.

She stood. "You can no longer forbid me to do what I feel is right. I have had to take over the control of this circus in the past week. You have not been well. I wonder if you truly forget things or if you are just trying to control me as you have in the past."

His face whitened as his anger faded. He fell back in the chair, putting his hand to his chest. "I don't know what you mean."

"Don't you?" Emma took a step closer and leaned across the desk. "You seem fine now, when you want to be. But if I were to ask you about my father's letters, what would you say then, Grandfather?"

"What letters?" He rubbed gnarled fingers against a place over his heart, as if the area pained him. Emma did not take the bait.

"The ones I found burned and torn on your desk the other day." She glanced around the room, but found no sign of the incriminating papers. A glance back at her grandfather caught a satisfied look on his face. Understanding dawned. "The ones you were getting rid of earlier when I was in town." She straightened away from the desk. "Never mind. I know now my father didn't desert me as you said. He wanted to see me. He loves me. He loved my mother, too. Once this mess is over, I plan to find him."

"You would leave the circus in the midst of a season? Such an action would mean the end of a brilliant career, Emmaline. I cannot believe you would be so foolish."

"You've held my career over my head to make me do your bidding for the last time. I'm starting to understand there are other things in this world. Other people. Different lives. If I can't be a tiger tamer, I'll do something else. But I plan to know my father. That's something I've always wanted more than this damn circus.''

Emma turned. She tensed, expecting him to get up and come after her. When he did not, she left the red wagon without looking back. She had spoken the truth and left nothing else to say.

Townsfolk flowed past Emma in a stream of humanity intent upon reaching the ticket taker and then the big top. A quick look around the back lot revealed she was the only performer not dressed for the show. Another delay to her imminent talk with Johnny. She hurried to her wagon.

An hour later, Emma took her final bow before the crowd. Destruction had not grumbled or balked once. The days they'd spent performing without Hope had at last come together to make their act into a show of professional quality and not a haphazard tumble of tricks. They had given, quite possibly, the best performance of their careers. As the applause flowed over her, Emma smiled and took a deep breath. She could smell success in the air. If she wanted to, she could probably soar with the eagles right now and never come back down to the earth.

Emma's gaze caught Johnny watching her from the front opening. He nodded, acknowledging her performance. His eyes warmed her with appreciation and so much more. Unfortunately, since her talk with Devora, she no longer trusted what she saw in Johnny's eyes.

When she'd told her grandfather there were other things in this world, she had been thinking of Johnny.

But now, standing amidst the adulation she'd craved since childhood, she wondered if anything other than this world would ever be exciting enough for her.

Emma waved one final time at the crowd and snapped Destruction's leash on his collar. Then, to continuing applause, they left the performance cage.

Emma berated herself as she put Destruction back into his wagon. She would do better to worry about saving her circus from their creditors, and her people from a supernatural force, than to wonder if she could survive elsewhere. First she needed to survive at all.

The answer to all her questions, the root of all her problems, could be the man she fantasized spending her life with. If he was the *teufel* as Devora said, what had he done? What was he capable of doing? To her people—and to her.

She'd thought he cared for her, believed she could see those feelings in his eyes whenever he looked at her. But when those eyes became the eyes of the wolf, would they see her as Emmaline or the enemy?

Emma waited until all the townies had returned to town. Then, when her people had assembled for their instructions in the tear-down, Emma climbed on top of Destruction's wagon and told them the news.

"The sheriff in Michel's Pond will not let us leave."

The crowd groaned.

"He is looking for townsfolk who are missing."

"We don't have them!"

Emma glanced at the fire-eater who had yelled the words from the back row. She waved her hand for silence as everyone else shouted their agreement. Her gesture, reminiscent of her grandfather's quieted them immediately. "I know that and you know that. Even the sheriff knows that after he searched our wagons today. Still, the people are missing.'' A movement near the red wagon drew Emma's attention. She looked out over the crowd, and her eyes met those of Sheriff Birkelund. She acknowledged his presence with a slight nod before continuing. "He knows a *mad wolf* has been following us and has killed four of our men. We will stay here until the wolf has been destroyed. The sheriff plans to help us remain safe.''

Her people turned as one and stared at the sheriff, then they turned back to her and nodded. They understood her message.

Keep our secrets. We will punish our own.

"Consider the next week a short respite from your work.''

The crowd dispersed to their sleeping wagons. Emma climbed down from the wagon. As her foot reached for the ground, strong hands grasped her waist. Destruction snarled a warning, which she silenced with a word. When she stood firm upon the ground, Emma turned and met the sheriff's astute gaze.

"Why just a week, Miss Monroe? You've been unable to kill the wolf over a period of two months. Why do you think you'll only be here another week?'' He glanced up at the first-quarter moon rising in the sky, then back at her. He raised his eyebrows and waited for her answer.

Emma stepped away from the sheriff. She still wore her costume, and its revealing nature made her uneasy in a strange man's presence. In the ring or with her people, her attire was accepted. In the real world, from which this man had come, she would be considered a scandal. Emma took a deep breath to steady her voice before answering.

"I assumed since you will be joining in the hunt, along with some of your men, we should not have to wait here more than a week. You do know what you're doing, Sheriff?"

He smiled at her taunt, recognizing her tone for what it was—desperation and frustration. "Yes, miss, I do. I hope you're right and we are able to clear this problem up in a week."

"Do you plan to hunt tonight, Sheriff?"

"No. I think we'll wait for the full moon. Wolves seem easier to find under the full moon. Have you noticed that, Miss Monroe?" He stared at her, waiting for an answer.

Johnny was right. The sheriff didn't believe the mad-wolf story. He knew. Somehow he knew the truth. Though he didn't plan to say so straight out.

Keep our secrets. We will punish our own.

Emma heard the words in her head, clear as a church bell in the winter air. She stared back at the sheriff. If she was ever going to learn to lie, now was the time. "No, I hadn't noticed that, Sheriff. But I'm sure you're more experienced at wolf hunting than I."

"Mebe." He looked at her for another long moment. She held his gaze. Finally he glanced away. "Well, I need to get back to town. I'll be by or have one of my men come by now and again."

Emma didn't answer. She understood his threat. *Stay here or I'll know.* Still, she found it odd he'd leave them alone for such large periods of time. Then again, they had nothing to hide until the full moon.

The sheriff mounted up and, with a final tip of his

battered Union hat, rode back toward town. Emma remained outside Destruction's cage wagon. The tiger paced back and forth behind the bars. Emma did the same.

"Where is he?" she asked the tiger.

Destruction grumbled and turned to pace back the way he had come.

"Very frustrating? I agree." Emma turned and followed the big cat to the far edge of the wagon, then back again.

Patience, Emma, she admonished herself. *He will come, and if he does not, you will find him.*

She turned once more and there he was. Even though she had been waiting for him, Emma still caught her breath at the sight of Johnny leaning against the wagon watching her. She remembered the first time she'd seen him, lounging in just the same way as he watched her. He looked so different now—his skin darker, his hair lighter, his body stronger, and in his eyes a subtle menace that had not been there before.

Or perhaps it had, and she had merely not seen the danger past the desire clouding her eyes. She could not help but be drawn to him despite her fears and uncertainties, and though she wanted to follow what her head told her and stay away from him, she could not.

He came toward her, stopping so close she could smell his male scent and feel the heat of his body next to hers. Without thinking, she swayed forward, and Johnny clasped her shoulders, holding her away from him.

"Emma," he said, his voice a husky whisper. "We need to talk."

"Yes." She looked into his eyes, and all her questions fled. Did his curse give him a supernatural power over her thoughts and desires? Every time she tried to question him, to force him to tell her the truth about himself, she found herself wanting to kiss him, to touch him, to learn everything he could teach her about life and passion and love.

He must have seen her desires in her eyes for he uttered a low curse, for himself or her she could not tell. Then, so slowly Emma ached with wanting, he lowered his head until his lips touched hers. The kiss was gentle, full of a sadness that made Emma pull him close and hold him to her heart. Her mouth opened in invitation, and his tongue traced a smooth path over her tingling bottom lip before dipping inside to entangle with hers. Her fingers clenched in his hair, terrified he would pull away and let the questions come between them. His answers could destroy everything, but she had to know the truth.

With a sigh, Emma released him and stepped away. Johnny let her go, watching her closely with his silver gaze.

"You know, don't you?"

Emma blinked at his direct question. "What?"

"What I am. Who I am."

She bit her lip. Now that he wanted to tell her, perhaps she did not want to know.

"Devora told you the truth, didn't she? She swore she wouldn't, but the old woman loves you. I suppose she couldn't let you get hurt despite her desire for me to kill the *teufel.*"

"Kill *it?* What do you mean? I thought *you* were the werewolf."

Johnny stared at her for a long moment, as if debating with himself how much to tell her. Then he swore and looked away. "I am."

Though Emma had heard as much from Devora, she still flinched when the admission came from Johnny's own lips. The lips she had so recently kissed. The lips that had slipped the blood of her friends—and that of children.

· A sob escaped her throat before she could choke the sound back. Johnny's gaze swung toward her. She wiped the back of her hand across her lips and stared at him in shock. His mouth tightened when he saw the horror in her eyes, and he took a step forward, his hand outstretched—an entreatment. She moved away, denial bubbling in her throat, and Destruction, sensing her panic, roared and threw his body against the bars of the cage, trying to get his claws into Johnny and pull him away from Emma.

Johnny wasn't close enough to the cage for Destruction to reach, but the sound of the tiger's roar and his frantic attempts to protect Emma made Johnny freeze. His hand fell back to his side.

"I wouldn't hurt you now, Emma. You have no reason to fear me under this moon."

Destruction continued to snarl and bang against his cage. Fearful the tiger might hurt himself, Emma stepped past Johnny to soothe the distraught animal.

"Hush," she whispered, reaching inside the cage to smooth the fur along the tiger's jaw. "I'm all right. Relax. Lie down."

The tiger did as she'd bid him, though he growled his displeasure. She allowed him to have the last word, knowing he would continue to mumble until he did. She turned back to Johnny.

John watched them, an odd expression in his eyes, one that looked like envy. When her brow creased in confusion, he gave a self-deprecating snort. "I'm jealous of a tiger. Stupid, I know, but I wish you could soothe the beast in me as you soothe Destruction and all the other animals here."

Emma didn't know what to say. The horror she'd felt moments before faded at the dark sadness shadowing Johnny's face. She had always been drawn to hurt creatures. She could no more deny his need for comfort than she could deny the need of a bird with a broken wing.

So instead of running away in terror from the admission that still hung in the air between them, Emma stepped closer and placed her hand upon his arm. The muscles flexed at her touch, and he looked from the tiger to her, a question in his eyes.

"Come with me," she said. "Away from here where we can talk."

He stared at her for a long moment, then nodded and followed her to one of the rock piles lining the farmer's field. They sat, close but not touching.

"Aren't you afraid to be alone with me?" he asked.

She shook her head. "As you said, I have nothing to fear from you under this moon. We need to talk, and I don't think we want anyone else to hear us."

"No, we don't."

She had taken him away from listening ears and watching eyes so she could question him. Now Emma wasn't sure where to start. Her grandfather had always told her to open with the most important act. Maybe the same applied to questions. "Why did you come to us?"

"The werewolf killed my brother, Peter, and marked me. Before he died Peter told me to come here."

"The creature murdered your brother, too?" Emma understood now the shadows of sadness in Johnny's eyes. "I'm so sorry."

He acknowledged her concern with a sharp nod, refusing any pity. "I thought you might be hiding the creature who killed him. Maybe keeping the beast as a sideshow oddity—until it escaped. When I came here, I didn't understand I'd been cursed, as well. Not until I changed."

Emma closed her eyes against the image his words brought to her mind. When she opened them and looked his way, Johnny stared out at the forest while he continued his tale. "I came to destroy the werewolf—and this circus."

Emma held her breath on the next question. "And you plan to still?"

"Kill it? Yes. Destroy the circus?" He turned and looked into her eyes, then shook his head. "Of course not. Once I came here, I understood you were all victims, too."

"Devora knew what you were?"

"Not at first. After the full moon, yes."

"And she didn't kill you herself?"

He lifted one shoulder in a half shrug. "I thought she might. But I'm not the only werewolf in these woods. The one who killed my brother and cursed me is here somewhere. Devora felt that my need for revenge would be a powerful motivator in destroying the one who has been stalking your circus. She hoped he might even come to me and reveal himself."

Emma didn't realize that the hope that had sprung

to life within her at his words showed on her face until Johnny's lips twisted in a wry grimace, and he shook his head. "He hasn't, Emma, or I'd have killed him already."

"Of course." Emma sat back and waited.

"Devora also gave me the chance to save myself. I must kill the werewolf, I and no other, to end the curse upon me."

Emma gave him a sharp, sideways glance. "Who told you this?"

"Devora confirmed what my father had hinted. I don't think he knew for sure what I should do. And the thought of what I would become probably scared him to death. He knew if he told me the truth, I might have killed myself instead of coming here. So he told me to kill the werewolf so my brother could rest in peace. If I'd done it before the last full moon, all our problems would have been solved with that one act. But I didn't have time."

Emma nodded, but her mind was not fully on his explanation. Instead, more questions filled her mind.

Should she tell him of the second cure? Or did he know of the legend already and lie to her again? Did it really matter? If she loved him, she could save him and countless others. The legend said the woman must love the man; not a word was said about the man loving the woman back.

Emma took but a moment to make her decision. Johnny had endured enough agony already over what he'd become through no fault of his own. She did not want him to place his hopes on a woman who did not know her own heart. Besides, to save him, she must shoot him when he had transformed into the wolf. He

281

would never allow her to brave such danger if he knew what she planned. If his cure worked, her interference would not be needed. She would keep the legend in Devora's secret book a secret.

"You believe killing the evil one yourself will end the curse?"

"It doesn't matter what I believe. I came here to kill the creature and I will." He sighed and looked up at the moon. "I have a week. I'll do my best to destroy him before then. Otherwise . . ." He broke off and looked at her, his eyes glowing under the moon's light. A shadow drifted across the moon, or was the shadow within his eyes? She could not tell.

"Otherwise?" she prompted.

"If killing the werewolf who marked me does not release me from the curse, I will have to die. By my own hand or another's, it doesn't matter which. But if I am not cured, then I cannot continue to live."

The thought of losing him to his own hand before she had a chance to help him frightened Emma so deeply she shouted, "No! You musn't do that."

He raised his eyebrows at her vehemence. "Who knows, perhaps the *jager-sucher* will come and end my pain."

Emma, who had been on the verge of continuing her pleas, paused when Johnny spoke the German words. "Hunter-searcher?" Emma translated.

"Yes. An ancient secret society that began in Germany. They are pledged to destroy the werewolves. It looks as if my brother was a member of this society. The last time we were together he hunted an evil one— the evil one who hunts us all. Before he could destroy the werewolf, it destroyed him and marked me. Have you ever heard of them?''

''No,'' Emma said slowly. She didn't think she had, yet something about the name tugged at her memory. ''Maybe my grandfather said something once.''

''He did. After I found you and him alone in the forest. I tried to question him, but he was in one of his vague moods. Devora said everyone from the old country is aware of them, though no one knows who they are.''

''Wait, you said your brother was a *jager-sucher?* How? He isn't from Germany.''

Johnny shrugged. ''The outfit we were in during the war, the 26th Wisconsin, was composed mainly of German immigrants. Perhaps he met one of the society then. I don't know. He disappeared after the war. The odd thing was, I saw him speaking with a tall blond officer right before he disappeared.''

''Why do you think that odd?''

Johnny watched her as he said the next words. ''Because the officer and the man who has been following this circus are the same man. The stranger your grandfather argued with.''

Emma gasped. ''The man who told me to stay away from you.''

Johnny frowned. ''You didn't tell me that.''

''I should tell you that? I should tell you he warned me you were dangerous? Wouldn't that be a bit stupid on my part? Kind of like sticking my head in the tiger's mouth?''

''I suppose, though you do it twice a day.'' He smiled at his joke, but the expression didn't reach his eyes.

"I know Destruction won't hurt me. You, I'm not so sure of yet."

The smile froze on Johnny's lips, and Emma cursed her thoughtless words. Though true, she had not needed to say them and murder the single smile Johnny had given her in the last several hours. She started to apologize, then stopped. No matter what she said now, she would only make things worse. "This stranger must be a *jager-sucher,* too."

"Perhaps. Or maybe the other werewolf."

"Why would you think that?"

"The way he watched you in the woods, as if you were the most important thing in this world to him. As important as his next meal maybe. If he were the *jager-sucher,* why would he be watching *you* like that? He should be looking for the werewolf."

Emma shivered at the picture Johnny painted. The stranger had been watching her in the woods when she was virtually alone, protected only by her grandfather, who had not been in his right mind at the time. Anything might have happened if Johnny had not been there.

"And," Johnny continued, dragging Emma away from her chilling memory, "Franz doesn't like him. What reason would he have to dislike someone who might be of help to him?"

"If this man were the *teufel,* why didn't my grandfather kill him?"

Johnny sighed. "I don't know. There are so many questions and secrets here, I can't begin to understand the truth. I only know my brother is dead. He died in my arms, and I won't let that sin go unpunished. Saving myself is second to obtaining revenge for Peter."

The hate upon his face made Emma wince. She could see how this man might turn dangerous between one moment and the next. "You must have loved your brother very much."

He glanced at her, and the blazing fury in his gaze receded, another emotion taking its place. "Yes, I did. I raised him after our mother passed away. Peter was full of life. He didn't deserve to die. Especially not the way he did."

"Neither did our people, nor the townsfolk the sheriff is looking for." The words came out before Emma could stop them, and she stared at Johnny wide-eyed. The love faded from his eyes and the shadows returned. For a fleeting moment she wondered how it would feel to have such love focused upon her.

"I don't remember what I did that night. I might have been the one to kill Wade. I awoke in the woods covered with blood."

"That's why you burned your clothes?"

The shadows died as his gaze narrowed on her. "How did you know about that?"

"Heinz told me."

"Heinz? How did he know?"

"He said he was leaving for the next town and smelled the fire."

"Hmm. Maybe he did. Or maybe he's the one who put the bloody clothes in my bag, hoping to place the blame on me."

"You're saying your clothes weren't bloody the morning after the full moon?"

His gaze slid away from hers, almost as if her question embarrassed him. "No, I—ah—I woke up naked. I found my clothes near the circus. Torn but not bloody. The clothes I burned were mine, but someone had put the blood on them.''

Emma frowned. ''Someone knows what you are.''

''The one who made me would know. Perhaps Heinz. I've wondered about him, suspected him. But no matter how I try to prove that the werewolf is him, I come up empty-handed.''

Emma shook her head. Though she would love to discover that the evil one was Heinz, she could not believe it either. ''He's been with us for years. If he's cursed, why wouldn't he have preyed upon us before now? How could he have hid his true nature so long?''

''I don't know, but I intend to find out. Why didn't you tell me before what he'd said to you? I knew you didn't trust me, I thought because I was an outsider. You suspected me of being the *teufel* and never said a word.''

''No. I didn't suspect you. You came to us after the first two killings. I never considered there could be two of you running about.'' She tilted her head and studied him. ''You didn't come to us from Illinois, did you?''

''No. I came from Andrewsville.''

She nodded. ''We were there at the beginning of our tour.''

''Two months ago when my brother was killed.'' Johnny spread his hands wide—a gesture of defeat. ''Now you know the truth, Emma. What do you plan to do about it?''

''Me?''

''Yes, you. You're in charge of this circus now. You have to ensure the safety of your people. If you have me killed, you will have eliminated half the threat.

Marcus will eliminate the other soon enough, and you can go on with your tour.''

Emma's heart thundered in her ears. Just the thought of ordering Johnny's death made her ill. But he was right. When the full moon rose, he would pose a danger to them all. ''You've gone to great pains to keep your secret from every one of us. Why tell me now? Why put your life at risk after all this time?''

Johnny looked away from her, staring up at the half circle of a moon hanging above them. ''Because I realized something today and knew I had to tell you before it was too late.''

''What?''

''I love you.''

Emma nearly fell off her rock in surprise. ''You can't be serious.''

He laughed. ''Emma, if there's one thing I am at this moment, it's serious.'' He looked at her then, and she saw the truth in his face, or maybe she saw what she wanted to see. Still, the emotion in his eyes fascinated her. Moments before, she'd wanted to see him look at her with love and now he did. It was as wonderful as she'd imagined. ''I love you, Emmaline Monroe, and if loving you means I have to die so there's no chance of hurting you, then die I will. By my own hands or yours.''

He stuck his fingers into a pocket of his blue jeans and withdrew several objects. He held out his hand to her, fingers closed into a fist. Emma leaned forward to see what he held. His fingers furled open, palm upward.

The mark of his curse shone red in the moonlight. Surrounding the scar, and shining with a different brilliance, rested three silver bullets.

Chapter Fifteen

"Take them," John growled, unaccountably irritated with her hesitation.

She looked up at him, her eyes awash with tears. "No."

Not wanting to frighten her further, he tried once more, in a softer, calmer tone. "Take them, Emma. Please. I don't want you hurt."

"What good will they do me? I—I don't have a gun," she lied.

"Yes, you do."

"I don't know how to shoot."

John recalled the shot that had stopped the tigress from killing him. "Yes, you do."

Emma wrapped her arms tightly about herself as if a chill wind had blown past them. She refused to touch the bullets. "I won't shoot you, Johnny. I can't."

"Why?"

"If Devora believed you were the best one to kill the werewolf, then who am I to say she's wrong? She lost her husband. If she can trust you to be the instrument of her revenge. . . I won't get in the way of what she wants.''

Fury pulsed within him, fueled by his fear for her. ''Dammit, Emma, I don't care what Devora wants. Didn't you hear I word I've said? I love you. I won't see you hurt. If you don't want to do it, then I will.'' He drew back his hand and stuffed the bullets into his pocket as he stood.

''No!'' she cried and jumped to her feet. She grasped his arm and pulled him around to face her, her eyes wide and frightened in her pale face. ''Promise me you won't destroy yourself. You'll do none of us any good by taking the coward's way out.'' He stared at her silently. She took a step closer and placed a hand on either of his cheeks, cradling his face. ''If you die, I'll be in more danger. There is still the other *teufel*. Swear to me you won't do anything foolish. We'll find a way to kill him and save you.''

God help him, but he wanted to believe they'd discover a certain way out of this mess for both of them. But he had only the word of a Gypsy, who had nothing beyond rumors and legends to placate him with. Did he dare risk Emma on those wisps of truth?

''Emma, I—''

''No, swear to me. I'll find a way out of this for both of us. You said you loved me. Prove it.''

The ferocity in her voice almost convinced him. She believed; could he? What if killing the one who marked him did not release him from his curse? What if he took a chance and risked the life that was a hundred times more precious to him than his own? God, he couldn't risk Emma. Somehow he would have to find a way to protect her until the truth of his own damnation became clear to him.

"Johnny?" She waited for his promise.

What was one more lie added to all the rest? "I swear," he said.

She let out her breath and released him, then held out her hand, palm up. "Give them to me."

John raised his eyebrows.

"The bullets. Give them to me."

He shrugged and dug the three silver bullets out of his pocket. She smiled and took them. She didn't know he had five more in his other pocket, and he didn't plan to tell her.

The fact that Emma had not returned his declaration of love had not escaped his attention. The omission pained him, but he could not fault her. How could he expect a beautiful young woman with her entire life ahead of her to love someone as cursed as he? She might want to help him, just as she could not keep herself from helping the other hurt animals in her world, but that didn't mean she loved him or could ever love him. Though he had admitted his cursed state, he had not told her his true occupation for a reason. He couldn't bear to see her withdrawal once she knew he was not of her world. She might dislike drifters because her father had been one, but a canvasman was still more a part of her world than a physician. The lie might be selfish on John's part, but until he left this world, he wanted Emma by his side for as long as he could keep her there.

Two voices, both male and raised in argument, drew their attention. They looked at each other, then began to run toward the red wagon. As they neared their destination, John recognized Franz and Heinz. He could not understand the nature of the argument being conducted in rapid German.

"Stop!" Emma shouted. When they did not, she tried the command in German. "*Aufhoren!*"

The two men looked at her, then both started speaking at once, still in German. Emma held up her hands. "*Sprechen das Englisch!* What is going on here?"

Heinz shook his head as if to clear away the German before answering. "Franz tells me we are unable to go to the next town."

"Yes, that is true."

"We must. I have marked the trail. I have promised we will come. Make the sheriff understand what he does to us."

Emma sighed. "I tried. He will not listen. The sheriff knows, Heinz."

Heinz cast a glare at John. "And this one knows as well, I take it. What happened to our vow to keep our secrets between ourselves?" He made a sound of disgust deep in his throat. "Who told the sheriff?"

"No one. I think he is a believer. He will not allow us to go on until the evil one is dead."

"Something must be done." Heinz turned back to Franz. "Once you would not have stood for this outrage. What has happened to you? You allow your granddaughter and her lover to control what you have worked your entire life to build."

Franz looked at Emma, then at John. Fury filled his eyes. He stepped toward John, his hands bunched into fists. John stood his ground. The old man had a right to be angry. Though he had not hurt Emma yet, he could not say he would not hurt her in the future.

"Francie, I told you this no-good would be nothing but trouble. He is fired."

Emma glared at Heinz and moved to her grandfather's side. "I'm Emmaline. And that's Johnny. We have done nothing wrong."

Heinz gave a snort of laughter. "She lies just as your daughter lied to you all those years ago. I've seen them kissing and touching when they think no one is watching. I wouldn't be surprised if they were rutting in the field just now."

John's fist caught Heinz on his painted jaw. The crack of bone against bone echoed in the night air. The clown fell to his knees. He put his hand to his mouth, then looked up at John.

"Does it make you feel like a man to hit me, Bradfordini?" He got to his feet.

"Watch your mouth, Kirshner, or I'll finish this."

The clown rubbed his chin. "I'll have to be watching my mouth now, thanks to you." He turned to Franz. "I will go into town and speak with this sheriff. If you cannot fulfill your duties to your people, someone must."

"Do what you wish," Franz said, his voice old and tired.

"I always do." Heinz glared at John once before turning to leave them. Seconds later the sound of a horse galloping down the road toward Michel's Pond came to them on the night air.

John glanced at Franz. The old man did not look well. His skin was gray and his eyes glazed. "I think maybe your grandfather should lie down, Emma."

She looked away from her contemplation of the road with a start and glanced at Franz. The old man's knees gave way. His eyes rolled upward and his lids fluttered; then he tumbled toward the ground. Emma cried out. John caught him before he hit the earth. Franz was unconscious when John lifted him into his arms.

John headed for the red wagon. Seconds later he had Franz positioned upon his pallet. He checked the old man over as best he could without his medical instruments. As far as John could tell, Franz had had an attack of some sort. Physician or not, John could do nothing until Franz regained consciousness. Then John could gauge the extent of the attack and its results.

Sitting back on his heels, John glanced up at Emma, who hovered in the corner staring at her grandfather with wide, panicked eyes. John sighed. He had hoped that Franz merely pretended to become ever vaguer as each day passed so he could keep John and Emma apart and his granddaughter under his thumb. But it looked as though Franz had not been acting at all. He had been losing his memory and his strength bit by bit. This attack would probably remove the remaining strands of the present from his mind, if it didn't kill him. With the full moon less than a week away, Emma did not need to worry about her grandfather's life hanging by a thread, especially when there was little she could do to prevent what now lay in God's hands.

"He needs to rest," John said.

She glanced at him once, then back at Franz. "I'll stay with him." Moving forward, she went down on her knees next to the pallet and took her grandfather's hand. She placed her cheek against the sun-browned flesh.

John left them alone.

At least her grandfather's collapse had removed Emma's attention from John's actions. He had to make a plan. He had so little time left.

If he could not discover the identity of the werewolf and destroy the beast by the night of the full moon, he would have to take drastic action. John put his hand into his pocket and jangled the silver bullets between his fingers. Their presence soothed him. No matter what, he would not hurt another human being. If he was still cursed when the full moon approached, John would do whatever he could to ensure the safety of Emma and the rest of the people he had come to care for. Then he would use the silver bullets in his brother's rifle upon himself.

Emma remained with Franz throughout the next several nights and days. Staying inside the red wagon while the moon became fuller and fuller each night, bringing them all closer and closer to the terror that stalked them, was nearly too much for Emma to stand. But her grandfather did not awaken, though at times his labored breathing deepened until he seemed to sleep in peace. When the full moon hovered a single night away, he was still unconscious.

There had been no reason to put on a show for the past week, since the people in Michel's Pond had already seen what Gerhardt Circus had to offer. A few of the circus people had come to the red wagon for instructions. Emma had told them to do what they wished until the night of the full moon. Johnny had come by a few times, checked Franz, kissed her brow and left. The sight of him had soothed her fears. If he had kept his promise and not harmed himself while she was preoccupied with her grandfather, she hoped he would not harm himself at all. She prayed that Devora's advice would save him. She prayed she could love him enough to break the curse.

The waiting was the worst thing. She had always been a woman of action. Living life every day. On the move, in front of the crowd. Now she just waited. Waited for her grandfather to awaken. Waited for the full moon. The waiting would drive her insane.

How had Heinz fared in town with the sheriff? She had not seen the clown since he'd ridden off, though she hadn't been out of the red wagon to look for him. Remembering Marcus Birkelund's face, she doubted that Heinz had gotten any further than she or Johnny had. Birkelund had seen a werewolf before. Emma was sure of it. The awareness in his eyes when he spoke to her told her the truth. She had seen one, too, and seeing one had made her believe.

She looked down at her unconscious grandfather and sighed.

One more night and this will all be over.

What then? her mind asked. *If you are able to save Johnny and your circus, what will you do then? He says he loves you. But does he tell the truth? Does he know of the cure, too, and hope your love will save him? Is his love based on what you can do for him, as all the love you've received in your life has been? If you do save him, then you love him. Will he stay here with you? If he won't, will you go? Can you exist anywhere but here?*

Emma groaned as the questions filled her mind. She put her palm to her grandfather's forehead, then kissed his brow and stood. She had to get out of the wagon for a moment or she would start to scream.

When Emma jumped to the ground, she saw Devora hovering in the door of her wagon. "Do you wish me to watch over him?" the Gypsy called.

Emma nodded, grateful for Devora's concern. But she could not stomach a conversation with the Gypsy right now. Emma hurried away from the red wagon before the woman came close enough to hail her.

The circus lot stood near deserted. A few of the sideshow oddities—the fire-eater and his daughter the sword-swallower, the bearded lady and her husband the hairless man—who never ventured away from their wagons sat outside in the warm night breeze. The clouds chased each other across the indigo sky, playing hide and seek with the nearly full moon. Emma avoided looking at the round orb, its presence reminding her of a ticking watch inching ever closer to the hour of death.

Her steps led her to the wagon where the canvasmen slept. As she drew near, she heard Johnny's voice.

"No! Stop, please. Dear God, don't let it happen again!"

The hoarseness of his voice, the utter pain in his cry, made her run the remaining steps and jump into the wagon. He lay alone inside, his bare chest glistening with sweat. One arm stretched across his eyes, as if shielding his face from the encroaching light of the moon through the open doorway.

He emitted a breath that sounded more like a sob, and Emma could no longer stand by and watch his pain. She went down on her knees and touched his shoulder.

His eyes snapped open and a growl of fury erupted from his lips. The sound, not quite human, sent a trill of terror down Emma's back. His fingers clamped upon her wrist in a punishing grip. One quick twist of his body, and she lay beneath him on the floor. Her heart pounded; fear spread throughout her chest. Johnny's eyes, unfocused and shining silver, stared at her but did not see.

Dear God, did we miscalculate the days? Is the full moon tonight? Must I watch him change before my eyes from the man I love to the beast I despise?

"Johnny," she whispered, hoping, praying, he dreamt the horror but did not live it.

He continued to stare at her without seeing her, and she watched, fascinated despite herself, the play of shadows behind the silver glow of his eyes.

He slept. He dreamt. But the images playing across the stage of his mind were memories, not fantasies. The black cloud, which had obscured the memory of his night as a wolf, lifted and allowed him to see the truth.

He watched, an observer of himself as he changed from man to beast. The process, which looked painful though he felt nothing in his dream state, was completed within seconds, and John the dreamer went along as John the wolf ran deeper into the forest.

With the abilities of the animal he had become, John heard the screams of dying men from a long way off. Even in his changed state, the sound made him flinch. But the burning, gnawing hunger in his gut soon sang throughout his body. Only blood would satisfy the craving; only blood would make the thriving agony cease.

Pausing, he lifted his nose to the breeze. The odor of living flesh drifted across his nostrils. He drew in the scented air, and some of the pain receded with the promise of release so close at hand. He resumed his journey, anxious to end the pulsing pain of his hunger.

He broke through the trees and stopped at the edge of the clearing. A field full of food. His tongue darted out, wetting his mouth in anticipation; then he raised his head to the moon and howled a death cry. The hoofed beasts scattered at the sound, and he leapt forward. The chase was on. The thrill of the hunt coursed through his veins, at one with the pulse of his blood. He could smell the animals' fear, acrid terror on the sweet winds of night. His eyes, able to see in the darkest tunnels of death, narrowed on his prey. If he could have smiled, he would have. Soon, warm, liquid life would flow into him and the gnawing pain would cease. He sprang into the air, catching his victim with ease, bringing it to the ground beneath him and . . .

"Johnny?"

The voice penetrated his dream-memory. He shook his head and willed the voice away. Something deep within him needed to experience the event once more; the soul-shaking thrill of the chase and the kill nearly obliterated any humanity he might have possessed. He fought against the voice calling him, wanting the dream-memory to return with a passion he had only experienced before with . . .

"Emma," he whispered, and opened his eyes.

She was there next to him. He blinked, but she did not disappear. Night had fallen while he slept, while he dreamt, while he remembered. The wagon was dark, but the moon lit the square of night visible through the open door. A silver halo framed her head as she bent closer. A red-haired angel, beautiful enough to tempt the devil himself. Beautiful enough to tempt a beast such as he.

John pushed away the thought, but a memory hung in his mind, like a great black bat in a cave. "I remember," he said. "I remember the last full moon."

Emma pulled away her hand, which had been resting on his bare shoulder, and sat back on her heels. She watched him, her eyes glinting in the semidarkness. "Who did you kill?"

He sat up, and she started, almost as if she meant to run. But she bit her lip and stayed where she was. John sighed. She might be willing to help him, but he still frightened her, and she should be frightened. He pushed his fingers through the tangled length of his hair. If she *should* be frightened, then why did the fact she *was* frightened anger him so much?

"Not who," he said, remembering what had fed his hunger in the dream-memory. "What. The zebra."

Her eyes widened at his admission. "You're sure?"

"Yes. I remember everything." He didn't tell her he remembered the thrill of the kill, the taste of the blood and the mind-numbing need for more. Those memories he would keep to himself.

"Who killed the others?"

"I don't know."

She narrowed her eyes. "You said you remembered everything."

"Everything *I* did. I was alone." He frowned, remembering the distant shrieks he'd ignored while his own pain raged. "I heard the others. A long way off in the forest. But I never saw anyone or anything else beyond the menagerie."

"Damn," she muttered.

299

"Yeah." Their problems would have been solved if he had only seen the identity of the one he needed to destroy to save himself. Instead, he was right back where he'd started. Nowhere. With his time running out.

One night and one day left.

She must have seen his dejection, for she returned her cool hand to his shoulder. He looked at her, and she smiled a soft, sad smile. "You didn't kill Wade or the other men. That's something."

"Yes, I suppose." He put his hand on hers, and she turned her fingers upward to twine with his. The contact warmed him. Too much. They were alone and he half-clothed. Memories of the last full moon fled his mind as other memories took their place. Memories of himself and Emma and all the times he'd touched her as lust raged within him. The lust he'd blamed on the beast he had no control over. Right now he felt the lust, and something else. The love. He loved her, and he wanted to touch her with love at least once before his life might end.

He looked into her eyes and saw his own need reflected there. He waited for her to run, but she did not. Instead, she leaned forward just a bit, her gaze moving from his eyes to his lips. He met her halfway.

"Johnny," she breathed against his mouth, her fingers spreading across his bare chest. He tangled his hands in her hair, turning her head so he could kiss her more deeply.

Her thumbs grazed his nipples, and they hardened at the innocent, accidental touch. Emma continued to explore his bare skin as he explored the taste of her mouth.

God, how could he have believed that all he felt for her was lust? The thought of never holding her like this again nearly tore him in two. John pulled his mouth away from hers and stilled her exploring fingers with his own.

"What's the matter?"

Her low, husky, voice sounded ripe with desire and confusion. The sound caused him to pulse with a need so deep and so sharp he had to clench his teeth to keep from throwing her upon his pallet and taking her right then. But he was still a man, not a beast, and he would not hurt her in this way. He could be dead on the morrow, and where would his death leave Emma? Alone, just like her mother had been alone. Though his desertion might be through no fault of his own, a desertion it would still be. He could not bear for her to hate him through all the years to come. There was time enough for them if he could manage to break the curse.

She offered her lips to him once more, her desires so new and fresh to her she only wanted more of what he had given her. John kissed her on the brow and brushed his thumb over her lips. She gasped at the sensation and took his thumb into her mouth, running her tongue over its tip.

John swore as heat surged through his groin. Where the hell had she learned that? He yanked his thumb from her mouth.

She opened her eyes and stared into his as she reached for his hand once more. Fascinated, he watched as she took his middle finger and suckled on it like an babe.

He couldn't breathe. How could something so simple make all his good intentions flee in the face of the overpowering want that consumed him? He reached for her, and she came willingly into his arms.

When she stiffened, he went still. Had she remembered what he was, what he would become? He could not fault her for her withdrawal, even though his body howled in fury. One of them had to start thinking more clearly.

"I'm sorry, Emma. This is my fault. I shouldn't—"

"Shh," she hissed and sat up. She turned to stare out the open end of the wagon.

Then he heard it. The sound of voices raised in anger, coming closer and closer to the circus. John scowled, then stood and made his way to the end of the wagon. Emma followed.

A pack of people swarmed in their direction. Torches bobbed in the hands of several men. John squinted against the flare of the flame, trying to identify the faces. He frowned when he recognized a mob made up of circus folk—performers, sideshow freaks and laborers. At the head of the pack walked Heinz Kirshner.

"There he is!" the clown shouted, pointing a finger at John.

John glanced at Emma. She had paled to ice white, her hair a flame surrounding it. When she turned to him, her eyes darkened with fear.

"They've come for you," she whispered. "What are we going to do?"

John didn't answer. He continued to stare at the mob without moving or speaking. Emma turned and disappeared into the wagon.

John heard her throwing things around as if she were looking for something. But he had no time to ask what she searched for. The clown and his minions had arrived, and they wanted his blood.

"Surrender, Bradfordini." Kirshner smiled, the expression ghastly when combined with his shining bald head and smudged makeup. "We know what you are."

John took a deep breath. The only way he'd get out of this would be to bluff his way out. They could prove nothing. Or at least he hoped they could prove nothing.

He folded his arms across his bare chest and leaned in the doorway. Damn, he wished he'd put on a shirt. He found it hard to look calm and in control when he faced a mob wearing his pants and not much else.

"What do you think you know, Kirshner?"

"You are the evil one who has been killing our people."

The crowd hissed and glared at him. John glared right back. "Where did you hear this?"

"A werewolf killed your brother. You were there. Tell us you were not."

John blinked. How had Kirshner learned about Peter? Then John remembered. Kirshner had gone into town to speak with the sheriff. Had Marcus told the clown the truth despite his promise to keep John's secrets? John found such a betrayal hard to believe, but it looked as though such were the case.

"I won't lie. A wolf with the eyes of a man killed my brother. I came here to destroy the creature who murdered him."

At those words, uttered in a calm, deadly voice, the crowd went silent. They sensed his fury and recognized truth when they heard it. Heinz glanced behind him with unease. His minions were not behaving as he wished. He attempted to rile them once more.

303

"You bear the mark of the wolf. You cannot lie about this. Show us your hand."

"Yes, show us your hand," a man yelled from the center of the crowd.

"Prove you're not the one," a woman spat from the front row.

"Show us!" they chanted.

Heinz merely smiled.

"I can't prove I'm not marked," John shouted. He held up his palm, and the crowd gasped. "Because I am."

Silence reigned for long moments. Then Heinz spoke. "We know what we must do."

"Silver bullets!" the crowd shouted as one.

John watched as they screamed themselves into a near frenzy. He waited for the shot to come. He had known his life could end this way, but he'd hoped to avoid it.

"You'll have to go through me first."

Emma's voice, strong, sure, cut through the frenzy beneath them. She moved from the shadows of the wagon and stepped in front of him. In her hands she held Peter's Spencer, the barrel pointed at Heinz Kirshner.

Chapter Sixteen

"What the hell do you think you are doing, Emma-line?" Heinz bellowed. "Point that weapon at your lover."

Emma resisted the urge to shoot the clown and silence his mouth for good. "He's not my lover. I won't let you murder an innocent man."

"Innocent? He has just admitted he is the *teufel*. You heard him." Heinz narrowed his eyes, and a smirk tilted his painted lips. "But you do not look surprised. Does this mean you've known all along what he is, and you have been protecting him?"

The crowd, which had been silent during their exchange, began to mumble ominously again. She had to make them believe in Johnny's innocence or she would lose him. She could not shoot them all if they chose to take him from her.

"No!" she shouted. "I didn't know. I found out today, just like you. But he is not the murderer of our friends."

"How do you know?" Helga and Heloise shouted

305

as one, the anger in their voices reminding Emma of the brother they had lost.

"Yes, how do you know?" Heinz repeated.

"He remembers what he did. He killed the zebra."

"So *he* says." Heinz smirked again. "Does he have proof?"

Emma bit her lip. She had no other proof but Johnny's word. She believed him, but then, she loved him. Or thought she did. The truth to her feelings would be proven soon enough—when she shot him. Emma winced and pushed the image from her mind. She would worry about the cure to his curse tomorrow evening, when the silver light turned him into a beast.

Johnny tried to step around her to address the crowd, but she shoved him back with the butt of the rifle. "Are you crazy?" she hissed. "They'll kill you."

"I'm not going to hide behind your skirts, Emma. They deserve the truth."

"Yes, Emma, let the boy tell us his truth."

Emma glared at Heinz. "Put the guns down," she ordered. Amazingly, everyone complied, much to the chagrin of the clown. It was Emma's turn to smirk.

Johnny stepped forward. "As Kirshner said, my brother was a victim of the werewolf. He told me to come to Gerhardt Circus. I believe he was a *jager-sucher.*"

"Ahh . . ." the crowd whispered their awe at the word.

"I will have my revenge upon the one who killed him. I believe if I kill the one who marked me, my curse will be broken. I ask you to give me the chance to have my revenge. If any one of you knows the identity of the one who changes under the full moon, I beg you to tell me.''

''Other than you?'' the clown asked.

Emma glared at him. Unfortunately, Kirshner was the only one of her people with anything to say. All the others remained silent, looking from her, then back to Johnny. No one knew the *teufel*'s identity or they would have shot the creature long ago.

Johnny sighed. ''All right. No one knows. Neither do I. But there is one day left until the full moon. If I am unable to find the evil one and destroy him by then, you can do what you wish with me.''

''No,'' Emma gasped. ''Johnny, you don't understand.''

The crowd roared their approval of his words, nearly drowning out Emma's plea.

''But what if you decide to run away where we cannot find you?'' Heinz asked once the crowd's roar faded. ''We might be safe, but others will die.''

''I'll be responsible for him,'' Emma said. ''This rifle is loaded with silver bullets.'' She took a deep breath and looked Johnny straight in the eye. ''If the full moon shines and he changes, I'll shoot him.''

Johnny returned her gaze, his own darkening with an emotion she could not decipher. They had one night left together. Time enough when they were alone for understanding.

The conviction in her voice must have convinced the crowd, for they mumbled their assent and dispersed. She was still their leader and they believed in her. She hoped she would prove worthy of their trust. When Emma turned to take Kirshner to task for assembling a mob, he had drifted away with the others.

"Thank you for defending me."

Johnny's voice, so close his breath brushed her ear, made Emma spin toward him. He grabbed the barrel of the rifle and held it away from his chest. She yanked the weapon from his grasp and jumped to the ground. He stood above her, his eyebrows raised in question.

"Come on," she ordered. "You'll have to come with me. I said I'd be responsible for you."

Johnny jumped down beside her. "Where are we going?"

"To check on my grandfather."

"And then?"

"To bed."

"Together?"

Emma, who had begun to walk toward the red wagon, stopped short and glanced back at him. Her face heated at the expression in his eyes. He wanted her.

She turned away and continued onward without answering. Seconds later he caught up with her. Before he could speak, Devora appeared in the doorway to the red wagon.

"He is fine, Emmaline," she said. "I will stay with him. You get some rest. You will have a hard day and night ahead of you."

Emma nodded. Devora was right. Even now, what she must do made her hands shake and a cold sweat break out on her brow. Could she do what must be done? Did she love him enough to save him? How could she know?

Johnny stepped past her. "Why did you tell her my secret, Devora?" he demanded. "You told me you wouldn't."

The Gypsy shrugged, and her bracelets snapped together with a tinkling sound, as if they were confused, as well. "The time for truth had come. She needed to know. I do what is right when the time is right."

Johnny swore under his breath and turned back to Emma. She saw the frustration on his face. But he had learned, as had she, that Devora could not be argued with.

Emma started toward her wagon. "Remember what I told you, Emmaline," Devora called. "You must believe."

Emma did not answer. She knew the cure. She just didn't know if she was strong enough to exact it.

They reached her wagon and Emma climbed inside. Johnny followed. While Emma lit a lamp against the darkness of the last night before the death moon, Johnny closed and locked the door. Emma turned with a gasp of surprise.

"Why did you do that?"

He took a step closer. She took a step back. She didn't like the glow of his eyes in the lantern light. They reminded her too much of the eyes of the black wolf she had seen a few months before. Emma shivered.

Johnny stopped coming toward her. "I want to talk to you. I don't want anyone interrupting."

"All right. Talk." Emma sat down on her bed, a pallet raised several feet above the floor on flat ticks stuffed with straw.

"I have one night and one day to learn the truth."

"I know."

"I need to be free to discover the truth. You can't keep me a prisoner here."

Emma blinked. She hadn't thought of that. But if she let him roam free, she would not be fulfilling her promise to be responsible for him. "You know I can't let you go, Johnny."

"Then you're sentencing me, and others, to death. I have to find him and kill him before I change again."

"How do you plan to discover in one day what neither you nor the rest of us could before now?"

"Devora said his symptoms will be stronger as the full moon approaches, just as mine are. I can feel them increasing as we speak." He inched closer to her, his eyes glowing even brighter than before.

"Devora says many things. How can we be sure she is right?" Emma held her breath, waiting for his answer, praying he knew more than she about Devora's powers.

"We can't be sure." Emma let out her breath on a pained sigh. Johnny frowned at her reaction, staring at her face while he continued. "But she knows more than anyone, so I've decided to trust her word."

"I suppose we have no other choice."

"No. At least I don't. I figure the *teufel* will head for the woods sometime. He would not want to be caught here during his change. If I place myself high in a tree with my rifle, I'll see whoever leaves."

"Anyone could leave."

"I'll know the one I'm looking for. I'll be able to smell the evil when the moon is full. I have before."

He took another step toward her. Amazingly, she could feel the heat coming off his body. His eyes glittered as he watched her. His tongue flicked out to wet his lips. Emma looked deep into his eyes and found she could not breathe when she recognized the desire, a desire that echoed her own.

She licked her lips. "Johnny?" she said—half question, half answer.

He sat next to her on the bed, but he did not touch her. "One of the symptoms of the wolf, little girl, is uncontrollable lust." His voice was a growl from deep within. The sound echoed in the quiet confines of her wagon and trilled along her spine, making her shiver with fear and something else. "The moon is almost full, and I can barely control what I feel."

"What do you feel?" she whispered, leaning toward him.

"I want you, Emma. I've wanted you since the first moment I saw you. I've been fighting it since then, but I can't anymore. Not tonight. Not when the beast is so close and you're right here, looking at me with those Little Red-Cap eyes. I can see you want me as much as I want you. But you don't know what you're asking. Why don't I disgust you? You know what I am, you should be running for your life. Why aren't you afraid of me? Of what I am?"

She reached up and touched his cheek, dark and rough with the start of a beard. "I never said I wasn't afraid. But there are other things I feel more strongly whenever we're together. Despite the beast sleeping within you, you are still you. I know what I want, and you're right, I've wanted it since I first saw you."

"You know what the wolf did to Little Red-Cap, don't you?"

"Yes. But the hunter saved her."

"There's no hunter to save you, Emma. Only the wolf who'll devour your soul."

"You put too much stock in fairy tales. Right now

it's just you and me. A man and a woman.''

He shook his head. "I'm not just a man, and you know it."

She merely smiled and lifted her lips to his. He groaned, obviously still fighting the passion that hung in the warm summer air between them. She tried once more, spreading her hands across his bare chest, fingers searching out and finding the increased beat of his heart. Then she voiced a plea from the very depths of her soul. "For tonight, you're still a man. You said you loved me. Show me. Make me love you back, Johnny. Please. For both our sakes, make me love you back."

He hesitated still, glancing at the closed door to the wagon. "I—I need—''

Her fingers on his jaw turned him back to face her. "You need what I need. Each other. Right now."

She saw the moment his need for her overcame his need to be gone. He sighed, a soft sound at war with the hardness of his jaw beneath her fingertips. When he leaned toward her, she gave a sigh of her own.

His mouth was as warm as sunshine in the chill of approaching midnight. She leaned into his warmth, desperate for more. Her lips parted, and she slid her tongue into his mouth, exploring the tastes and textures of the man in her arms.

She walked her fingertips over the warm, taut flesh of his back. With a curse on his lips, he kissed her harder. She wanted to feel his flesh against hers, but her costume kept her from him. Almost as if he read her mind, he began to unbutton the fastenings at the back of her neck. In moments her costume slithered down her arms. Underneath she wore a thin chemise, cut in half at the waist to accommodate the shortness of her skirt. His lips left hers, gliding down her neck, following the path of the material. His thumbs hooked in the straps of the undergarment, and soon the chemise joined her costume, leaving her bare to the waist.

The lamp illuminated his face as he raised his head to look at her. Their gazes caught and meshed, his hot, hers a bit shaky. She wanted him, needed him, but she did not know what to do next. He smiled gently, the expression softening the flaming desire on his face. Slowly he reached out and touched her breast, his thumb grazing the peak. The nipple hardened beneath his hand. He bent forward, his long hair hiding his face from her view so that when he took her nipple into his mouth, she started at the unexpectedness of it. A slight push, and she fell back upon the bed. He released her long enough to remove her costume and chemise, baring her entire body to his avid gaze. Despite her naiveté with the act of love, she did not feel any embarrassment when he looked upon her nakedness. Instead, her skin warmed. When he returned his gaze to hers, she ached with the need to be touched. He got to his feet, then removed his boots and pants until he stood naked before her.

She had never seen an entirely naked man before. Her gaze wandered over the lean muscles of his arms and stomach, pausing a moment to study the light brown hair matting his chest, then moving lower to the darker hair at the juncture of his thighs. Her eyes widened at the proof of his desire, and her gaze flicked up to his.

He joined her on the bed, taking her hand and guiding her fingers around him. Fascinated with the contrasts—hardness beneath smooth skin, pulsing heat within her cool hand—she stroked him, learning intimacy through touch. Then it was his turn to groan. He pulled her curious fingers away and rolled on top of her, fitting his body to hers.

For a long moment they stared into each other's eyes, and Emma's heart pounded in a strange, uneven rhythm. He had such beautiful eyes, so light in color, yet so dark in emotion. He'd said he loved her. Was love what she saw shining in his eyes? How did he know he loved her; perhaps he just wanted her? Emma pushed the disturbing thought aside. Johnny was a man more experienced in life than she. If he said he loved her, then he did. Or at least he believed he did. And wasn't believing the same thing?

She reached up and touched his cheek. He turned his mouth toward her palm and licked the center. The moist heat made her shiver and arch her hips against him. She gasped in surprise at the sensation flooding her body when her most secret part rubbed against his hardness. Moist heat of another kind flooded her, and her breath came in harsh pants as she strove to discover what her body already seemed to know.

He rose above her, positioning himself between her thighs. He probed at her entrance, and she opened wider, wanting him to be a part of her before she exploded with need.

"I love you, Emma," he said. "Always remember, I did love you."

He drove his hips forward, breaking through her barrier and burying himself deep within her. Emma bit her lip to keep from crying out at the sharp pain. He held himself still while her body adjusted to his. The pain was fleeting, leaving her as quickly as it had come and making her ache all the more for the release she sensed at hand.

''Please,'' she whispered, and arched her hips.

He groaned but followed her lead, withdrawing so far she ached to have him return, then filling her so completely she didn't know how she had ever lived without him. The speed of his thrusts increased, and she matched his movements with her own. When he stiffened and pushed into her one last time, she looked into his eyes and saw the truth there. He did love her.

Just before the world faded with her own release, she felt it, too. She loved him. But would her love be enough to save his life?

For both our sakes, make me love you back.

The echo of Emma's plea pulled John from a pleasant doze. What on earth had she meant by that? Obviously she wasn't sure she loved him.

He couldn't blame her. Why would she? A monster slept within him, waiting for the silver-tinged night to awaken the beast.

Yet her voice when she'd pleaded with him made John think there was more to her words than the words were saying. She'd sounded desperate. As if her loving him were a matter of life and death.

She was so naive. Making love to her, and that's what the experience had been for him—love—could not make her love him. Nothing could accomplish that but the hand of God.

He almost laughed at the thought of God having a hand in his life. He was cursed, perhaps forever, through no fault of his own. If allowed to continue on, with each successive full moon he would become more the demon of legend—an evil, murdering, lost soul—forever cast away from the light of heaven. Yet, if he had not been cursed, he would never have found Emma.

John looked down and love filled his heart. She slept against his side, secure within his arms. It didn't matter if she loved him back. If he died tomorrow—John glanced at the small slat of daylight pushing through the crack at the bottom of the wagon door—make that tonight. If he died tonight, he would die knowing he had not left this world without loving someone.

Emma was far too trusting, sleeping in his arms as if he were a normal man. He had to get away from her before he hurt her—or worse. She'd taken responsibility for him with her people, sworn she would watch over him so no one else suffered. He hated to do it, but he would have to take advantage of her trust and make an escape.

Her fragrance enticed him. He wanted to make love to her all over again. He wanted to sleep with her every night and wake up with her every morning. He wanted to share her life, within this circus or in their own home. He wanted a future and the happily-ever-after that was an impossibility for a man who was no longer merely a man.

A slight tapping on the wagon door made him frown. His hearing, which had grown less acute as the moon waned, had begun to improve in the last few days. He listened again. Yes, someone stood outside the wagon. He could hear them breathing.

Disengaging himself from Emma, John stood and dressed quickly. Then he crept to the door and cracked it open. Half expecting to find an irate Franz with a shotgun, John was surprised to see Marcus Birkelund awaiting him outside. The sheriff motioned for John to join him.

The circus folk slept, exhausted from their mob activities of the night before. John risked a quick glance back at Emma. She slept on, her long red hair tousled across her face, a bare arm flung outward as though beseeching him to return to her. He closed his eyes against the sight and joined Marcus on the ground.

"What is it?" he asked.

"Just checking the area. Making sure you were all still here."

"How did you find me?"

"I asked at the common wagon, and they said you were with the boss lady."

John frowned, wondering what else the men had told Marcus. If they'd told the sheriff what John had admitted, he would not be long for this world. John studied his old friend, but Marcus did not behave as though he'd discovered John's secret. The thought of secrets made John remember the sheriff's broken promise.

"What did you tell Kirshner, Marcus?"

"Kirshner?" Birkelund turned toward John, his brow creased in confusion.

"The clown. He came back here after talking with you and got the circus folk worked into a mob."

"What about?"

John hesitated. Sharing Kirshner's accusations with Marcus could get him shot. But if he wanted to follow the clown and destroy him, he needed to have Marcus's understanding. "He knew about Peter. He told everyone that since I was there when Peter was killed, I must be the werewolf.''

''Hmm.'' The sheriff looked at him long and hard. He tapped his fingertips on the barrel of the gun strapped to his hip, then gave a small shake of his head. John relaxed when Marcus removed his hand from his gun. ''I didn't tell him a thing about you, John. He wanted permission to move on, I said no. He was furious and stalked off. I saw him just now, when I arrived. He's still mad, because when he saw me, he took off into the woods.'' Marcus pointed in the direction where he'd seen Kirshner disappear.

''But how . . .'' John's voice trailed off as a sudden realization hit. He had suspected before, but the chain of events and timing of the murders had made this truth an impossibility. Though he still did not understand how, John knew the truth with a surety that made him blink. ''It's him,'' he whispered. ''I knew it.''

''Share it with me then.''

John glanced at Marcus. ''The clown is the werewolf. How else would he know I was there when Peter died, unless he was there, too? The only other being in the woods that night was the wolf that killed my brother.''

''Why didn't you figure this out before?''

''Because Kirshner's also the advance man, and he was always ahead of us, marking the trail, when the murders occurred. For him to accomplish his job, which he did, he would have had to be in another town when people were being killed. Even with the increased abilities a werewolf has, he couldn't have been in two places nearly at once. But he was. If I could think like a damned wolf and not like a man, I'd know how, too.'' John turned away.

Marcus grabbed his arm and spun him back. ''Where the hell are you going?''

''To get my rifle. He's not getting away this time.''

''I'll go with you.''

''No!'' John took a deep breath. He had to go alone. He couldn't risk having anyone but himself shoot Kirshner. He had to break this curse or lose Emma forever. ''I need you to stay here. He's been preying on these people for some reason. He'll come back here to feed. I know it. Take care of them. I'll follow the *teufel*.''

''Killing him is my job, John.''

''He murdered my brother right before my eyes. You have to let *me* do this, Marcus.'' John looked into his friend's face and begged. ''Please. I loved Peter, and this animal took him away from me.''

Marcus looked at John for so long he feared the sheriff would refuse. John held himself tense and ready. If Marcus denied him, he would do whatever necessary to insure that he went into those woods alone—even knock the lawman unconscious.

Finally, Marcus nodded. ''All right. Go. You deserve the chance to have your revenge. But if the thing comes here, I'll kill it.''

John nodded. He clasped his friend on the shoulder in thanks. Marcus turned away, striding toward the open field of menagerie animals where he could watch the forest from the ever-present pile of rocks at the edge of the field. John crept back into the wagon.

His rifle, loaded with silver bullets, leaned against the wall just inside the door. He grasped the weapon but paused before leaving. He needed to look upon Emma just once more.

She slept as he'd left her, peaceful, trusting, beautiful. God, he loved her so much he wanted to die thinking he might never see her again. But if he could not break the curse upon him, then never seeing her again would be the best thing for Emma. He didn't dare touch her, though he wanted to with all his soul. When she awoke, it would be best if she thought he'd betrayed her trust. If he didn't return, she could hate him and perhaps go on with her life. If he did return, he would explain the betrayal and hope she could understand and forgive him.

John left her safe and asleep, then went to hunt the werewolf.

Chapter Seventeen

"Emmaline!"

The voice, like the buzz of a bee, penetrated Emma's rest. She swatted at the pest, wishing it would go away and leave her in peace. She was happy, for some reason, content and warm in her bed. Why couldn't she just stay here forever?

"Get up, girl. Your grandfather has disappeared."

Emma sat up with a jerk. She shook her head to clear her mind of the tumbled images: Johnny saying he loved her; Johnny making love to her; Johnny in her bed all night, holding her in his arms. No one held her now. She opened her eyes searching for him.

"Bradfordini is gone. Disappeared into the forest along with Franz."

Devora stood in the open doorway. The sun had risen, though a thick cloud cover lay across the sky. Emma guessed the time was past noon. Her gaze flicked to the place she'd last seen the Spencer rifle.

Gone. Just like Johnny Bradfordini.

"Bastard," she spat. "I'll kill him for this."

"Yes, you will. Wasn't that the plan all along?"

Emma pushed her hair from her eyes and stared at Devora. The Gypsy's black gaze swept over Emma's tousled nakedness. Emma pulled the blanket up to her chin. She didn't like the tone of the woman's voice. She had trusted Devora to guide her in the correct direction. Maybe her trust had been misplaced. "Is this your revenge, Devora? You get Johnny to kill the *teufel,* then you have me kill Johnny? Your hands are clean, yet you've gained vengeance for Wade? Did you know Johnny remembered what he did that night? He didn't kill Wade."

"So he says. You are too trusting." Devora shrugged. "I have no motives beneath my truth. You saw the book. The cure is as real as you make it. Everything depends upon you."

"If I love him enough."

"Yes."

Emma sighed. She believed she loved him. But could she kill him to save him?

"Johnny's gone, you say?"

Devora nodded.

Emma frowned. "And Grandfather, too?"

"Yes."

"You were supposed to keep watch over him. What happened?"

The Gypsy sighed. "I slept. When I awoke, he had gone. The sheriff is here. He arrived early this morning. He says he saw nothing, so Franz must have left in the night, before the sheriff came to watch us."

Emma swore and jumped out of bed. She dressed in a hurry, clothing herself in an old pair of blue jeans and a cotton shirt she often used when working her tigers. After braiding her hair into one thick link, she headed for the door. Devora stopped her with a slash of her hand and clash of her bracelets.

"What are you doing?"

"Looking for my grandfather. He can't be allowed to wander the forest. I have to find him before nightfall."

"The sheriff will not allow anyone to leave the circus."

Emma swore again. "Can you distract him?"

Devora smiled, a slow, secret, conspiratorial smile. "Certainly."

Emma nodded once and turned away. She didn't care what Devora did, as long as she did it quickly.

"Wait," Devora's voice commanded, and Emma turned back. The Gypsy gripped a Navy Colt in her hand. Where the gun had come from, Emma had no idea. She looked into the old woman's face. "Take it. The gun is loaded with what you need."

Emma reached for the Colt. The weapon was heavier than she'd expected. With a nod of thanks, Emma jumped to the ground. She assisted the Gypsy from the wagon. One glance around the area revealed Sheriff Birkelund sitting on a pile of rocks in the menagerie field. He smoked a cigar and stared at the forest, the road to town, and the circus in turn.

"I will talk to him and keep his attention away from the circus," Devora said. "You slip into the woods behind the wagons."

Emma nodded. As she turned to go, Devora stopped her with a gentle touch on the wrist.

"Despite what you think, I want what is best for us all. Only you can save him. I have dreamt you will hold your love in your arms as he dies. I thought this would be a bad thing, and I didn't want you to hurt as I have hurt. But now I see, he must die to be reborn.''

"You've seen that he will be reborn?'' Emma's voice trembled with hope.

Devora shook her head, and Emma's heart tumbled. ''I have seen his death and your pain. The cure rests upon your belief in the power of love. You will break the curse or he will die. For him, either one is better than the alternative. For you . . .'' She shrugged, and Emma shivered at the implication.

If she did not believe enough, he would die, and she would be left alone forever. The thought of a life without Johnny made the truth quite clear to Emma.

She did love him. She had to save him. She must believe.

Emma tightened her grip on the gun and turned toward the forest.

The approaching full moon caused a sharpening of John's senses and aided him in trailing Heinz Kirshner. He could hear the man ahead of him in the forest. He could smell evil on the breeze. But despite John's heightened senses, the clown was able to remain out of John's reach throughout the day.

John, intent on following Heinz, soon lost any sense of his whereabouts within the forest in relation to Gerhardt Circus. He could not smell the animals, so he was not very close. Yet he sensed others near, so Kirshner did not lead him in a direct line away from the circus. John had not thought the man would. The clown would return to the circus in his guise of the wolf to feed. If John did not kill him first.

Besides losing direction, John also lost track of time.

He'd left after dawn, but the hours blended into each other. The day was overcast, the dense foliage of the forest making the path he trod dark. On several occasions he tried to determine the height of the sun, but could not.

The scent of fresh water wafted across John's face, and he paused. Despite the lack of direct sunshine, the day was hot, stifling, and sweat streamed down his face. He followed the air trail and soon broke through the dense trees and into a small clearing where a creek bubbled and gurgled with life. John fell down on his knees and dunked his face beneath the clear surface. He burst from the water, shaking his head and sending droplets flying around him. Cupping his hands, he drank until he appeased one thirst. When the moon rose in an hour or so, another thirst would pulse within him, and water would do nothing to quench that need.

The coolness of the creek bank soothed him, and he lay his cheek against the earth. He had been awake most of the night—making love to Emma, then watching her sleep as he berated himself for his stupidity and inability to control the lust within him. But the lust of the beast combined with the love of the man had been too much for him. If he must die tonight, at least he'd held the woman he loved in his arms one time. Despite his best intentions, John's eyes drifted closed, and his consciousness wavered in and out for a time.

"I hope you didn't think you could sneak up on me."

The sarcastic voice came from somewhere above him, and John jerked his head up, his heart pounding. Had he slept? Or rested for a moment? The shadows had increased around him. Because a storm approached? Or had night leapt through the final boundaries of day?

He jumped to his feet, grabbing the rifle he'd placed on the ground. He strained his eyes against the darkness, thankful his superior eyesight had returned as the full moon neared. Despite the shadows, he could distinguish Heinz Kirshner perched upon the branch of an evergreen tree about fifty feet above the ground. John started to swing the rifle to his shoulder.

"Ah, ah, ah," Kirshner admonished. He lifted his arm, the gun in his hand pointed at John's head. "Do you want to die, Bradfordini? I do not think so. At least not yet." He motioned with the pistol. "Put the rifle down."

John did as he'd been told. Kirshner was right. He did not want to die. At least not yet. Not until Kirshner lay dead, and then only if John found no hope of a return to his normal life.

"You've been leading me on a chase all day, haven't you?" John asked.

Heinz laughed. "Of course. You couldn't possibly think I didn't know you were behind me. You crashed through the trees like an elephant, boy."

John remained silent. He had thought he followed so quietly. But then Kirshner's hearing was better than most—better than John's, it seemed.

"Evil bastard," John snarled, furious with himself for letting down his guard. He had to figure a way out of this mess. He had to kill this man somehow.

The clown's face melted into an affronted expression. "Evil?" He tilted his head, studying John, then sighed. "I suppose I am. Now. But once I was like you. A normal man with a job, a family. But when one such as we took my family from me, I cared little for anything else.''

John blinked in surprise at the clown's admission. He had not considered what had made Kirshner into an evil one. ''A werewolf killed your family?''

''Isn't that what I said? I was marked like you. I agonized, just like you. But then I saw immortality, or as close to immortality as can be found on this earth, within my reach and I agonized no longer. You see, every full moon you become more the wolf and less the man. Nothing matters but the hunt and the kill. You lose your scruples, and you don't even care.''

The picture Heinz painted was not a pretty one, but John had no doubt the clown knew of what he spoke. ''You know why I'm here.''

''Of course. Your brother. And yourself. I didn't mean to make you like me. I would have killed you, too.''

''Then why didn't you?'' John spat, surprising himself with the vehemence of his voice.

Heinz raised his eyebrows, but he answered the question. ''You knocked me a bit senseless with your rifle. By the time I came around, you were awake. Delirious, but I suspected you weren't bad enough off that you couldn't still shoot me. So I had to retreat. I'd like to say I regret killing your brother, but I can't. He would have killed me. He trailed me from one end of this state to the other. I'd had enough of him.''

''He was a *jager-sucher?*''

Kirshner nodded. ''Irritating society. There is one who has been after me for years, but I change shape like the clouds, and he has not been able to find me. But I think he has come for me now.''

"The blond stranger."

"Very good. He sent your brother after me. Now he has come himself. Little does he know, I came to Gerhardt for a purpose. To kill him."

John frowned. A hole gaped in the midst of this tale. "When did you come here?"

"Three, maybe four years past. I travel a lot." He pointed a finger at his face. "The makeup helps. I can change the pattern or take it off, and no one recognizes me from place to place."

"You've been with Gerhardt for so many years, yet you've only killed their people in the last few months?"

"It's not a good idea to eat where you live, boy."

"Then why did you do it?"

"To catch a *jager-sucher*. I knew he'd come if people began to die here. He would no longer send his minions. He is the one I want. He is the leader. The great hunter. If I kill him, the rest will scatter like leaves in a winter wind. They will need years to regroup. By then I will be so powerful, no one will stop me."

"What do you mean?"

The clown shook his head. "You haven't been one of us long enough to understand. With every full moon you become more the wolf and less the man."

"Both you and Devora have told me that."

"But she never truly understood what that meant, and neither do you. The increased abilities—sight, smell, speed, hearing—you've noticed those?"

"Of course."

"They get stronger, boy, with every full moon. And they last longer. Eventually, though you return to the

328

shape of a man, you keep the abilities always.''

Understanding dawned in John's mind. ''That's how you were able to kill, mark the trail and be in the next town before anyone got there.''

''Yes. My speed is beyond what you can comprehend. My hearing is impeccable. Each time they attempted to set a trap for me, I heard their plans on the wind.'' He laughed. ''Mere mortals don't stand a chance against me.'' Kirshner looked at John and shook his head. ''You don't either. You should have left me alone, boy. You would have been better off.''

''You knew who I was all along.''

''Of course. And I tried to get rid of you at first. I released the tiger, hoping she'd kill you. She always smelled the wolf in me and it infuriated her. I thought she would go right for you. But she did not, and Emmaline saved you. Then I put the bloody clothes in your bag, planning to institute a search, find them and have you destroyed. But you were too quick for me there. Last night I brought the mob to kill you. But . . .'' He shrugged.

''Emma,'' John said.

''Yes. She's becoming quite an irritation.''

John didn't like the way the clown said ''irritation.'' He narrowed his eyes. ''Leave her alone.''

The clown didn't even acknowledge the warning. ''I've been this way a long while, and I'm getting lonely. Emma would make a lovely mate, don't you think? Franz isn't long for this world. And if he lasts too long, I'll help him out of it. Then Emma will be in charge of the circus. Once she's like me, she won't allow these nasty little hunting parties. I'll even forgive her ill-advised indiscretion with you, though I'll have to punish her for it.''

Bile rose in John's throat at the images the clown's words conjured up. ''You'll not touch her.''

Heinz laughed. ''I won't hurt her. I want her, too. Besides, you have nothing to say about who I touch or anything else. Or haven't you figured things out yet? The reason I'm answering all your questions is because you won't be around to tell anyone my secrets. You're the sacrifice, boy. Tonight you will be offered up to the *jager-sucher*. He'll kill you. I'll kill him.''

John had already decided that Heinz meant to kill him. But to let the stranger do it? Why leave such a thing to the chance of another? ''Can't you do your own dirty work, Kirshner?''

''I'd love to. Unfortunately, you must be killed with a silver bullet. I can't touch them. The stronger the wolf within us, the more the silver hurts us. I can smell it in your rifle. The *jager-sucher* will have to do the deed for me.''

''You're saying you don't have silver bullets in that gun?''

The clown smirked. ''Of course not.''

John dove for his rifle, which lay in the damp earth next to the creek bed. His fingers circled the barrel, and he pulled the weapon toward him. As he straightened, the clown's maniacal laughter filled his ears. John frowned. What could be so funny now?

He tried to lift the rifle to his shoulder, but his strength deserted him. The weapon dropped to the ground. John's knees buckled as pain ripped throughout his body. He landed on his back in the cool, damp mud. What had soothed him moments, or perhaps

330

hours, before now felt like so much wet earth. The clown continued to laugh, but the sound came from a long way off. The world spun in slow circles, but John could still see the source of his pain.

Kirshner had been talking for a reason. And not to let John in on his secrets or boast of his power. No, the clown had answered all John's questions to distract him from the one thing that would have made John desperate enough to kill without a care for his own life.

He *had* slept. Too long.

Though the night had not yet fallen completely, a sliver of silver shone through the clouds just above the highest treetop and cast an eerie glow over John's face.

"Sorry, Bradfordini, but it's too late now. You're changing, and so am I. Guess what? I smell blood. And you know whose blood it is? Little Red-Cap's out here looking for you. Poor thing's lost in the woods." He laughed, but this time the sound resembled a gurgling growl. "I'll race you to her."

John moaned. He'd failed. Failed Peter not once, but twice. Failed his patients by leaving them, never to return. But those failures were nothing when compared with his present failure. This time the woman he loved would suffer.

Kirshner's laughter died away on the breeze, but John barely noticed. He was too preoccupied with the pain ricocheting in his head. He had forgotten how much the change hurt. Or maybe he had chosen not to remember. If he had remembered, he might have killed himself to avoid the agony.

The sound of clothes ripping shrieked in his ears, ears that lengthened, as his nose lengthened. His face felt as if it were being split in two. Hair sprouted from his flesh, each strand a blaze of pain. Long, canine teeth scraped his lips, drawing blood as they grew. He cried out for the agony to stop, but instead of words a long, shrill howl erupted from his mouth, drifting up toward the clouds, which parted to reveal a circle of silver surrounded by an indigo sky.

Chapter Eighteen

Emma was lost.

She couldn't believe it. She'd lived in these woods all her life. Or maybe not in these woods exactly, but she'd been traveling through them since childhood. How could she be lost?

But lost she was. She had been trying to talk herself out of that fact for the past several hours, but as darkness approached, she had to be honest. She hadn't the vaguest idea where she was or how far she'd come from the circus.

She had spent the day searching for her grandfather and for Johnny. She had found no sign of either—as if the two had disappeared from the earth. Perhaps one or both had returned to the circus. But if so, their return did her little good, since she didn't know where the circus was.

The moon had risen and with it her fear. Danger stalked her within these woods. Emma clutched the pistol tighter. Her arm ached from carrying the weapon all day, but she didn't dare put it down, or even tuck the pistol into the waistband of her pants. She more than anyone knew the speed at which a wild animal could strike. Should the werewolf come, she would need every second available to aim and fire the gun.

"What am I going to do?" she whispered.

By now, the circus folk would have returned to her wagon to take Johnny. When they found her abode deserted, they would no doubt form a hunting party and head for the woods. If the sheriff allowed them to. If she was lucky, they would find her before a werewolf did.

She would do best to sit down and wait for them to come. Emma cringed. She could not just lie down and wait for her death. She had to keep moving or risk going insane.

When the howl began, Emma froze, her heart increasing in rhythm with the scale of the sound. She swallowed the lump of fear at the base of her throat and headed toward the noise. Soon, another sound reached her ears.

Gurgling water. She licked her lips in anticipation of a cool drink and increased her pace. Up ahead, the trees thinned and Emma saw a clearing. She pushed through a section of low bushes and came upon a creek. Her joy at seeing the clear water faded to horror at the sight of the creature that stood on the opposite bank.

The black wolf bent over his fresh kill. The blood on her grandfather's face made Emma gasp in horror.

"No!" she shrieked. "Get away from him!" The wolf looked up, and its human eyes blazed evil. Emma did not care. She rushed forward, lifting the Colt and pointing the barrel at the animal. Her arms shook, but she grit her teeth and pulled the trigger.

The force of the blast knocked her several steps

back. When she opened her eyes, the creature still stood. The man-wolf stepped into the creek. Legs stiff, hackles raised, the animal advanced upon her. The eyes of the beast, those horrible human eyes, remained fixed upon her face. She could feel the animal's hunger, which fed on her fear.

Emma fumbled with the gun. As she steadied her hands, the wolf crouched to leap. Before she could fire again, another figure burst through the trees.

A second wolf, this one with fur a shade between brown and gold, fell upon the black wolf's back.

Johnny! Emma wanted to shout. *Get out of my way!* But he would not hear her in the midst of the fight that must be to the death.

Snarls and growls drowned out the pleasant gurgling of the water over the rocks. Emma tried to aim once more at the black wolf, but the two figures rolled over and over, making a clear shot impossible. When they stopped tumbling, the black wolf held the brown wolf down, his teeth snapping at the animal's throat. Emma sighted along the barrel.

Johnny's voice seemed to echo in her head. *To break the curse I must kill the one who made me. Only me and no one else.*

Emma hesitated. If she killed the black wolf, would she destroy any chance Johnny had of being cured?

To break the curse, the one who loves the man must kill the wolf.

Emma flinched as Devora's voice swirled around her, so loud it seemed the Gypsy stood in the clearing behind her.

Which cure is the true cure?

While Emma stood, indecision blocking her actions,

335

the black wolf fixed his teeth upon the throat of the second wolf and bit down. A shriek of fury and pain erupted from the brown wolf. Emma bit back a sob as the animal went limp. The black wolf lifted his head, blood streaming from his mouth, and stared at Emma.

She knew those eyes. Hatred flowed through her, strong and sure. The evil bastard had killed Johnny before she'd had a chance to save him. Emma's shaking hands became steady on the gun. When the black wolf charged her, she pulled the trigger.

Click.

Emma stared at the rifle in shock.

Misfire.

She looked up just in time to see the black wolf leap into the air. Emma closed her eyes and waited for death. The silence of the clearing thundered in her ears. She could almost hear the creature's teeth snapping for her throat.

A gunshot cracked through the forest. The wolf yelped, a sound of pain and surprise. A heavy thud and something fell to the ground. Emma gasped. Her eyes snapped open. At her feet lay the black wolf. She stared in amazement and horror, unable to believe what she witnessed. Inch by inch, he changed from wolf to man, the fur on his face becoming human flesh beneath black and white greasepaint, his nose and ears shortening, his body twisting and writhing into human form, the wound in his side bleeding the life out of both the man and the beast.

When the change was complete, Heinz Kirshner stared at the full moon, but he did not see it. His eyes were fixed, as dead as the man himself.

Emma tore her gaze away from the horror at her feet.

336

She stood alone in the clearing. Alone but for the bodies of two men and one wolf. She frowned. Had she been wrong? Was the brown wolf merely a wolf and not Johnny? Had Johnny shot Heinz and broken the curse? Was she relieved of the burden of killing her love to save him?

"Johnny?" she called, praying he would appear from the forest holding the gun that had killed the *teufel.*

"No. Not Johnny," a voice answered. Emma brought her gun up and pointed the weapon in the direction of the sound. The blond stranger stepped from behind a tree. He pointed at the brown wolf. "There he is."

Emma shifted toward the fallen animal just as it staggered to its feet. The wolf turned to Emma and lifted his head. Her breath hitched in her throat, a painful sigh. She'd know those eyes anywhere. Silver-blue. Beautiful, be they the eyes of a man or a wolf.

The sound of a gun being cocked made her flinch. She looked at the man who had killed Heinz. He aimed his rifle at Johnny.

"No!" She ran forward until she stood in the line of fire. "You mustn't."

The man frowned. "Get out of the way, Emmaline."

"No." She took a deep breath. "I'll do it."

"You will not. You almost got yourself killed, or worse, just a moment ago. I know what I'm doing."

"So do I." Emma looked the man straight in the eye. "I won't let you shoot him. You'll have to go through me first. I'll do it or no one will."

He stared back at her for a long moment as if gauging her resolve. Something flickered in his eyes, an odd emotion, so out of place in the situation that Emma could not give a name to its source. The stranger gave a short nod and the emotion was replaced by determination. "Use this." He held out his rifle toward her.

Emma hesitated. Did this man understand what she needed to do and the tools she must have to do it?

"Take it," he snapped. "It's loaded with silver bullets, and the damn thing fires when you pull the trigger. Give me yours." He snatched the pistol from her hand and shoved the rifle into her stiff fingers. "If you mean to do this, Emmaline, do the job right."

She turned back to the wolf and lifted the gun. Johnny's eyes stared into hers, and she swallowed against the agony.

You must believe. Believe in the power of love.

"I believe," she whispered. "I believe."

She bit her lip hard and tried to pull the trigger. An image of Johnny lying at her feet with a hole in his chest assaulted her. She imagined watching him as his blood seeped into the Wisconsin earth. Emma's eyes watered and the world wavered.

What if I'm wrong?

She started to lower the gun. A flash of movement, the snarl of a beast in pain. Emma's eyes cleared, and she watched in horror as the wolf launched itself at her.

The snarl exploded in her mind, sounding too much like the words *Save me!*

A gun exploded. The wolf jerked once and fell to the ground. Emma stared in shock at the rifle in her hands. Had she fired the shot?

Reaching out a shaking finger, Emma touched the barrel.

Warm.

She had fulfilled the prophesy. But would shooting Johnny save him as he'd begged her to?

The gun dropped from her aching hands, and Emma fell to the ground next to the wolf. She waited for the animal to change to a man. Nothing happened.

She shoved at the wolf's shoulder. The body rolled forward and back, as limp as death. Her hand came away bloody, and she stared at the glistening red patch on her palm in horror. Then fear made her furious. "Change, damn you! Change!"

A boot appeared beside her and Emma glanced up. The stranger stood over them, his gaze fixed upon the wolf. "He's still breathing."

Emma followed the man's gaze. He was right. The wolf still lived. Emma reached out and smoothed the fur on the animal's head. The wolf's eyes opened—Johnny's eyes. Emma put her arms around the wolf's neck and pulled the animal to her.

The stranger put his hand on her shoulder, holding her back. "Don't get too close."

She yanked herself from his grasp. "Get away from him," she shouted. "He has to change. I shot him. He's cured now. He shouldn't be a wolf anymore."

The man said nothing. Emma sat back and rested the wolf's head in her lap. She held him there long after his breathing stopped, and his silver-blue eyes stared at the falling moon, though they no longer saw anything of this world.

Sheriff Birkelund and the hunting party from the circus discovered them as the sun peeked over the trees. Her people whispered. Emma glanced up, her gaze drawn to the circle of folk around the body of her grandfather. She gently laid the wolf on the ground, then got to her feet and crossed the distance to Franz. The people fell back, then closed their ranks once again around her and him.

Pain filled her. Everyone she loved was gone. She had tried to save them, and she had failed. She touched her grandfather's face. So cold. She could do nothing for him now. Just as she could do nothing for Johnny.

What had happened? She had believed. She loved him. She had done as she'd been told, just as she had done all her life, and still Johnny was dead. She wanted to be dead, too. What did she have to live for? The circus? She gave an hysterical laugh. What had once been her entire reason for living now seemed as important as the dust on the wind.

"Emmaline?"

The stranger stood before her. He held out a hand and helped her to her feet. She frowned at him in confusion.

"Who are you?"

"Karl. Karl Monroe."

Emma blinked. The name meant something to her. If she could think through the fog of pain, she'd know who he was. A word appeared in the mist. A new word, but familiar nevertheless.

"Father?" she asked.

He nodded. Emma blinked harder and faster, but the black curtain that threatened her consciousness would not recede. Her knees gave way, and the stranger caught her as she fell, scooping her up against his chest and holding her like a child.

"Yes, Emmaline, I'm your father."

* * *

Emma awoke to a darkness so black she could feel the absence of light in the coolness of the air on her heated face. Something moved within the darkness. She turned her head toward the sound, amazed to discover that her fear of the unknown had vanished. She doubted that she'd be frightened of much again in her life. Before she could examine the reason for her belief, she slept once more. Slept only to dream.

In the world of her dream, two men she loved waited. Dead men. Her breath hitched on a sob.

"Ah, *mein Liebchen,* do not cry for me." Her grandfather walked forward and enfolded Emma in his arms. "I can be with your grandmother and my darling Francie now. I will be much happier here." He kissed her brow and turned away, walking down a long, light-filled tunnel where two figures awaited him. The women waved to Emma, then embraced her grandfather before all three disappeared.

She turned to the second man.

"Johnny," she whispered.

He smiled, the smile that always broke her heart. The expression did the same to her in this dreamworld.

"I'm sorry," she said. "I believed I loved you enough to save you. But I killed you. I'll never forgive myself."

He shook his head. She started toward him, but he faded. Just before he disappeared, he changed back into the wolf and ran away.

Emma awoke with his name on her lips and tears streaking her face. She still existed in darkness. A sob escaped her throat.

"Emmaline?" The bed on which she lay dipped as someone sat next to her. "Are you all right?"

A stranger's voice, yet not a stranger truly. *Her father*. What was he doing here? She hadn't the strength for this now.

"I'm fine. Please leave me alone."

Pained silence came from the darkness, followed by a sigh. "You've been sleeping for a day and a night. You should eat." He sighed. "I'm not very good at this."

"Just go away."

"You have every right to hate me. I can't blame you. But . . ." He broke off with a curse.

"You tried to see me, to write to me. I know. But Franz wouldn't let you."

"He told you?"

"No, I found some letters. I understand. You had a life of your own. You didn't need a child in it."

"No! That wasn't the way I felt. I wanted you to be safe. With me, you would always have been in danger. Hell, I put you in danger as it was without even trying."

The darkness enhanced the emotion in his voice, calling out to her, stirring curiosity within Emma. She tried to stifle the curiosity, afraid that any emotion would bring back all the pain she'd somehow managed to bury, but found herself unable to force the prickling need to know from her mind. "What do you mean you put me in danger?"

"Kirshner hunted me. He came to Gerhardt because he found out somehow that I came every summer to see you. But the last two years I spent on a hunt in Germany, and I couldn't come. I sent Peter Bradfordini, but Heinz killed him before he arrived to keep a watch over you. To make sure I came, Kirshner began

342

to kill at this circus. He knew I'd come if you were threatened.''

''You're a *jager-sucher.*''

''Yes. After your mother died, I didn't want to live either. I didn't leave her, Emmaline. I went away to look for a job. You were so little, and she was still weak. I shouldn't . . .'' His voice broke and he paused for a moment, coughed, then continued. ''I shouldn't have left, I know, but we needed the money. When I came back, she was dead and you were gone. I couldn't take care of a child. You were better off with your grandfather, so I left you here. But I went a little crazy, losing you both like that.'' He shifted in the darkness, his hand brushing against her before drawing away, almost as if he were frightened to touch her too long. ''The society searches for men like me. Men who think they have nothing to live for and don't care if they die. By the time I wanted to live again, it was too late to get out, and I didn't want to. I'm good at my job. I want to destroy the evil that multiplies with every full moon. Now, too many of them know me. I can never stop. Not only do I hunt, but I'm the hunted. I can't stay here long, Emmaline. It's too dangerous for all of you.''

Emma considered the life her father had led, the choices he'd made. She couldn't say she approved of his abandonment, but she understood devotion. Once, she'd been devoted to the circus. Now she couldn't seem to work up enough emotion to care whether the Gerhardt Circus survived or not.

''You loved him, didn't you?''

Emma flinched at the low-voiced question. Pain flooded back into her soul with an agony that left her gasping. Her father fumbled in the darkness until he found her hand. She let him hold her fingers until the pain receded enough so she could speak. "Yes. But my love wasn't strong enough to save him. I'll have to live with my failure for the rest of my life."

"We don't know if there's any way to break the curse. You did what you thought best. He wouldn't have wanted to go on living a cursed existence. He was a man who saved lives."

Emma searched for a meaning to his words. She could find none. "Saved lives?"

"Yes. He was a physician. A damned good one, from what I could discover. Not the usual sawbones who knows nothing about people and cares even less."

"Physician?" Emma pulled her hand from her father's, her mind stumbling over the information.

Johnny had lied to her from the first, but when he'd told her he was a werewolf, she'd thought that was the extent of his secrets. He'd held another secret back, and his betrayal cut her deeply. Even if she had been able to save him, they never could have had the future she'd envisioned. A man of his social status and advanced education would never have spent his life in a traveling show, and she would never be accepted in the real world. If he'd been a drifter as he'd claimed, they might have had a chance.

He'd said he loved her, and maybe he had. Or maybe he'd just claimed to love her, hoping that in her naiveté she would love him back enough to break the curse upon him. Little did he know that he had not needed to lie. She loved him anyway. Still, the death of another dream pained her, despite the fact that any future with Johnny lay in the grave beside him.

"Where is he?" she asked.

Her father cleared his throat, a sound of discomfort she didn't care for.

"Have they buried him? I want to see the grave."

"Emmaline, when you fainted, I brought you back here. The others, they took care of Franz and Heinz."

"Yes. But what about Johnny? Where is he?"

"Gone."

"Gone? What do you mean gone?"

Emma heard her father shift with unease. She didn't need to see him to know that his mouth tightened with suppressed fury at what he had to tell her; she could hear the anger in his voice. "When the sheriff went back for his body, it wasn't there."

Hope lightened Emma's heart. "You mean he might be alive?"

"No, sweetheart, he's not." The hand that patted her in the darkness did so with a fumble but gave her no less support and affection for the awkwardness of the gesture. "Wild animals took him. We found a lot of blood and fur. Drag marks and animal tracks."

"I don't have a body to bury? I wasn't even left with that much?" Emma turned onto her side, away from her father, and his hand dropped from her shoulder. "Leave me alone. I want to remember him before the memories are gone, too."

She feared he'd argue, but after a long moment of silence, he left the wagon without speaking or touching her again.

Emma relived every moment she and Johnny had spent together—every smile, every touch, every word. She didn't know how long she stayed in her bed, refusing to answer every summons. When Devora finally shook her awake, daylight poured through the open door of the wagon.

"Time to get up, girl."

"Go away." Emma pulled the blanket over her head. Devora snatched it back and cuffed her on the ear. "Ow!" Emma sat up, blinking at the light. "What do you think you're doing?"

"You might be able to frighten the rest off with your commands. They think you're the boss now. I, however, know you must earn such a right, and you are not earning the right by hiding from your responsibilities."

Emma fell back on the bed and closed her eyes. "I don't care. You be the boss."

Devora sat on the bed and yanked Emma up by her shoulders. She shook her until Emma's eyes snapped open. The Gypsy's face darkened with anger. "Do you think I don't know how you feel? Do you think you are the only one who has lost someone they love to this evil? What about Helga and Heloise? What about your Johnny and his brother? I wanted to die when Wade died. But you are alive and you have to go on. People are depending upon you. They're lost without Franz. You are their leader now. If you don't get up and lead them, they'll drift away and you'll have nothing left."

Emma jerked away from Devora's hands. "I don't care."

"Yes, you do. When the fog clears from your mind, you'll need something to occupy your life. If you don't have this circus, then you *will* want to curl up and die. You have no other talents, Emmaline. You're a tiger tamer. You'd better get out there and save your world. Otherwise all you've gone through will be for nothing.'' Devora stood and walked to the door, where she turned back and fixed Emma with another dark look. ''Your grandfather is being buried in ten minutes. They'll expect you to say something. If your world has crumbled, so has theirs. Get up and be the woman your grandfather raised you to be.'' With those final words and a look of disdain, the Gypsy slammed the wagon door behind her.

Emma stared at the ceiling. She wasn't going to do it. She would not be the leader of this circus. Just because her grandfather was dead did not mean she would take his place. The mere thought made her remember how he had died, and she did not want to remember that. Still, if she was not going to be their leader, she needed to tell them so.

Emma forced herself from the bed. She stared at her clothes. She possessed nothing black except a costume, studded with silver beads. Emma took the material between her fingers and rubbed the beads as she considered her options.

Why not?

She would preside at the funeral of Franz Gerhardt, the greatest showman in circus history. He had made her a tiger tamer and a tiger tamer she was. She would go to his final show dressed as he would have wanted her to dress. And she'd take the damn tiger, too.

Ten minutes later she stood over the fresh grave of her grandfather with Destruction resting at her feet. The circus folk watched her. She stared back.

What on earth should she say to them?

She looked in turn at Devora, who scowled at her and gave a ferocious gesture indicating she speak, then at her father, who smiled his encouragement, but also nodded for her to speak. She sighed. She had dressed herself befitting the woman her grandfather had raised her to be. As Devora had said, now she must act like that woman.

Emma took a deep breath and hoped what she had to say would be enough. "My grandfather gave his life to this circus. He loved it and you with all his heart. You know he was not himself in the past few months. The troubles we've had pained him. The loss of his friends was agony." She paused and took another deep breath, focusing on the freshly turned earth. "You wonder what will happen now. So do I. I will be honest, I have no desire to continue with the circus."

The circle of people mumbled in displeasure and fear. Their world would dissolve without someone to lead them, and they knew it. Emma glanced away from the grave and looked into the faces of those she had known all her life. Her family. The only family she had left now; all that was left of the world she had fought to save.

Emma scowled, and the crowd's mumblings increased with their unease. They were like children, lost without someone to care for them. What choice did she have? She would be their leader.

"Have no fear." Her words and tone made them go silent once more. "Like you, this is my life. I could not exist anywhere else. So we will go on. We will try to forget the man who fooled us all into trusting him. The one who nearly destroyed our world with the evil that consumed him. And we will remember those who tried to help us." She looked up and met the gaze of her father once more. Love shone from his eyes. All her life she had wished for someone to love her just because she was Emma. This man did. She would take the gifts she had left and hold them close to her heart. They were all she would have for many long, lonely nights and days to come.

Devora began to sing, and the rest of the circus folk joined in. The words of the song, which had been sung over every grave they'd left along their way, rose toward the sun shining in the clear summer sky. Emma listened and for the first time heard their meaning.

"Amazing grace, how sweet the sound that saved a wretch like me. I once was lost, but now am found, was blind, but now I see."

And she did see. She had held love in her arms for a brief time, but that dream of love was not for her. This life she had been trained to live was all she had left of any dream.

But once every month she would spend a night remembering the man who would forever be a part of her full moon dreams.

Epilogue

The next full moon

The dream came again, bearing down on her fast and hard from the blessed peace of sleep. She struggled against the too-familiar images. Not strong enough, her mind succumbed to the inevitable.

Dream and reality merged. She dreamt, yet the world was exactly as she knew the world to be in reality. Emma rose from her lonely pallet and left the wagon. The circus slept in the silver-tinged night, resting in preparation for their move onward in the morning as they resumed their interrupted tour. She had said good-bye to her father that morning, waving as he rode away to fight more evil in other parts of the country. They had spent a month together, and his presence had soothed some of the pain in Emma's heart. He would return. He had promised. Until then, she would be alone.

Who was she trying to fool? She would forever be alone in the ways that truly counted. She would never again allow herself to love someone so completely that when she lost him, a part of her died. She had already lost a large part of herself to Johnny Bradfordini. She didn't think she had much left to lose before Emmaline Monroe was gone, too.

Once before they left this place forever she would return to the clearing where her love had died in her arms, even if her return was in a dream.

She hurried through the forest, pushing aside the thick foliage as she made her way toward the scene of so much death. Funny, she could almost feel the coolness of the night air upon her face, even though she dreamt the feeling. Could this perhaps be real?

No, if she truly walked the night, how could she find the clearing? She'd been lost the night she came there and had left the area unconscious in her father's arms. Yes, she had to be dreaming. But this dream she would experience to its fullest.

She broke through the bushes along the creek and came upon a bright circle of light, enhanced by the intense darkness of the surrounding forest. The heat of the day combined with the cool night had created a mist that swirled around and above the water. The opposite bank was obscured from her view. Emma didn't care. She had come to see one last time the place where love had died.

The area revealed no trace of what had occurred one month ago this night. The blood and fur and drag marks her father had spoken of had washed away with the rain and wind. The grass had burst through the earth once more and covered the site where Johnny had died. Emma went down on her knees anyway and smoothed the place where she had held him when he breathed his last.

351

She couldn't cry. Not anymore. She'd cried every night since he'd died, and she was through crying. She had taken this dream visit for a reason. She had come to say good-bye.

"Good-bye," she whispered.

The wind swirled the mist across her face. Damp air and the smell of a man.

"Hello," a voice answered.

Her breath caught in her throat, hope and fear at war inside her. She was dreaming, therefore he could not be real. Still, she wanted to see him with a desperation that frightened her. If she did see him, would she ever return from this dream land? Perhaps she'd want to stay here forever.

Emma turned her head. A figure, a man not a wolf, wavered in the fog on the opposite bank. He moved forward, emerging from the mist and stepping into the creek.

She remained silent as he approached her. The mist followed him, swirling around his feet, then around her as he neared.

He said nothing more, just reached out a hand to help her to her feet.

Warm flesh enveloped hers. She frowned. This dream was too real. She had been right. She did not want to leave. She'd rather stay here with the dream-Johnny than go back to her dry, empty life.

His eyes, still silver-blue, stared at her as if he were as amazed as she that they were once again together. He lowered his head, and she held her breath until his lips touched hers, terrified she would awaken before she experienced his kiss again. Their breath mingled, warm and moist, as real as the ground upon which she stood. Or was it the bed upon which she lay? Emma did not care. She wanted to make love to him once more, even if their lovemaking would not be real, before he disappeared back into the mists of death.

She circled his neck with her arms. Her mouth opened, and she kissed him with all the pain and passion she thought she had killed with her month of tears.

They didn't speak, allowing their hands and their mouths and their bodies to say all that needed to be said. The grass that had cushioned Johnny's dead body now cushioned their naked forms as they made love with an abandon only a dream could afford.

His long hair fell forward, curtaining their faces from the moon's light as he kissed her, fitting his body over hers. She arched toward him, begging without words for him to become a part of her. With a curse that sounded more like a prayer, he came into her, and she gasped at the sensation of oneness she'd thought never to experience again.

Tangling her fingers in his hair, she held his mouth to hers as their tongues mated along with their bodies. They climaxed together—tensing, stilling, releasing.

He pressed his mouth to her neck and spoke one last time. "I love you, Emma. I'll always love you."

The tears she'd thought no longer possible streamed down her cheeks. God, why did she have to dream this? She'd go insane if she had to dream about loving him over and over again for the rest of her life. When she awoke and he was still dead, she wouldn't be able to go on.

She turned her wet cheek to the side and rubbed the tears into oblivion against his soft hair. "I love you, too, Johnny. I should have told you before." She sighed, and drifted back toward a deeper sleep. There, she'd told him; even if her words had been dream-words, at least she'd finally said aloud the secret she would now lock away forever in her heart.

When Emma awoke she was, as she'd known she would be, back in her bed inside the wagon.

Back? She laughed in self-depreciation. She'd never left. Johnny was still dead, just as she'd known he would be once she returned from fantasy to reality. And just as she'd known that she wanted to die, too, rather than face another empty day and another night of make-believe love.

Emma glanced out of the open wagon doors. The day had not begun yet, the dawn just peaking over the trees.

Wait a minute.

Why were the doors open? She never left them open at night.

Destruction roared, a sound of welcome more than fury. Emma got out of bed and threw on her traveling dress. She went to the back of the wagon and peered across the back lot until her gaze lit upon the tiger's cage.

A man stood with his back to her, whispering to the tiger. Emma couldn't breathe. He looked so much like . . . but no, this man could not be . . .

Destruction caught sight of her and roared another welcome. The man turned; a sob escaped Emma's throat. She jumped from the wagon. Her feet tangled in her skirts, as always, and she yanked them free so she could run.

One leap and she landed in his arms, kissing the face she'd thought lost to her forever. He held her chin still with his hand and kissed her full on the mouth.

When he released her, she sagged against him. He held her close, and she heard his heart beating beneath her cheek, slightly fast, as was her own, but beating nevertheless.

Johnny was alive.

"How?" she whispered.

He flexed and released his shoulders before he spoke. "I was dead, but then later I awoke, as if I'd slept, not died. There were other wolves around, real wolves. They had dragged me away from the creek. I was no longer a wolf and my wound had healed. They scattered when I got up. Then I found my clothes, and come morning I walked out of the forest."

Emma stiffened, then backed away from his arms. "You mean you were alive and you didn't tell me?" The joy that had consumed her at his touch faded when she recalled her father's words. This man was not of her world. Never could be, even if he was real and not a dream as she'd believed.

"I couldn't come to you, Emma, until I knew for certain the curse had been broken. Before I lost consciousness, I heard you tell the stranger—"

"My father," she interrupted.

His eyebrows raised in surprise but he did not comment. "Your father, then. I heard you tell him about the cure your love could exact." His gaze warmed her face, but she did not allow herself to soften. "But I wouldn't put you, or anyone else here, at risk again, so I went home."

"To your patients," she spat.

The flash of surprise across his face told her he had not expected her to know his truth. "Yes. I did what I

355

could for them. I'd been away for a month and people had died because I wasn't there." He took a deep breath. "But I had to come back to you if I could. So I spent the past month searching for another physician to take my place in Andrewsville."

"Why?"

"I love you. I always will. I told you last night." He smiled and allowed his gaze to drift over her body. "You couldn't have forgotten already."

Her eyes widened. "Last night? That was—"

"Real? Oh, yes. Very real. I came back to the place I'd last seen you. I wasn't sure you'd still be here, but it was a good place to start. I waited for midnight with a gun at my side. When the moon reached the highest point, and I felt nothing more than an intense desire to hold you in my arms, I knew you had cured me. I had just started for the circus when you came." He held out his hand. When she stared at him without moving, he frowned and let his arm drop back to his side. "You told me you loved me last night, Emma, and you must to have cured me. What's the matter?"

Fear of the unknown arose in Emma. She had fallen in love with Johnny Bradfordini, canvasman. She did not know Dr. Bradfordini at all. She might believe in her love for him, but to believe in any future for them would only mean losing him twice. The second time would be more final than the first. She almost wished he had never come back and given her hope for the briefest of moments. She had to tell him the truth, make him understand and leave her alone with her memories. "I can't live in your world, Johnny. I might try, but it would never work. You and I, we're not the same."

He rolled his eyes. "We've had this discussion already. I'll tell you the same thing I told you then. You're a woman, I'm a man. We're not supposed to be the same. That's the beauty of it." She began to speak, and he held up his hand to stave off her words. "And don't even try to give me your Lutheran-Catholic, German-Italian argument. After what we've been through, what we've overcome, I don't give a damn about anything but us, and you shouldn't either. I want to stay here and make a life with you."

Emma made a sound of exasperation and turned away. "How long before you feel the need to return to your normal life? How long before you tire of this life and leave me to it? I can't lose you twice, Johnny. I just can't."

He moved so quickly and silently she jumped when his arms encircled her from behind. "And you won't. I'm not leaving. You can't push me away anymore. I learned so much here. How to love—a woman and a place. All my life I've taken my responsibilities too seriously, putting everyone else ahead of anything I might want or need. Peter was always the adventurous brother, and I admired him for it. I thought I was drawn to the daring in him because I loved him so much. But living in the circus I came to understand, I admired Peter's daring because I wanted to live life and not just observe others living it. I've never felt so alive as when I lived here. With you."

She wanted to believe. But a lifetime of being loved for what she could do and not who she was made her wary. "I can't see you cleaning up after the elephants when you've been trained to save lives."

His arms tightened and released, a brief hug. She heard the amusement in his voice, though he didn't laugh outright. "No cleaning up after the elephants. I draw the line there. I'll help any other way I can. But I still plan to use my training. I can practice medicine anywhere. With our people and with those we meet on the way. I'll do more good traveling through remote areas than I ever could in my staid little house in Andrewsville."

Emma turned in his arms. He meant what he said. She could see the truth in his face. Could she believe in the power of love one more time? She had believed once and saved Johnny's soul. If she believed this time, she could save her own. Emma smiled and allowed the truth of her love to shine in her eyes.

They had both lost people they loved to an evil they did not understand. But together they had destroyed the evil, and despite their losses, they had found each other.

"Shall we make a pact?" he asked.

She tilted her head, studying the glint of amusement in his silver-blue eyes. "What kind of pact?"

"Nothing but good dreams from now on? For us and for all those who visit Gerhardt Circus?"

"Nothing but good dreams for us." She considered the notion, then nodded her agreement. "And nothing but good dreams for all who visit the Gerhardt-Bradfordini Circus."

Destruction roared his approval. They both started, then laughed. Johnny's eyes gleamed with love as he kissed her, sealing their pact.

AUTHOR'S NOTE

The circus in Wisconsin has a long history. From the early 1800s, countless traveling road shows and later rail shows traversed the state. Today, the circus continues to travel Wisconsin by truck and trailer. In writing this book I was aided by the Circus World Museum in Baraboo, Wisconsin. Here one can see many of the circus wagons from hundreds of years ago, restored to their original beauty. There are also posters, photos, and best of all the Robert L. Parkinson Library and Research Center, which possesses an incredible collection of information on circuses from the past and around the world. If you are ever in the area, take a trip to The Circus World Museum: 426 Water Street, Baraboo, WI, 53913-2597. During the summer months they have a daily show on the back lot. And if you happen to be in Wisconsin in July, the entire circus—animals, wagons, horses and everything in between—is moved by train from Baraboo to Milwaukee for the annual circus parade through the streets of downtown. This parade is much bigger than the parades of old, and the excitement remains. For all of you who, like me, can't get enough of the circus, I hope you enjoyed this book. Let me know what you think at:

P.O. Box 736
Thiensville, WI 53092